Sign up for our newsletter to hear
about new and upcoming releases.

www.ylva-publishing.com

Other Books by C. Fonseca

Where the Light Plays

Food
for *Love*

C. FONSECA

Dedication

For Jane and my sisters.

In memory of our grandmothers, mothers, and aunts who shared
their stories and their recipes, and who are my inspiration.

Acknowledgements

To many people the Bellarine Peninsula, where the story is set, is all about vineyards, restaurants, the sea, and the surf. But it is also a popular cycling destination, and home of Tour de France winner, Cadel Evans, who founded the annual professional Cadel Evans Great Ocean Road Race.

The Bellarine is the traditional land of the Wathaurong tribe, and I acknowledge them as Traditional Owners. I pay my respect to their elders past and present.

Thank you to my betas. Gill, your support and encouragement has been invaluable. I'm grateful to my friends Paula and Julie for their attention to detail and making this a better book.

I am indebted to Astrid, Daniela, Amanda, Lee, and the Ylva team. Working with you on my second book—who would have thought it possible?—has been a pleasure. Michelle, my editor, was there for me when I needed her most—even though our time zones were out of sync. You were always patient and kept me focused on the essential ingredients.

Thank you to my readers. I write about my little corner of the world: you live and read from far and wide. I am grateful for your comments and encouragement.

Jane, I couldn't have written this book without your love, persistence, and reassurance. I continue to learn from you daily. You are my shelter in a storm, my ray of sunshine on a cloudy day.

When I initially thought about writing this book, I knew it would be an emotional journey. Cooking is a creative connection to my family and our heritage. Writing about food draws on childhood memories of cooking with my mother Theresa, Auntie Poppy, Auntie Olga, and my sisters.

I am fortunate to live in Australia, with its culturally diverse population. When food is prepared and shared with love, it brings us together, nourishing our bodies and souls.

Prologue

In second position, with the French rider only fifteen seconds ahead and only dead-flat tarmac left to ride, Jess knew she had a good chance to win: her body soared with adrenaline, and she could almost taste victory.

The one hundred and fifty-three-kilometre course had had multiple sections of bone-jarring cobblestones. She'd ridden her bike as hard as possible to smash the three steep artificial climbs and gained a favourable place in the lead group. But now, the canal city of Hoogeveen, where the Ronde van Drenthe race began and ended, was finally in sight.

She hoped her team had made the right decision. Holding her back until now—picking up the workload for Jess so that she'd have fresh legs for these last three kilometres was a risky move. There was only a one-minute gap between the breakaway group up front and the approaching main field of riders. A team in that bunched-together group could still propel their lead sprint rider for a surprise dash to the finish line.

It's time. Jess pumped her legs hard. They rotated rhythmically—almost effortlessly, as though powered by an unknown source. No pain.

"Go for it, Jess," Bruce yelled from the support vehicle.

No time for thinking. Jess was flying. Nerves like steel.

It was within her reach. Jess would move up, overtake the lead rider, and win the race. There were only seconds between their wheels as they approached the final sprint. She could do this. For herself, and for her team.

But then, before Jess could fully comprehend what was happening ahead, the lead rider's bicycle kicked out from under her and wobbled, and she headed towards the barrier.

"Watch out!" A warning blast in Jess's earpiece from the team car came too late as the riderless bicycle flew in the opposite direction, across the road—towards Jess.

In a flash, things became chaotic. A loud roar erupted from the crowd on the sidelines.

As the mangled bicycle bounced across the road, Jess swerved, zigzagged, and desperately attempted to stop her slide, powerless to do anything but just hold on. Her bicycle shuddered when the missile clipped her front wheel, and she sailed head first over the handlebars. *Oh hell.*

As Jess somersaulted into the air, she heard the *whoosh* of riders passing, then metal scraping on the ground, and then came the smell of burning rubber.

She lay in a crumpled heap. Her leg stuck out at an awkward angle—entangled in the bicycle wheel. Her shoulder hurt like hell, and there was a strange numbness spreading down her arm.

"Don't move."

On her back, staring up at the sky—thick, grey clouds pressing down—Jess heard footsteps running towards her. She tried to lift her head.

A hand rested lightly on her upper chest. "Stay still, Jess." She recognised the voice of Bridget, the team doctor.

Jess clenched her teeth. She was in pain—but she really wanted to win this. *Get back on the bike. The finish is so close. Move, Jess.* "I'm okay," she murmured.

"Sure. Sure, you are," Bridget said. "Lie still so I can check you out." She began to cut away at Jess's skin suit.

"Medic. Stretcher. Move, *please*," one of the paramedics shouted.

Jess attempted to roll onto her side and straighten her leg. It would be easier if she could lift her arm. *Damn, it hurts.*

"Lie still," Bridget repeated. "Jess, it's okay. We've got you."

Jess grimaced when she glimpsed her twisted leg through the tattered remains of the red, blue, and white racing shorts. It finally dawned upon her that she was in trouble.

She saw the dream of a win fade as blood from a large gash near her knee covered her leg and spread on the asphalt beneath her, and her vision blurred.

Chapter 1

London, England.

"Ten more minutes, and we're done," said Cassie Jones, the rehab centre's lead physiotherapist.

As far as Jess was concerned, she was done half an hour ago. Ten minutes was an eternity. The once simple, painless act of pumping her legs on the stationary bicycle now felt like hours of climbing the steepest course in the Alps.

Finally, Cassie moved beside her to indicate the session was over, and she slowed to a stop. Jess pushed her sodden hair from her eyes and wiped her forehead with the back of her sleeve. She glanced down at the hand that rested on her thigh, avoiding eye contact with Cassie. "You are right. I am so done." Jess sighed. It had been another gruelling afternoon session of physical therapy, stretching, and exercise.

Cassie moved even closer and dragged her hand from Jess's thigh down to the hem of her shorts. She traced the thin, raised line across her bare knee and gave her a slow smile. "You're doing way better than we expected. It won't be long before you're back out there, collecting another bunch of medals."

"Sure." Jess slid off the exercise machine and walked haltingly across the room. She reached for the towel and mopped at her face and neck. As the nagging pull of self-doubt and worry gnawed at her stomach, Jess doubled over, leaning heavily on the balance bar. How long would it be before she was back to her old self? Before she got back to racing, got back her rhythm, and regained her full strength? What if she didn't?

Jess pushed herself upright and pulled the towel over her head. She wasn't ready to face the possibility of never being able to race again.

"Hey, are you okay?" Cassie snaked her arm around Jess's shoulder. "You'll feel better after you've had a shower. Then, since you are my last client today, you could join me down at the Rose and Crown for a drink or two. How about it, Jess? You deserve it."

A protein smoothie in front of the television had seemed like a good option, but it was Friday night, and Cassie was high-spirited and a lot of fun away from the rehab clinic. She glanced up into the woman's eager hazel eyes.

Jess shook her head and stepped back, out of Cassie's embrace. "Hmm... sorry. I really am done. You've worn me out."

"Oh. That's my fault." Cassie frowned. "Serves me right, then. Maybe some other time?"

"Maybe," Jess said. "Tonight's not a good night for me anyway. My sponsors arranged an appearance at South Ham Ladies' College tomorrow, and I haven't yet prepared my presentation."

"No problem, Jess. That is perfectly understandable. Another time. Good luck with your preparations." She smiled and backed away. "You do like to cut things fine."

Jess collected her gear and dragged herself to the locker room. *What is wrong with me?* It was Friday night, and she had just turned down a date. Her social life was in the doldrums, and she couldn't seem to pull herself out of this negative space. She sighed. This wouldn't have happened a few months ago.

But the truth was Jess knew that after a couple of drinks, she'd end up blubbering on Cassie's shoulder, recounting the devastating news about Ben's recent death. She didn't need that. Anyway, it wouldn't be a good idea to start something with her physiotherapist.

Jess hated public speaking, but being here wasn't just about maintaining a favourable image or giving supporters a return for their investment. It was about giving back. She put down her notes and lowered her gaze to the auditorium across the sea of young faces.

Today, she was addressing three hundred teenage girls about herself and her career. *Well, what's left of it.* Jess's passion and commitment to the sport was her driving force, encouraging women to get active and make cycling part of their lives.

Nearing the end of her presentation, Jess drew a bolstering breath. "I'm taking a break in my pro cycling career because of the injuries I sustained in the Netherlands." She didn't have to recount the details of the crash or the extent of her injuries—that would be pointless and unnecessarily distressing for her audience. She clutched the podium tightly and forced herself to focus on the students.

She tried to ignore the restless movements of some of the girls who clearly had more important things on their minds. Jess couldn't expect everyone to be engrossed in her talk. Overall, though, they were curious about her life as an elite cyclist. She answered their questions and incorporated a short account of the list of races she had won—her Palmarès—and about some of the famous, colourful characters she'd met on the international circuit.

"Enough about me," Jess said. "I'm here today to tell you about a nationwide scheme. Un-Chained is an organisation that encourages girls and women of all fitness levels to participate in the joy of cycling." When Jess glanced around the room, she noticed the intense look from a young student in the front row. She sat bolt upright in the chair and her lips set in a straight line. *Too thin*, Jess thought. Did she suffer from lack of self-esteem and anxiety as Jess had at her age?

"Cycling is an incredible sport," Jess continued. "You can do it on your own—you can do it with a group of friends. It's great for fitness. It gives you the physical preparation, emotional strength, and mental toughness through life to deal with the unexpected. Do it just for fun or take it further. Competitive cycling can take you all around the world. Participating in one of Un-Chained's activities is an opportunity to make new friends, experience an amazing sense of freedom, and build your self-confidence." Jess pointed to the table by the main entrance of the auditorium. "Please, help yourself to the information packs outlining our programmes. Registration forms are inside."

"You have all been wonderfully attentive." Jess smiled. "Thank you so much for inviting me to your school today. Good luck. You never know—I may see some of you on the circuit one day. You'll have to catch me if you can." Jess gave a slight bow at the waist to a hall full of giggling girls.

She collected her notes as the students rose to their feet and showed their appreciation with polite applause. They filed out of the hall, and Jess noticed the girl who'd earlier drawn her attention pick up one of the information packs and tuck it under her arm.

Jess glanced down at her watch. "Okay, I did it," she told herself. Even if she'd managed to reach only one person today, it was worth the effort. The appearance had gone better than she'd hoped, and Doctor Waters would be pleased. Her rehabilitation psychologist encouraged Jess to stay connected with the cycling community and continue her volunteer work while she recuperated. Today was another step in the right direction.

Heels clicked authoritatively on the wooden stage. The dean was fast approaching with her hand outstretched. Dressed in a smart navy business suit, with her platinum hair pulled into a daring topknot bun, her every move spoke of strength and assuredness.

"Thank you, Ms Harris. It was a real pleasure. The girls will benefit greatly from your knowledge and experience." Her eyes danced with interest as she glanced over Jess from head to toe. "And humour."

"It's been *my* pleasure, Dean Holcombe."

"Please call me Kathryn."

"Thank you, Kathryn," Jess replied. Uncomfortable under the dean's scrutinising gaze, Jess shifted her weight from one foot to the other. She'd dressed in a classic white button-down shirt and tailored black linen suit to present as professional and capable, but as Jess stood in front of the dean, she was back at school and fourteen years old again.

"If you're free later this evening, would you care to join me for dinner?" Kathryn asked. Her imposing voice pulled Jess from her thoughts. Had the dean truly invited her out for dinner?

Jess cleared her throat. "I'm sorry. That would have been lovely, but I have an engagement this evening."

Kathryn smoothed her skirt with one hand. She didn't quite manage to hide her disappointment. "Never mind. Perhaps another time. It's been a pleasure to finally meet you."

"Thank you for the invitation, and for the opportunity to address your students. I hope I've sparked their interest in cycling."

Kathryn arched an eyebrow. "I'm sure you've sparked their interest," she said.

Jess reached behind the podium to collect her trench coat and briefcase as she surreptitiously looked towards the nearest exit. She'd raced at the elite level for over six years, and despite her manager's official announcement about the respite in her professional career, reporters still followed her about, hoping for a snapshot that showed her in some vulnerable or compromising position.

As Jess made her way to the door, she looked back at Kathryn, who was still watching her. Jess nodded and smiled once again before she left the building. If she hadn't made plans for an early supper with Jonathan, maybe she would have accepted the dean's invitation.

Thankfully, the spacious ground-floor bar was still relatively empty, and Jess easily located Jonathan seated at a table for two at the back of the room.

When he noticed Jess, Jonathan stood up and moved towards her. "Here you are at last."

She smiled, comforted to see his welcoming face. "I am sorry I'm late." She unbuckled her trench coat, slipped it off her shoulders, and threw it over the back of the chair that he pulled out for her. "You look so different without your beard." Jess leaned forward and ran her fingers along his angular jaw line. "What made you finally shave it off? You've had it for years."

Jonathan rubbed his chin. "Maxine. She gave me an ultimatum. Either I cover the beard when I'm near Rupert or shave it off. It was giving him a rash."

"Well, it suits you. You look handsome. Who'd have thought becoming a father would shave a few years off you?"

"Thank you." With a low chuckle, Jonathan drew Jess into his arms, and she held on tightly, enjoying the strength of her friend's embrace. "How are you?"

Jess released him. "I feel so lost," she said, and settled into the chair. "I still can't get my head around what's happened. I can't believe Ben's gone." She stared down at her hands to avoid the look of sympathy she saw crossing Jonathan's face. "God, I literally have no family left now."

"You have us, Jess. Me and Maxine," he said.

Jess looked up and held his gaze.

"Wine?" Jonathan didn't wait for her response. He poured it into a glass and placed it in front of her.

"Just what I need." Jess gulped a generous mouthful. Anything to relax the jittery, sick feeling in the pit of her stomach.

"Do you mind if we stay down here and have something light?" He glanced around the casual dining space. "I did snag us a table in the restaurant upstairs for later, just in case you preferred a more substantial meal." He raised his eyebrows. "On second thought, what was I thinking?"

Jess shook her head. "It's been quite a long day, and I'm tired." She swept her hair to one side and massaged the base of her neck. "Here would suit me fine."

They'd agreed to meet for supper at The Wells, in Hampstead, near Jess's apartment that bordered the rugged heath with its acres of woodland as well as cycling and running tracks. But by far, the best feature of the hilltop flat was the outstanding views over London—on a clear day.

"Good. I could use an early night myself." He stifled a yawn and excused himself for it. "Maxine was exhausted last night. I was on pick-up-and-deliver-Rupert-for-feeding duty." He shrugged his shoulders. "I almost forgot about your lecture this afternoon with the young *ladies* at South Hampstead. How did it go?"

She peered over the top of the menu and cleared her throat.

"I tried to answer the questions as honestly as I could without giving too many details about the crash." Jess sighed. "I *hate* public speaking."

"Even though you naturally command attention." Jonathan sat back in his chair and gave her a long, appreciative gaze. "Even Maxine has remarked on it."

Jess glanced at the menu again before tossing it aside. "Actually, the dean asked me out to dinner tonight."

"And, yet, here you are with me, a boring old man with nothing to entertain you with except baby pictures." He smirked.

She made as if to smack him from across the table. "You *browbeat* me into this meeting." But she couldn't keep up the pretend scowl for long. "Jonathan, you can show me all the pictures of Rupert you want."

"Are you trying to avoid dealing with Ben's estate?" he asked. "I know it's a difficult time, but we have to talk about it. You can't put it off any longer."

She shut her eyes and rubbed her forehead with closed knuckles.

"There is no way around it. You do realise going to Australia to meet with your brother's executor and the lawyers is the sensible option. How long has it been since you were there?"

"I was eleven when I left. Haven't ever been back, apart from a brief stopover in Sydney a few years ago on my way to the New Zealand championships."

"It will be a shock, going back after all this time."

With a long, slow draught from her glass, she swallowed past the knot of emotion lodged in her throat. "What choice do I have?"

"You will fly in to Melbourne," he said. "The legal firm will have a driver pick you up at the airport, and they'll arrange a hotel in the city for the night. The appointment with Ben's solicitor can be the following afternoon. That gives you a chance to recover from the long flight."

He's right. It is manageable. There's no excuse for not going.

"Do you have any friends in Melbourne?" He glanced up at her, then reached into his leather satchel and removed the papers he had brought with him. He searched through them. "How far away is the restaurant? Ah, what's it called again?"

"It's named Ailie." Jess raised her eyebrows. "I looked it up. It means *light of the sun*. The restaurant is on the Bellarine Peninsula, seventy minutes' drive from the city, so not exactly close. I've kept in contact with a few cyclists on the international circuit, and some of them may be in Melbourne, but I doubt I will have time to connect with anyone."

"So, you will go." Jonathan refilled her glass. "Do you have someone to look after your apartment? Do you need me to keep an eye on anything?"

"My next-door neighbour"—Jess tapped his hand gently— "but thanks for asking."

He leaned across the table and squeezed her forearm in a comforting gesture. "Have you heard anything about Ben's memorial service?"

Jess looked at him in the eye. "Do you think it was wrong of me to not go?" she asked quietly.

"No, sweetheart. Well, you were out of hospital, so perhaps you could have gone. It was the shock, I think. You weren't ready. It would have been too much on your own."

"I just couldn't go to the memorial service." Jess exhaled deeply. "But I will go now. You are right. He was my brother, and I owe him that much." She spoke carefully to conceal the depth of her sorrow.

"This business of his investment in the restaurant is unclear. The paperwork you sent me sheds no light on their arrangement, and his will was never updated when the restaurant was registered four years ago. I dare say you will find out more when you get there. Considering your estranged relationship with him, it is odd that you're the only beneficiary. Do you know anything about Lillian McAllister, the owner of the restaurant?"

"She's a chef. I need to do some more research before I go."

"Okay. Maybe Lillian was also his girlfriend?"

"No, she wasn't. At the time of the accident, Ben was travelling with his girlfriend." Jess lowered her gaze. "She was the other victim when the jet ski flipped."

"Oh. That's horrible, Jess," he said. "I suppose it could take a while to get everything sorted. Prepare yourself for a longer stay, if necessary."

"If I must." She sighed. "Apart from my volunteer work...I haven't decided what's next."

"Early days yet. What's the latest from the specialist about your long-term prognosis?"

"We're hopeful. Depending on how long I'm in Australia, I'll find a gym so I can keep up my strength training and continue with my rehab programme. Whether I get back to elite level—or not—is up to me. It might have been my second-last year on the circuit anyway. The accident may have just brought it forward." The weight of declaring that to another person sat heavily on her chest.

"Seriously?" Jonathan shook his head. "But you're only twenty-nine."

"The average age of the competitive cyclist is creeping down. I could continue for a few more years, but given the limited amount of time you can push your body in this sport, not much longer, certainly not at that level. It's just not sustainable."

"But Jess, cycling has been your life—your passion."

"Yes," she whispered. Adjusting to the world outside competitive cycling would be incomprehensible, to put it mildly. "I would miss the buzz. I already miss my teammates." She tapped her fingers on the table. "But after my time in rehab, I've had some thoughts about putting my degree to use." She looked up to gauge Jonathan's reaction.

"Are you thinking of *working* as a physiotherapist?"

"Maybe."

"Do you even have experience doing that? I mean—other than the occasional volunteering at the children's physio clinic?"

"I've only had limited experience," she admitted.

"I know you love volunteering at that place, but—" Jonathan looked up. "Jess, your real love is racing. How are you going to cope with this forced hiatus?"

She shrugged. "I don't have a choice. I could rush back in and chance an early return, but I face a higher risk of permanent damage and *never* being able to race." Jess placed a hand over her glass as Jonathan attempted to refill it with wine. "Thanks, but two glasses is my limit these days."

"All right, all right. I'm sorry I went on about it." He tucked into his hearty meal of burger, chips, and mound of coleslaw. Pointing his fork at her plate of salad, he said, "You need to eat more. No wonder you're built like a reed. A baby bird could out-eat you."

"Hah," she said. "Just for that..." Jess leaned across the table and stole one of Jonathan's chips.

He pushed a few more of the fried potatoes to the edge of his plate, within her reach. "Seriously, take all you want. Between sitting all day at work and watching over Rupert at night, I certainly don't need the extra calories." He paused. "By the way, Ashley sent me a copy of your contract. It says they've agreed to put it on hold, but when you return from Australia, team management expects you to keep in the public eye as an athletic goodwill ambassador to keep your sponsors happy. You'll do volunteer work like the physiotherapy clinic, only a lot more of it."

It could be worse, she thought. Better than rushing back into racing before she was ready. "What about my company endorsements? I don't want the funds I'm raising for all those charities to dry up."

"Ashley is negotiating the individual endorsements," he said. "We'll see. But if your contract with the team is suspended, unfortunately that salary—no matter how meagre—stops. It's a good thing you don't rely on it to live, Jess."

"Well, thanks to you and my inheritance money you look after." She smiled. "I'm fortunate to have you as my accountant."

"Thank you. And as your accountant, I'll need copies of any additional paperwork once you see Ben's lawyers in Melbourne."

"Yes," she said. "I'll e-mail you anything new."

He tapped at one of the papers in his hands. "What about this Lillian McAllister?" he asked. "I didn't get a chance to look her up. Do you think you need to worry about her? What *was* the nature of her and Ben's relationship?"

"I don't know. Jonathan, you are asking a lot of questions." She stretched her neck to ease her tight muscles. "Obviously close enough friends for him to have loaned money for her business. I guess she will have to pay it out." She tilted her head at him, then sighed. "Unless I decide to go into the restaurant business."

He almost choked on his last piece of potato. "Really, Jess? Think about it: you and food—not exactly a match made in heaven. You hardly ever cook, or even eat anything. I've seen the inside of your refrigerator. As your accountant and your friend, I strongly advise you not to call me in a month and tell me you've become a restaurant owner. Get it settled as soon as possible."

He was absolutely spot on. She knew a little about sports nutrition, but naught about the restaurant business.

No. For now, she had to take one thing at a time. One day at a time.

Jess checked the time and shifted around in the oversized leather armchair. "I get tired of the press asking me how I'm progressing and not knowing the answer. The specialist hasn't given me a set date when I can return to racing." Jess leaned forward and scrubbed at her forehead. "There are good and bad days. Sometimes I feel useless. I lie awake at night and can barely crawl out of bed in the morning. But on the days I ride, I feel better."

Doctor Waters tapped the pen on the side of her notepad, crossed her legs, and pulled her skirt over her knees. "Will you have access to a bicycle in Australia?"

"I am going to buy one. There's no way I'd feel comfortable on a borrowed bicycle," she said. "A girl can never have too many of them, and I've learned that I get pleasure and joy from cycling, just for the sake of it."

Doctor Waters looked at Jess over her black-framed glasses. "I'm pleased for you. You've made great strides."

"Thanks to you, I've accepted that moving on is a work in progress, not a quick fix." With Doctor Waters' help, Jess had avoided sinking into severe depression. She had resisted seeing her at first, because her physical rehab regime was so intense, but confusion and despair led Jess to make the first appointment. She found Doctor Waters to be non-judgemental and positive in her practice, and she was helping Jess manage her anxiety while her body mended. This was her only way forward, because Jess never wanted to revisit the dark times when, for a short time as a desperate twelve-year-old, she'd succumbed to self-harm. She clutched her right thigh automatically, then quickly smoothed her hands over her sweater to hide her action from the therapist.

Jess stared out the fourth-floor London office window to avoid meeting the doctor's perceptive gaze.

"You are a strong and resilient woman, Jess," Doctor Waters said. "No longer the twelve-year-old you remember." After a brief pause, she continued with, "Autumn has come early to London, and the plane trees in Kensington Park are beginning to turn golden brown. The view is one of the main reasons I have this office."

"Strange to think it is spring in the southern hemisphere," Jess said.

The psychologist smiled. "You're going *home* to Australia."

Jess turned to her. *Home*—what did that mean? Everything was silent, save the tick-tock of a large antique clock on the sturdy wooden mantle. Jess crossed her arms tightly in front of her chest.

"You've made huge positive changes in the last few months." Doctor Waters walked with Jess and pulled the door open. "I will see you when you return." She briefly squeezed Jess's shoulder, smiled, and retreated into her office.

Jess thought about the doctor's choice of words, calling Australia home. Without her mother or her brother there, how could it be home? Wasn't home family? But home was also a sense of place—perhaps Doctor Waters was right.

Chapter 2

Bellarine Peninsula, Southern Victoria, Australia.

USUALLY, HER MORNING RUN HELPED lighten her thoughts, but today Lili McAllister's legs were heavy under the weight of her worries.

Her heart beat strong and steady beneath her hand. The five-kilometre run to the foreshore, with its gradual incline up and over the sand dunes, had worked her calf and thigh muscles hard, and it was still another ten minutes to Portarlington, where she'd told herself she would turn back. So much for this run helping her get her act together.

Stop wallowing in your own grief, she told herself as she watched the sun rising above the treeline to the east. Its warm rays were like fingers caressing her skin. *Time to focus on your own family, Lillian McAllister. And your staff.*

Lili had done a Google search of Jessica Harris after she'd received information from Ben's lawyer, and her name alone had given Lili countless web links to troll—though most of the hits seemed to be speculation and idle gossip. Still, Ben's sister was clearly a celebrity, and an alluring one: half-British and half-Indian, with sultry dark eyes and a graceful, athletic figure that had placed her in *Sports Magazine*'s list of most beautiful sportswomen. She featured heavily in online and print media social pages too.

Obviously, a prima donna. She had the potential to make Lili's life difficult. Just thinking about her soon-to-be houseguest made her queasy.

She took a deep breath, turned back onto the gravel path that wound through the reserve, and jogged towards the small coastal township. She'd grab a quick coffee and check her mailbox at the local post office before she ran the track home.

An hour later, after her shower, Lili drove the outer farm road to Ailie. She stopped the Subaru on top of the rise and rolled down the window to scan the undulating verdant farmland across to her restaurant—where it stood with its solid red-brick base and high glass windows that reflected the surrounding gardens and tall gum trees. She looked past Ailie to the valley of grapevines, down to the shimmering blue of Port Phillip Bay and the You Yang hills in the distance. Lili sighed deeply. They'd worked so hard to create Ailie, and now it defined her. This was *hers*. She was suddenly overcome by fierce protectiveness.

She entered through the main door and spied her staff clustered around the bar counter. She ducked into her office, threw her keys and wallet into her desk drawer, and headed into the dining room.

"Hi, everyone," Lili greeted. She manoeuvred through the group and stopped beside Alex, who wrapped her arms around her and gave her a quick hug.

"Here we go. The first staff meeting for the spring season. Are you ready for this?" asked Alex.

"Ready as I'll ever be." Lili shrugged and turned to the small group. "Please, take a seat." She waited while most of her team settled into their chairs, while a few chose to stand and lean against the bar.

"I'm right here." Alex squeezed her forearm, and Lili appreciated the reassuring gesture from her sous-chef.

Lili raised her hand, and the chatter around her ceased. "Thank you." She squinted in surprise at the sight of her father, standing with his arms crossed in front of his chest, at the back of the room. She acknowledged him with raised eyebrows before continuing to address her staff. "It's great to see you all." Lili buried her hands deep into the pockets of her trousers. "We were on annual leave when we received the news about Ben, and I appreciated all the phone calls and e-mails I got from you reaching out. Thanks to those who were able to make it to the memorial service."

Owen reached into his pocket, pulled out a handkerchief, and dabbed his eyes. The front-of-house manager had been recruited by Ben, and they'd shared a weird passion for early Hitchcock movies.

Lili offered him a sad smile and took a deep breath. "Ben was my mentor, and he helped me build this business. Ailie has a lot to live up to." She looked towards the Trip Advisor Certificate of Excellence and the *Gourmet Traveller* award that graced the restaurant wall above the bar.

Alex stepped closer and placed her arm around Lili's shoulders.

"We have a great team, and I'm very proud of all of you." She leaned into Alex, taking comfort. "Let's make Ben proud."

Josh, their second-year apprentice chef, held his glass of water aloft. "To Ben."

"To Ben," the others repeated, and waited silently for Lili to continue.

"You've seen the new rosters. Please let Alex know if there are any problems." Lili smiled and turned to Owen. "Now comes the fun part. I'll hand you over to Owen, who will take us through the main reason we are all here, to brush up on the latest hygiene and safety handling procedures."

Later that afternoon, after the staff left, Lili made her way to the garden where she took a seat on the shaded terrace. She turned at the sound of footsteps to accept a steaming cup of chai tea Alex handed to her. "Thank you."

"No problem," Alex said. "I heard from Haley this morning. She promised she'd be back by the time we opened."

"That's good news, but it's disappointing she won't be here for the staff party."

"Did you know she broke up with Grace? According to Haley, they had a huge disagreement on the first day of their cycling trip in South Australia."

Lili rolled her eyes. "So, she's single again."

"I don't imagine that will last long." Alex smirked. "You know Haley: she's young, and in the end her number-one priority in a relationship is to have fun. I honestly don't think she gets serious about any of her girlfriends. Anyway, how do you think the meeting went?" She sat down beside Lili on the garden bench. "You were great."

"Yeah, thanks. No point worrying everyone." Lili pushed her hand through her newly cropped hair. She was still getting used to the short, layered haircut. She'd needed a change, and her hairdresser convinced her the new look would be a confidence booster. As a chef, wash and wear was unquestionably a sensible choice.

Alex blew the heat from the top of her cup, releasing the spicy aromas of star anise, cinnamon, and ginger into the air. "Hmm…this is an excellent blend. It goes well with the new organic honey you brought in."

"It does. It's beautifully silky and toffee flavoured." Lili sipped the soothing tea, glad of the change of subject. "I have an idea for a bush honey panna cotta accompanied with star anise-infused fruit or berries. It came from Mei's mum, Huan. She told me she's been making a Chinese egg-custard tart flavoured with star anise. I thought the aniseed flavour would add a delicate layer to the dessert."

"I'm all for it. Sounds amazing," Alex said. "It's a bugger about the money you owed Ben. I guess you owe it to his sister now."

"The agreement was made between friends. Ben was so generous and never put a time limit on repaying him. He believed the restaurant would be a success and he'd eventually get his money back."

"He had great faith in you."

Lili sighed. "There's no way I can pay it in a lump sum."

"Have you spoken to the bank?"

"Not yet." Lili put down her empty cup and angled herself over the raised garden bed to thin out the weeds that threatened to suffocate the horseradish plants' young, crinkled leaves. "I have a big enough mortgage already."

"Let's hope you can come to an agreement with Ben's sister. You've worked so hard, and things are on the up." Alex knelt beside Lili, picked up a short-handled cultivator hoe, and broke clumps of rich, dark soil with steady movements. "I'm sorry I can't help. I would if I could. We are still so tied down with Tash's student loans, and we'd like to buy a house in the next few years."

"Don't be ridiculous. I would never expect you to lend me the money." Lili nudged Alex in the ribs. "But thanks."

Alex put down the hand tool. "How are you doing?"

"I'm okay."

"I mean it, Lili. How are you doing, really?"

"There's a huge gap in all our lives that nothing will replace." Lili rolled her shoulders as if to shrug off her sorrow. "Even though lately he spent less time here and more time travelling, it's hard to imagine *never* seeing him again. Ben was a part of our lives."

"I miss him too," Alex said. "Damn it, I miss that cheeky grin and his offbeat humour." She wrapped her arms around Lili tightly and then released her. "Is Ru still asking a lot of questions?"

"Not so much. The service helped, though. Sometimes, she picks up the memorial card and stares at his picture. But I don't know if she understands the finality...of death." The informal gathering on the beach had been simple yet significant, and had given Lili, her daughter, and Ben's friends a tangible way to express their grief.

"Will you tell her about Ben's sister—that she has an aunt?"

"She's only four years old. I guess with me being an only child, she's never known a *real* aunt or uncle," Lili said. "If Jessica Harris is only here for a short time—if she just breezes in and out of Ru's life—Ru won't understand. I've decided to wait until I've met Jessica, and then I'll figure out how to tell her. There's been so much to deal with, so much to do."

Lili took a deep breath and was energised by the earthiness and the hint of salt in the air. She dusted soil from her hands. She never tired of being in the edible oasis that Ben and her mother had helped her establish. "I have a few more things to take care of in the office before I go. Why don't you head home now?"

Alex nodded. "I'll go soon. When do you expect *her* to arrive?"

Lili shrugged her shoulders. "I got a call from Ben's lawyer. She should get here either today or tomorrow."

"Are you okay with her staying at your place?"

"I don't think I have a choice. Mum and Dad don't have the space at the cottage." Lili tossed the bunch of weeds to the side. "Mum's a darling. She's already prepared the guest room. Anyhow, this way I can keep an eye on her."

"Do you think that's necessary?" Alex grabbed her jacket from the back of the bench. "You'll be sharing the house until who knows when with someone you don't know."

"It will be fine," Lili said, trying to convince herself more than Alex. "I just hope she doesn't stay long. The lawyer thought she'd want to take care of things quickly and return to London in a week or two."

Alex fished into her pockets, searching for her car keys. "So, how much do you know about her?"

"Not much. Although I did Google her."

Alex raised an eyebrow. "And?" She glanced down at her watch. "Oh damn, I have to rush home. Ring me later." She headed for the gate. "Tash has to attend some function at the hospital, and I'm going to be late—once again." She blew Lili a kiss. "Good luck!" she called as she disappeared through the courtyard gate.

"Thanks, bye." Lili waved, picked up the hand trowel, and dug it into the ground with force. "I need it."

Ben's sister had made the front-page news before and after her accident. Maybe the tabloids had painted a distorted view about the cyclist in describing her grand lifestyle. But what if some of it was true? Lili leaned forward to yank a bunch of nettle weed from the pebbled path.

"Ben," she said to the sky, "I have a feeling your sister is going to be as much of a challenge for me as she was for you."

Chapter 3

"WHAT THE HELL?" JESS'S SMALL yellow rental car jerked to a squelchy stop on the muddy road. "Well, this is just bloody marvellous."

She turned her head and looked back to where she'd come from. The incline gave her a panoramic view of the ocean and the rolling hills in the distance. But she sure as hell wasn't going anywhere.

She'd followed the GPS directions, hadn't she? Jess was one hundred per cent sure that the instructions were to turn left. There'd been no sign on the roadside, so she'd relied on the car's fancy electronic device. That was a mistake: the gravel road had turned into a dirt track. She never had much luck with the bloody things.

The rental, a Mini Cooper convertible, was a lot of fun to drive. The car yard had even delivered on their promise to make available an ingenious rear-mounted bike carrier, on which she had secured her newly purchased carbon bike. With the top down, the wind in her hair, and the warmth of the sun on her skin, it had been all systems go.

Until this happened. Jess pushed open the door and stepped outside the car. Her right foot sank into thick sludge. *All systems stop.*

Jess groaned and kicked what was visible of the front wheel. She should have opted for a four-wheel drive. Looking down at her shoes, she was thankful that her black leather boots were only partially immersed in the sticky brown goo. She scanned the paddocks around her. There was not a human to be seen, just a few cows grazing in a distant field.

She crouched low, checked the half-submerged black rubber tyre, and thumped the side of the car with her fist. Her boot slipped as she lost her balance. Using the exterior mirror, she worked herself into an upright position, only to have her boot slip out from beneath her again. She fell back against the side of the car. Her once-pristine white knee-length Bermuda shorts were streaked with brown clay.

"*Fuck*," she yelled, kicking the tyre. "Honestly." She kicked harder. "*Ouch*!"

"Darling, I really don't think that's going to solve your problem," a voice called out.

Jess snapped her head up and turned. She hadn't heard anyone approach.

The new arrival scratched his ginger hair, dismounted his horse, and stood a few feet away from her. A medium-sized black-and-white dog ran between them, stopped beside the man, and sat at attention.

"Good girl, Rhona. Stay." He tipped his hat to Jess and placed it back on his head. "G'day." The large hat shielded his eyes from the sun, partially hiding them.

Jess shaded her face with her hand and tilted her head to see under the wide brim. "Hello." She wiped her muddy hands on her ruined shorts.

"Got yourself in a bit of a mess, eh?" He slowly circled the car, a bemused expression on his face. "You are bogged." The dog followed close behind him.

Jess looked on in surprise. Well, that was stating the obvious.

The rugged giant hunched over to inspect the tyre. "Oh, she's stuck, all right." He stood up to his full height and laughed. "Not to worry, love. We'll be able to get her out for you." He pointed to her bicycle on the back of the car. "Nice wheels."

"Thank you. That's really kind of you." Jess reached into the car for her map. Rhona barked, approached her, and nuzzled her hand.

"Rhona, come," he called, and the dog immediately returned to his side.

"I'm lost," she said. "If you could just point me in the right direction?" She felt a gentle nudge at her back. Now what?

The horse nudged Jess's shoulder and whickered softly. She couldn't help but reach out and stroke its beautiful grey coat.

Her rescuer chuckled as the horse pushed into her shoulder again. He grabbed the reins. "Leave the lady alone, Dora."

Jess pulled her mobile phone out of her pocket. "I do have an address," she said. "I'm looking for Faodail." She pronounced the property's name phonetically and glanced at the farmer.

He smiled. "Scott McAllister at your service. You have arrived at your destination, Faodail Farm."

Jess met his gaze. "I have?"

"You are Jessica Harris, Ben's sister?"

"Yes, I am."

The mare nuzzled her hip. Jess frowned. "Did you say *Scott McAllister*? Are you related to Lillian McAllister?"

"That's right, love. I am her father, Scott. And these two scruffy creatures are Dora and Rhona. This is Faodail Farm," he repeated, and gestured widely across the rolling paddocks.

She detected pride in his voice, edged with a touch of sadness.

Scott turned back to Jess. "I'm so sorry about your brother. Ben was a good man. We all miss him a lot." He touched his hand to the rim of his hat in what appeared to be a sign of respect. "You look like him," he said. "Mind you, he didn't have your proper British accent."

She cast her eyes to the ground. The painful knowledge that this farmer, a stranger, knew her brother better than she did, cut through her like a knife.

Jess must have appeared uncomfortable, because when she looked up, Scott had turned his attention to the car.

"It's unlikely that anyone will come by, but just in case, I'd lock up. I'll get you to the house first and come back for the car." He pointed to her bicycle. "I guess we'd better take that fancy bike of yours."

She couldn't see any sign of a farmhouse. "Is it far?" She passed him the map. "Can you show me here where I went wrong? I shouldn't have relied on the GPS."

He chuckled. "Useless things. Ah, I see what you've done. You've come off the main road and onto the old stock road. It's a common mistake." He pointed on the map. "We are here. Our cottage is near the main entrance, off McAllister Lane, the road you should have taken. You'll be staying here." He indicated to a spot further up the lane.

"Won't I be staying at the farm?"

"Yes, you will. My wife Helen and I live in the cottage. Helen thought you'd be more comfortable staying at the hilltop with Lili."

"The hilltop? That's very kind, but I don't want to cause her any trouble," she said.

26

"No trouble. Lili's place is modern and spread out. There's loads of room for a visitor, with great views over the bay. Helen's set up the guest wing for you. We thought you would appreciate a bit of privacy."

"What about Ben's house? Can I stay there?"

"Ahh..." He looked sheepish. "Your brother loved to do three things. One was to cook, which he was bloody good at—excuse the language." He squinted in the bright sunlight and adjusted his hat. "Two, he loved to travel, and he did every chance he could. And three, he was a keen surfer. Ben shared the house with a mate near 13th Beach, about a half hour's drive away. It's not really a place you'd want to stay, though." He raised his eyebrows. "There's not much room."

"Oh, okay." Lillian's house did seem the better option. If it got awkward, she would take herself to a hotel.

"I think I'd better get you to Lili's. She won't be back for a bit, but Helen should be there." He peered at her boots. "You can have a shower, change out of those clothes."

Jess glanced at the disabled car. She didn't like to leave it there in the mud.

"Don't worry, it will be fine. I'll come back with some help and bring the car to you."

"Thank you. If you set me in the right direction, I'll walk the bicycle—"

Scott laughed and slapped at his knees, while Rhona barked excitedly and ran around in circles.

"What did I say?"

He gently seized hold of Dora's shiny mane and held her steady. "The house is a half-kilometre trek across the paddock." He pointed to Jess's shoes. "We don't want you falling down a rabbit hole or into a pile of cow dung, do we? Are you accustomed to horses?"

"What are you suggesting?" She pushed the sunglasses onto her head to hold back her windswept hair. It had been a long time since she'd been on a horse, but Dora looked like a Clydesdale—thankfully sturdy, and hopefully a reasonably comfortable mount. "I have ridden, years ago."

"Okay, then. I'll adjust the stirrups for you," he said. "Do you need a hand up? Dora's slightly taller than an average horse."

"No, I'll be fine, thank you. What about my bicycle?"

"No problem. I'll walk it to the house." He loosened the fastenings on the back of the car and lifted the carbon bicycle high into the air with one hand. "It's as light as a feather."

She stepped towards the horse, put her foot in the stirrup, and hoisted herself onto Dora's back. The mare shifted under her, and Jess repositioned herself in the saddle. She gritted her teeth, careful to hide her discomfort. Dora was at least sixteen hands tall, maybe more, and rather wide to sit astride comfortably.

As if in sympathy, Dora lifted her head and neighed gently.

"Steady, girl," Scott said.

"Yes, steady girl," Jess murmured. She never imagined she would arrive at the farm on the back of a draught horse.

Dora trotted along, and Jess began to enjoy the gentle rhythmic sway from her elevated perch. Scott walked beside her with the bicycle resting easily on his shoulder. Rhona trotted ahead, leading the way. Jess was content to listen to Scott chatter about Faodail Farm and his family.

"Ru's going to wonder whose flash bicycle this is. She's been pestering her mother for a bike since her last birthday," he said cheerily. "If she doesn't try to get onto it herself—she's only four, you know—we'll be right. Although Ru is plucky...she may try."

Did she miss something? Who was *Ru*? Jess looked down at Scott, who spoke so fast his accent made the ends of his words sometimes indistinguishable. It had been a long time since she'd been back to Australia. She'd have to pay better attention.

It was a good thing there wasn't another soul in sight. Jess imagined she looked ridiculous, sitting perched on top of this large creature, wearing filthy Bermuda shorts and ankle boots, being transported across the paddock. They passed under the welcoming wrought iron Faodail sign and through the gate, and followed a red dirt road flanked by a white post and rail fence. An English-styled garden bordered a picturesque timber home painted green, with a wide front veranda.

"That's our cottage," Scott said.

They continued along the road that curved around a stand of tall eucalyptus trees and then climbed gradually upwards before levelling at the top of the rise.

"That's where you'll be staying." He pointed to the crescent-shaped, single-storey timber house that seemed to float on the hilltop.

"It's very modern," Jess said, surprised.

"Lili helped with the design," he said in a proud manner. They stopped near a slate-tiled carport at the bottom of a flight of stairs that led up to the house. He held on to Dora, and Jess dismounted carefully but misjudged the distance and winced as her leg took her full weight.

"Are you okay, Jessica?"

"Yes, thank you." She stretched her back. "It's been a while."

"Since you've been on a draught horse?"

"Since I was on a horse of any kind." She stroked the gentle mare and gazed up at the black timber-clad house. "It's quite unique…and the views must be lovely from up here."

Movement on the upper level caught her attention, and a small child appeared on the sun deck.

"That's not Grandpa riding Dora. Who is it, Gran?" The piercing high-pitched tones of the child's voice drifted down. "Look, Grandpa has a *bicycle*."

"Hello, my little pumpkin." Scott placed Jess's bicycle against a low stone wall, then secured Dora to a post. He turned to Jess. "Come on, then. I'd better introduce you to the family. Then you can get cleaned up."

He strode ahead, mounting the stairs two at a time, and Jess followed him up to the landing.

The little girl, clothed only in bright-pink pyjama bottoms, scampered towards Scott.

A woman appeared with a matching pyjama top in her hand. "Ru, come back here. Your mum will be home soon. Let's get you dressed. What are you looking at?" she exclaimed, breathlessly. "Well, I'll be…"

"Hello, love," Scott greeted.

"Grandpa, Grandpa," Ru repeated, holding out her hands to Scott. She bounced up and down, and the soles of her red slippers tapped on the floorboards.

He scooped his granddaughter into his arms and held her against his chest.

"And why is my husband grinning like an old fool?" the woman asked, placing one hand on her hip.

Jess stepped around Scott. There was no way she could hide her mud-streaked clothes and boots, so she didn't try.

"Jessica, this is my wife, Helen. And this little devil is our granddaughter, Ru." He ruffled the girl's hair. "Helen, may I introduce Jessica Harris."

"It's lovely to meet you, Jessica, but what on earth happened to you?"

"Unfortunately, I took a wrong turn, and my car is stuck on the stock road," Jess said. "I am fortunate that Scott and Dora arrived to save me."

Helen turned to her husband. "Take Jack with you when you pull it out. I saw him down in the orchard."

"I'm on to it, Helen."

Jess studied the couple as he leaned forward to kiss Helen's cheek. She was her husband's complete opposite. While he was broad shouldered and rugged, her features were petite and fine boned. Her shoulder length, ash-blonde hair, flecked with grey, framed her face. She smiled and held out her hand to Jess.

"Welcome."

"It's a pleasure to meet you, Mrs McAllister." Jess took Helen's hand in a firm handshake and let it go.

"It's Helen, please."

"Thank you, Helen." Jess met her direct gaze.

"Oh my, you look so much like your brother." Helen pulled Jessica into a firm embrace. "I'm so sorry for your loss."

Jess froze, uncomfortable with the sudden physical contact. After a few seconds, she slowly extricated herself from Helen's arms and stepped back.

"Who are you?" asked Ru in a tiny voice as she leaned out of her grandfather's arms and tugged at Jess's sleeve.

Jess gazed into a pair of sparkling caramel-brown eyes. "Hello. I'm Jess."

"And I am Ru McAllister. How old are you?"

"Ru, mind your manners." Helen shook her head.

Scott lowered his granddaughter to the ground. "Listen to your gran, pumpkin."

Helen coaxed the bright pyjama top over Ru's unruly head of curls. "Jessica is our guest. You know better."

Ru pointed to Jess's clothes. "But Gran, look, she's covered in mud. When I get dirty, you make me have a bath. Let's help her take a bath," she said in a very matter-of-fact tone.

Scott snorted. "On that note, Helen, I'll leave you to sort this. I'll take Dora to the stables. We have a car to rescue." He cleared his throat. "Jessica, I leave you in good hands. The girls can show you around. We'll be about an hour. I'll lock your bike safely in the garage."

"I'm so sorry. I've caused a lot of trouble." Jess sighed. What a way to arrive—not exactly a good first impression.

"It's no trouble at all," he said.

"I'll find you some clothes to change into." Helen smiled at Jess. "You're taller than Lili, but I'm sure there's something in her wardrobe that will fit you."

"Come on, Jess." Ru tugged on her hand. "I'll show you to your room. I helped Gran make the bed, and we put clean towels in your bathroom and everything. Mama said you were staying in the guest room. Her room and mine are way over on the other side of the house." She waved her arms above her head. "Will she mind if *Jess* wears her clothes?" Ru asked her grandmother.

"Darling, this is Jessica," Helen corrected.

"Jess is fine. In fact, I prefer Jess." She looked down at Ru, who held her hand tightly as they stood at the entrance of the house. She bent to remove her soiled boots with one hand.

"Jess," Ru said with a mischievous grin that accentuated her cute dimples. "You can borrow Mama's clothes."

"Thank you, Ru."

Just inside the entranceway, Helen stopped and said, "The house is shaped like a boomerang. It's easy to make your way around." They moved forward into what Jess guessed was the sitting room, with a corner freestanding wood stove and dark-polished floors covered with a geometric rug in shades of grey. "It's divided into three spaces. The living areas, home office and kitchen are in the centre, with the master suite and Ru's bedroom at one end. The guest rooms are at the other end."

Floor-to-ceiling windows showed a rear sundeck that overlooked rows of distant grapevines and glimpses of the ocean beyond. Jess lingered a moment to take in the view. "This is lovely," she murmured.

"Your room is right through here."

She followed Helen and Ru into a generously sized bedroom which enjoyed the same outlook and shared balcony.

Ru released Jess's hand and threw herself onto the large bed, bouncing dangerously close to the edge.

"Miss McAllister, off immediately," said Helen, firmly. She scooped Ru into her arms and placed her onto the wooden floor. "The bathroom is through here." Helen rolled open the barn-like door, revealing a modern bathroom and a soaking tub.

"Thank you." Jess stifled a yawn, but Helen caught it.

"We'll leave you in peace and let you clean up."

Jess glanced at her watch. Five thirty-five. "I'm sorry. I didn't get much sleep last night. Guess I'm still on London time. It will be great to have a quick bath, if you don't mind?" This time she didn't try to hide her yawn.

"You must be exhausted. Please make yourself at home. There's a dressing gown in the wardrobe. I'll find you something to wear and leave it on the bed." As if sensing Jess's discomfort, Helen added, "There's no one else here. Relax and enjoy your bath. When you finish, make your way to the kitchen. I'll have a snack ready."

The announcement was a relief; she'd have space to herself at last. Ru's presence—and everyone making a fuss over her—was overwhelming.

Ru also yawned, and Helen took her hand. "Come on, sweetie, let's get dinner and then it's your bedtime."

"Bye, Jess." Ru smiled tiredly and waved, allowing herself to be towed through the doorway.

Jess sighed as the door clicked behind Helen and Ru. She welcomed the thought of a hot bath and twisted her hair into a loose knot.

She reached into the wardrobe for the white towelling robe and held it to her face. Helen had thought of everything. It was thick and soft, and promised comfort after a couple of wearying days.

Fifteen minutes later, she rested back against the curved porcelain tub and surveyed the room. Someone had good taste. It was eclectically modern—uncluttered, stylish. Jess hadn't known what to expect when she'd first heard the word *farm*, but she found herself pleasantly surprised. She bent her knees up and submerged herself into the gloriously hot water. Her aches and pains eased as a pleasant tiredness enveloped her.

The information she'd foraged on Lillian McAllister before leaving London had given her a surfeit of facts about the chef's professional life but very little about her *personal* life. Given that Lillian—*Lili*, apparently—had ended up back home, Jess wondered why she had served her apprenticeship in Sydney, not Melbourne. Perhaps it made sense because she'd finished at the top of her class from a Sydney culinary institute.

The online photo she'd seen of a beaming Ben and Lillian from years ago, posing together for an article about a programme pairing experienced chefs with female apprentices, had clutched at Jess's heart. Ben had looked so happy. Lillian had too. And no wonder: she was primed to be head chef in a prestigious Sydney waterfront restaurant—so why leave it all? When Jess had been doing her research on Lillian, the fact that a year or so later Ailie had opened its doors on the Bellarine Peninsula had seemed an odd little mystery.

But it seemed obvious to Jess now what had brought Lillian home. She'd fallen pregnant. Ru's mellow-brown skin and dark, curly hair set her apart from her fair-skinned mother and grandparents. Jess's mind flashed back to the online photograph of Lili and Ben. Was it possible that they had been a couple once, and Ru was Ben's child? She shook her head. *No way.*

He would have told her, three years ago when he'd made that surprise appearance after her race in Spain. She recalled how she'd lost the race, was in a grumpy mood, and made little time for him. But despite her behaviour, surely he would have told her if he'd become a father.

The hot bath made her drowsy, and she could no longer focus on any particular thought. She flicked the tap, adding more hot water to the tub. The sun was setting, the sky turning pink. She gazed dreamily out the window. The clouds, broad on the bottom and fluffy on top, were outlined with silver.

When the water started to cool again, Jess pulled the bath plug and reached for her towel. She was incredibly tempted to slip between the sheets of the large, comfortable-looking bed, but that would be impolite. Maybe she could rest for ten or fifteen minutes—just a short nap on top of the bedclothes. Jess fell backwards on the quilt and closed her eyes. "Hmm, that feels so good," she said aloud.

A while later, Jess woke on the bed, dressed in a bath robe with no memory of how that had happened. She glanced around, disoriented by the unfamiliar surroundings.

Oh, I'm at the farm. She yawned and stretched, thankful the sleep had alleviated the stiffness in her shoulders and lower back. Helen had invited her to the kitchen for a snack. Damn, how long had she been asleep? She snatched the loose drawstring pants and black T-shirt that Helen had left on the bed and dressed quickly. Jess shook out her tangled bed hair and caught sight of herself in the mirror. Her eyes were red and edged by shadows despite the long soak and nap. She steadied the slight tremor in her hand. "It's nothing. I'm just tired," she murmured to herself.

The borrowed top, emblazoned on the front with bold white text—*Guess my super power*—fit tight across her shoulders and everywhere else. She looked in the mirror to read the back of the T-shirt. *Yes, CHEF.* Jess raised her eyebrows. The sooner she got into her own clothes the better.

If she had a choice, she wouldn't leave the room until tomorrow. After a full night in that heavenly bed, she would be much more prepared to face—whatever. But she did want her luggage; she'd have to go and find it.

Jess left the safety of her room and stopped at the end of the hallway to gaze through the large window. The sun dipped behind the horizon, and a hint of sea mist had settled over the treeline, amongst the neat rows of vines that surrounded the McAllister property. There might be time to sample the local wine during her stay. Jess had been amazed by at least half a dozen signs for wineries along the highway between Geelong and the farm.

The sky was painted a dusky blue and streaked with pink and violet. Quite different from a week ago when she'd watched the dipping orange sun mirrored in London's shimmering city buildings from her flat's terrace. Jess sighed and reluctantly made her way towards the kitchen where an increasingly loud and discordant metallic rapping echoed down the hallway. *What on earth?*

A woman stood at the stove, facing away from Jess. Large over-ear headphones perched atop her cropped blondish hair. This *must* be Lillian. Dressed in checked cotton trousers, charcoal singlet, and bare feet, she moved to music only she could hear.

Blame it on her drowsiness, or just the gentle sway of the body in front of her—Jess stood mesmerised. Lillian held a long-handled spoon in one hand and a metal whisk in the other, and used the utensils like a pair of drumsticks, beating out a rhythm on a group of pots and the stainless-steel benchtop. She stopped her drumming abruptly and turned a half circle to face Jess.

"Oops—" The utensils clattered to the floor.

"Sorry." Lili tugged the headphones off her head and placed them on the kitchen bench. She stared at the stranger who was yet familiar, thanks to her previous Googling. "Jessica?"

"Lillian?"

"Lili. I prefer Lili."

"Okay. And I prefer Jess," she said.

Jess stared at Lili, her eyes dark and broody. Her arms were crossed tightly in front of her chest. The borrowed T-shirt was stretched across Jess's shoulders, and the cotton drawstring pants came to just above her muscled calves. The tabloids didn't do her justice. She was even more beautiful in real life.

"Sorry I scared you." Jess lowered her gaze, then picked the fallen utensils up off the floor and extended them helplessly toward Lili. "Where do I—"

"Here, let me." Lili grabbed the utensils—perhaps more aggressively than she'd intended—and threw them in the sink, where they clattered loudly.

"I did call out," Jess said, after the silence between them had obviously become too much. "I wasn't sure if Helen was still here." She tilted her head to one side, then gestured to her clothes. "Not exactly my size. I hope you don't mind? Your mother was kind enough to lend me something to wear."

Jess seemed to be struggling either with tiredness or perhaps embarrassment. "I'm Ben's sister," she said unnecessarily, then turned red. "Of course, you already know that."

God, she did look like Ben. Lili stared, unable to think of what to say. Jess had the same lustrous dark-brown hair, large, expressive eyes, and high cheekbones. She pinched the bridge of her nose in that familiar nervous habit, just like her brother. But dressed in Lili's clothes, with a bewildered look on her face, Jess appeared to have none of Ben's cheerful, carefree disposition.

Lili took a slow breath. "You have my deepest sympathy, Jess. I am so sorry," she said. "If there is anything I can do to help, please let me know." She ran some water over the utensils in the sink. "I should apologise. I didn't hear you come into the kitchen. I use headphones so I don't disturb Ru."

"No problem. Do you know where my luggage would be?"

"Yes. Dad left your things by the front door." Lili pointed to the leather suitcase, matching carry-on, and two duty-free bags. "Would you like a hand?"

"No, thank you. What about my bicycle and car? I didn't get a chance to ask where they'd been parked."

"Dad's locked them both in the garage, safe and sound."

"Thank you."

"Are you sure I can't help you with your bags?"

Jess shook her head. "I'll manage."

"Okay then." Lili hesitated. The woman looked ready to drop, but if she didn't want her help, she wouldn't push. "You must be hungry. Can I get you something? I've made some vegetarian laksa, I was about to serve—" Lili lifted another bowl from the shelf.

"I'm not hungry. After a decent night's sleep, I may feel more human."

"How about something to drink?" Lili offered. "A local apple cider or glass of wine?"

Jess stifled a yawn and muttered, "Goodnight, Lillian...Lili. I'm beat. Can we talk in the morning?" She moved towards her pile of luggage. "It's been a long day. If you don't mind, I'll head back to bed."

Lili nodded. "You'll be able to hear the ocean if you leave the window open. It may help you sleep."

"I do hope so. I'll see you tomorrow."

"Yes, see you in the morning," she said, watching Jess skilfully juggle the numerous bags under both arms and walk towards her room.

Lili sipped her drink. Its fresh apple sweetness didn't taste right after her brief encounter with taciturn Jess. *Guess I could have handled that a little bit better. She does hold control over your financial future, Lili.* She set aside the bottle and reached for her bowl of soup. Maybe she should have coaxed her more into sharing a meal. She decided to leave a note on the kitchen table telling Jess to help herself to fresh fruit, biscuits, or anything in the fridge.

It wasn't much, but it was all Lili could think to do right now to reach out to her stand-offish and reticent houseguest. If Jessica Harris was like this when they'd only just met, what was she going to be like when it came time to sort out their awkward financial situation?

Chapter 4

THE FAINT ROAR OF THE ocean and rustling wind in the trees had lulled Jess to sleep last night. She'd managed a few good hours of undisturbed rest. Stretching lazily, she watched sunbeams dance along the white bedroom walls—like musical notes across a staff. Jess rolled across the sun-warmed mattress and reached for her phone on the bedside table. Six forty-five. She threw aside the duvet, swung her legs off the bed, and pulled the white T-shirt down over her well-worn grey pyjama shorts.

Eager to get her bearings, she pushed open the door and stepped outside onto the deck. The sky was a painter's canvas. Wispy silver clouds with ribbons of fading oranges and reds hung over the property that stretched out below her with clusters of trees forming a surprisingly verdant foreground to the distant bay view. She breathed in the sweet, damp scent of eucalyptus gums and savoured the fragrance of slightly sulphuric, briny sea air. Although Jess had lived in the countryside as a child, it had been miles from the ocean.

Leaning against the doorframe, Jess winced as pain shot through her leg. She hadn't fully adjusted to the time difference or the stresses of the long-haul flight. She bent and stretched her left knee a few times to relieve her tight muscles. The local roads looked steep enough to provide a moderate workout and put her new carbon-frame bicycle to the test.

A bird's harsh screech and a flash of blue and red drew Jess's attention skywards. Exuberant child's laughter followed, punctuated by a high-pitched squeal. Jess turned towards the sound as the little girl skipped along the deck next to her.

"Good morning, Ru."

Ru waved her arms and pointed to the brightly coloured birds. "Look, look," she yelled.

"Yes, I see them. Are they king parrots?"

"No, Jess. It's rosellas." Ru tugged excitedly at the hem of Jess's shorts. "They have blue cheeks."

"I always did get them confused," Jess said, staring at her for a moment. "Are you out here alone?"

"*Cussik-cussik. Cussik-cussik*," Ru cried out, imitating the rosellas. She shook her head, seemed to contemplate her answer, and scrunched her nose. "I am allowed out on the deck by myself but *no* further. Mama said so."

"Okay, good to know. Where is your mother?" Jess sat down on the step, and Ru joined her.

Ru bit her bottom lip and pointed to the other end of the house. "My mama is still asleep. I tried to wake her. She opened one eye, said 'ten more minutes, please', and fell asleep again." She jabbed at the symbol printed on the front of Jess's T-shirt. "What is this?"

Oh. The *Un-Chained* T-shirt she'd slept in. "That's a bicycle wheel."

"I want a bicycle." She reached over to trace the surgical scar on Jess's left knee and gently prodded the two incision marks on either side of the slightly raised skin. "Does it hurt?"

Jess flinched at the unexpected touch. She gazed into Ru's concerned eyes and shook her head. "They don't hurt anymore."

Ru kissed her palm and pressed her damp hand to Jess's scarred knee. "Poor Jess."

"Don't worry, I'm okay." She took Ru's hand in her own and squeezed.

Ru sat pressed close against Jess's side, and together they watched flocks of rosellas and galahs diving, making spirals, and swooping through the treetops.

Ru toyed with a delicate chain around her neck, and sunlight glistened on the polished surface. A small heart-shaped pendant hung on the chain, partially obscured by Ru's pyjama top.

One glimpse of it, and Jess froze. It looked exactly like the blue filigree heart that had always hung from her mother's neck and she'd played with as a child. She reached out and brushed the locket with her finger. The silver was slightly tarnished, but the turquoise face was smooth and still in incredibly good condition. And it was definitely her mother's.

Jess had always assumed the precious locket had been buried with her. But then, she'd been too young when her mother died to be included in on those sorts of questions, she supposed. Someone must have given it to Ben when she died. But who?

"*Jess?*"

She felt a gentle tug on her arm, and only then did it register that she'd grasped onto the locket so tightly, she was pulling Ru towards her.

"I'm sorry." Jess loosened her grip and turned over the small piece of jewellery. The Sanskrit symbol of Vajra was etched into the silver, just as she remembered. "Where did you get this, Ru?" she asked.

"Mama gave it to me. It was a special present from Ben after he went to heaven." Ru's eyelids half-closed. "It was in an envelope with my name on it." She sighed and eased the locket out of Jess's hold. "Mama cried a lot when she put it around my neck. It's mine, Jess. The envelope said, *Aruishi Helen McAllister.*"

"Is that your name? Aruishi?" She clenched her fist so tightly, her nails dug into the palm of her hand.

"Yes. That's why I got the envelope with the locket." Ru placed her hand over the pendant, as though to protect it.

Jess stared wide-eyed at Ru—Aruishi—for several seconds. Her dark hair, dimples, and big brown eyes. And that smile. How had she failed to notice the resemblance to her own mother? And Ben? God, now that she thought about it, Aruishi was so much like her brother as a child.

"Aruishi, can I please have a closer look at your locket?"

"Sure." Aruishi lifted it over her head and handed it to Jess. "You look funny."

"I just want to check…" Jess slowly unclasped the tiny catch to reveal a small black-and-white photograph of her mother, Aruishi Annand Harris. The other side of the locket held a faded snapshot of two children. She stared at the miniature portrait of a boy with his arm protectively around his young sister. Ben and Jess.

Jess took a slow, drawn breath, closed the locket, and placed it around Aruishi's neck. She carefully tucked it back and patted her pyjama top.

"Why are you sad?" Aruishi reached out and touched Jess's face.

"Ru, where are you?"

Aruishi turned her head towards her mother's call.

"Could you come inside now? Please?" Lili's voice was stern.

"It's Mama." Aruishi tugged on Jess's arm. "She will make you better. She gives great hugs."

"*Aruishi*, I'm waiting…" This time her voice was louder. Insistent.

"You'd better go inside," Jess urged.

Aruishi kicked the wooden step with the toe of her red slipper.

"Go on, your mother wants you." Jess gave her a gentle push, and Aruishi ran inside.

She closed her eyes. Why had no one told her Ben had a child? Why had *Ben* never told her? She had a niece. She was an aunt.

Several moments later, Jess stood under the shower, gripped the tap, and increased the heat until the room filled with steam. *He should have told me. He should have.*

All right, she'd been making excuses, refusing to meet up with Ben for nearly twenty years, except for that one occasion in Spain, when he'd turned up unannounced. She'd kept him at a physical and emotional distance all that time. *And you think that you deserved for him to tell you?* Now she had lost her chance to reconcile with him. Forever.

Jess flinched at the burn on her skin and turned the tap to cold, her mind stuck replaying a loop of that last day in Melbourne in 2000. The departure gate at Tullamarine Airport. Her father pulling on her arm to board the plane to England, pulling her along like one of his suitcases as Ben watched through the glass security gate. Her muscle memory still felt the gut-wrenching emotional pain from that day when she and her father had turned the corner of the aerobridge and Ben vanished from her sight.

Unlike Jess, who had had no choice, Ben had *chosen* to stay in Australia after their mother's death. How could he have picked his chef's apprenticeship over her? Who left his baby sister, not even a teenager, to fend for herself in a new country, especially without her mother?

Seeing the locket again after all this time released a flood of traumatic memories, ones she really didn't need now that she had *this* news to deal with: he had named his daughter after their *mother*, for God's sake, and he had never told Jess about it.

A flash of ice-cold water jolted her, and she jumped out from under the spray, shutting off the taps altogether. She stared at the tile wall and it hit her: she'd thought her entire family was gone.

Now there was Aruishi.

Aruishi sprinkled her porridge with chopped dates and cashews, and stirred the mixture roughly with a circular motion, while she sang at the top of her voice.

"I love your singing, but we have a visitor. Jess was really tired, and we should let her sleep for as long as possible." Lili planted a kiss on Aruishi's forehead. "Sing quietly, please."

"Jess is already awake," Aruishi whispered, adding a few slices of banana to her bowl.

"Oh? And how do you know that?" She placed her hands on her hips. "You didn't wake her, did you?" Lili lifted Aruishi's chin until she held her gaze. "Did you disturb her?"

She shook her head. "No, Mama, I promise. She was already awake. We watched the birds on the deck."

"When?"

"Earlier." Aruishi squeezed her eyes shut in an almost wink and scooped a heaped spoon of porridge into her mouth.

"Okay," Lili said. She hadn't seen Jess on the deck earlier.

"Mama?"

"Yes, sweetie?"

"Jess is sad."

Lili squatted down beside her daughter. "Yeah, she is. Did Jess say something to you?"

Aruishi brought her shoulders up to her ears in an exaggerated shrug. "I showed her my heart, and then she looked really sad." She pulled the silver locket from inside her T-shirt and held it out to Lili. "Why did it make her sad? Does Jess know Ben's not coming back?" She stared at Lili, her eyes wide.

"Yes, baby, she does know." Lili tugged at her ear. *And she's just found out she has a niece.* Why had Lili been so dense? She should have realised last night that Jess hadn't a clue. Ben hadn't told her. She should have put the locket away until she had a chance to tell her.

"I miss Ben."

Lili blinked back her tears and tugged Aruishi into her arms. "I miss him too."

41

Aruishi held on to her. "You need to give her one of your special hugs, Mama."

"Maybe later." Lili tightened their embrace. She considered Aruishi's suggestion that sorrow could be resolved with a simple hug. If only things worked that easily. She could no more imagine hugging Jess than drinking a cup of cold instant coffee. But Aruishi was right: Jess really did need a hug.

Lili lingered outside the guest bedroom door. She took a deep breath and raised her hand, ready to knock. Should she wait for Jess to come out of her room? No, she had to do it now. She knocked firmly.

"Jess," she called. She waited for an answer, then knocked again. "Jessica…can I come in, please?" She turned the handle and stepped inside. The room was ultra-tidy, the bed immaculately made. The only indication that Jess had been in the room at all was the clothes she'd borrowed, neatly folded on the dresser.

Lili walked onto the balcony and closed the sliding door, leaped off the deck, and headed for the north paddock that led down to the beach. She strode the quarter kilometre across the field, taking a chance that she'd find Jess near the water. Visitors to the farm found it hard to resist the gently undulating slope that led to the water's edge.

When she arrived at the boundary gate, Lili checked to the left, where five hundred metres along, the creek flowed through a narrow lagoon and crossed the sand. No sign of Jess; just a few pied oystercatchers digging for treasure amongst the reeds. She walked back along the wire fence and searched right, towards the wooden jetty.

Lili spotted Jess, striding along the beach. Even from this distance, she noticed her lean, wiry figure and the way she moved with the confidence and lightness of the athlete that she was.

As if sensing she wasn't alone, Jess looked up, clearly surprised to see Lili, and she raised her arm.

Lili waved back. Dreading the conversation she knew they had to have, she held the metal gate open and waited for Jess to pass through.

Before she had time to fasten the gate, Jess turned sharply and glared at her. Her lips were clamped together in a thin line, and her eyes flashed.

"Why didn't you tell me?" she asked in a slow, measured tone. "About you and my brother's relationship? You had his child." Jess leaned towards Lili intimidatingly, her arms crossed tightly in front of her chest.

"Whoa…hang on—" Lili held her hands up.

"Are you going to stand there and deny that Aruishi is Ben's child?" Jess demanded. "*Aruishi?*"

"Hold on. Just give me a chance to explain."

Jess scowled at her. "Were you and my brother in a relationship?"

"No."

She looked startled and took a step back. "So, you're denying she's Ben's child?"

"No. Yes, Aruishi is Ben's child."

"Make up your mind."

"Look, it's not what you think."

"Not what I *think*? I don't know *what* to think."

Lili leaned heavily on the gate. "What is your problem?" She pointed a finger at Jess and said, "You know what? It's not my fault you were estranged from your brother—"

"She's four years old, and I didn't even know she existed," Jess snarled.

Lili blinked and lowered her gaze. "It's not my fault. You don't understand," she said through clenched teeth.

"I feel like a total fool. Why didn't your parents tell me yesterday? I mean, they introduced me to your daughter and didn't bother to tell me. Does she know who I am?"

Lili looked out over the bay. "She does know Ben has a sister. She just hasn't put two and two together—she *is* only four."

"You could have told her who I was when I arrived."

"I can understand that you're upset, but how could we have known Ben hadn't told you? I'm so sorry you didn't know." She kept her voice low. "Look, I'm not prepared to stand out here and have you yell at me. We can discuss it back at the house. Helen is with Ru now and taking her to play group in around fifteen minutes. We'll have the place to ourselves."

Jess nodded stiffly and moved alongside her.

Lili held up her hand. "I'll go ahead," she said. "Meet me in half an hour."

How was it possible that Jess's life had tilted off its axis so spectacularly? The crash. Her injuries. The danger of losing her career. Her brother's death. And now this.

She closed her eyes as a gust of wind blew sand in her face. "Damn it." She never let anyone see her cry.

The earth seemed to mock her. Sunlight glistened on the tranquil water, and the fragrance of the fresh grass under her feet taunted her with memories of her childhood and happier times. She dusted herself off and headed back along the shale path to the house.

Ten minutes later, Jess stood on the deck outside her room and stared at her reflection in the window. There were dark circles under her eyes, and her windswept hair resembled a bird's nest. She wanted to return home. For the sake of speed and simplicity, she should let Lili set the terms for repayment of the money owed to Ben's estate and get the hell out of here. But now she had a niece. What was she supposed to do with that information?

Jess leaned over the basin and splashed water on her face. She traced her finger along the thin line near her collarbone, then bent down to touch the incision marks and scarring from her knee surgery. The doctors had assured her the scars would fade in time.

She pulled up the hem of her running shorts and brushed her palm across the small marks along the top of her thigh. The cuts were marginally raised and only barely visible. She hadn't cut herself for a very long time, having found refuge in her sport and music. Her life had changed, and she'd come away from that dark, lonely pain—but Jess knew her triggers and acknowledged she was heading for a roller-coaster ride that in the past would unquestionably have tested her mettle.

Jess brushed out the tangles and tossed her hair over her shoulder. When she'd first arrived in England, her hair had been so long that it had touched her lower back. Her mother had always liked it that way. But on her own, it had been hard to look after and impossible to make into the two braids her mother had woven so deftly for her every morning.

On the last day of school, before she was to return to her father's home in London, Jess had caught the bus to the town barber and got it chopped off—super short. She'd read about the Hindu ritual *mundana,* and even though she wasn't a newborn and she wasn't Hindu, she'd wanted her hair to be shorn to signify that religious ceremony—freedom from the past and moving into the future. Eventually, it had grown back with a slight crimp, and it now rippled below her shoulders. She tucked a loose strand of hair behind her ear and glanced into the mirror again. Composed. Calm. Collected. Years of practice at keeping her feelings hidden allowed her to mask her emotions. It was time to face Lili.

From the door of the light-filled office, Jess watched Lili hold a pencil between her perfect white teeth. She gazed through the window, her shoulders slumped, as if she carried an enormous weight upon them. She wore a coat of vulnerability at that moment—contradicting the resilience and toughness Jess imagined it took to run a successful business. What could Jess anticipate from this woman?

Lili spun around in the chair. "I really do wish you'd stop doing that."

"I'm sorry."

Lili's china-blue gaze bore into her. "That is the second time you've crept up on me." She pointed to the empty chair across the desk, and Jess sat.

"I regret what I said before. I had no right to make accusations." Jess crossed her legs, sat upright in her chair.

"And I am so sorry you didn't know about Aruishi."

"Ben never told me he had a child," she said. "After our father's death from a heart attack six years ago, we should have grown closer; we were all the family we had. But that didn't happen. And none of that was your fault. I'm sorry too." She tucked her hands under her thighs. "Had you separated from each other?"

"What?" Lili squinted and tilted her head to one side.

"You weren't travelling with Ben when he died. And he had a girlfriend, the one who died in the accident with him."

Lili stood up and paced the floor. "Ben and I were very good friends, but we were never *together*. We loved each other like family, but we were never lovers."

"I don't understand," Jess said.

"Ben and I were never a couple." Lili twisted her hands together in her lap. "I'd been in what I thought was a steady two-year relationship with my partner Dani when I met your brother. I wanted to have a baby, and Dani agreed we would do that." Lili sat back in her chair. "With Dani's promotion, both of our careers were stable enough for me to take maternity leave." Lili shrugged her shoulders. "But things don't always work out the way you expect."

Jess tilted her head. Ah, she supposed this was how Ben fit into the picture. "Was there some kind of problem with you falling pregnant?"

"No," Lili said emphatically. "I was fine. No, we wanted Ben to be the one to help us. Dani was totally there when Ben agreed to be the donor. Your brother had become a close friend—he was an easy choice." She took a deep breath before continuing. "My first trimester went smoothly, and I sailed through without any sickness. It's hard to pinpoint exactly when things started to change between me and Dani. At week fifteen, Dani failed to show up for an appointment with the gynaecologist. Things went downhill from there."

"Oh," Jess said. She thought she had it now. "Ben agreed to be the donor because your partner was infertile?"

"What?" Lili narrowed her eyes. "What makes you think Dani was infertile?"

Lili looked even more confused than Jess was at this point. Then, suddenly, her face lit with some kind of recognition. "Oh, Jess, wait a minute. I think there's something you don't understand here."

Jess crossed her arms. "Well, I certainly don't understand why a perfectly fertile couple needed help from my brother having a baby."

"Uh, we needed help because *neither* of us had the sperm required," Lili said with a grin.

"What?"

"Jess, Dani is a woman—I'm gay."

It had never once occurred to Jess that Lili could be a lesbian. But now that Jess looked her over, little things started to fall into place. She had a slightly muscled, naturally toned body—definitely gorgeous, in fact. Her hair was short and practical. None of these necessarily meant anything, especially on their own. But now that she thought about it, there was something about the way that Lili interacted with her that was a clue: her gaze when she talked to Jess was direct, and maybe even a little searching. Once Jess was alerted to it, she could remember how when she and Lili had first met, she had noticed and forgotten immediately how Lili had given her the same kind of flickering glance that Jess recognised she did herself with women of interest, as if somewhere in the back of her unconscious mind

Lili was looking Jess over and weighing her options. She probably should have guessed.

"So, wait. Your girlfriend Dani—"

"Short for Danielle," Lili supplied.

"Okay, so you're saying that Danielle agreed to Ben getting you pregnant, let you go through the first trimester, and as soon as it started getting real, dumped you?" Jess would have been furious with this Danielle woman. "What a bitch."

"Well, it wasn't as simple or as blatant as all that." Lili sighed. "At least not at first. Dani started working longer hours, coming home late more and more often. I finally confronted her, and after avoiding the question some, she admitted she'd made a terrible mistake and that a child was not in her future. She didn't want to be a parent after all."

Jess raised her eyebrows. "Four months pregnant. Jesus, what did you do?"

"What could I do? I kept working. I needed to earn a living."

"Where was Ben?"

"He was working in South Africa. Right from the start, our agreement did not involve parental obligations on his part." She gave Jess a shrug. "At seven months, I stopped work, and my parents coaxed me back to the farm."

"You returned home."

"Yes, and then Ben turned up just before Ru was born." A blissful smile graced Lili's face. "She was such a beautiful baby. Blame it on postnatal melancholy, or just stupidity, but I was naïve enough to think Dani might show up, knowing Ru would have been born by then, would see her and want to get back together. It was irrational of me to think that." Lili sighed. "I did get an e-mail wishing us luck and informing me about her accepting a job transfer to London."

That must have been a harsh reality check. "What about Ben?"

"Oh, Ben stuck around. He didn't seem to be in his usual rush to keep moving. He was fantastic and helped us fix up the house so Ru and I could move in."

"This house was already here?" Jess asked. "It looks newly built."

"Mum and Dad were in the process of building it as a holiday rental, to make a bit of money in their retirement."

"That's quite a sacrifice on their part."

Lili tilted her head, levelling her gaze. "They did offer. I used my savings for the redesign and to finish the build. Everyone pitched in. We came home from the birth centre and moved straight here. The renovation wasn't finished, but it was liveable. Ben helped select finishes and appliances. As I said, he was fantastic. After putting up with me for a few months, I'm sure Mum and Dad were happy to reclaim their cottage. It wouldn't have been much fun for them living with a new baby."

"Hmm..." Jess looked around the room. "Well, this is a great house."

Lili stood up and walked over to the window. "It is perfect for Ru and me." She stared outside. "And my parents are close by whenever I need to be at the restaurant." After a moment, her tone pitched upwards. "Hey, listen. Are you hungry? Let's have lunch. At Ailie." She tapped the window pane with her fingers. "You should see it sooner or later. It's technically part yours at the moment."

Jess guessed Lili was ready for a change of subject, but she couldn't help taking the bait. She had yet to see this place that had so captured her brother's attention. She surprised herself by grinning back at Lili, despite how awkward and unresolved the subject of the restaurant was between them.

"Sure," she said, standing up. "Why not?"

Chapter 5

LILI'S BLONDE HAIR GLEAMED IN the sunlight that picked up the red highlights. Jess stared at the short, lustrous strands, unexpectedly captivated yet again. But they were indeed beautiful in the light of this sunny day. She found herself wondering what it would be like to run her fingers through them.

Really, Jess told herself, *the minute you find out she's a lesbian, you start gawking at her highlights. You're as ridiculous as the tabloids say you are, Jessica Harris.*

"Jess?"

She blinked upon hearing her name. "Yes?"

Lili gestured for Jess to follow her under the arched courtyard entrance covered in rambling yellow roses that laced the air with a heady fragrance.

They had ambled along the farm's dirt road, through a stand of sheoke and manna gum trees, and across the grassy hillside. After a brisk ten minutes, they reached the top of a rise into a service area outside a high brick wall that appeared to be the staff carpark and delivery entrance.

Jess followed Lili around a rustic rectangular brick and greying-timber building, along a path that meandered through vegetable and herb plots of different sizes. She stood back and admired the abundance of plants, some growing on metal and wooden supports, while Lili harvested an assortment of spring salad greens of various hues and textures.

As they reached the terrace, Lili pointed to the restaurant's large windows that overlooked the kitchen garden. "The veranda and main dining room have views of the You Yang ranges and the Melbourne skyline across the bay," she said. "We can seat thirty-five to forty guests. But we've hosted stand-up parties for up to three times that number."

Jess pointed towards an old stone chimney with a blackened fireplace. "That looks like a really old stack. Not something I'd expect in a restaurant garden."

"It's all that's left of my grandparents' cottage, which was gutted in a fire years ago, but the chimney survived. Dad took it down stone by stone and resurrected it here."

"He did a good job," Jess said. "Your father told me his parents settled here from Scotland."

"Yes. After the Second World War." Lili moved to a stone bench and ran her finger over the raised letters of a carved plaque with a Scottish thistle emblem. "*Faodail*. It means *a lucky find*. I guess they considered this land their lucky find." Lili lifted her face up towards the sun and twirled the silver helix cuff that adorned the top of her left ear. "Ready for some lunch?"

Lili turned, and Jess found herself staring into those clear blue eyes. *Seriously, quit it. You were fighting with her half an hour ago.* She nodded in agreement. "Does this garden provide a lot for the restaurant?"

"Not everything, but it supplies us with *most* of the required herbs, salad leaves, and a selection of vegetables." Lili placed her armful of pickings on a table in a shady corner of the terrace and brushed her hands on her trousers. "Beyond the garden walls, we have an orchard that produces apples, stone fruit, and quince, and there's a small almond grove. Also, we grow our own blueberries, strawberries, and blackberries in season. A lot of restaurants have kitchen gardens." Lili reached into a raised planter and picked a handful of jagged leaves.

"But it's worth it, right? You wouldn't be doing all that work otherwise."

"Oh yeah." Lili smiled broadly. "It's worth it for many reasons."

"Is this rocket?" Jess showed her the bit of plant she'd snipped off with her fingers.

"Wild rocket. It was once regarded as a weed, but its mustard flavour adds a punch. I thought I'd use it in our lunch salad."

"A salad from weeds? I don't know about that." Jess bit tentatively into the dark-green leaf. "It has a peppery bite."

Lili arched her brow. "I'm sure I can tempt you, or at least I can try. Follow me." She retrieved a set of keys from the pocket of her trousers.

They entered through double-height glass doors into the dining room, where old wooden beams framed the white vaulted ceiling.

"Welcome to Ailie." Lili gestured with an outstretched arm. Her face shone with pleasure.

The stylishness of the interior surprised Jess. Modern but unpretentious pale-coloured wood tables and contemporary upholstered chairs were arranged to take advantage of the sweeping views. They were a marked contrast to the rustic, exposed red-brick walls and iron chandeliers. She guessed the rough-hewn ceiling beams were remnants of the original building, and they added a warm and honest feel to the interior space.

Lili led her past a sleek stone counter with a row of vintage barstools and a colourful bar alcove, through a set of swing doors into the kitchen.

Like the dining room, it was filled with natural light. The shiny metallic equipment, polished surfaces, and gleaming copper pans hanging over the workbench looked amazing.

"Wow, this place is much more upscale than I'd imagined. It's so clean and gleaming and bright."

Lili poked her head out from behind the refrigerator door. "I'm sorry, did you say something?"

"I was just saying this place is impressive," Jess said. "When do you open again?"

"We'll reopen for the season next week." Lili pulled a kitchen stool over to the stainless-steel bench and patted the seat. "Sit. The kitchen is the nerve centre."

Jess sat as commanded. "I can only imagine." She tilted her head towards the stained-glass panels in the bar wall. "Don't you mind being on display?"

"It goes both ways. We get to spy on the dining room as well. Anyway, chefs love to put on a show." Her cheek dimpled, and the corners of her eyes crinkled when she smiled. "Well, I do." She wrapped the strings of the indigo apron around her waist and tied it at her front. Lili moved swiftly around the work space, putting a match to the iron griddle and collecting a mixing bowl and whisk, then reached under the workbench to retrieve a red metal toolbox.

Here in the kitchen, she was so clearly sure of herself. Her manner and voice transformed from cautious to confident. Lili selected two knives from her toolbox and set them on to a rectangular cutting board. She hummed softly as she worked and flashed a smile that Jess couldn't help but return.

"The fennel should be tender but crisp." Lili moved the lightly charred vegetables to one side of the griddle. She peeled and segmented an orange, brushed the griddle again with olive oil, and placed the fruit down. Within seconds it hissed and sizzled, releasing a fragrant scent of roasting citrus. "I'll grill this just until the sugars start to caramelise." She threw a few ingredients into a bowl and whisked them together. "Olive oil, lime juice, and seeded mustard." A handful of walnuts and balsamic vinegar were tossed around in a pan with butter.

She grinned at Jess, who leaned closer and smiled back at her. Lili placed the wild rocket into a bowl.

There was a jar on the bench waiting for Lili. Jess picked it up and stared at the contents.

"May I?" Lili lifted the jar out of Jess's hand and opened the lid. "It's a crumbly feta with just a touch of lemon myrtle. Balances the sweet and savoury flavours in the salad perfectly." She used her fingers to break the cheese into the bowl, and reached for the toasted walnuts. "Now for the finish. The nuts are for richness and crunch. And the mustard dressing is for zing."

"Do you always bother to make such a fancy lunch for yourself?" Jess asked.

"No. Not usually, but I'm not by myself." Her fine eyebrows raised just a fraction. "It's a version of the Roasted Fennel and Orange Salad from the menu. Same ingredients, just not as intricately plated." Lili removed her apron and tossed it on the bench. "Come on, let's sit outside." She collected two bowls, some cutlery, glasses, and a pitcher of iced tea from the refrigerator and gestured towards a small cloth-covered basket. "If you grab the bread and serviettes, lunch is ready."

Jess followed Lili out to the terrace. She focused first on the black T-shirt stretched across Lili's shoulders, then travelled down to her slender hips clad in low-slung trousers. Unlike elite cyclists who obsessed in their pursuit of leanness, Lili was graced with gentle curves and toned muscles, more like a dancer's. Well-proportioned, healthy, and strong.

Lili turned around and raised an eyebrow. She held Jess's gaze for a fleeting moment and set the food down on a table under the green canopy of dappled shade. "Sit, please," she said.

Jess placed the bread basket in the centre of the table and lowered herself into the chair opposite Lili.

"So, what about the restaurant?" Jess busied herself with unfolding her cloth napkin and placing it onto her lap.

Lili's expression brightened. "As much as I could talk for hours about the day-to-day inner workings of my restaurant, come on—let's eat."

"Okay, but actually I meant how did the restaurant come to be *here*?"

"Oh." She jabbed a fork into the greens. "Well, after Ru was born, my parents asked me to consider opening a restaurant or café here on the farm."

Jess recalled the framed photograph she'd just seen in Ailie's kitchen, one of newborn Aruishi with Scott and Helen McAllister standing over the bassinet. Jess knew instantly why it was there, in such a pride of place in Lili's restaurant. In the photo, the new grandparents' faces were filled with wonder. Lili had been right when she talked about Aruishi being a beautiful baby.

"They had it all worked out. Since Dad closed the dairy a few years ago, the old milking shed and brick courtyard had been wasting. They reckoned it was an ideal site for a restaurant, investigated a planning permit for the renovation, and engaged a draughtsman for some ideas."

"They clearly had faith in your abilities," Jess said. "But, um, if you don't mind me saying, it's not exactly Sydney, *or* Melbourne. Isn't that what you were used to? Big city? Fast pace?"

"It's what I thought I wanted, but my circumstances changed." Lili met her challenging glance. "My parents' generosity and promise of assistance with Ru gave me the opportunity to reconcile duelling responsibilities— work and family. It was the ideal solution. And this area has always been popular with tourists, especially since the Peninsula re-established itself as a wine region. It was decimated by a deadly vine disease in the 1870s."

"I saw lots of signs for restaurants, and there are wineries everywhere. In fact, we are surrounded by grapevines here."

"That's because we lease our land to a vineyard," Lili explained.

"How did Ben fit into this?"

"When I told him the idea of converting the milking shed into a restaurant, he was pretty enthusiastic. I drew up plans of my own, based on the draughtsman's structural blueprint. He agreed it was a great opportunity to establish a restaurant away from the pressures of big-city competition and offered to help financially right from the start." Lili stopped abruptly as if she were aware she'd waded back into thorny territory. "I don't know why. Maybe because of Ru."

"I'm sorry I jumped to conclusions about your relationship with Ben." She was.

Lili waved a dismissive hand. "Happens to the best of us." She stood up. "How about some tea now?"

Lili stretched out her legs under the table and sipped her tea. She was a good observer, and her guest intrigued her. Jess picked at her food self-consciously—like someone who didn't acknowledge the pleasure of eating.

When Jess let down her guard, her brown eyes were warm and rich as the Peninsula's soil, complex as the finest espresso.

"Lili."

"Hmm?"

"Thank you." A small frown creased Jess's forehead. "I've emptied my plate. I didn't think I could eat it all, but I have." She sat back and draped her arm over the back of the chair. "You seem to like what you do. Why did you become a chef?"

"I *love* what I do," Lili said. "Growing up, I wanted to be a farmer like Mum and Dad. We've always had a vegetable garden and fruit trees." Lili breathed in deeply, enjoying the mixture of fragrances on the terrace: lavender, the piquant sweetness of oregano, and the sharpness of lemon-scented thyme. "I love having my hands in the dirt. Pulling up potatoes and carrots, and picking fresh silverbeet and green beans. In summer, there was an abundance of berries to make tarts or jam. On weekends, we'd bake a variety of breads and cakes. The house was always filled with the most delicious smells. It wasn't until my last year at school that I considered a career in cooking. I love experimenting with new ingredients, and we have a wealth of produce right here on the Peninsula."

"And yet you left to pursue your career elsewhere," Jess said. "You went to Sydney."

Lili gathered and stacked their dishes, then refilled their glasses with iced tea. "I had to. It was hard to find the type of restaurant I wanted to work at on the Peninsula, one that would take on a female apprentice. I applied through a rural scheme and was lucky to receive a scholarship to a school in Sydney. And how do you know this about me?" She cast a deliberately playful suspicious glance over at Jess.

"I did look you up on Google."

"Really? Don't believe everything you read online."

"Why not?" Jess shrugged her shoulders. "Your CV reads well. Anyway, you can't blame me, I knew nothing about you."

"Okay, then, I have to admit." Lili bit her lip. "I looked you up too."

"Then it's my turn to ask you not to believe everything *you* read online." Jess gazed at her tentatively. "I dare say, if you read anything you *didn't* like, you wouldn't have allowed me to stay in your home."

"It was quite a colourful read. I can say one thing: They love you in the tabloids. And you seem to enjoy the company of glamorous women."

Jess narrowed her eyes. "I don't read the gossip columns. Most of it is lies or misconstrued."

"Not all. I read about your father and his Olympic medals, and about you following in his footsteps."

"I was never a track cyclist."

"But you did win medals at more than a couple of road events. At junior and world championships. In Argentina, Italy, and America. Also—"

"Lili, please don't."

"I'm sorry. I didn't mean to—"

"It's okay," Jess said. But her tone didn't sound all that convincing.

"I am sorry about your accident. I can't imagine how hard it is to come back after something so horrific."

"Well, I guess I haven't come back yet." She grimaced. "At least not into the competitive arena." Jess's voice had definitely turned strained.

"But you still ride. I saw your flash bike in the garage."

"Yes, I still ride. At present, it's recreational and for rehabilitation." She rested back in her chair. "And for fitness—to build strength before attempting competition again."

Lili bit her tongue. She knew from Jess's demeanour not to recount more.

"So, how about you?" Jess asked. "You've collected a couple of trophies of your own *and* were employed by one of Sydney's best restaurants."

Well, at least she seems to be trying to improve the mood. That's a good sign. And this seemed like safer territory, maybe. "You *did* read up on me, didn't you?" She tried smiling, giving her a little cheek. Maybe Jess would laugh. "Yes, I was lucky. Sydney was where I met Ben, you know." Some positive memories about her brother couldn't hurt either.

But suddenly Jess was drumming impatiently on her knee with her fingers and draining the last of her tea. "Yeah, about Ben. Listen, should we talk soon about the loan?"

"I have all the paperwork if you—" Lili began but stopped midsentence when Jess held up her hand.

"I have copies. The lawyers provided all the financials."

"Oh. Okay, then. Right." Lili stood, picked up the dishes, and headed inside to the kitchen.

"Lili," Jess called out and followed her.

"Yes?" she asked without turning around. She put on her gloves and turned towards the sink.

"I thought you would want this settled so I can get out of your way."

"You are right," Lili said flatly. "I do." She turned on the tap with full force and gasped as water sprayed her face. *Damn.*

"Is there a problem?"

Lili tugged off her gloves and wiped her forehead with the palm of her hand. Wasn't money always a problem? She turned around to face Jess. "No, there's no problem," she said woodenly. "I'll be prepared by the time you've sorted through Ben's stuff."

Jess stood and walked towards her. "Excellent," she said. "What about Aruishi? Have you told her that I'm her aunt?"

"No," Lili snapped, then lowered her voice. "I haven't."

"Don't you want her to know?" Jess pinched the bridge of her nose.

Jess's obvious distress surprised her. She took a deep breath and steeled herself for what she was about to say. "It's hard to explain the situation to a four-year-old. I'll tell her, and then you'll be gone. I need time to think

about the best way to handle it. After Ben died, it was so hard to explain…
that he wouldn't be coming back." Lili crossed her arms.

Jess held up her hand. "I understand."

But she looked suddenly distant. Or something. Something not good.

Great, Lili thought. She'd alienated her yet again. "Well, good," she
said. "We should probably get going. Ru will be back at the house soon."

"Right." Jess's voice sounded stiff. "We should."

Lili bustled around the room for another minute, adjusting a stack of
paper serviettes on the bench, avoiding Jess's gaze and trying not to look
too eager to escape the whole money conversation. She picked up her keys
and shook them as a wordless signal to Jess, then walked briskly towards
the door. Jess, of course, had no choice but to follow. In the midst of this
chaotic, tense situation between them, Lili took some dark comfort in that.

Chapter 6

LILI ENTERED HER KITCHEN TO find Jess at the dining table, bent over a thick folder of papers. As she leafed through the pile, she sipped from a small espresso cup. Jess's dark hair, twisted into a single braid, was draped over her shoulder. She placed the coffee cup on the table and twirled the end of the braid through her fingers.

She was smarting from their argument yesterday. But Jess—in her brightly coloured, snug-fit cycling jersey and bib shorts—still got her attention. The woman could easily grace the cover of *Sports Illustrated* or *LOTL*—in fact, she probably did. Or something British like *Diva* or *Sports Monthly*. Those thick-framed reading glasses just made her more... interesting.

She stifled a yawn and rubbed her eyes. "Good morning, Jess. The coffee smells good."

Jess sat upright. "Good morning." She held up her cup in one hand. Her gaze seemed to be inspecting Lili. Testing the waters, perhaps? They hadn't talked to each other since yesterday afternoon at the restaurant. "I hope you don't mind, I helped myself to your espresso machine."

"No, of course not." Lili moved in behind the kitchen-island bench and reached for the bag of Ethiopian blend. Strong. Just what she needed. "You don't have to ask."

"Well, I didn't." Jess looked up and stared at her intently. "Is that okay?"

"Yes," she said. "I just said you don't have to ask."

When Jess arched her eyebrow, Lili sighed. "Oh, never mind." She flopped into a chair across from Jess. "Looks like you've been out this morning."

"No, not yet." A flash of pleasure briefly lit her brown eyes before the mask came down.

Lili noticed the slight flutter at the corner of Jess's eye and the way she tapped her fingers on her thigh, but nothing in her voice betrayed what she was thinking.

"I would like to go to Ben's house this morning," Jess said abruptly. "Helen left me a note to say you'd arrange my visit with the housemate."

"I've done it. Nathan, the tenant, is away on a job for a couple of days, but he knows you want to access the house. The key is under the Buddha statue on the front porch." What would Jess do with Ben's house in the long term? She knew Nathan was keen to keep renting it, but Lili doubted Jess would hold on to the property.

"Thank you for that." Jess stood and placed her papers neatly into the folder. "I'll make my way to the house later this morning."

"I'll prepare you some breakfast before you go."

Jess shook her head dismissively. "No thanks. Coffee is all I have in the morning."

"Haven't you heard breakfast is the most important meal of the day?"

From the look on Jess's face, she didn't care. "Not for me," she said, turning to walk away.

She wasn't about to argue with Jess. Lili stood still for a moment, her arms braced on the edge of the bench. Then a pang of guilt changed her mind. "Jess."

Jess halted and turned back to Lili. "Yes?"

"I could go with you, if you'd like?"

"I'm sure you have a lot to get done here, with the restaurant opening soon. I'll be fine." She continued towards her room.

"That's that, I guess," she said to herself. Lili reached overhead and removed a cereal bowl from the cupboard. "Well, I'm going to have breakfast." She stubbed her toe on the edge of the skirting board and swore loudly. *When will you learn? She doesn't want your help.*

After two espressos and a large helping of granola, yoghurt, and fruit, Lili threw her nightshirt into the laundry basket and turned on the shower. Her mother had telephoned fifteen minutes earlier and offered to keep Aruishi occupied for the rest of the morning. She was a lifesaver.

After she had stepped out of the shower and grabbed her towel, Lili patted her face dry and glanced in the mirror. *I look a wreck.* Was she imagining it, or were the tension lines around her eyes more visible today?

The papers that seemed to occupy Jess this morning were presumably about Ben's estate and the loan. She didn't want to pry, and she'd been in no shape to discuss the matter then, but Lili wished she'd been brave enough to ask how soon Jess expected to be paid.

Lili reached for the aspirin high up in the medicine cabinet. She needed to cement a plan, and she'd like to do it quickly without jeopardising her staff or the restaurant. She didn't have a business loan with the bank, so she'd have to borrow additional funds on her existing home loan. And because she was essentially self-employed, Lili would need evidence of her assets and earnings for the last few years.

Her first step would be to make an appointment with the bank manager; it was long overdue.

Jess glanced in the rear-vision mirror, took her foot off the brake, and reversed back to the entrance of the property. She'd been thinking about Lili's dishevelled appearance in the kitchen earlier that morning as she'd tugged self-consciously at the hem of her nightshirt and ran her hands through her short, tousled hair—and, of course, she overshot the driveway.

The house, partly hidden by a stand of scrubby trees, had a rusted galvanised iron roof. She manoeuvred the car down the bumpy driveway, parked in front of the garage beside the deck of the timber shack, exited, and climbed the stairs to the small porch. She pushed her sunglasses up to her forehead and checked out her surroundings. This was the place Ben had called home.

Why had it taken so long for her to come back to Australia—to her brother? Jess sighed deeply and extracted the small key from underneath the statue, relieved it was exactly where Lili had advised. She turned the key in the door and ducked under a row of colourful Tibetan prayer flags, then walked straight into a living room and was assaulted by a mixture of smells. A woodsy, earthy odour mixed with petroleum and some kind of resin. It was musty. The house itself—with timber floor boards, white cabinetry, and a sparse scattering of furniture—was surprisingly tidy. A large mounted photograph above the fireplace, of a surfer and his board suspended in mid-air, dominated the space. It must have been Hawaii or another South Pacific island, because the combination of the light, of giant emerald-green waves, and of high mountain peaks was breathtakingly beautiful. Jess stepped closer. Lean and muscled, Ben arched above the wave. She was mesmerised by the image, the sublime stillness and physical beauty captured by the camera. This was her brother, and yet he was a stranger.

Jess wrenched herself away from the photograph. Was her brother's bedroom the one on the left or the one on the right? She opened the door on the left. Oops, wrong room. Luckily, Nathan wasn't home. She opened the door on the right. A large bed consumed the midsized room, and one wall was lined with a stack of brown boxes, each labelled by black marker. She counted—how could the life of a man in his thirties be packed into twenty-two boxes? Jess was faced with the unbearable task of sorting Ben's belongings. She sat down heavily on the end of the bed. Combing through his personal effects seemed too intrusive right now.

She should have taken Lili up on her offer to help, but Jess couldn't deal with the look of sympathy in Lili's big blue eyes, and her obvious determination to get things done and make everything right.

Without allowing herself another moment for reflection, Jess scanned the labels and put aside three boxes, labelled *photos and stuff*, *documents and letters*, and *family*. She would no doubt learn a lot about Ben and their past from the contents of these boxes—when she was ready.

Jess lifted the three large cartons and carried them to the car one at a time. It was more than the physical weight of the things inside that made her journey back and forth to the Mini agonisingly slow.

After she'd loaded the boxes, Jess wandered the short distance down a shale path, over the dunes, and down to the water's edge. She kicked off her running shoes and enjoyed the damp sand and cool seawater washing between her toes. The beach was deserted except for the screeches and flaps of seagulls hopping along the strip of pale-gold sand.

She sheltered her eyes and gazed back towards the shack. Ben's home was small but well located, so near to 13th Beach, popular with surfers and only four kilometres from the seaside village of Barwon Heads.

She understood why Ben chose to live here, in this peaceful coastal environment—he'd grab his board and be in the waves in five minutes. It was also only a thirty-five-minute drive away from the McAllister farm and his daughter. From Lili's description, Ben's involvement had been purely altruistic. Having relinquished all parental obligations, Ben had obviously wanted to be simply near Aruishi—he was interested in her welfare and in her future. Although Ben travelled widely and worked in many cities across Australia, it seemed significant that his main place of residence was here, close to his daughter.

Sadness welled up inside her. The beach was bathed in sunlight, and a gentle wind lifted loose strands of hair from her face. She collected her shoes from the sand and slowly made her way back to the shack.

Jess re-entered the house and stood before the image of her brother. Ben's joyful face and the huge wave and the shimmering silver light evinced a timeless, ethereal tranquillity to the photograph. She wanted to remember him like this.

Chapter 7

JESS REACHED OUT AND GRASPED at nothing.

The thrust of an enormous roaring wave sent the ghostly figures of Ben and her mother catapulting into the air. A scream stuck in her throat. Paralysed by her inability to stop the inevitable, a dread washed over her.

Sweat rolled into Jess's eyes as she blinked them open. She sat up and swung her legs off the bed as a strong cramp knotted in her calf. She winced, limped to the window, stared into the darkness, and placed the length of her trembling body against the cold glass. Beyond the tree line, shadows painted the night and fed her terrors.

"Jess?" Lili called out from behind the door. Her knock had been soft but persistent, and Jess could no longer ignore her presence.

"I'm okay. Please go away."

"Can I come in?" Her tone had shifted from tentative to firm.

The door slid open, and light from the hallway streamed into the room. Lili stood silhouetted in the doorframe.

"I'm okay," Jess repeated in a choked voice. She tightened her arms around her torso and stared, momentarily transfixed by the shimmer of light around Lili's head.

Lili strode into the room, grabbed the blanket at the end of the bed, and wrapped it tightly around Jess's body. It was comforting yet smothering at the same time.

"Thank you." She pulled the blanket high around her shoulders, aware her tank top was damp and clinging to her body.

"You're shivering." Lili rubbed her hands up and down Jess's arms. "Let's sit down." She placed her arm around Jess's shoulder and helped her move to the edge of the bed. "I heard you—"

Jess flinched as Lili sat down beside her and lowered her gaze to where Lili's hand rested on her thigh, near the edge of her sleep shorts. What was she doing?

"I heard you scream. I'm a light sleeper. Probably a mother thing," Lili said in a slow, steady voice. "My room is at the other end of the deck, and sound travels through the open windows."

She wasn't flirting, was she? Despite Lili's touch, she was just being a nice person, Jess thought.

"I'm sorry I woke you." Jess loosened the throw around her shoulders. "I hope I didn't wake Aruishi," she said. "I am okay. Please check on your daughter and return to bed."

"Don't worry about Ru. She sleeps through almost anything." Lili had removed her hand from Jess's leg, but her proximity was disconcerting.

"I am really tired." It was a genuine struggle to keep her eyes open.

Lili reached out and brushed Jess's cheek with her fingers. "Can I get you a glass of water?"

The intimacy of it startled Jess. "I have water," she said lamely, and pointed to the bedside table, feeling a bit flustered. "Thank you for your concern, but really, I'd rather just go back to bed. It's after two. I think we should both get some sleep, don't you?"

"Okay…if you're sure." Lili stood, tugged at the hem of her nightshirt, and backed away.

No, she wasn't at all sure, but Lili didn't need to know that. "Go back to sleep," she said, looking towards the window. The tremor in Jess's hand had eased, but she couldn't hide the tremor in her voice.

"I'm just up the hall if you need me," Lili said softly. She closed the door on her way out.

Jess crawled in between the sheets, rolled onto her back, and drew the covers up to her chin. It would have been safer to stay at a motel. The sympathy she read in Lili's gaze left her exposed, scrutinised. And while she was here, trying to get through this unpleasant, emotional business of Ben's estate, she certainly didn't need pity.

She woke several hours later, irritable and sluggish. Recalling last night how Lili had attempted to come to her rescue, she wondered for a moment whether *that* had been a dream as well. It wasn't easy to admit, even to herself, but she had been comforted by Lili's presence in the early hours of the morning.

After an awful night, the best remedy for Jess's low mood was exercise. And the best exercise was going for a ride. She stopped in the entrance hall, glanced at herself in the mirror, and rubbed her eyes. Surprisingly, there was little sign of the dark circles she'd expected. She picked up the garage keys from the sideboard. The sooner she got on her bicycle and headed into the countryside, the better.

Aruishi marched down the hallway, heading straight for Jess. "Hi, Jess. Are you going riding right now?" She jumped up and down on the spot.

Jess put the keys back on the dresser and crouched beside Aruishi, who gazed at her with a mix of innocence and determination. She couldn't help but smile—albeit tiredly. "I am, Aruishi. How did you guess?"

"You've got your bike stuff on," Aruishi said, pointing at Jess's outfit. "The tight shorts that make your legs sexy."

Jess put her hand out and steadied herself against the wall. "Oh. Who said that?"

"Mama told that to Alex."

Obviously, one had to be careful what they said in the presence of a four-year-old. Apparently, her clothing sponsor's streamlined, skinsuit, body-hugging jerseys, and leg-gripping bib shorts designs were appreciated not only by cyclists. She wondered what else Aruishi had overheard. "I'm just heading out for a ride. Do you have anything special planned for your day?"

Aruishi touched the wraparound sunglasses that hung from a cord around Jess's neck. "Mama and I are spending the morning together. We're cleaning Dora's stall before I go to kinder," she said, tugging at the cord.

Jess wrapped her hand around Aruishi's sticky fingers. "That will make Dora happy. I hope you have fun at kindergarten."

"I always do," she said with a slight frown. "Um, Jess?"

"Yes, Aruishi?"

"We have show-and-tell. Not today, but some days we do."

"Well, you're the lucky one." Where was this leading?

Aruishi sighed and looked down at her feet. "Last time, I took my shell bracelet that Ben brought me from Hawaii. It has beads like a turtle. It's special."

"Oh, is it a good-luck bracelet?" Jess asked.

Aruishi nodded. "Yes, that's what I said. It's special. Ben gave it to me." She placed her hand on Jess's shoulder. "Can I take you next time?"

"Where, to kindergarten?"

"Ah-ha. To show-and-tell."

"You want to take *me* to show-and-tell. Is that allowed?" Jess slowly stood up, and her knee made a cracking sound.

"Ouch, what was that?"

"It's nothing, just my funny knee. Why do you want to take me to show-and-tell?"

"I want to show you to the kids. Come with me, now. I want to talk to you about it. It's serious." Aruishi took her hand and tugged her down the hallway.

Jess allowed herself to be chaperoned to the living room, where Aruishi directed her to sit in a leather armchair in the far corner. She pulled up a tiny wooden chair and sat directly in front of her. The leather creaked as Jess shifted to get comfortable. She sat upright, giving Aruishi her complete attention.

"Mama told me that you're my Ben's sister," Aruishi began. She was the epitome of concentration with cheeks slightly flushed and eyebrows furrowed.

Jess took a deep breath and let it out slowly. *When had that happened?* "That's right, Aruishi. I am Ben's sister."

Aruishi pointed a finger at Jess. "You are my Auntie Jess."

Lili must have decided the time was right to tell Aruishi. Jess wished Lili had given her the heads-up, allowing her time to prepare for the *Auntie* conversation, but still, she was thrilled.

Aruishi, meanwhile, seemed to have a perfect handle on the entire situation, passing out instructions to Jess like she was four going on twenty-four. Jess wanted to pull Aruishi into her arms and cover her earnest face with kisses.

"I am your Auntie Jess." She blinked away the tears that threatened and raised her hand to touch the locket around Aruishi's neck. "Did you know my mama's name was Aruishi? This was her locket, and it has her picture inside." Jess wiped her eyes with the back of her hand. "You were named after her."

"Don't cry, Jess. Auntie Jess." Aruishi placed her hands lightly on Jess's chin and patted her face. "Ben told me I have beautiful brown eyes like his mummy. That's why he gave it to me in an envelope. It was his mama's, and now it's mine."

That did it. Jess couldn't stop the tears from rolling down her cheeks. She wrapped her arms around Aruishi and hugged her gently.

"Don't be sad," she said, tightening her arms around Jess's neck. "Mama said it's a happy discovery. I'm happy to discover you, Jess."

Jess's sunglasses dug into her clavicle, and she flipped them over her shoulder. She leaned back and glimpsed tears in Aruishi's eyes. She pulled her back in for another hug and buried her face in her niece's curly hair. "Me too, Aruishi. I'm so very happy to have discovered you."

"Is everything all right here?" Lili asked.

Jess looked up, and wiped away her tears. How long had she been standing in the doorway?

Aruishi sat back onto her chair and spun around. "I told Jess she's Ben's sister. She's got to come to show-and-tell with me."

Lili placed her hands on her hips and grinned. "She doesn't get her bossy nature from me."

"Oh, really?" Jess raised an eyebrow.

"I've never had an auntie before. Auntie Jess is new and interesting," Aruishi insisted.

"I think it's up to Jess, don't you?" Lili moved closer and placed her hands on Aruishi's shoulders. "Looks like Jess is ready for a ride. She's got her cycling clothes on."

"Yes, the sexy shorts you told Alex about."

Lili looked up at the ceiling as a deep blush surfaced on her cheeks. "Right, it's time to clean Dora's stall. Go and grab your old cardigan, and I'll meet you at the front door."

"Okay." Aruishi turned back to Jess. "Show-and-tell. You must come with me." She shrieked with laughter and ran out of the room.

Jess shook her head and stared down at her hands. "You told her."

"Yes. Only this morning. I'm sorry, I didn't have a chance to let you know."

"No, I'm glad she knows." Jess pushed herself out of the chair and adjusted the mesh bib on her outfit, suddenly self-conscious. "I'd better get on my way."

Lili shoved her hands in her pockets and scanned Jess slowly, from head to toe and back again. "How do you find our country roads? Totally different from those hedgerow lanes in England?"

Jess glanced at Lili and felt the smile bloom over her face. "The hills aren't as challenging as what I'm used to, but I love the distinctive smell of the native trees here." She pushed aside the memory of walking the eucalypt-lined roads around Wylie as a child with her mother. "And I love the breathtaking ocean views," she added.

"But you've ridden all over the world." Lili pursed her lips in thought.

"Hey, I'm enjoying exploring the Peninsula's back roads." She shrugged. "If it's a good enough training ground for Cadel Evans, a Tour de France winner, it's good enough for me."

A pleased smile curled the corner of Lili's mouth. "Enjoy your ride."

"Have fun cleaning Dora's stall." Jess reached for her keys and turned for the door.

"Oh, Jess?" Lili called out.

"Yes?"

"Be careful exploring those back roads."

"Thank you. I will."

After loading and securing the bicycle on the rear mount of the Mini, Jess threw her bag onto the back seat of the car and checked the Map-My-Trail app on her phone for directions.

Twenty minutes later, Jess pulled into the foreshore carpark in Portarlington. She leaned against the car as an assortment of boats moored along the concrete pier gently rocked in the sea breeze, under a sky spattered with wispy clouds.

The route she'd chosen today was a twenty-six-kilometre round-trip, and according to the app, the undulating course would be a relatively tame ride.

Jess slipped into her clipless, recessed rubber-soled shoes and stashed the car keys in the saddlebag under her seat, which held a spare inner tube and a patch kit. She tucked an energy bar into the side pocket of her short-sleeved jersey and attached a water bottle on the bike frame. Finally, she gathered her hair back into a ponytail and fastened the helmet.

Fifteen kilometres into her ride, her heart pumped steadily and her leg muscles had loosened. The carbon fifty-six-centimetre frame was exceedingly comfortable. The bike-fit specialist in Melbourne had adjusted it to her exact requirements. Free and flying along the quiet coastal road, her lungs filled with air, the tension in her neck and back became a distant memory.

In competition cycling, she'd pushed her body to extreme limits. Her muscles screamed; her shoulders ached. Saddle sore and beyond exhausted, nothing in the world mattered more than her legs turning beneath her as she chased that white line to the finish.

Dismounting her bicycle at the top of a rise near Shortland's Bluff, Jess reached for her water bottle, took a large gulp, and gazed out towards Black Lighthouse and the red-bricked walls of Queenscliff Fort. She recalled an excursion to Queenscliff with her mother and brother. She'd been about nine years old and remembered sitting on the old wooden jetty, teasing the seagulls with her paper-wrapped package of hot chips. Ben had been fussy about what he ate even in his early teens, preferring to prepare and cook his own food. But on this occasion, he'd relented and selected a serve of crispy sliced potato cakes and thick, golden battered fish. When their bellies were chock-full of the salty, crunchy treats, he'd used his pocket money to buy them all a chocolate-topped ice cream cone each.

As a doctor in a small country town, her mother had always been busy. The rare chance of a road trip to the coast and time together as a family was a precious memory.

Jess lost the joy of eating and sharing food after the death of her mother. But her earliest recollections of preparing and eating with her family were happy ones—like Lili's.

Her mother's best friend, Doctor Usha, was often present on these occasions. It had been particularly difficult as a five-year-old to wrap biscuit dough around a tiny sausage. But Usha had exercised amazing patience in helping Jess prepare piglets-in-the-blanket and other treats.

She'd loved the kitchen of their country cottage. Usha and her mother had told dazzling tales about India—stories of women who went from door to door, manually grinding fresh spices and chilli powder, and the sweet sellers balancing large silver platters on top of their heads, piled with golden balls of besan ladoo, crispy layers of soan papidi with pistachios, or deep-fried orange spirals soaked in cardamom syrup.

Where was Usha now? Jess realised she'd like to meet up with her before she headed back to England. She made a mental note to herself to check on Doctor Usha Joshi's whereabouts.

A loud horn from the Queenscliff–Sorrento ferry announced its departure, and a veil of melancholy overcame Jess as she walked her bicycle down the hill. Here she was, back in Australia, after nearly twenty years' absence. It was a very different place without her mother and brother. She wasn't nine years old anymore.

Chapter 8

LILI WAS ACTUALLY RELIEVED HER offer a few days ago to help Jess sort through Ben's stuff had been rejected. She must have been crazy to think she'd have time to spare with the restaurant reopening in just three days. Thankfully, she had already updated the employee manuals, completed all building and equipment maintenance checklists for the safety inspector's visit, and spent hours with Alex finalising Ailie's new menu. When she thought about how exhausted she was, she reminded herself that Faodail Farm was surrounded by some of Victoria's best vineyards, farmgate producers, and provedores. It was worth the intense amount of time and effort it took to nurture relationships with her suppliers, worth it to reflect on her menu, her connection with the land and sustainability, and her respect for the local region.

How to raise capital to pay out Jess was an additional burden, but she tried to focus on the present moment. Tonight's staff party, in the courtyard garden at Ailie, was a chance for them all to simply enjoy each other's company.

Josh, the apprentice chef, assisted by her father, was already turning out a delicious assortment of pizzas and dessert calzones for the hungry mob. Alex and her partner, Tash, dispensed pots of beer, cider, and juice from the mobile bar, housed in a 1975 Airstream caravan borrowed from friends who owned a small brewery.

"Good work," Lili called out to Owen. Their front-of-house manager was responsible for the sparkling fairy lights adorning the trees, the decorated tables, and the background music wafting through outdoor speakers.

He grinned and saluted her with his glass.

Lili headed to the terrace to check on her mother. Helen had managed to corral the half-dozen ankle-biters—all under eight years old—in a secure section of the garden where they could safely eat, drink, and play while their parents enjoyed the party.

"Hey, Mum, how are you doing?" Lili lifted Sophie, the line cook Tim's two-year-old, onto her hip.

"All under control." Helen swiped a child's sticky mouth with a damp towel. "Can't go wrong with pizza. It's a good turnout tonight. Everyone seems happy enough." Helen looked around, surveying the crowd. "Has Jess showed yet?"

"Ah, not so far." Lili grabbed a pudgy little hand as Sophie smeared the remnants of a strawberry custard calzone across her face, catching the collar of Lili's raw-silk, jade-green shirt. "That is…icky."

"Oh dear. Why don't you get yourself inside and sponge that off? The berry syrup will stain the fabric."

"Are you sure Jess said she would come?" Lili pulled the collar away from her neck.

"Yes, she did. She's spent a lot of time at the shack these last couple of days. It must be difficult to sort through Ben's personal belongings on her own." Her mother shook her head. "I did offer to help, but she refused."

"So did I," Lili said. "I haven't seen much of her lately. She's been holed up at the shack and in her room. To be honest, Mum, I think she's having a hard time." Lili was glad to share her concern over Jess's behaviour. "She keeps to herself and disappears for hours on her bike. I never see her eat at home, so I hope she's getting nourishment from somewhere."

"Maybe I should talk to her."

"I don't know. She's such a loner," Lili said. "Anyway, where is Aruishi?"

"Mama, look who I found."

Lili spun around at the sound of Aruishi's breathy voice. Aruishi had her hand firmly planted in Jess's as she dragged her captive towards them.

"I'm so glad you came, Jess," Helen said. "It is such a beautiful night to be outdoors."

Lili stooped to plant a kiss on Aruishi's head. Turning to Jess, she said, "Glad you could make it."

"Mama, what's that?" Aruishi pointed to the smudge on Lili's shirt.

"A little accident. I'm about to go clean up." She held out her hand. "Would you like to come with me?"

Aruishi shook her head and held on to Jess.

"Okay, then." Lili looked at her mother.

Helen raised her eyebrows.

"I won't be long. Ru, don't wander off again. Please stay with your grandmother."

"Okay." Aruishi stared up at Jess and tightened her grip on her hand.

"I'll keep an eye on her," Jess said.

Lili took a deep breath, forced a smile, and turned on her heels. "Thank you."

In the restroom, she sponged the tacky residue carefully from her collar and checked in the mirror. Hardly a trace. She patted down a stray wisp of hair and rechecked her appearance. Satisfied, she made her way outside.

She lingered in the shadows on the terrace to observe the party and soon spotted Jess and Aruishi, sitting together on a bench under the apricot tree. Lili sighed. Aruishi seemed entranced by Jess, who held a napkin around a slice of pizza and offered it to her. Whatever Jess said made Ru grin. The sight of the pair sitting so close took Lili's breath away. They were so alike; they could pass for mother and daughter.

In the evening light, Jess's hair, pulled back and clipped, shone a glossy, rich brown, almost black, highlighting her strong arched eyebrows and pronounced cheekbones. Her athletic body—lean, muscled, and physically powerful—was an exceptional sight out of her usual spandex and lycra, and she wore calf-high burgundy boots, black denim jeans, and a simple white merino crew.

"You're staring."

Lili jumped as Alex stepped beside her. "I'm not."

Tash appeared behind Alex. "You are," she agreed, and the pair giggled.

Alex leaned back to rest her head against Tash's shoulder. "Not that I blame you."

"Don't gang up on me." Lili huffed.

"The woman is hot." Alex poked Lili gently in the ribs.

She nudged her friend back. "Actually, most of the time she's cool and distant. How does she manage to look so—"

"Scorching," interrupted Alex.

"Alex, really. *Aloof.* That's the word I was looking for."

Tash leaned forward and whispered in Lili's ear, "Don't let that cool exterior fool you. I've only just met her, but I think there's a lot going on behind the mask."

"You think so?" Lili asked. She couldn't take her gaze off Jess.

"I do," Tash said.

"I caught Jess in her running gear on my way to work yesterday, and let me just say…" Alex fanned her face, as if overcome by heat. "Those Nike shorts and racerback crop top leave little to the imagination." She whistled. "Rock-hard abs."

Tash cleared her throat. "Well, even if you haven't, Ru's certainly taken to Jess." Her gaze remained fixed in their direction.

"She's totally besotted," Lili said. "And that's what worries me. What happens when Jess goes?"

On cue, Jess looked up and raised her eyebrows. It was obvious the three of them were staring. As Lili locked gazes with her, Jess appeared ready for flight, her body suddenly transformed into a well-tensioned bow.

Lili lifted her hand in a hesitant wave and smiled. With what appeared to be equal deliberation, Jess returned her greeting. Lili caught a hint of a smile.

"Come on, Alex, let's get back to our bar duties." Tash squeezed Lili's shoulder. "It is cute seeing Jess and Aruishi together, Lili. Ben would be chuffed."

"It's as though he planned it this way," Lili said.

"Eh?" Alex put her arm through Lili's and pulled her close.

"I don't know, just thinking out loud."

"Ru has the Harris magnetism, and those remarkable chocolate eyes. But she's so like you too. She has your determination and stubborn chin." Alex grinned and rushed off after Tash before Lili had a chance to whack her on the arm.

"How about pouring some drinks for our thirsty guests?" Lili called.

The paper lanterns cast a mellow glow through the garden as soft, moody jazz piano chords merged with the rustle of leaves, night-bird calls, and the whisper of distant waves. The other guests had left, and everything was cleaned up. Lili, Alex, and Tash sat along a table near the warmth of the wood-fired oven.

Jess sat at the other end of the table, watching the glow of the dying embers. She was thousands of miles from familiar territory, but after her emotional week she welcomed the soft lighting and intimate music, and its sedative effect.

These people were strangers, but they were Ben's colleagues and friends. Jess imagined him sitting here, sharing an ale and a yarn about his latest surfing adventure or entertaining them with a tune on his guitar. She'd been surprised and pleased to find the instrument, with a pile of sheet music, at the shack. When Jess had started piano lessons at age six, Ben showed no interest in playing anything at all. There was a lot she didn't know about her brother. However, the more she sorted his belongings, the more she discovered.

She'd pored through albums and hundreds of loose photographs. Some had handwritten notes attached; some just had a date and location scribbled on the back in pencil. Her bedroom at Lili's was strewn with files and pictures. Ben had collected a lot of family memorabilia, and slowly Jess had begun to piece together the fragments of their early life together. When the visual assault sent her emotions into a tailspin and it all got too much, she'd take off on her bicycle, sometimes pushing herself until eventually physical exhaustion cleared her mind and provided some inner peace.

A cool hand rested on her shoulder. Jess sat upright and turned. "Alex." She blinked and combed her fingers through her hair.

Alex squeezed her shoulder. "Sorry. I didn't mean to startle you. We're taking requests. Would you like a cup of tea, coffee, or something else?" She smiled and stepped back. "You seemed miles away."

Jess glanced at her watch. It was after midnight. "Just a little tired. Thank you, but I think I'll go back to the house."

Lili appeared directly in front of her. "Stay," she said. "The hot drinks won't be long, and then I'll walk back with you." Her eyes flickered warily.

Walking across the field to Lili's house on her own in the dark didn't appeal at all. Jess nodded in agreement. It wouldn't hurt to stay a little longer.

"That's great," Alex said. "What'll it be then? Tea, coffee, or hot chocolate?"

Half an hour later, Lili and Jess walked along a path lit by moonlight. Jess inhaled deeply, savouring a hint of sweet spice from Lili's perfume, carried on the night air. She'd avoided Lili for the last few days as she'd been sorting Ben's stuff, and Lili had not sought her out either.

This was probably the reason, Jess thought, for the awkward silence between them.

"Lili," she finally said when they'd reached home, not saying a word to each other. She said it perhaps louder than she'd intended.

"Yes?" Lili stopped at the top of the stairs and turned to face her.

"Amongst Ben's belongings, I found several documents to do with his work. I wonder if you have time to go through them with me?" Jess asked. "I'm not sure what is important or not."

Under the glow of the porch light, Lili's face was a combination of irritation and weariness. "I can't tomorrow. I have an appointment in Geelong." She turned and unlocked the front door. "Can it wait?"

"Don't worry, it can." Jess knew her disappointment probably showed, but Lili had grown so distant, Jess figured she'd have to break the ice. "Have I said or done something to annoy you? You asked me to walk home with you, but you haven't said a word."

"I couldn't let you walk home by yourself," Lili said. "And I haven't been avoiding you. You're the one who's been avoiding me. I've had a lot on my plate, and you've either been busy at the shack or kept to yourself, in your room."

"I didn't ask if you'd been avoiding me. Have you been?" She shot Lili a pointed glance.

"No," Lili said. "As I've just said, I have not." She turned her back on Jess and walked inside, cutting off any further chance of conversation.

Jess stood on the deck and looked up at the clear sky, full of stars. A low blanket of sea mist hung in the valley below the house, and the air had taken on quite a chill. She sighed, stepped inside, and made her way to her room.

Chapter 9

LILI UNFASTENED THE HARNESS AND lifted Aruishi out of her booster seat. She set her down on the paved driveway in front of her parents' home. Aruishi charged up the path, climbed the stairs, and ran through the open screen door.

"Walk, don't run," Lili called, to no avail. She picked up Aruishi's yellow backpack and the cake box from the back of the Subaru and followed her inside the house.

The home had been extensively renovated a few years ago, but her parents' 1950s farmhouse still retained its retro charm. They'd kept the large bay window in the front sitting room, with its unrestricted views of green pastures and vineyards. This had been her favourite place to daydream, sitting on the old floral-fabric-covered sofa at the window. Lili felt herself grin, delighted by the happy memories the cottage evoked. The saggy couch had long been replaced by two leather recliners, but the view remained largely unchanged.

"Hello, darling. Up with the birds this morning, were you?" Helen pointed to Lili's running shorts. "Or should that be *running* with the birds?"

"Oh, Mum." Her mother's attempts at humour were better some days than others.

"Do you have time for a coffee?"

"Thanks, I've already had two today." Lili bent to kiss her cheek. "Good morning. Where did Aruishi disappear to, so fast?"

Helen wriggled her eyebrows. "It's *Angelina Ballerina* time." She pointed her thumb in the direction of the sunroom.

Lili poked her head around the doorway and chuckled. Aruishi was in front of the screen, dancing and humming along with the television show. "Last week it was the Wiggles. She really loves singing along and takes any chance she can to plunk the keys on Grandmother's piano at the restaurant."

"Have you thought about starting those piano lessons yet?" Helen asked.

"She's too young," Lili said. "I don't think she'd be able to concentrate." She didn't have the time or skill to teach Aruishi, and lessons with a piano teacher weren't in the current budget.

"You started piano lessons with your grandmother when you were four. If it's the cost, your father and I can help."

"You're doing more than enough already." As far as she was concerned, the subject was closed. But Helen had been on at her about piano lessons for months. "Lessons can wait till next year."

"Here, let me help you with that." Helen tossed a tea towel over her shoulder and lifted the box from Lili's arms. She inhaled deeply. "If it tastes as good as it smells, it will be delicious."

"I whipped it up before my run this morning. It's not long out of the oven."

"You *were* up early, then." She peered at Lili. "You look tired. What's up?"

"Just a few things rattling around in my head."

"How are things going with Jess?"

"Not now, Mum. Can we talk about it later, please?" Lili sighed.

Lili had had a horrible couple of nights. The evening of the staff party, her anxiety about meeting with the bank manager the next day had made her bitchy with Jess. She hated that. Last night, after the depressing meeting, she'd totally avoided her and tossed around in bed all night. Eventually, she'd given up any thought of sleep, crawled out of bed at dawn, scribbled down an idea for a new dessert, threw together the ingredients, and baked a cake.

Now she followed her mother into the bright yellow kitchen and deposited Aruishi's bag on the dining chair. The kitchen often smelt of baked bread or scones. Its enamel wood-burning stove provided the house with warmth in winter, and Helen produced jams and relishes for Ailie's kitchen throughout the year, using the slow, cast-iron hotplate. This morning, the combined aroma of fresh bread and espresso from the copper stovetop coffee maker was mouth-watering.

"What have you been baking?" Lili asked.

"Mixed seed and honey loaf. Ru's favourite, spread with avocado."

"Lucky girl." Lili smiled. With a little added crumbled feta cheese or vegemite, it was one of her favourites too.

"If you can wait ten minutes, the bread will be out of the oven."

"I'd love to, Mum, but I really can't stay." Lili lifted the cake out of the box. "I don't think running with Ru in the stroller is going to be an option much longer. She's getting more fidgety and impatient."

Helen chuckled. "Well, that's understandable. You can always drop her here. Or give me a bell, and I'll be over. As you know, I'm awake early myself."

"I'll figure something out. You'll have your hands full three days a week when Ailie reopens and I'm working in the kitchen, *plus* other times when I must be in the office. Ru needs me around as much as I can be. Once she starts school, we can reassess things." Lili didn't mean to be short with her mother, but lack of sleep had made her cranky this morning.

"Well, just remember your team at that restaurant is a solid bunch, and trustworthy. In the first year, Ben was a huge help. But it's you. For the last couple of years, *you've* put in the long hours and trained the staff." Helen walked over to Lili and embraced her. "Your father and I are flexible. Take advantage of us now, while you can."

"Thanks, Mum." Lili returned her mother's hug.

"Will this cake be on the menu?" Helen asked when Lili let go.

Lili scratched her forehead. "Maybe, for the high-tea trolley. It's a brown-butter almond torte—gluten-free and sweetened with our luscious dark-pink quinces."

"And what's this?" Helen asked, and opened the first lid to reveal a soft-pink syrup.

"Bramble berry drizzle. Slightly tart. It cuts the sweetness of the caramelised quince."

"Sounds divine."

Lili removed the lid off the second jar. "Vanilla bean custard," she said. "I need your opinion. Would you and Dad try it tonight and let me know what you think?"

"We will, with pleasure."

She walked towards the sunroom and found Aruishi springing up and down on the chesterfield. "No bouncing on the furniture, Aruishi McAllister." She picked her up, twirled her in the air, and sat her on the sofa. "I'd better get going, Mum," she called.

"Mama, you are perspired," Aruishi said, pulling Lili's damp T-shirt.

"Yes, I have been *perspiring*, and I need a shower. Be a good girl for your gran."

"Yucky." Aruishi parked at the edge of the sofa, nodded distractedly, and went back to singing to the television.

Helen walked Lili to the car. "How did you get on at the bank yesterday?"

"Okay." Lili climbed into the wagon and opened the window.

"Just okay?" Helen asked.

"I'm really sorry, can we talk about this later? I'm going to be late." Lili blew her a kiss and turned the key in the ignition.

Helen put her hand through the window and squeezed Lili's shoulder. "You're not alone. You know your father and I will help any way we can."

"I know, Mum. I'll ring you later."

Lili put the car into reverse and backed down the driveway. She glanced at the dashboard clock. She only had twenty minutes to shower and dress before she met up with Jess.

The bank manager was not the guy she'd dealt with previously. Angelica Costa was new. The third bank manager in three years. She'd been kind, but all the same, Lili was put out by the change. Angelica explained that even though her business was successful and had enough revenue to cover operating expenses, as things stood, the bank couldn't increase her home loan. Did she have another source—her parents, for example? Lili wouldn't ask her parents for more money. They dreamed of an overseas trip—a barge cruise through the Canal du Midi, from Marseilles to Paris and then on to Scotland to visit family. She would not take a cent of their holiday fund.

Angelica Costa suggested the executor of the estate may accept a long-term payment option, or a part share in the business. *Yeah, right; and pigs might fly!* There was no way she was handing over any part of her restaurant to someone with little food knowledge and no experience in the hospitality industry. But she had to face reality. How could she convince Jess to accept the long-term payment option?

Lili had planned to do more with the kitchen garden in the future, to use the restaurant and garden as a learning centre one day a week. She'd mapped a programme that included gardening workshops and cooking-skill classes to build an awareness for the environment and healthy eating. She didn't expect it to be a huge money earner at the beginning, but any increase in revenue would help pay back the loan. She just hoped Jess would agree to longer terms than she might be expecting.

Water lapped against the old pylons under the wooden pier as Jess sat sipping her espresso at a café table at the edge of the jetty, enjoying the warmth of the sun on her skin. She'd met with a real estate agent in Barwon Heads who'd organised a market appraisal on Ben's property. Jess left his office with data on its investment potential, median house prices, and expected rental income for the area. She reflected that none of the supplied information made her decision whether to sell or not any easier.

She could return to the UK and let the lawyers here tie up the loose ends of Ben's estate. They could handle the sale of the property and his car. But for both her and Lili's sakes, Jess wanted the loan settled before she returned to London.

"Can I get you another coffee?" the waiter asked with a hopeful smile. "Or perhaps something to eat?"

Declining both offers, she gathered her belongings before setting off to wander along the boardwalk that flanked the white sandy beach and wide river estuary. Jess couldn't recall being brought to Barwon Heads as a child. When her father had returned to England after the divorce, her mother worked even longer hours, and family trips to the coastline had been rare.

Jess did remember the appealing coastal town as it was portrayed in the television show *Sea Change*. She and her friends had watched it at boarding school in England. The series was partly filmed at the very café on the Barwon Heads jetty where she'd just been sitting. Jess grinned, recalling how the other girls had drooled over David Wenham's character, Diver Dan, while Jess favoured the sultry Laura, a beautiful city lawyer who became the magistrate of the fictitious town, Pearl Bay. It had been compulsive viewing for Jess and helped her stay connected to Australian popular culture and the landscape.

Her phone buzzed with incoming mail. Jess took it out of her pocket to check the sender. It was the Wylie Medical Centre, in reply to her query about the whereabouts of Doctor Usha Joshi, her mother's childhood friend from a Christian-run orphanage in Pune, India. It seemed she no longer practised medicine in Wylie, Jess's birthplace, but the telephone number with a Victorian prefix they'd supplied should get her in contact.

Amongst Ben's photographs, Jess had found pictures of her mother with Usha bundled together with a letter, handwritten in such a scrawl that it was hardly decipherable. It was from Usha to Ben, dated April last year. The fact that Ben had kept in contact with their mother's friend stirred so many memories. Jess was eager to meet with Usha. She could barely remember the time of her parents' divorce, and hoped Usha could shed light on that period, although it would be painful.

The smooth water under the pier and light air had a calming effect. It was as though she could see things clearly for the first time since she'd arrived. She didn't want to leave. Not yet. She would extend her stay in Australia. Not too long. Just long enough to connect with Usha and spend as much time with Aruishi as possible, to hopefully establish a bond which would continue after she flew back across the globe. A bond for life.

One of the photographs was of her mother and Usha standing in front of the giant passenger ship that would transport them across the world to Australia. They would have been younger than Jess was now. Their long black hair fell over their shoulders in tight braids. They wore colourful salwar-kameez—the traditional baggy trousers and fitting dress tunic of northern India that had been adopted by women all over the continent. Jess liked the style, and it was obviously more practical for travelling than a sari.

They'd been fortunate to receive sponsorships, and graduated from a medical college in Pune. Usha and Jess's mother were granted residence in Australia on condition they practised in country Victoria for a minimum of five years. They'd both settled in the small town of Wylie.

If the Englishman Benjamin Harris Senior hadn't tumbled off his bicycle during a cycling tour of Australia, requiring stitches—he and Doctor Aruishi Annand would have never met. Jess sighed. Their whirlwind romance had lasted only six years.

Jess drove into Faodail Farm and continued up the tree-lined lane to Ailie. She collected the leather folder of documents from the rear seat and hurried across the courtyard. She was fifteen minutes late.

Through the kitchen window, she spied Lili leaning back against the bench, her hands moving quickly as she talked to someone out of Jess's view. Lili looked totally at ease as laughter and gesticulations accompanied her speech.

Jess turned the handle, walked through the French doors, and stepped into the kitchen.

Lili's expression shifted from happiness to uncertainty. It was obvious that Jess's arrival instantly changed her mood.

"Hi, Jess. How are you?" Alex asked. She looked from Jess to Lili and back to Jess. "How's your day?"

"I'm well. I had a productive morning, thank you." Jess turned to Lili. "But I am sorry I'm late."

"Don't worry, so was Lili," Alex said as she smashed thick slices of avocado onto a toasted bagel. "I'm making Lili a snack. Would you like something?"

"No, thanks." Jess's stomach rumbled, and she coughed to hide the noise. She should have eaten something with her two coffees this morning. When she looked up, Lili had her head tilted to one side as she appraised her. Jess took a deep breath and released it slowly. "Please go ahead and have your meal. I'll wait on the terrace. I don't need lunch." Her stomach rumbled loudly as if to punctuate her words. How embarrassing.

Lili reached into the under-bench refrigerator and pulled out a bagel. "What would you like with it?" She pointed to an array of ingredients on the benchtop. "You have choices. But let me suggest Mum's apricot-and-ginger preserve with aged cheddar, or my favourite—vegemite and avocado."

Alex turned the split bagel that was toasting under the open grill.

"Vegemite and avocado? Strange combination," Jess said, moving closer to Alex, who removed the bagel from the grill and spread layers of vegemite and avocado onto the golden surface.

Jess's mouth watered. Of course she should eat. Why was she being so obstinate about it? "Hmm, I will have half a bagel like that…if that's okay, please?"

After adding a quick twist of freshly ground pepper, Alex pushed a laden plate along the bench to Lili and another one with two halves towards Jess.

"Don't knock it till you try it. This is one of my go-to favourites." Lili leaned casually against the bench, picked up her bagel, and bit into it.

"Sorry. I don't think my mother ever knew how to spread the right amount of vegemite on our sandwiches. She was originally from India." Jess smiled. Why did she just say that? Obviously Alex and Lili knew her mother was from India. Jess and Ben had suffered some weird sandwich combinations in their school lunchboxes. Salami and jam rolls. Curried mince, mayonnaise, and lemon pickle. "I could never convince anyone to swap."

"Oh, really?" This time when her gaze met Jess's, Lili's face relaxed. "Didn't most kids have vegemite sandwiches at school?"

"Probably, but not half an inch thick with Kraft cheese and parsley."

"Oh." Lili smiled. "You saw for yourself, this has only a thin scraping of vegemite."

Jess bit into the crunchy bagel. "Hmm…"

"Hmm? That's it?" asked Lili, her eyebrow raised.

Jess shook her head. "It's good."

"Told you."

"No, it is good. The avocado is creamy, the vegemite a little salty. Goes well with the bagel."

Alex leaned forward and wiped Jess's chin with a kitchen towel. "Sorry, you have a little avocado—"

Jess stepped back involuntarily. "That's okay, I've got it." She put her hand to her face.

"Oops." A flush crept across Alex's cheeks. "I'm out of here," she said sheepishly. "See you both soon."

"Thanks Alex, see you tomorrow." Lili cleared the ingredients from the bench and gave it a quick wipe down. "Actually, Jess, I'm done here for the day." Lili pointed to the folder Jess had placed on the benchtop. "Let's do this in my office at home. Bring your bagel with you, if you like."

"That's fine with me. The Mini's outside. I'll meet you back at the house." Jess stared at the remaining half of her bagel, picked it up, and headed for the door. "It would be a shame to waste it."

Looked like there had been no need for the mad dash back to the restaurant after all.

Lili drummed her fingers across the top of her desk and watched Jess leaf through the papers on her lap. Lili was ready. Couldn't they just get on with it? She swivelled around to stare out of the window. The wind had picked up since this morning, and the distant waves were topped with choppy whitecaps. "That does look like a storm coming in." Perfect weather to suit her mood, now that they were back to business.

"Lili."

She looked back to meet Jess's penetrating stare.

"Are you ready?" Jess sat back with an anticipatory look on her face.

Lili quickly nodded her head. "I am."

Jess held up a piece of paper and waved it between them. "This document outlines Ben's initial investment in your restaurant and the proposed interest on pay-out." She peered at Lili over the top of her reading glasses.

"I have the figures." Lili clenched her jaw. She knew the figures off by heart; she could recite them backwards in her sleep.

"Okay, then," Jess said. "Then let's just agree how to do this."

"Do what?"

"Settle the loan."

"I'm sure you think it's just a walk in the park." Lili tapped her fingers on the desktop, again. Why should she expect Jess to understand her situation? The sooner she could fly back to her glamorous life in London, the better.

"Pardon me?" Jess asked, with her eyebrows raised. "The sooner this settles, the sooner I will be out of your hair. Isn't that what you want?"

Lili sighed. "Yes."

"Are you positive? You don't sound sure."

She crossed her arms in front of her chest. "It's just that I haven't had enough time to—"

Jess cut her off. "That is exactly why I suggest you talk with your accountant. Then we can decide on how and when."

A flash of lightning lit the room, followed by a slow rumble of thunder, and a stream of rain splattered across the window.

Jess flinched. Her eyes widened.

"There's a storm moving in—" Lili's phone rang, and she lifted it from her desk "It's Mum, I need to get this."

Jess jumped to her feet and moved her chair into the middle of the room, further away from the window.

Lili ended the conversation with her mother and slipped the phone back onto the desk. She turned to Jess. "Are you okay?"

"Yes," Jess snapped, and sat up abruptly as a crack of thunder echoed through the study.

Jess's gaze darted around the room—she was nervous of the storm, or afraid, or both.

"Mum called to let me know she and Ru were enjoying the weather event." Lili got up to move in between Jess and the window. "Wow, the sky is really dark except for the lightning flashes." Lili loved thunderstorms. She scanned the sky. She loved the turbulent clouds, the crackling sound, and the drama and energy of a spring storm.

Another sharp clap of thunder rattled the window. "Isn't Aruishi frightened?" Jess asked.

"And here comes the heavy rain," Lili said. "It will be great for the garden." She smiled and returned to her desk. "Ru loves thunderstorms—if she's indoors with her teddy bear and a blanket. Rumble, Thumble, Boom."

"Pardon?"

"We need to introduce you to *Rumble, Thumble, Boom*. It's a book about a boy and his dog and overcoming his fear of thunderstorms." Lili saw a thinly veiled vulnerability in Jess's eyes and posture. She wanted to comfort her but held back. Jess might misread her gesture and slap her. "You obviously don't like thunder and lightning?"

"No." Jess raised her eyebrow and pushed the papers across the desk towards Lili. "Can we get back to this?"

"Sure."

"Do you agree with the principal and interest due?" Jess moved around uncomfortably, rubbing the back of her neck.

"It's what Ben and I agreed." For goodness sake, Lili was aware of the sum and the agreement between Ben and herself.

Jess glared at her.

Lili wiped her sweaty palms on her trousers and sat back in her chair. Her anxiety was not about the weather. "I don't have the money to pay you back in a lump sum." She had to shout to be heard over the howling wind.

The boom of thunder rolled across the lower valley, and rain hammered the iron roof. Lili recognised the sharp crack of a gum tree splitting, followed by a deafening crash.

Jess cupped her hands over her ears.

Lili got up and went to Jess, took her hands, and gently moved them away from her ears. "Listen, you'll be okay if you stay in the house. I have to check what's going on outside."

"Okay, be careful. Sorry I can't help you."

Jess retreated to the safety of her room after Lili left to investigate the loud crash. She wished she wasn't so wimpy. Lili was out in the thunderstorm by herself amongst all those eucalyptus gum trees and shallow root systems. Jess's mother had died during a fierce storm when high winds downed a tree; it had fallen across her car, killing her instantly. Jess lay on her bed, trembling, and pulled the blanket up to her chin. She took slow, deep breaths and practised the meditation technique she'd learnt from her therapist to push those terrifying memories away.

Finally, the storm seemed to be abating, and rain no longer lashed the bedroom windows. Jess left the sanctuary of her bed to collect her laptop from the dresser. Lili said she couldn't repay the loan—that was a surprise. She scrolled through her inbox and found a new e-mail from Jonathan. She hoped he'd managed to find the data she'd requested. If anyone could unearth information about Lili's financial situation, Jonathan could.

She clicked on his e-mail, read the accompanying letter, and opened the attached PDF document. Apart from Ben's investment, Ailie had been co-financed by Scott and Helen through their self-managed superannuation fund. Ailie, on paper, was in the black, running on profitable earnings. Per the last financial statement, the restaurant had increased its turnover by fifteen per cent since it opened. The figures were good, and over the next two years the projections estimated a further increase in net profit. So what was Lili's problem?

Jess scrolled down the page. "Ah-ha…"

There was a substantial mortgage on her house, and Lili was in debt to her parents. It must be tough keeping a business afloat, employing eighteen people, as well as raising a child on her own. The financial pressures would be enormous—something Jess never had to worry about.

Although her father had taken little interest in her—at least it seemed that way to Jess—he'd bequeathed a large portion of his estate to her. Her inheritance and investments gave her a secure future.

Lili was not so lucky. Jess hadn't considered Lili wouldn't have the funds to pay off the loan. She'd been so busy feeling sorry for herself, she'd never considered Lili's predicament. She'd behaved like a selfish brat. Ben had died suddenly, and Lili had lost her friend. Now, here she was—pressuring Lili to pay back the loan.

Her phone rang, jolting Jess out of her funk. Jonathan's number came up on the screen.

"Good evening, Jess. Sorry it took longer than expected to find the information you asked for."

"Good morning, Jonathan. Thanks for your e-mail." It was good to hear his voice, even if he was miles away. "Lili can't repay the loan right now."

"She told you that?"

"Actually, she yelled it at the top of her lungs."

"Did you have a fight?" He sounded alarmed.

"No, there was no fight." She snickered. "There was an enormous thunderstorm, and she raced out to check on a fallen tree."

"Okay. I hope she's all right," he said. "So, what do you want to do?"

"What do you mean, what do I want to do? I was hoping you would give me some suggestions."

"There are choices. But in the end, you should decide, rather than have the executor make the decision for you." Jonathan's cough was followed by a sneeze. "Sorry, Jess."

"No, I apologise. You mentioned you were feeling poorly in your e-mail. This can wait."

"No. I'm okay, it's just a head cold." Jonathan cleared his throat. "Whatever you decide, you need to tell Lili and put her out of her misery. Your best options are P, G, or B."

"GBP? Explain."

"*PGB*. Payment plan, gift it, or barter." He coughed again. "Jess, I think a payment plan is the only option for Lili. Forget the bartering; I don't imagine she'll let you have a share in the restaurant. She has enough on her plate, pardon the pun. As your accountant and friend, I'm not going to encourage you to wipe the debt. But it is up to you."

"Payment over time was my thought as well. Something that doesn't put her under too much pressure. Lili is proud; I can't see her taking on a partner—especially me." There was pride, and there was the fact that Lili had her daughter's future to consider. As Aruishi's aunt, Jess had the opportunity to take the pressure off and help them both.

"Many people won't accept help, even when they need it," Jonathan said in a croaky voice. "By the way, don't forget, I'll not be contactable next week."

"That's right. Your conference in South Africa. You'd better be over your cold by then."

"Indeed." He laughed. "Boot camp at the Londolozi Game Reserve. Just me and fifty other bean counters. If you don't hear from me, I've been eaten by a lion."

"Boot camp, my arse. I've heard about the place. Luxury accommodation and fine cuisine."

"Okay. I am looking forward to the little ecotourism jaunt, but I don't like being away from Maxine and Rupert. Now, back to you. Talk to Lili and see if she agrees to repayment over time. I can't see she has any other option. Once that's settled you can come home."

"Yes." Jess hesitated. "On that topic, I'm not sure I'm ready…"

"You're not ready to come home?" he asked. "Is it Aruishi?"

"There are some things I'd like to follow up on." Jess paused. "But yes, you are right about Aruishi. I would like to get to know her better. She follows me around. I think she likes me."

"How does Lili feel about that?"

"That's another matter. Lili is protective of her daughter, and I'll have to work hard to earn her trust." Lili assumed she was merely a celebrity playgirl on wheels. Jess aimed to prove her wrong.

What was expected of an aunt? There was so much to learn. Maintaining a relationship with Aruishi after she returned to England depended on her building a strong bond with her niece and winning over her mother.

"I understand you want to spend time with Aruishi. Can you extend your visit?"

"As long as I keep up with my exercise programme and push myself. I'm all for taking time to decide what I want to achieve for the next chapter of my life."

"You do have a lot of things to think about," Jonathan said. "You're currently living with Lili. Do you think she'll have you longer?"

"I don't want to outstay my welcome," she said. "Ben's shack is an option, but I'd have to ask his housemate. It's not that big, and Lili did mention his girlfriend spends time there."

"That could be awkward."

"Yes, you know me and awkward."

"Talk to Lili," he said. "I've got to go. I have a meeting in fifteen. Best of luck, and we'll reconnect when I'm back in London."

"Thanks, Jonathan."

"Anytime," he said. "And Jess, take it easy on yourself."

"I will." She ended the call.

Chapter 10

AT FIVE-TWENTY IN THE EVENING, Lili strolled through Ailie's tranquil dining room. The lighting was elegant and welcoming—not too bright. Whimsical arrangements of field flowers with shimmering silver-greys and bright whites graced the sideboards. Their fragrance, as per Lili's instructions, was delicate, not overpowering.

She ran her finger along the centre table that seated twelve. It was set with simple white porcelain, silverware, linen, and sparkling Italian glass. Even though the food was the heart, the décor influenced the diners' total experience. It had to be perfect.

"Everything to your satisfaction, Chef?" Owen gave her an exaggerated bow from the waist.

"Excellent," Lili said, and smiled at each of her waiting staff. "The room looks brilliant. And Mei, please thank your mum for the flowers. She's done a great job."

Mei shrugged. "Mum's really glad to have the work."

Owen handed Lili a copy of the in-house printed menu. "Can you talk us through the last-minute changes to tonight's menu?"

"Yes," Lili said. "We harvested an abundance of fresh peas this morning. So today's starter will be chilled spring-pea soup shots with goat cheese gougères."

"Gougères?" Haley looked unsure for a moment, then grinned. "Ah, they're those little cheesy puffs, right?"

"Right. Little choux pastry puffs made with silky goat curd."

"Yum."

"Come back just before service so you can try one," Lili said. "Then you'll know first-hand what they taste like."

Haley and Mei nodded in unison.

"Tuckerberry Hill delivered a tray of strawberries on our doorstep early this morning, so at the other end of tonight's menu we have a bush honey panna cotta, served with cinnamon and star anise-spiced strawberries. Alex made the most amazingly thin layers of salted, nutty butterscotch brittle for the garnish."

"I bet that'll be popular," said Haley.

"If you are all done, Lili," Owen said, looking at his watch. "We need to get ready to welcome our guests." He buttoned his waistcoat, straightened his tie, and turned to the servers who followed his lead. Haley adjusted Mei's tie and evened her own shirt cuffs. They looked slick in soft charcoal button-down shirts and black straight-cut trousers. Grey denim aprons topped off the look.

Lili reached towards the kitchen swing door and felt a light tap on her shoulder. She turned around to face her attractive young server. "Hi, Haley. Do you have another question?"

"No, it's not a question about the menu. I'm sorry I missed the staff party last week. I was looking forward to meeting Ben's sister. I've followed her career for years. She's awesome." Haley fixed Lili with an eager gaze. "Do you think I'll get to meet her before she goes?"

Lili smiled. "I'm sure she'd enjoy meeting a fan. I'll see what I can do." She pushed through the servery doors and welcomed the sight and smell of her kitchen gearing up for service. As she stepped into the room, she nearly collided with Alan, her dishwasher, as he dashed across from the locker room.

He smiled shyly and looked at his watch. "Sorry, Lili. I'm late."

"That's okay. I'm glad you're here."

He gave her the thumbs up and moved towards the utility room.

Lili looked around at her dedicated team. A restaurant was only as good as its staff, and she was blessed to have one that operated so well, despite not being arranged in the classic hierarchical kitchen structure. They were a small group—*a family*, she thought to herself. Everyone had their strengths, but each chef had to know how to make, and plate, every dish on the menu.

Alex gently stirred the sauce simmering in the pan on the stove. "Cracking storm yesterday," she said as Lili approached her.

"Powerful. It rattled the windows. How did your place fare?"

"All right. Tash was at work, and I hate being alone in storms."

"You're not the only one," Lili said. "Jess really freaked out. I thought she was just grumpy about our meeting. I was anxious about talking to her, and it surprised me how edgy she was. There was a huge crash when lightning struck one of the large gums near the cottage. I didn't know if Dad was out there."

"Oh hell, Lili. I had no idea. Was he okay? What about the tree?"

Lili shook her head. "Yeah, Dad's fine. He was in his work shed. The tree was a bit of a mess, but thank God it missed the cottage."

"And Jess?" Alex asked.

"I was such a fool." Lili slapped her forehead with her hand. "It wasn't until I was outside that I remembered how Ben and Jess's mother died. She was killed by a fallen tree during a thunderstorm when they were kids."

"Damn. How was Jess when you got home?"

"She was in her room. I did knock on the door to check on her."

"And?"

"She looked okay and acted like nothing was wrong, asking me about the storm damage." Lili grabbed a clean spoon from her jacket pocket. "May I?"

"Of course." Alex moved aside.

Lili closed her eyes and inhaled. The aroma was heavenly. She swirled the spoon through the sauce, lifted it to her lips, and tasted it. She let the sauce rest on her palate and then tasted it again. The red onion and beetroot reduction would accompany the spring lamb cutlet, caramelised fennel, green-pea tendrils, and savoury olive oil torta. "Perfect."

"Thanks, Lil." Alex took a napkin from her pocket and dabbed at her forehead.

"A little bit sweet, a little bit tart," Lili noted. "It won't overpower the lamb or the other accompaniments on the plate."

Alex smiled. "Oh," she said with raised eyebrows. "How did the meeting go?"

"The storm put a stop to it. We haven't reached an agreement yet."

"But did you tell her—"

"Yes. I told her I didn't have the money."

"Flying *duck*." Alex's voice rose.

The kitchen grew silent.

"It's okay, everyone." Lili nudged Alex's arm. "Check your stations. Twenty-five minutes to show time." She leaned closer to Alex. "Let's finish this conversation later, without an audience."

Alex nodded. "Where *is* Jess tonight?"

"At the house. She's going to watch Ru later so Mum can pop by."

"Whose idea was that?" Alex asked.

"Jess offered. I hope Ru won't play up," she said with a frown. "I don't know if she's had much experience with children, but she's so sweet with Ru, I didn't have the heart to say no. If things get out of hand, I've told her to call Dad."

"Scott will charge to the rescue if required."

"I'll ring Mum now and see if Ru is settled." Lili rested her hand against her office door.

"No problem." Alex set the double boiler near the bain-marie at the end of her station. "Anything else you need me to do?"

"Check on Nora and let her know we have six confirmed vegetarians. And the flavour is subtle in the kale and potato gnocchi, so we need to be sparing with the Otway truffle in the hazelnut butter drizzle. It is heavenly but intense."

"I'm on it."

Lili entered the office, then stuck her head back through the open door to call out to her apprentice. "Josh."

"I'm right here, Chef." He walked towards her.

"Good. You're working alongside me tonight. It's time you got some plating experience."

"Yes, Lili." He grinned.

"Remember, plating food is an art. We keep it simple, using colour, shape, aroma, and texture to achieve balance." She returned his smile. "Help Nora set the shot glasses and plates for first course. I'll be with you soon." She turned back to the office to call her mother.

"Yes, Chef."

Jess removed her glasses, laid them on the kitchen table, and rubbed her eyes. She'd read the executor's e-mail twice to be sure, but it was clear she wouldn't be able to sign the papers online. She'd have to go to their office in

South Melbourne to complete the paperwork in person. Well, she might as well achieve two goals with one trip. She'd drive to the city and return the hire car at the same time. The Mini was fun, but Ben's Jeep Wrangler was sitting in Scott's garage collecting dust. The four-wheel drive was bigger than she was used to driving, but now that she'd decided to extend her stay in Australia, it made sense to have a more practical vehicle for rural conditions.

"Can I *please* have a glass of water?"

"Aruishi, where did you spring from?" Jess looked up with a start. "Your gran put you to bed ages ago."

Aruishi smiled sweetly, her brown bear dangling from her arm. "I'm thirsty." She looked down at her feet. "I'm hungry too."

"Hungry? Didn't you have enough dinner?" Jess closed her laptop and beckoned for Aruishi to come closer. "Tell me what you'd like to eat." She patted the seat beside her.

Aruishi dragged her feet and placed her brown bear on the chair. "Boris wants milk and honey."

"Okay, but what would you like?" She plucked an avocado from the bowl in the centre of the table. "How about your favourite, avocado on toast?"

She shook her head and stamped her foot. "I hate avocado."

"How about a cracker with peanut butter? Or honey?" Jess stood up. "Come on, let's have a look in the pantry."

Aruishi put her head to one side, then gave it a determined shake. "No."

What was safe to feed a child at night-time? Would Lili even want her eating this late in the evening? How would Jess know? It was her first time babysitting Aruishi. Maybe this wasn't even about food and she just wanted attention.

It wasn't like she was experienced with children.

"What if I read you a story from one of the books your grandmother left beside your bed?"

Aruishi ignored Jess's question and grabbed the bear. She ran around the kitchen, squealing, and tossed Boris over her head.

Jess lurched forward and snatched the bear out of the air just as her phone rang. Before she could get to it, Aruishi picked it up from the table and swiped the screen.

"Hello," she said. "Yes, Gran, it's Jess's phone." There was a few seconds silence. "Ah-ha. No, Gran. I couldn't sleep. I'm starving, but Jess won't give me anything to eat. Boris's tummy is rumbling. I am being a good girl. Okay." Aruishi held the phone out to Jess. "It's Gran. She wants to talk to you."

Jess took her phone from Aruishi and sighed. "Helen?"

"Hello, Jess. Is everything okay?"

"Um…it was," she said, reaching out to scoop up Aruishi, who was pirouetting on top of a kitchen stool. It tipped over and crashed to the floor while Aruishi dangled gleefully from Jess's arms.

"What was that?" Helen asked.

"Sorry, I knocked over one of the kitchen chairs."

"Ru was fast asleep when I left. When did she wake up?"

"Not long ago." Jess sat down at the table and lifted Aruishi onto her lap. "I think she's hungry. At least that's what she told me."

Helen laughed. "I gave her a full serve of veggie noodles and some yoghurt and berries. She ate the lot."

Jess could imagine Helen shaking her head. "So, I shouldn't feed her anything?" She held the phone close to her ear as Aruishi played with the zipper on Jess's windcheater.

"No. Why don't you just offer her a drink of water?" Helen said. "I'll be there as soon as I can."

"I'll read her another story. That may settle her," Jess said. "I'll be okay. You don't need to come."

"The little person is pulling a fast one. It's Lili's first night at the restaurant in a while, and I think Ru wants attention."

"But…"

Helen chuckled. "Don't worry. I'm heading over to Ailie anyway. I'll just call by and tuck her in."

"Okay, Helen. If you're sure?"

"See you soon."

Jess tucked the phone into her pocket. She lightly rested her cheek against Aruishi's head and was surprised that the little girl appeared to be asleep in the crook of her arm. She carefully shifted into a more comfortable position. Jess didn't dare move from her seat until Helen got there.

Helen walked into the kitchen with Scott trailing right behind her. She whispered in Jess's ear, "We'll take Ru back to bed."

"Hopefully she will sleep through. I'm so sorry you had to come over." Jess released her hold of the now-angelic sleeping child.

Scott lightly ran his hand over Aruishi's curls. "No problem. We won't be long."

Aruishi snuffled faintly as Scott lifted her from Jess's lap, cradled her securely in his arms, and followed Helen out of the room.

Letting out a sigh of relief, Jess stood and walked around to stretch her legs. How could a four-year-old move so fast? It was frightening, really. She could have fallen off that stool and hurt herself.

"Oh *Christ*." She powered down her laptop and packed it away in the messenger bag. She sat down on the couch, hands tucked under her thighs and waited.

"She's fast asleep, didn't stir at all," Helen said, walking back into the room. "Scott will stay with her for a few more minutes just to be sure. I guarantee she won't wake up again tonight."

"Thank goodness. I feel terrible I had to disturb your and Scott's evening. Thank you. I'll be okay now." Jess hoped Aruishi slept through, because she didn't know what she'd do if she woke up again.

"Jess, are you interested in coming to the restaurant with me?" Helen asked.

"Now? I promised Lili I would look after Aruishi until she got home." Jess hadn't done a very good job of it so far.

"Yes, you did, but you'd be doing me a favour. As you know, it's Ailie's first night after the winter break, and they're booked to capacity." She sat down on the couch beside Jess. "No matter where your brother was—whatever corner of the planet—he would ring Lili and wish her luck. It will be different tonight." Her eyes filled with sadness. "I'm going over to make sure Lili's okay." She patted Jess's knee. "It will be nice to have you along."

"What about Aruishi?"

"Scott can watch the football game here and keep an eye on his granddaughter," Helen said. "Why don't you change and come along with me? I'll let Scott know."

She nodded. Of course they were missing Ben tonight. It was the right thing to do.

Jess got out of the car and waited at the passenger-side door. She was having second thoughts about coming to the restaurant. They were not planning to eat, so what were they doing here? Helen wanted to check on her daughter, and Jess could understand her concern, but Lili might not want to see her here.

"Ready?" Helen asked.

Too late to change my mind now. She followed Helen through the rear courtyard and into a side entrance of the building. They walked past Lili's empty office and staff room, then along a short corridor into a cosy foyer.

Helen squeezed Jess's shoulder. "If we sit at the bar, we can observe things without getting in anyone's way." As if sensing Jess's self-consciousness, Helen smiled warmly. "You look lovely. Your V-neck sweater is a gorgeous shade of pink. Is it cashmere? It looks so luxurious. Come on, let's see if Owen will pour us a drink."

Glancing at the tables seated with elegantly dressed diners, Jess was thankful she'd taken time to change out of her jeans and windcheater. She held her head up and tucked both hands deeply into the pockets of her linen trousers, aware of the curious glances she received.

"Take a seat," Helen said, pulling herself up onto a bar stool.

Jess slid onto the stool beside her. "The diffused light from the metal-wheel chandeliers transforms the restaurant." The delicate glow and the flower arrangements were intimate and welcoming. "Up to now, I've only seen it during the day."

"Yes, I think Lili did a tremendous job. She wanted it to be a little laid-back and minimal, but I think it's stylish. Ben contributed some fantastic ideas as well."

"I am impressed."

"It is a good-sized room. Even though the place is packed, it's not cramped or noisy," Helen said. "The tables are well-spaced, and the large windows bring the garden indoors."

Helen was right. The subtle lighting on the terrace and in the garden extended the diners' view, making the restaurant feel more spacious. On a balmy summer evening, it would be lovely dining on the terrace under the stars.

The bar was situated to the left of the room, between the dining area and the kitchen. The back-lit open shelves behind the service counter were filled with bottles of multi-hued beverages. Squares of coloured glass were randomly placed between the shelves, and Jess recalled peering through them from the kitchen last time she was here. On the wall, directly above the bar, a large, moody seascape portrayed a stormy sky with heavy rolling clouds and beams of sunlight glistening on the turquoise sea. Jess peered at the signature and made out the name *A. Rey*. "I love the painting, Helen. Does the artist live locally?"

"She and her wife have properties at Hakea, on the Great Ocean Road. Andrea and Caitlin married in Ireland recently, and the wedding party was held here at Ailie. They were so impressed with Lili's efforts—the wedding fare was splendid; I wish you could have seen it—that they gifted Andi's painting to Lili."

"What a special gift," Jess said.

"It does look fabulous in this setting."

Jess began to ask about the couple when she noticed a piano occupying the corner of the room close to the terrace.

"A baby grand? I can't believe I didn't notice that before."

"They only brought it back from the piano technician yesterday. What a drama it was to move. Two strong men and lots of ropes." Helen chuckled. "All because of some moisture-stabilisation problem. Hopefully it won't have to be moved again."

"Moisture can damage the wood and alter the pitch."

"Yes, so I believe. Do you play?"

"I'm out of practice."

"Lili used to play, but she doesn't have time these days." Helen sighed. "It was my mother's piano, and has been fully restored and tuned. Feel free to play it when the restaurant is closed."

The restaurant manager approached them with a bottle and two glasses in hand.

Jess had been briefly introduced to Owen at the staff party. She'd stayed mostly in the background that evening, watching the close-knit group from a distance.

"Owen," Helen said. "I hope that wine is for us."

"Definitely." He smiled and poured dark rose-coloured wine into the stemmed glasses. He was elegantly dressed. His hair, thick and fair, was brushed back from his wide forehead. "It is nice to see you again, Jess."

"Owen is our restaurant manager extraordinaire." Helen grinned. "Who, as well as looking after the dining room, brings to Ailie his exceptional knowledge of wine and beverage."

"Welcome to Ailie." Owen handed each of them a glass. "Scotchman's Hill Pinot Noir. It's a local favourite."

She tilted her head, taking in his accent. "Thank you, Owen. What part of London are you from?"

"East Finchley," he said.

"My flat is in Hampstead," she said. "Practically from the same neighbourhood."

"Mind you, I was twenty when I left. I've lived all over the place since then."

"And now, we are very lucky to have you here." Helen raised her glass to Owen before taking a sip.

"And I'm lucky to be here, Helen." He turned to Jess. "What do you think of the wine?"

"Hmm, it reminds me of ripe plums, with a bit of spice. I like it."

Helen excused herself to greet a diner who waved at her from across the room. A server joined Owen behind the bar. Like him, she was smartly dressed, although the attractive young woman's outfit was completed by a full-length apron. While she spoke to Owen, her gaze strayed to Jess several times and a knowing smile formed on her slightly pouty lips. She hadn't been at Lili's staff party—of that Jess was sure.

Jess held her gaze as she came around the bar counter and stood before her. "Hi. Jessica Harris?" she asked. "I'm Haley. It's totally awesome to have you right here. Right here, on the Peninsula, I mean. I saw you win in South America two years ago—you were amazing." Haley held out her hand.

Jess raised an eyebrow and accepted Haley's handshake. "You were there?"

A flush crept across her cheeks, and she let go of Jess's hand. "No. No, I wish," she said. "I saw you on TV."

Jess smiled. "Ah…that was a great race."

"It was a great year for you all-round, wasn't it? And that tour—two individual medals in the one event. Wow."

"Our whole squad did well. It's not just about individual medals." It was the first time she'd been approached by a cycling enthusiast since she'd been in Australia. There was a hint of flirtation in the way Haley engaged her.

Haley leaned close enough that Jess could take in her faint floral scent. "Oh, I know that...but I can't believe I'm meeting you in the flesh," she said, reaching out to touch Jess's forearm.

Jess didn't flinch from Haley's touch. She looked down to where Haley's hand lightly caressed her.

"Haley. Can you help Mei, please?" Owen frowned from behind the bar.

Haley withdrew her hand. "Yes, of course." Turning to Owen, she tilted her chin defensively, then flicked her head back to Jess and grinned. "It's so good to meet you. I hope we can...talk again?" She stood to attention and clasped her hands behind her back.

"Yes. That would be nice," Jess said as Haley returned to her station. She was cute, in a fresh-faced, bright-eyed, eager kind of way. Jess had to admit she didn't mind the attention from someone who clearly followed the women's cycling circuit.

At the sound of loud laughter, Jess spun her barstool around as an elderly couple were seated at the central table. They were greeted with handshakes and hugs by the other members of their party.

"Wouldn't it be nice to have met the love of your life at twenty and be celebrating sixty years together?"

Jess jumped at the soft tone of Lili's voice in her ear and her warm breath against her face.

"I am sorry. I didn't mean to startle you." Lili remained close beside her. "Mr and Mrs Hubert are celebrating their sixtieth wedding anniversary."

"Quite an achievement," Jess said. "It's hard to imagine *any* relationship lasting that long."

"Is it?" Lili's blue eyes sparkled, and she lifted her chin as though truly interested in her response.

"Yes." She took a gulp of wine. Jess didn't know many marriages that lasted even half that length of time. Her parents had divorced before she turned three.

"That's unfortunate." Lili smiled sadly and stepped back as Helen joined them at the bar. "Mother," she greeted.

"You must be pleased with the turnout tonight," Helen said, and turned to Jess. "So, what do you think?"

Jess placed her glass on the bar counter. Lili's expectant gaze unsettled her. "It's not what I imagined."

Lili raised her eyebrows. "Oh?"

"I've only seen the restaurant in daylight, and empty." Jess gestured towards the kitchen. "This is a new experience for me. I like that I get a glimpse of the kitchen in action through the small windows beside the bottles. The serene atmosphere of the dining room is quite a contrast." She looked up to meet Lili's curious stare. "The diners get to experience the food preparation without the noise or heat.

"Spot-on. Very observant." There was just a hint of a grin.

Jess held up the menu and bit her lip. "Do people just trust you to serve them…whatever?"

"They do," Lili said confidently. "Our degustation tasting menu is a great way to experience new flavours, be adventurous—give up control a little."

Was Jess being teased? She gave Lili an appraising look. She liked what she saw. Dressed in a pristine white jacket with off-centre zipper and front pockets obviously tailored to fit her body, tapered black trousers, and polished work boots, she looked the part. Certain of herself and capable, Lili radiated energy.

"Lili." Helen tugged at her jacket.

Lili quirked an eyebrow and glanced at her watch. "Time for action." She lifted her shoulders in a playful shrug. "We're flexible. We cater for special dietary requirements, and there's always a vegetarian alternative for each course. Our motto is fresh, seasonal, and simple."

"Chef. We're good to go," Owen said from behind the bar and then signalled to Mei, who poured a pale pink liquid into aperitif glasses arranged on a tray.

"Okay. Please let Alex know we start in ten. I'll do my walkabout now." Lili bowed to Jess and headed to the Hubert family table. She welcomed the elderly couple with a hug and a handshake, then moved away.

Lili had that look—the look Jess once knew so well: the look of success. The look of a winner. Did she get tense before a big night? Did Lili's hands tingle with excitement, or nerves? Did Lili, like Jess at the start of a race, enjoy the thrill of a challenge? Did she, too, experience the adrenaline rush of the build-up and the sprint to a finish line?

Jess admired the way Lili moved from one group of diners to the next, shaking hands with a few guests, smiling at others along the way. The whole process took less than ten minutes before she slipped back into the kitchen.

Conversations, the clinking of glasses and silverware, the swish of the revolving door between back of house and the dining room hummed around Jess.

"I'm ready to go now," Helen said. "If you want to stay longer, Owen will keep a watch out for you."

Jess drained her glass and reached for her jacket. She would have liked to stay a little bit longer—to have another glass of wine and observe how Lili's degustation menu was received. Lili appeared so sure the diners would be entranced by her selection, and Jess was curious to witness their reaction. "No, thank you. I'm ready to go," she said reluctantly.

There was something compelling about Lili the chef. Her self-assurance was attractive. Jess was sure she'd made the right decision. She'd go to Melbourne tomorrow, meet the executor, and sign the papers. Stage one completed.

Chapter 11

THE MOMENT SHE ENTERED THE café, Jess identified the delicate figure of Usha Joshi from the way she sat, always upright, those thin-framed glasses perched on the edge of her slightly bent nose.

Jess's memories were hazy, but she would never forget how important a role this woman once played in her life, especially the day her mother died.

Usha had collected her from school after lunch break. The fierce storm had kept everyone inside, and the driving rain made it impossible to get from the schoolhouse to Usha's car without getting soaked. Ben had sat shivering in the rear seat, arms crossed tightly against his chest, his face unreadable. Jess had tugged at her seatbelt, the fabric choking her so she could barely breathe. During the fifteen-minute drive, Usha had stared straight ahead, concentrating on manoeuvring the car along washed-out roads as rain lashed the windscreen. Jess had caught sight of the bright-blue neon sign above the hospital emergency entrance. The nightmare had begun. It was a lifetime ago, almost nineteen years.

Jess walked past empty tables now with an odd assortment of chairs, a worn leather couch, and side tables piled with magazines. Under the focused beam of a retro pendant light that hung directly above her, Usha's hair looked grey, but she still wore it braided in one single plait down to her waist. As she looked up from her magazine, Usha's soft brown eyes—with just a few laugh lines visible at the corners—gleamed in recognition.

Jess's throat constricted, and unshed tears stung her eyes.

Usha pushed back her chair, stood, and held out her arms to Jess. "Come," was all she said. She wrapped her arms around Jess's waist. They were strong arms, just as they had been that day in the emergency room. The doctor had shaken his head, and Jess would never forget Usha's sharp intake of breath as she'd gripped Jess's forearm so tight to stop her from running.

She lowered her head to Usha's shoulder, and they stood together for several moments, oblivious to their surroundings.

"Child," Usha said quietly, "we are lucky the café is empty this morning. This is a small town, and people will gossip about us."

Raising her head, she edged back to look down into smiling eyes. Usha winked, then rested one hand on Jess's forearm.

Having Usha hold her so tenderly, being unable to resist, and allowing herself to be comforted in this way was so far from her experience of the last nineteen years, she nearly fell into the chair that Usha held out for her.

"Let us share some tea and talk a little."

They sat across from each other at a small table near the window.

Usha turned sideways in her chair as a robust middle-aged woman approached their table with a menu in hand. "Ah, Jess, this is my friend and the café owner, Maddie. Maddie, this is my dear Jessica, whom I have not seen for a very, very long time."

"Welcome."

"Thank you. It's nice to be here."

"Doc," Maddie said, "I'll take your order and leave you two to catch up." She turned to Jess. "What can I get you?"

"Earl Grey, please. Black." A cup of tea was just what she needed to steady her nerves.

"Make that a pot, please," Usha added. "And a couple of those fresh cinnamon scrolls. You don't have to twist my arm today, they smell so delicious."

"Two cinnamon scrolls and a pot of Earl Grey tea coming up," Maddie said, then headed towards the counter.

"I couldn't."

Usha held up her hand and shook her head from side to side. "Of course you can. They are very good. I do not like to eat alone. Let us spend some time together and share some food." She reached across the table and squeezed Jess's hand. "I have waited a long time for this day."

"I'm so sorry—"

"Don't be sorry. You are here now," she said. "After the divorce and your father returned to England, you and your brother and mother were my family. You were just a child when she died and your father came to Australia and took you away. Some things are different between us, yes. But some things never change." Usha waved her hand between the two of them. "You are still family."

Jess gasped at the power of Usha's words and slowly met the woman's steady gaze. "You and Ben stayed in contact." She hesitated. "I am glad he wasn't alone."

"I was his guardian until he turned eighteen. So, yes. We did. It was good for me too, Jess," she said. "When he moved to Melbourne, we lost touch for a year or so. Ben wanted to prove he could make it on his own." Her eyes twinkled. "He was a man. He didn't need me to watch over him."

"Did you know about Aruishi?" Jess was unable to hide the pain in her voice.

"I'm so sorry he didn't tell you." Usha cast her gaze downward. "I didn't even find out myself until that beautiful child turned two."

"But why? Why did he keep it from you?"

Usha twirled the end of her braid with her fingers. "I think he was embarrassed," she said eventually. "In your e-mail, you said you knew about the arrangement between Lili and Ben, that he'd relinquished his parental rights?"

Jess nodded.

"I don't know why he thought I would not approve of their arrangement. He was helping a good friend, and Lili is a wonderful mother to Aruishi."

"I wish I hadn't kept him at arm's length." Jess sighed.

She held Jess's gaze. "Your brother always moved from one place to another, and he wasn't the best communicator."

The same could be said of herself. "I was so angry that he didn't come with us. He left me alone with my father. I didn't even know that man." Jess looked away before Usha glimpsed the tears welling in her eyes. "I couldn't forgive him," she whispered.

Usha reached for her hand and gently squeezed her fingers. "I'm so sorry."

Jess willed herself to get a grip of her emotions. "So, how did you find out about Aruishi?"

Usha picked up a spoon and stirred the tea before pouring it carefully into their cups. "Ah, Ben was overseas. Hawaii, I think. I received a telephone call in the middle of the night. Aruishi had been taken to Geelong Hospital."

Jess almost dropped her teacup. "What on earth happened?" She carefully placed her cup on the saucer.

"Aruishi was admitted with respiratory syncytial virus. Usually the symptoms are minor, just like a cold. But it developed into bronchiolitis, and she was struggling to breathe."

Even though Jess knew her niece was in good health now, her hands trembled, and she tucked them under her thighs.

"Lili called Ben in Hawaii to let him know. Ben rang me. He was frantic with worry."

"It would have been hard being so far away."

"Yes, but he was also worried about Lili. Her parents were on holiday in Scotland."

"Lili was on her own?" Jess bit her lip. She couldn't imagine how traumatic it would be to have a child admitted to hospital. "She must have been out of her mind."

"Yes, she was. Ben first asked me if I could go to the hospital to check on a friend's child. When he told me the girl's name was Aruishi, I understood immediately. I asked him directly, and he confirmed that Aruishi was his daughter."

"What a shock."

"Yes, but I went to the hospital immediately. Aruishi was receiving supplemental oxygen and fluids to prevent dehydration. Her breathing had settled, but she looked so small and helpless. When I arrived at the child's bedside, Lili looked as though *she* would collapse, she was so pale and exhausted. It took me a long time to convince her Aruishi was stable."

"I'm so glad you were there for Lili. I didn't know that you knew each other. Do you keep in touch with her and Aruishi?"

Usha nodded. "When Ben returned, we dined together at Lili's restaurant. I met Lili's parents, Helen and Scott." Usha reached into her bag for a handkerchief. "It was Lili who came to give me the news of Ben's accident. She asked me to speak at the memorial service." She dabbed at her eyes. "They are a very loving family who cared very much for Ben. And that child, Jess—she is something else. Aruishi—she is so beautiful, just like you were at her age." She smiled at Jess. "Just like you are now."

"Thank you, Usha." She rubbed the back of her neck. "It's scary, really how quickly Aruishi's got under my skin. I've only just met her, but it's like I've known her all her life."

Usha nodded, encouraging Jess to continue.

An idea popped into her head. "I would like to do something special for her, so she doesn't forget me when I go back."

"She's not going to forget you, Jess."

I hope not. "She's really keen on having her own bicycle. Aruishi is fascinated not only with my racer, but also my cycling kit," Jess said, smiling. "I caught her attempting to climb onto my bicycle and stopped her just in time. Imagine if Lili had seen her."

Usha's eyes widened just as her phone sounded an alarm, and she grimaced.

"Does that mean you have to go?" Jess asked, disappointed. It was surprisingly easy to talk to Usha, even after all these years.

"I'm afraid so. I can't keep my patients waiting," she said. "I thought you would be more comfortable to meet here at the café first. But before you return to England, you must come to my home, and I can cook for you." She smiled again.

"Only if we can cook together, like we used to…"

"Yes, like we used to. Anyway, we will meet again so you can tell me about your life and sporting achievements—and, when you are ready, about that terrible accident." Usha shook her head as if to shake off the thought.

She raised her eyebrows. After their mother died, Usha had moved into the house with Ben and Jess. She'd cooked all their favourite foods, trying to encourage them to eat. She'd held Jess when her nightmares woke her. She'd done everything for them until Jess was taken away.

Jess sighed heavily. Usha had followed her career and knew about the accident. "I was so selfish. I failed to respond to any of the birthday cards you sent when I was at boarding school."

"Jessica, don't be so hard on yourself," Usha said. "You were just a child. None of this was your fault."

She was glad Usha was so forgiving and that she had the chance to have her in her life again—and correct some of her mistakes.

Usha stood and gestured to Jess's empty plate. "I told you: Maddie's cinnamon scrolls are irresistible."

She'd eaten the entire sweet roll filled with raisins and nuts. Jess pushed away the empty plate, got up, and reached for her satchel. "Let me take care of this," she said.

Usha pulled Jess into a hug. "It is already taken care of." She loosened her hold and stepped back, gazing into her eyes wistfully. "Now, promise you will visit me before you leave."

"I promise," she said, and meant it.

"Good. That is very good."

As she watched her walk away, Jess noticed Usha favoured her right leg. What could have caused the slight limp? Arthritis, perhaps. Or an injury. Jess frowned; there was a lot she didn't know about Usha's life.

As Jess parked the Jeep into the McAllisters' garage, she drummed her fingers absently on the steering wheel—tapping out a beat to a song playing on the radio. Ben's four-wheel drive was a lot roomier than the Mini. She was pleased with the result of her shopping trip to Simon Emmett's CycleMania in Geelong, and turned around to admire the item she'd carefully stowed away in the back. Simon's sister, Haley—and that was a surprise—had rushed to serve her.

She jumped out of the driver's seat. If her smile was any wider, she'd resemble a clown. *Thank you, Haley.*

"Hi." Lili walked into the garage. "You're back."

"Yes, hello," she said, standing beside the rear door. "I met Usha at a coffee shop in Drysdale."

"Fantastic, I bet she was pleased to see you."

"She's shorter than I remember." Jess grinned. "It was wonderful to catch up with her after such a long time." She opened the rear door and hoisted the small alloy-framed bicycle—gloss-white and lavender—out of the car and set it on the concrete floor.

Lili circled around Jess and stopped in front of the child's bicycle. "What is this?"

"It's for Aruishi."

"You can't go buying her expensive gifts." There was an undercurrent of annoyance in Lili's voice.

This was not how Jess had imagined Lili reacting to the gift. Not at all.

"She mentioned she'd never had a bicycle of her own." Surely, Lili wouldn't object to Jess giving it to Aruishi?

"She's four years old."

"Yes, I know. It's from CycleMania. Haley was very helpful."

"You went to Simon's shop? In Geelong?" Lili's steely blue eyes seemed to pierce through Jess.

"Yes, Haley helped me choose the safest Australian-made bicycle for a four-year-old. I didn't know it was her brother's shop. It was a pleasant surprise to see her there," Jess said.

"I bet it was." Lili walked around the bicycle. "Haley only works at Ailie part-time," she said. "It's beautiful. But you shouldn't have."

"I thought I could teach her to…ride."

"Did you even think to ask me? Dad and I are restoring an old bike for Ru. As a Christmas present."

That rusty old thing Jess had noticed in the corner of the garage, covered with cobwebs, wouldn't be safe for Aruishi. "Oh hell. I'm sorry."

"No. You obviously didn't think to ask." She shook her head.

Jess reached into her jacket pocket for the executor's letter. Hopefully, this would improve Lili's mood. She handed it to Lili.

"What's this?" she asked, taking the envelope from Jess's hand. "Really, Jess, you should have talked to me first about the bike before spending your money."

"You'd better open the letter."

Lili ripped open the envelope and pulled out the document.

Jess slowly pushed the bicycle around in circles, waiting for Lili's reaction.

"What have you done?"

"What have I done?" Jess asked, knowing exactly what she'd done.

Lili waved the paper in front of Jess's face. "I don't understand. You're Ben's sole beneficiary. You are entitled to all the money."

Why was Lili making it so complicated? It was really very simple. "I can explain," she said.

"This says the loan's been written off—fully repaid." Her eyebrows furrowed. Lili blinked, and then blinked again. "It was you."

Jess shrugged.

"Why did you do it?" Lili asked suspiciously. "Throwing your money around like a game of Monopoly."

Jess backed up a couple of steps and leaned against the car. "It is what Ben would have wanted," she said. "I've heard that he meant to—"

"How could *you* know that? *You* couldn't know that."

"Does it really matter?" Jess looked down at the child's bicycle. She ran her hand over the small lavender-coloured handlebars. "I just know."

"I can't let you," Lili said.

Although Lili's voice was now soft and controlled, Jess heard uncertainty for the first time. She straightened her shoulders and took a deep breath. "Yes, you can. Ben was your friend. He must have cared for you very much if he agreed to be the donor. My brother was Aruishi's biological father." She lowered her tone. "He cared about both of you." She sighed. "It's what he would have wanted." *Like it or not, I am Aruishi's aunt.*

Jess placed the new bicycle into the storage locker, next to her own bicycle, and fastened the latch. "I'll leave it up to you. You decide whether Aruishi can have the bicycle or not," she said. "And if you decide she can't, I'll take it back. No problem." Her voice quivered. "But as far as the loan is concerned, that's not negotiable. It's written off."

Lili stared at her with her mouth half-open.

Jess grabbed her jacket from the front seat of the Jeep and headed towards the house. But then she stopped and turned back. "Oh, just so you know. I'm going to Melbourne with some friends tonight and I probably won't be back until late."

What would have been the right thing to do—according to Lili? Jess turned on her heel and took off again. "I did it for you and Aruishi," she muttered through clenched teeth. She'd made things worse. Jess couldn't understand why Lili was so unhappy with her.

Lili stood rooted to the spot like a fool and took a few deep breaths. What just happened? What just happened was that she'd lost her cool. Jess had bought Ru a bike costing a few hundred bucks *and* written of Lili's debt of over a hundred and fifty thousand dollars—and she hadn't even thanked her. Everything had happened so fast.

Damn. She was already running late, and going back to the house to get her car keys would mean she couldn't avoid Jess. Even looking at her right now would be too intimidating.

You're such a coward. She'd walk to Ailie, even though it meant making Alex wait.

When she arrived, Alex looked up from the computer screen. "Lili, I'm glad you're here. You wanted to know when Mac came in with the order of sea scallops. It has arrived."

"Good." Lili sighed with relief. "I'm glad to be here."

"Prep for tonight's menu is on track," Alex said.

"That's great," she said absently.

"Tim and Sara are both rostered to cover the extra tables on the terrace. We're in good shape." Alex peered at her with concern. "Hey, are you okay?"

Lili leaned against the wall, letting her bag fall to the floor. What could she say? She should have gone after Jess and thanked her. "I'm such an idiot." She buried her face in her hands and rubbed her temples.

"Now I'm worried," Alex said. "What did you do?"

Lili's gut twisted with guilt as she recounted the exchange from half an hour ago, hardly pausing to take a breath in the telling.

"Stone the crows," Alex said.

"Yeah, well…"

"You must be ecstatic the debt is wiped. I would have thrown my arms around her and kissed her profusely."

Lili shook her head. "You would."

"I'm sure Jess is right. Ben would have done this for you and Ru," Alex said. "Absolutely. But you do realise that Jess didn't have to do it."

"I know." Was it insecurity or pride that had caused her to act like that with Jess? She regretted her disgraceful reaction. "I don't know what got into me. I'll talk to her later and apologise." She rubbed the back of her neck.

Alex began to speak, then hesitated. "You'll have to wait, anyway. Haley was just here," she said.

"Oh? She's not working today, is she?"

Alex shook her head.

"Then what was she doing here?" Lili couldn't remember making an appointment with Haley.

"She came to drop off some gear on her way to your place to pick up Jess. But I guess you know that, right?" Alex raised her eyebrows. "Haley and her cycling buddies are taking Jess dancing at Mother's Attik in Prahran."

Lili's mouth fell open, but she quickly swallowed the sarcastic remark that threatened to spill off her tongue. It wasn't her concern if Jess wanted to go with Haley to the lesbian dance venue in Melbourne, was it? Then why did the thought of Jess partying with her sultry employee upset Lili so much? "Well, I hope they have a wonderful time." She shrugged.

"Hey, this is new." Alex narrowed her eyes. "Are you jealous?"

"No," Lili snapped.

Alex grinned. "Not that I blame you. You have this stunning *single* woman under your roof. And need I remind you—you're a beautiful, awesome single woman too."

As though Jess's beauty should matter. But it did seem to matter.

Not that she would let Alex see that. "Don't be ridiculous. Let's get to work."

She gave Alex a gentle push through the office door. "And stop smirking."

Haley and her friends were genuine biking enthusiasts, not like some of the obsessive and overexcited fangirls who had followed Jess around everywhere during the height of her career. Only halfway to Melbourne and they'd already asked a million questions on every conceivable topic.

"Hey, Jess. What do you do about saddle soreness? You know, so you don't wear out your...parts."

"Oh, Tori, haven't you got padded bike shorts?" Haley asked from the driver's seat.

"Sure, I just want to know if Jess has any secrets she wants to share with us," Tori said.

"Secrets. Yeah, tell us some of your secrets," another voice called from the back seat. Jess missed who.

Haley turned to Jess. "I'm really sorry about those three back there."

"Padded shorts are a must, but you need the right saddle fit. Some riders need more padding for their rear," Jess said over her shoulder.

"You wouldn't want a numb bum, would you, Haley?" Tori giggled.

Haley sent Jess a sideways glance and sighed heavily.

The venue was something else. It was crammed with women. The music was insanely loud, and Jess got a rush of energy as soon as they hit the dance floor. She appreciated the sea of diverse faces and the anonymity of being in an unfamiliar city. Apart from a few snippets of shouted conversation, she did very little talking with her stream of dance partners, and that suited her fine. A few months ago, she would have let her hair down and partied harder—but not anymore.

She wasn't a big drinker, but the girls persuaded her to spin the cocktail-flavour wheel, and she obligingly drank one lethal mixture of Absolut vodka with cranberry, orange, and peach schnapps. That was enough for her. Jess left the game of chance to Haley and her friends, and for the rest of the night stuck with crisp, refreshing Coronas with a wedge of lemon. The beers and a lot of sparkling water were enough to keep her lightly buzzed.

"I love this song. How about it, Jess? It's my turn." Haley gazed up at her with baby-blue eyes. She tugged at Jess's hand and pulled her towards the dance floor.

Why not? She appreciated Haley's attention and enjoyed the young woman's energetic gyrations.

How would Lili dance? she wondered. Would she ever have time to go clubbing? What would it take for her to let loose, have some fun? There was something freeing about moving in a crowd of people you didn't know, amongst hot, writhing, sexy bodies. What would Lili be like in one of these places—exasperating, strong-willed, *intense* Lili? She was angry at Jess, and all Jess had tried to do was make life easier for her and Aruishi. *Lili is so obstinate.*

Haley's arms wound around Jess's waist, pulling her close. She seemed out for a good time; she was uncomplicated, and Jess could handle that right now. With a slick dance move, Haley sent Jess into a spin, then grabbed her determinedly around the waist and locked her lips with Jess's.

After a few moments, Jess ended the kiss and removed herself from Haley's grasp. "Cheeky," she said with a laugh.

In the early hours of the morning, four of them piled back into the car. Tori remained behind, having hooked up with a woman from the club. They stopped to pick up a drive-through breakfast on the outskirts of the city. Haley and her friends feasted on bacon-and-egg burgers and French fries in the car, while Jess chose the largest takeaway coffee she could buy. It was black and strong, and tasted like it had been brewing for half a day. She looked over her shoulder. "Looks like Bec and Claire have crashed," she told Haley. "I now have the solemn task of keeping you alert."

Haley laughed. "I'm wide awake and stone-cold sober," she said. "It was a full-time job keeping *you* safe from all those women."

"Terrific job." She prodded Haley's thigh. "Much appreciated."

In Geelong, they coaxed the dozing pair out of the car and into their flat, arriving at the farm around five a.m.

Jess reached into the back seat for her jacket and then turned back to Haley. "Thanks, that was—"

Before she could catch a breath, Haley snaked her arm around Jess's neck and pressed their lips together. Jess didn't have a moment to react before Haley slipped her tongue into her mouth.

Jess placed her hand lightly on Haley's shoulder. "That was unexpected," she said. In truth, it was not at all unexpected. Haley had stuck close by Jess all evening and kissed her, playfully, more than once. She was clearly interested in more than dancing.

Perhaps Jess shouldn't keep resisting when pretty, interested women presented themselves to her? She drew Haley closer. "I like it," she whispered in her ear before her lips found Haley's once again, and their mouths found an easy rhythm.

A harsh light illuminated the car's interior, and they sprung immediately apart. Jess squinted into the darkness. "Lili?"

"I don't see anyone," Haley said. "It must be a sensor light." She attempted to pull Jess back. "Hey," she said dreamily.

Jess extracted herself from Haley's grip and edged closer to the door. "I think someone turned a light on." She hoped Lili hadn't seen them. Not that it should matter. But somehow it did.

"You're so sexy, Jess." Haley let out a deep sigh.

Jess forced a smile. "Thank you for tonight."

"Yeah, it *was* a good one. And it doesn't have to end."

"Haley." Jess reached for her hands. "I really enjoyed myself, but I need to call it a night. You are a great dancer, and your friends Tori, Bec, and Claire are a hoot."

"They're the best. I had a great time too." Haley gave her a small smile. "Another time?"

"Yes," she said. But she knew she didn't sound entirely convincing. "Another time." She waited until Haley met her gaze. "I'm dealing with a multitude of changes in my life right now."

Haley gripped Jess's forearm. "I'm sorry, Jess. I wasn't thinking. With losing Ben, and everything else."

"Thank you. No need to apologise," Jess said, stifling a yawn. "I don't know about you, but I'm exhausted. Are you sure you'll be okay to drive home?"

Haley gave her a cheeky grin. "I could say no. Then what would you do?"

Jess raised an eyebrow.

"Just kidding. I'm fine. Which is a good thing, really." Haley looked down at her watch. "In five hours, I have to meet up with my brother for a sixty-kilometre loop around the Peninsula."

Jess had the door open and was half way out of the car. "Lucky you."

"Hey, Jess?" Haley called.

"Yes?"

"Maybe, you'd like to come riding sometime?" Haley hesitated. "With our bike group. It would mean a lot to have you along."

She leaned into the car. "I'd love to. Drive safe." Jess pressed the car door closed and stepped back.

Haley pumped her fist out the driver's side window. She started the car and tooted the horn before driving off.

So much for not drawing attention. Jess looked up at the house and shook her head. She couldn't see any sign of Lili. Maybe it was just the sensor light acting strangely.

The first orange rays of sunlight were dancing on the landscape. A blanket of fog sat just above the trees, and the air was cool and dewy. Jess sighed tiredly and climbed the stairs to the house.

Chapter 12

HELEN UNBUCKLED ARUISHI'S CAR SEAT and lifted her out. Aruishi nodded drowsily and rested her head on her grandmother's shoulder. "Lili, you grab the bags, and I'll carry this sleepyhead into the house."

"Not a sleep head," Aruishi mumbled, wriggling her feet.

"Can you walk in by yourself, then?" Helen asked as Aruishi slid out of her arms.

They'd spent a leisurely two hours at the farmers' market, perusing the goods and visiting the animals at the Children's Farm. Lili and Helen sampled artisan breads, local free-range meats, cheeses, and other gourmet treats, while Aruishi fed the baby goats and geese, and enjoyed a ride on Mickie the donkey. Lili was chuffed, having made a great bargain with a second-hand dealer for a large, rusted iron rooster weathervane that would look amazing mounted in the restaurant's kitchen garden. He'd promised to deliver it to Ailie early next week.

As she placed the string bags filled with produce onto the kitchen island bench, Lili felt a tug on the hem of her shirt.

"Can I please tell Auntie Jess about my ride on Mickie?" Aruishi rubbed her eyes and yawned.

"Hand over your mouth, please," Lili said, glancing over to her mother, who raised her eyebrows.

"Yes, Mama." Aruishi placed her hand over her mouth. "But can I check if Auntie Jess is awake?" she mumbled through her hand.

Lili pinched her nose between her fingers. "I don't think Jess would want to smell you before you have a bath."

"I'll get things started," Helen said, coming to Lili's rescue. "You smell like Mickie the donkey, and you're covered in straw and mud." She ruffled Aruishi's curls.

"Do I really smell like Mickie, Gran?" Aruishi lifted her pink windcheater up to her nose and sniffed.

"Maybe just a little. But you'll smell like oranges after your bath."

Aruishi took her grandmother's hand. "Okay, then I'll tell Auntie Jess later when I smell like oranges." They walked towards Aruishi's bedroom hand in hand.

Now it was Auntie Jess this, Auntie Jess that. Lili groaned and began emptying the bags of fruit and vegetables onto the kitchen table. She wished she hadn't been curious last night and turned on the carport light when she'd heard a car pull up. But she had—just in time to see Jess and Haley all over each other.

"What did Aruishi want to tell me?"

Lili staggered backwards. The apples and grapefruit she'd been holding rolled across the kitchen floorboards. "Damn," she muttered. "I *really* wish you'd stop doing that."

"Doing what?" Jess asked.

Lili couldn't stop staring at Jess, who lounged against the doorjamb, her dark hair tousled like she'd just got out of bed. Her eyes were heavy-lidded, rich, dark-brown—almost black.

"Frightening me to death." Lili lunged for an apple as it rolled off the table and plummeted to the floor. She reached down and picked it up.

"Sorry. Let me help you." Jess bent down on her knees and scurried across the kitchen floor, scooping the spilled fruit into her arms. Lili tried hard not to focus on Jess's drawstring pyjama shorts and her muscled thighs, or the sleeveless jersey that fit like a glove. Lili wasn't blind. In fact, she had twenty-twenty vision, and it was hard to take her eyes off perfection.

What am I doing? I'm ogling a woman who clearly isn't interested in me. Lili shook her head to rid herself of the image of Jess and Haley in the car. Jess had been partying—and goodness knows what else—with Haley just a few hours ago.

"Lili, could you tell me where to put these, please?"

Lili bit her lip and reached for the wire fruit bowl. "In here. Please put them straight in here."

Jess painstakingly placed the eight apples and three grapefruit into the bowl. "There you go. Hopefully they're not bruised."

Like my ego. Lili lowered her eyes. "Thanks for your help," she snapped.

"No problem," Jess said, taking the last apple from Lili's hand and placing it gently on top of the pile. "Anything else I can help you with?"

"No, thanks." As Jess shrugged and turned to leave, Lilli swallowed hard and added, "Jess, wait. I owe you an apology."

"For what?" She turned back to face Lili, her eyebrows raised in question.

"For my reaction to Aruishi's new bike. And for my rudeness."

"Okay, no problem." Jess stared, obviously waiting for her to continue.

Lili tucked her hands into her pockets. "I also want to thank you for your generous—"

"Auntie Jess, you're awake," Aruishi called as she emerged from the hallway, naked and dripping with water. She ran towards Jess with Helen close behind her, clutching a towel in one hand and Aruishi's clothes in the other.

"Ru, get back here, you scamp." Helen lunged towards Aruishi, who threw her arms around Jess's legs.

"It's all right, Gran. I can make a noise now. Jess is up."

"Aruishi, let go of Jess," Lili said, perhaps a little too desperately. "Please."

Helen wrapped the towel around Aruishi and scooped her up in her arms. "Sorry, Jess. Now your clothes are wet."

"Um, it's okay. I'm happy to see you too, Aruishi."

Aruishi squealed. "I had to have a bath because Mickie got me dirty." She bobbed her head up and down dramatically.

Helen sighed. "Good afternoon, Jess. How was your excursion to Melbourne?"

"It was rather late." Jess stifled a yawn with her hand before she took a seat at the kitchen table. "But a lot of fun. It felt good to let off steam on the dance floor."

"Yeah, I bet," Lili murmured under her breath and shoved her hands even deeper into her pockets.

Helen tilted her head to one side, glancing quickly from Jess to Lili with a frown. "Maybe you should go along with Haley and her friends sometime, Lili."

"Yes, Mother." Lili grimaced. It might be what Jess liked, but, really, what made her mother think she'd go clubbing with Haley?

"Anyway, I'll let you take over from here, Lili." Helen passed Aruishi into her arms. "Ru, are you going to tell Jess about the animals at the market?"

"Yes! At last." Aruishi wriggled in Lili's arms and turned to Jess. "I've been to the children's farm with the animals, and I had a ride on a donkey named Mickie. He's not as big as Dora, but. And I fed the geese and the baby pigs, and I got covered in mud and stuff."

"Slow down, Ru. I don't think Jess understood half of that." But Lili was actually grateful for the distraction from her thoughts about Jess and Haley. She placed Aruishi on the floor and held the towel around her.

"Yes, Mama." She tugged on Jess's hand.

Jess laughed. "Did you enjoy your ride on Mickie?"

"He was really smelly." Aruishi pinched her nose. "Some of it rubbed off on me."

"So, that's why you had a bath." Jess leaned down to Aruishi's height and kissed the top of her head. "You smell lovely now."

The gesture towards her daughter was disarming, and despite everything from yesterday and today, Lili would have been sucked in if her mother had not interrupted her thoughts.

"Sorry to be a nuisance." Helen handed Aruishi's clothes over to Jess.

Lili gave her mother a flicker of a scowl, which Helen seemed to be blithely ignoring. "I'm off home. The McPhersons are popping in for afternoon tea. Hope you three enjoy the rest of your day." She kissed Lili on the cheek.

"Thanks, Mum," she said with a small wave of her hand, then turned back to Aruishi. "If you've finished telling Jess about the animals, after you get dressed we can go to the beach." Lili brushed stray curls away from Aruishi's eyes. "Maybe build a fort in the sand? Like the one at Queenscliff."

"Yes, okay, if Jess can come." Aruishi placed her hands on her hips and turned to Jess. "Can you come with us to the beach and help make a fort, please?"

Jess visibly bit her bottom lip. "I'd love to, Aruishi, but I was about to get ready for a long ride. If Lili takes a photo with her phone camera, I'll be able to see a picture of the fort when I get back. How about that?"

Thank goodness Jess had the sense to realise now was not the time to play happy families in the sand.

"Good idea," Lili said, and twirled Aruishi around and marched her towards the bathroom before her daughter had a chance to argue.

Chapter 13

"TABLE EIGHT: FOUR PORK, TWO ravioli," Lili called, and watched Sky, her third-year apprentice chef, place perfect dollops of apple puree, just off-centre, onto four hand-thrown ceramic plates. She followed with a measure of broad beans to the left of each circle. Lili then lifted the small rectangle of roast pork belly and placed it until it was just touching the puree and spooned the apple brandy reduction onto the plate—she preferred this traditional, rustic finish rather than a smear or painterly streak. The twice-cooked pork was soft and tender with a golden crispy skin. The bright green of the broad beans, the pale yellow of the puree, and the dark caramel glaze finished the dish. Lili positioned the plates under the infrared lamp beside two shallow earthenware bowls of goat's cheese ravioli with lemon butter, white asparagus, and a sprinkling of red currant jelly cubes—topped with a popping green fried parsley sprig.

"Pick up table eight." Lili reached for the table plan on the shelf above the serving station and looked up, straight into Haley's eyes.

Haley smiled. "Good to go," she said, placing two plates along her left arm and picking up one of the vegetarian bowls. Owen was close behind. He collected the remaining meals and followed Haley through the kitchen doors.

Lili hadn't thought again about Jess's night out until Haley had come bouncing into the kitchen at the start of her shift. She was in high spirits, full of praise about Jess, and couldn't stop talking about how much fun they'd had at the nightclub.

Lili's imagination ran riot, with visions of Jess and Haley cosying up on the dance floor, a variant of the scene Lili had witnessed in the car. It didn't help that she'd barely seen Jess since her night in Melbourne.

"Chef, we have a problem." Nora stood beside the servery with a deep frown on her usually cheerful face.

"Yes? What is it?" Lili asked calmly.

"Eddie was dismantling the electric slicer." Nora shook her head. "He's cut his finger quite badly. I think he'll need stitches."

Oh no. "Is he okay?"

Nora shrugged. "I hope so."

"All right. Thanks, Nora." Lili took a deep breath. "Alex, relieve me, please."

Alex spoke briefly to Sara, the assistant pastry chef, and took over Lili's place at the servery. She picked up the clipboard. "Sky, you'll assist Sara," she instructed the apprentice chef. "Next course in fifteen minutes, people."

"Yes, Alex," Sara and Sky called in unison.

Walking briskly towards the utility area, Lili took her phone out of her jacket pocket and pressed the preset contact for the local after-hours doctor, who picked up after just a few rings. She explained about the accident and asked him if he was available for an incoming patient that might require stitches.

Blood splatters dotted Eddie's apron and the white tiled floor. She grabbed a pair of sterile gloves, a roll of paper towels, and a clean cloth from under the nearest workstation. Eddie was perched on a low stool with a cloth stained dark red around his right hand. He looked pale and visibly shaken.

"How are you feeling, Ed?" She placed her hand on his shoulder.

"A bit queasy," he said. "I'm sorry, Lili. I totally forgot to wear the mesh glove."

"Guess you won't forget next time." She crouched beside him. "Will you let me look? I'll be as gentle as possible."

He nodded.

"Here's the warm water." Nora placed a basin of water and the first aid kit on the floor beside them.

"Thanks, Nora," she said. "Okay, here we go."

Lili gently removed the stained towel, exposing the deep gash between Eddie's thumb joint and forefinger. She cleaned away the blood with alcohol wipes and pressed a clean, soft cloth firmly against the wound.

Eddie flinched.

"Sorry." She removed the cloth and quickly wrapped a strip of gauze around the wound. "You need to hold this around here. That's right, use a bit of pressure. Not *too* tight."

"Will I need stitches?"

"Probably. Doctor Travis will take care of you." Lili stood and called Nora to one side. "Can you please drive Ed to the medical centre in Portarlington? I'll call back and let him know you are leaving now."

"No worries. I can drop him home after and make sure he's okay."

"Thanks. I'd go myself, but I'm closing up tonight."

"It's no problem. I'll just grab my keys," she said. "I don't know how long it'll take."

"Don't worry, I have you covered. Take everything with you, and go straight home after seeing to Ed."

"Are you sure?"

"Definitely. Now, get your things, and I'll help him collect his gear. We'll meet you out the back." Lili threw the gloves and soiled towels into the waste bin and helped Ed to his feet. "Come on. The doc will have you fixed up in no time."

Eddie looked down at his shoes. "I'm sorry. I feel like a *total* twit. Who's going to finish off my work?"

"Don't worry about it. I'll take care of everything." She squeezed his shoulder reassuringly. "Let me know how you get on."

Jess parked the Jeep alongside Lili's bright-orange Subaru in the rear carpark at Ailie. She hopped out of the driver's seat, walked through the dimly lit courtyard, and heard the clinking of glass. Probably bottles being emptied into the recycling bin. As she got closer to where the intense beam of a spotlight lit the service area, she saw Lili jumping animatedly on a large cardboard box.

"Has it been that bad a night that you're taking it out on a carton?"

"*Christ*, Jess." Lili clutched her neck, then pulled earphones out of her ears. She was blurry-eyed, and a sheen of sweat covered her forehead. The front of her apron was patterned with stains, like a quirky Jackson Pollock abstract. "It's nearly midnight. What are you doing here?"

"I had dinner with Aruishi and your parents. Helen finally managed to put Aruishi to bed, after I read her the same story four times. Then Helen brought out some old photograph albums, and time got away from us."

Lili picked up the squashed box and tossed it into a four-wheeled recycle bin. "Mothers," she muttered, shaking her head and shrugging. "Well, that would have been fun for you."

"It was, actually. You were a cute kid, and a gangly teenager with braces. You've changed," she said, and looked away. Even in her dishevelled state, with her hair damp and sticking out at odd angles, there was nothing gangly or awkward about Lili now.

Lili frowned. "Yes, well, I'll have something to say to Mother about that."

"Don't be too hard on her. I loved going through the photographs," she said. "Helen mentioned what happened tonight, and you still weren't home when I got back to your house, so I thought I should come over and see if you needed help."

"Thank you. I'm just about done," Lili said. "Alex and Mei stayed on to help."

"That's good. How is your kitchen hand?"

"Ed will be fine. Six stitches. He's lucky he didn't sever a tendon. If all goes well, he'll be back at work next week."

"That's good. I am glad he'll be able to return soon."

"It could have been worse." Lili sighed. "The accident reminded me I need to schedule a refresher on the safe use of machinery, knives, and blades." She tilted her head towards Jess. "Don't suppose you could help me with these bins? I almost forgot to put them out."

Jess helped Lili roll the two wheelie bins to the outside of the courtyard gate.

"Thanks." She nudged Jess with her shoulder and quickly stepped away.

Jess looked up, surprised. "No problem." She followed Lili inside and down the corridor towards her office. "What else can I do?"

"Follow me around and make sure I don't fall asleep on my feet," she said.

"Okay."

Lili turned back to face her. "Just joking. But thank you for helping with the bins. I'm nearly done here." She rubbed her lower back and twisted from side to side. "I really do need a hot shower. And a whiskey."

"Are you sure I can't help you with anything else?" Jess repeated.

"Only if you're any good at massage and have magical hands." Lili pressed the back of her neck.

Jess briefly squeezed her eyes shut. "As a matter of fact—"

Lili stifled a yawn with her hand. "Relax. I'm joking." She managed a tired smile. "But since you're here, you could give me a lift home. I'll leave my car and walk over in the morning."

"I can do that," Jess said.

Things had been so strained between them, and yet Jess found the idea of being around Lili tonight, even for a short while, strangely agreeable.

"Just give me five," Lili said. "I'll get my stuff together."

She relaxed into Lili's comfortable office chair and waited.

Jess studied the photograph of Aruishi, Lili, and Ben at the beach that sat on the Danish-styled sideboard in Lili's living room. It was the only photograph she'd seen of the three of them together. Aruishi appeared a lot younger—maybe two years old—and sat on Lili's shoulder, her hands clenched in her mother's hair. Ben stood slightly behind them with a huge grin. All three of them looked happy.

She took a sharp intake of breath, with the now-familiar ache in her chest, as she noticed the framed memorial card with Ben's photograph. Seeing the date of his passing made it so final.

"Would you like to join me? I'm having that whiskey."

Jess wiped her eyes with the back of her hand before turning around, relieved to find Lili standing with her back to her at the drinks cabinet.

Freshly showered, Lili had changed into loose-fitting striped pyjama bottoms that sat nicely on her hips and a white tank top that showed off her toned shoulders. As Lili reached for glasses from the overhead shelf, Jess looked away before she caught her staring. She sat down heavily on the sofa. "I'd like that."

"You have a choice. Aberlour 16 or Suntory Hibiki."

"I'll leave it to you. I'm not familiar with either," Jess said.

Lili placed two curved glasses and a squat bottle on the coffee table in front of them and sat down at the other end of the sofa. She poured a small measure in each glass and handed one to Jess. "I'll introduce you to the Scottish Aberlour, then. Spicy with a gentle oaky splash. Tell me what you think."

Jess sipped the dark amber fluid and coughed as the warmth hit the back of her throat. "Oh…" She drew a sharp breath.

Lili laughed and held up her glass. "*Slow*," she said, drawing out the word. "Tilt the glass slightly towards your lips. Just sip a small amount—only to cover the surface of your tongue. Even good whiskey will burn if you take a gulp. Hold it in your mouth for ten seconds, and you should begin to taste the sweetness—like raisins. After you swallow, open your mouth slightly, and you'll taste other floral and plum flavours."

Lili sipped from her glass. "Hmm…"

Jess's gaze rested on Lili's mouth—the curve of her slightly parted lips, her sweet smile. She swallowed hard and coughed again, even though she'd yet to attempt a second taste.

"Sip really slow," Lili said.

Lili edged back into the corner of the couch and stretched her legs out in front of her to ease her achy lower back. It was nice of Jess to call by the restaurant to check on her. Unnecessary, but a pleasant surprise.

Jess lifted her glass and tried to emulate Lili's movements. When she pursed her ruby lips and sipped the honey-coloured spirit, she didn't cough this time, and a rosy blush flushed her cheeks. Sultry. Despite herself, despite all the tension between them lately, Lili was entranced.

"Hmm…I do like it," Jess said in a squeaky voice.

Lili laughed and found herself leaning over to give Jess's forearm a gentle pinch. "You'll be a single malt connoisseur in no time." She winced as the sudden movement tugged at her back. She rubbed at the tender spot on the left side of her waist.

Jess placed her glass on the table. "Your back is still bothering you, even after the shower."

It was a statement, not a question. Lili couldn't deny what was obvious. "Yeah, it was a long day on my feet."

"Has it been giving you trouble for long?"

"Only since I caught Ru from sliding off the donkey at the market."

"Ah, that would do it." Jess stood up and dragged the leather ottoman in front of the couch. "Can you remember if the pain was sudden or has worsened gradually?"

"It was like a pull. It hasn't been too bad, but being on my feet for so long today hasn't helped." Lili tilted her head and stared at Jess. "Why are you asking so many questions about my back?"

Jess returned to the couch, pulled the ottoman footstool between her knees, and patted its padded surface. "Sit. I'll check it."

"Thanks, but all I need is a good night's sleep. It's a bit tender, so I don't think I can stand to be touched." Lili didn't want to risk making the situation worse if Jess didn't know what she was doing. The idea of a gentle massage was tempting, though. As was the thought of Jess's warm hands on her back... *Hmm.*

"I may be able to help. Sit." Jess patted the ottoman again. "I'm not just saying that. I have a BSc in physiotherapy. I've completed over one thousand part-time clinical hours, and part of my course included remedial massage."

Lili knew she was staring at Jess with her mouth wide open. "Aren't you a career athlete? How on earth did you have the time?"

Jess grinned. "I began competitive cycling in school and rode for the university team during my three years of physio studies in London. After that, I transitioned into sports physiotherapy, working part-time with British Cycling. I trained, cycled competitively, and got my degree. I sometimes volunteer at the Children's Clinic in London. Trust me, Lili, I'll be gentle." Jess raised her eyebrows, and this time she nudged the ottoman with her foot. "What have you got to lose?"

"You're full of surprises." That was an understatement. Jess was always creeping up on her, surprising Lili with her seemingly limitless talents. She scooted to the edge of the couch and moved onto the four-legged ottoman in front of Jess. *What do I have to lose? My mind—or more?*

"Okay, just relax," Jess said, her hands resting on Lili's bare shoulders.

Lili flinched at her touch. It was a reflex action—Jess's hands were warm and strong, just as Lili had imagined.

"Relax," Jess repeated gently, and applied more pressure, her thumbs gently pressing into the knots in her shoulders. "You're so tense."

"Ah-ha."

"Drop your head forward, and slowly move your chin to your chest. That's it," she said, and Lili complied. "The shoulders and neck are connected to the heart chakras. Feel how the tension drains away as you lift your heart centre up and soften your jaw. It releases pent-up tension from your whole body." Jess's low voice soothed.

Lili dropped her shoulders and allowed her body to relax. "You learned this while becoming a physio?"

Jess laughed quietly, and her hands stilled. "No, from a Buddhist yogini."

"So, natural therapy combined with traditional practice? I thought all physios were hard taskmistresses."

"It has its place. Physiotherapy is about recovery, rehabilitation, and pain management." Jess moved her hands to Lili's lower back. "Here?"

"Yes, there. On the left. Yep. That's the spot."

"You've had no numbness or tingling in your legs? No pain anywhere else?"

"No…" Lili said slowly as Jess explored her lower back with practised fingers just under the hem of her tank top. Lili sighed and then flinched as Jess's hands dropped away suddenly.

Jess cleared her throat. "No other problems that you know of?"

"None at all." As a chef, Lili believed in a healthy body image and liked to set a good example. She took pride in keeping fit. Allowing anyone to witness her fallibilities was not her style, especially when that person was Jess.

"Good. I'm just going to try some soft-tissue massage to increase the blood flow. It should ease your pain." Her voice was steady and confident. "Do you feel comfortable with that?"

"Ah-ha," Lili murmured and leaned back into Jess's hands as they curved around her waist. She relaxed as the tension left her body. "That feels good." She sighed. If she were a cat, she'd be purring.

"It's working, then," Jess whispered close to her ear. "Now just stretch to the right. And now back against my hand again. Good. I think we're done. How does it feel?"

Lili couldn't answer immediately. Her cheeks heated and warmth spread through her entire body. Lili chastised herself about the direction her mind was taking. Jess was just being professional.

She leaned forward, away from Jess's hands, stood carefully, then moved back to her place on the sofa. She took a deep breath and let it out slowly. "Thank you, that feels so much better. I mean…thank you."

"You're welcome. Hopefully, you will sleep well tonight. But you may need more soft-tissue massage and some stretching soon"—she lowered her gaze—"if you feel comfortable with me helping with that?"

Lili reached for her glass and finished her drink in one gulp, hoping the whiskey burn would bring her back to her senses. "Sure. Thanks, Jess." She sighed again. "You do have magical hands."

Jess cleared her throat, and looked down into her glass.

"Oh, I'm so sorry." Lili put her head in her hands. "Please tell me I didn't just say that aloud."

Brilliant. She'd managed to embarrass them both. If she sank into the couch and disappeared, it would be a blessing.

Chapter 14

FOR THE PREVIOUS FEW NIGHTS, Jess had not been visited by her demons and had slept through peacefully until around six a.m. Not last night. But last night, her restlessness hadn't been due to bad dreams.

She'd crawled into bed at one-thirty, spent hours tossing and churning over Lili's surprisingly flirtatious behaviour, and hardly slept at all. It had been extraordinarily hard to maintain a professional reserve with Lili during her massage and manipulation session. Lili was exhausted, in pain, and vulnerable, and Jess had had to disregard her friendly flirtation and not act on the pleasant sensations that surfaced as she ran her hands over Lili's tense muscles. But it was difficult to ignore the signs that something might be changing between them. Was Lili beginning to understand that Jess's motives for paying off the debt and buying a bicycle for Aruishi were well intentioned, with no hidden agenda?

She got out of bed, showered, and made her way to the kitchen. Lili wasn't there. There was a note on the bench, informing Jess she'd gone for a surf, after which she'd collect Ru from her parents and take her to kindergarten in Portarlington. The massage must have helped if Lili could surf this morning.

Twenty minutes later, after two coffees and a banana, Jess sat on her bicycle, glanced down at her gloved hands, and smiled. *Magical hands.* She'd helped relieve Lili's discomfort, and that actually made her happy. Jess turned onto the open road and pedalled the gradual incline. It was a long hill, and she directed all her energy to her legs. She kept the top part of her body still, staying light on the pedals, and moved her legs rhythmically. The smooth riding technique meant she'd have plenty of energy after she crested the hill. She slid forward on her seat and positioned her hips just right to produce the best muscle force, given her tall height.

Since her accident, hill climbing had become the most challenging. A good warm-up and climbing fitness were the keys to improving her speed and power. Cassie in the rehab centre had told her that over and over. And so, to maintain her strength, Jess chose a hilly route at least once a week. For a proper workout, she'd have to drive out to the Barabool Hills near Geelong or over an hour into the Otway Ranges. Challambra Crescent, the torturously steep road in Geelong that had been part of the 2010 International Road Cycling Championship route was another option, but not for today.

Coming to the end of her thirty-one-kilometre loop, Jess had the Portarlington Pier in sight, and her GPS watch guided her to the Foreshore Reserve. At the edge of the park, Jess dismounted and reached into the saddlebag for her phone. Should she take a chance and text Lili? She looked left towards the shops and cafés. Oh, what the heck. Jess pressed the messenger app and typed.

Hi. If you are near Portarlington, are you free for a coffee?

It was more than a minute before her phone chimed a return message.

Yes. Just dropped off Ru. A coffee would be good. Where are you?

Jess texted back.

Foreshore Reserve. Near the carpark. Where shall we meet?

Jess's jersey and shorts weren't the most appropriate café gear, and she scowled as a trickle of sweat ran down her back. She'd feel a whole lot better if she could shower and change into fresh clothes, but she'd messaged Lili on impulse. Thank goodness she'd taken time to pull her hair into a fishtail braid this morning, which lessened the damp hair and helmet-head look.

She received the directions.

Keep coming along the main road. Portarlington Bakehouse. Table out front. I'll order. Espresso, hot milk on the side. Right?

Just as Jess spotted the well-signed weatherboard bakery with its red-brick chimney around three hundred metres up the street, it occurred to her that Lili remembered how she took her coffee.

Perfect.

Perfect in more ways than one. Agreeing to meet her for coffee must be a sign that Lili was comfortable about their interaction last night.

It took her a couple of minutes to wheel her bicycle to the bakery and secure it to the bicycle stand. She removed her gloves, tucked her helmet under her arm, and strode towards the sidewalk table where Lili sat under the shade of the Bakehouse awning. Her friendly smile was a welcome sight.

Jess had a way of carrying herself that was casual and sexy. How did she manage that?

Maybe being in the public eye, with all the social pressures that went with it—as if Lili would know anything about that—gave her self-assurance beyond her twenty-nine years. She appeared both insouciant and mature on the outside, but during the storm, Lili had got a glimpse of pain and turmoil within. She was beginning to form a picture of what lay beneath Jess's cool and controlled surface.

Jess was smart. A physiotherapy degree was not an easy one to get. Lili had never considered that, as an elite athlete, Jess would have bothered to pursue another career, but that was clearly a stupid assumption.

Yeah, smart, but also beautiful.

And as Jess slid elegantly onto the bench seat across from her, that last part was reinforced. How did anyone manage to look so good in stretchy spandex?

"Hi," Jess said.

"Hello, how was your ride?"

"It was great." Jess nonchalantly tossed her braid over her shoulder and removed her wraparound sunglasses.

She became engulfed in the fathomless deep pools of Jess's eyes. *Look away. She's interested in Haley—not me.*

"Lili." Jess tilted her head to one side.

"Yes?" Lili sat up straighter.

"Thank you for the coffee." Jess added a dash of hot milk into the espresso cup and slowly stirred. "You went surfing. How was it?"

"Sensational. Thanks to you, I loved being out on the water this morning." She grinned. "Perfect waves." Lili was grateful for Jess's help, and it was pointless being churlish about Haley and Jess, she supposed.

"I'm glad I could help. Your back better?"

Lili put her arms above her head and stretched from side to side. "Virtually pain-free."

"Don't overdo it for a few days."

"I won't," Lili said. "Honestly, I feel good."

"I'm glad." But Jess looked uncertain. Then she suddenly smiled. She pointed to the laden plate on the table in front of her. "And whose is this?"

"It's mine, but I'll share. The croissant is filled with frangipane, and look at these toasted almonds on top. Flaky and golden—pure indulgence—give it a try."

"It looks good. But I'll stick to coffee."

Lili scooped out a smidgen of pale-yellow cream filling with a piece of the pastry she'd broken off and held it out to Jess. "Go on, I insist. It's nutty and luscious, their speciality, rivalling any French bakery."

Jess leaned forward, and Lili popped the morsel into her mouth. She chewed delicately and licked the powdered sugar that dusted her lips.

Lili momentarily closed her eyes and caught her bottom lip between her teeth as she recalled last night and Jess's lips as she'd sipped the whiskey.

"Definitely indulgent. That cream is rich, and probably loaded with a thousand calories." Jess wiped her mouth with a napkin and sipped her coffee.

"But it is yummy. Anyway, everything in moderation. You've probably burnt off loads of energy on your ride. You need to refuel."

"It wasn't a taxing circuit." Jess grinned. "Only thirty kilometres."

She stared at Jess. "Just a ride in the park, eh?" She pushed the plate with the remaining croissant closer to her. "On second thought, I think this is yours." She looked over at where Jess had parked her bike. "So, have you always been good at sports?"

"I took part in a lot of different sporting activities when I was young. I tried everything. Track and field, gymnastics, netball, swimming."

"I can imagine. You were a country kid from Wylie, weren't you?"

Jess nodded.

"I bet you were involved in Little Athletics. Probably won a load of medals?"

Jess pushed the plate back towards Lili and ran her finger around the edge of her cup. "I remember getting a few ribbons in track and field."

"What about cycling?" Lili asked.

"I actually didn't get on a racing bike until after I arrived in England."

"Really? Wasn't your father a medal winner too? A gold medal winner." Jess pursed her lips. "Yes, he was."

Hmm. She'd struck a nerve. Should she go further? It seemed to hurt Jess to talk about her parents, but talking might help with the burdens she carried. If only Jess would open up to her.

"When did you start competitive cycling?"

"The boarding school I attended focused on both sports and academia. We were encouraged to take part in interschool competitions. My life changed after I started cycling."

"How so?"

Despite looking uncomfortable, Jess held Lili's gaze. "It saved my life. It made me feel a part of something. After my father took me to England I was...lost. In a dark place. I did some stupid things." She rubbed her knuckles over the tops of her thighs.

Lili's heart lurched at the thought of Jess alone in a foreign country without her mother and brother. According to Ben, soon after their mother had died, Jess had been taken to England by their father. The anguish Jess had experienced at that time was evident even now.

"I'm glad you found refuge in cycling. Your father did the right thing, enrolling you in that school."

Jess tilted her head to one side, as if contemplating Lili's words. "It didn't seem like it at the time. But I guess you're right."

"He must have been proud of you? Following in his footsteps?"

"My father didn't spend a lot of time with me. He was pleased when I began cycling, but couldn't hide his bias against women's involvement in professional sport. Old school, I guess. Even though his own cycling career was nearly over, I didn't get a lot of encouragement from him."

"Oh, I'm so sorry, Jess." Was Ben Senior jealous of his daughter's success and her physical attributes? If his son had been a sportsman, rather than a chef—he'd once called young Ben a sissy—things might have been different.

"Don't be. As you said, he gave me a good start, and I inherited some of my competitiveness and drive from him."

"You've achieved a lot already," Lili said with an encouraging smile.

"Thank you. I'm ready for more coffee, and maybe another bite of your croissant." She looked up at Lili with a twinkle in her eyes. "How about you? Another coffee?"

"Yeah, that would be great." Lili watched Jess walk into the bakery and couldn't avoid focusing on her shapely behind. She smiled to herself, scratched her forehead, and contemplated her newly acquired appreciation for lycra.

Appreciating her physical beauty was one thing, but Jess was being so sweet and hadn't even mentioned Lili's outburst in the garage about the bicycle and wiping the loan. *I really have to apologise, for real, and now would be a good time.*

"Coffee won't be long," Jess said as she settled back on the bench across from her.

"Thanks," Lili murmured. She bit into the soft skin of her thumb, then quickly drew her hand away from her mouth and gripped the edge of the table. "I'm sorry."

"Sorry?" Jess gazed at her.

"Yes, again, I am very sorry for my behaviour in the garage."

Jess frowned. "You mean about Aruishi's bicycle?"

"Yes, but not just that. I am apologising for my reaction to the letter explaining you've wiped the loan. I was in shock. It was so unexpected. I'd been sick with worry about coming up with the money, but it was my problem to deal with... Then it was taken out of my control." She looked away briefly. "I reacted so badly. I'm sorry."

Jess blinked and slowly nodded her head. "I understand that now. Thank you for explaining. I shouldn't have just handed you the letter. You were already upset about the bicycle surprise. I should have explained what I had done and why."

"Okay," Lili said. "Can we start again?"

"Um, what do you mean?" She smiled but looked confused.

"This afternoon, when I bring Ru home from kindergarten, can we give her that beautiful new bike?"

"Really? Are you sure?"

"Café latte?"

They both looked up, startled at the server who'd approached unnoticed. He held out a coffee glass.

Jess turned towards Lili with a smile. "That will be hers."

"Thank you." Lili looked quickly back to Jess. She reached across the table and grasped her hand. "Yes, I am very sure. Ru will be over the moon."

Aruishi stared at Jess with her hands on her hips. "What is it?" she asked, looking from Jess to Lili and back again.

"Your mother and I have a surprise for you," Jess said, and winked at Lili.

Jess followed them along the narrow, meandering creek that skirted a gently sloped, wildflower-filled pasture. Crisp sea air filled her lungs, and afternoon sunshine warmed her skin. Aruishi walked slightly ahead, holding her mother's hand, and glanced back at Jess every few seconds. Jess quickened her pace, caught up with them, and fell into step beside Lili.

"It's going to be impossible to keep her off that bike," Lili whispered as Aruishi let go of her hand and skipped ahead. They reached Scott's garage door, and Lili inserted the key and flipped a switch on the outside wall. The roller door opened, and Aruishi ducked inside.

"I hope she likes it," Jess whispered back.

Aruishi stood inside, her arms crossed, looking in every direction. "I don't see anything new, Auntie Jess." She twirled around. "What's my surprise? Tell me," she insisted.

Lili leaned against the parked Jeep, smiled at Jess, and shrugged. "If you stand still, Ru, you will see for yourself."

When Jess rolled the bicycle out of the lock-up and into view, Aruishi squealed and clapped her hands. "Ooh! Jess," she said. "It's a bike…a beautiful bike. Can I get on, can I get on now?"

"I'll help you," Jess said. "Oh, wait one second, I almost forgot." She held up one finger and walked back to the lock-up. She removed a small cardboard box and placed it on the floor. "This is for you too, Aruishi."

"Another present?" Aruishi gripped Jess's arm but turned to look at her mother. "Another present, Mama. Am I the luckiest?"

Lili's eyes twinkled. Her joyful laugh filled the space. She went to Aruishi, crouched beside her, and helped her open the box. "You are definitely the luckiest, munchkin." She lifted the purple helmet out of the box and carefully placed it on Aruishi's head. "Um, I'm not sure how this works."

Jess stepped up and adjusted the magnetic buckle so it was a snug fit. "Is that comfy?"

Aruishi nodded. "Thank you, Jess, you're the best auntie ever." She grinned and climbed onto the bike while Lili gave her a steadying hand.

Jess looked up and met Lili's approving gaze. Lili silently mouthed, *Thank you.*

"It has lots of wheels," Aruishi said in a serious tone, pointing to the training wheels. "I can go for a ride outside now?"

"After you practise a bit in here and get used to it," Lili said. "Perhaps when Jess has time, she'll teach you the rules and take you for a ride around the farm."

"Okay, I will get used to the bike." Aruishi took off and circled the interior of the large garage.

"I'd be happy to give Aruishi lessons." Jess turned in a circle to follow her around. "Maybe tomorrow? Umm, I have an appointment this afternoon to view an Airbnb in Portarlington."

"Why?"

"I've decided to stay a bit longer in Australia. I can't continue to take advantage of your hospitality."

Lili's forehead creased. "What are you talking about? Do you feel uncomfortable here with us?"

"No, Lili. I just don't want to overstay my welcome." She rubbed the back of her neck. This was turning out to be awkward. "I'd like to spend more time with Usha Joshi. I haven't seen her in years, and we have a lot of catching up to do. And Aruishi…" She looked down at the ground.

"Jess, you can stay here. Unless you want to go?" Lili looked uncomfortable. "Ru and I would like you to stay. After all, you did promise to give her lessons—she'd be learning from the expert, wouldn't she?"

"But I don't know how long I'll be here before I return to the UK."

"That's okay." She looked at her quizzically. "I did wonder, though. Don't you have a job, or something or someone to go back to?"

That was a very good question, and not one she could answer with conviction. Especially at this moment. Especially to Lili. "Nothing that can't wait," Jess said.

Lili looked like she wanted to ask more questions, but thankfully, she didn't. "We're agreed, then," she said. "Please go and cancel that appointment."

Jess let out a relieved breath. She did want to stay at the farm, but she'd have to answer Lili's questions about her life back in the UK eventually. She was bound to ask again.

"I'm hungry." Aruishi climbed off her bike and clutched the strap under her chin.

Lili leaned forward and unclipped the magnet. "Okay. First, let's thank Jess for your presents. Then we'll put them away safely."

"Thank you for my bike and my helmet, Auntie Jess." Aruishi threw her arms around Jess's legs. "I can't believe it. My friend Max will be so jealous. We've both wanted bikes, and now I have one."

"You're welcome."

"Can Auntie Jess come with us for fish and chips?" Aruishi let go of Jess and tugged her mother's arm.

"Why don't you ask her?"

"Come with us, Jess," Aruishi said. It wasn't a question, more like a plea, her eyes wide and expectant.

"Yeah, come with us." The corners of Lili's mouth quirked with an amused smile. "The fresh fish and crispy chips are really good. We always eat at the foreshore reserve so we can people watch, and afterwards we take a walk along the pier."

Lili's phone buzzed. She grabbed it from her pocket and checked the screen. "We'd better hurry and put your bike away, Aruishi. Tash and Alex are already in Queenscliff."

Memories were sometimes painful and you wanted to push them away. But Queenscliff. Fish and chips with her mother and Ben. These were happy memories she wouldn't mind revisiting with Lili and Aruishi.

Jess walked beside her niece, helped roll the bicycle in next to hers, and hung the helmet on the wall hook. She fastened the door and turned to Lili. "I will tag along, if you don't mind? It is a lovely evening for a stroll, but first I'll make that phone call. Again, if you are sure?"

Lili raised an eyebrow and flashed Jess a beaming smile. "Yes." She hitched one shoulder at Aruishi. "What do you say, Ru? Should we let Jess tag along?"

"Yes. She must come. *Please*." Aruishi skipped towards the garage door. "Come on, Jess," she called loudly.

"How could I refuse?" Jess asked. "Your daughter is very persuasive."

"I wonder which side of the family she gets that from?" Lili smirked.

Chapter 15

THE NEXT MORNING, JESS SET up a makeshift street scene on the paved farm road using an orange traffic cone, an old tyre, and a wheelbarrow to teach Aruishi about bike and road safety.

"Can Crumpet, Cream Puff, Elsie, and Patch be like pretend cars?" Aruishi pointed to the four jersey cows in a nearby paddock. "Jack is over there." She pointed to the farmhand. "Ask him to open the gate and let them through, Auntie Jess."

"That's a very bad idea. No, we can't let the cows out of the paddock." Jess stifled a laugh. Aruishi would not be on a road with traffic anytime soon, but she needed to learn about obstacles, especially cars. "Just pretend the wheelbarrow is a car."

"But it's not moving."

"Pretend it is a parked car," Jess said.

"It's a very small parked car. With only one wheel."

Jess couldn't fault her logic. "Yes, Aruishi. Stay in a straight line, no weaving about. I'm right behind you."

Aruishi turned around and called out, "I'm not weaving."

"Eyes in front. Watch out for that…wheelbarrow."

They completed the session with no major crisis, Aruishi finally agreeing to place both hands on the handlebars and not turn around. Although she'd been involved in programmes that instructed people of all ages to ride, after two hours instructing Aruishi, Jess was exhausted. It was different with her niece; there was more at stake.

After they parked their bicycles side by side in the garage and stowed away their helmets, Aruishi threw her arms around her, and Jess was content.

Later, on the drive over to Usha's house, she checked the rear-vision mirror frequently. Initially, Aruishi had chattered nonstop, but she'd dozed off ten minutes after they'd left the farm and was still sound asleep.

"Where are we?" She asked as Jess lifted her out of the booster seat and onto her hip.

"We're at Usha's house," Jess said. "Do you remember what I told you?"

Aruishi rubbed her eyes and nodded. "Doctor Usha."

"That's right. You've been here before with your mama, haven't you?" Jess struggled to balance Aruishi on her hip and reach into the back seat for the large carry bag.

"Ah-ha, I've been here with my Ben too," Aruishi said, clinging onto Jess's shoulder. "Can I give Usha the flowers?"

"Yes, please do." Jess placed the bag over her shoulder and scooped up the bunch of flowers Helen had picked especially for their visit. She eased Aruishi onto the footpath and took a firm hold of her hand. Aruishi reached for the flowers with her other hand and held them out in front of her.

The door swung open, and Usha held out her arms. "Welcome," she said, smiling broadly.

Jess leaned in to Usha's hug.

Usha placed her hand on Aruishi's shoulder. "Who have we here? You must be Aruishi?"

"Yes, I am. I've met you before." Aruishi handed her the flowers. "These are for you. They're from Gran's garden, but we brought them."

"Silly me. Of course you've been here before." Usha took the bunch of red and yellow roses mixed with bright-orange tulips. She lifted them to her face, taking in a deep breath. "They smell wonderful, and they remind me of a sunset. Thank you, Aruishi, and Jess. Come, come." She ushered them through the door and inside the house. "I must put these in a vase straight away. Let's go to the kitchen," she said. "I thought you could both help me make puris this afternoon."

"Puris? What's that?" Aruishi tugged Usha's free hand.

Usha glanced over her shoulder at Jess. "Do you remember, Jess? How your mother and I taught you to make the deep-fried bread?"

"I do. How could I forget? After Mum died and you moved in to our house, Ben and I would help you cook." It was a bittersweet memory.

Aruishi knelt on a chair beside Usha at the kitchen table. "That's right, child. Press the dough a little with your hand. Then we can roll it flat," Usha said. She flattened the round ball with the palm of her hand, lay it on the board, and placed her hands over Aruishi's on the wooden rolling pin. "If we turn and roll, turn and roll, it will be a circle."

From her workstation at the other end of the table, Jess watched as Usha patiently gave directions to Aruishi—just as she had done when Jess was a child. Aruishi looked up wide-eyed as Usha added the last puri to the stack under a tea towel.

"That makes twenty." Aruishi held up both hands.

"That's ten," Jess said.

Aruishi opened and closed her hands and waved them in the air. "Twenty," she yelled. "What can I do next?"

Usha wiped her hands with a paper towel and placed them on her hips. "Next, my dear child, is that you can stay right here and watch while Jess finishes the potato bhaji and I fry the puri. Then we can eat."

"Puri and bhaji," Aruishi repeated five times, and rubbed her stomach.

"Shush, Aruishi." Jess cleared one end of the kitchen table, pulled out colouring pencils and a large notebook from the carry bag, and placed them on the table. "Do you want to draw for a while until we eat?"

"Can I draw Usha a picture of us on our bikes?"

"Oh, I'd like to see what your new bike looks like," Usha said.

"Okay." Aruishi opened the notebook and grabbed the box of pencils.

Usha stepped beside her. "That is a beautiful locket you are wearing, Aruishi."

"It has pictures in it." She held it out for Usha to take a closer look.

"I know this locket, although I haven't seen it for a long time. Would you mind if I held it for a moment?"

Usha clasped the jewellery in the palm of her hand and closed her eyes. "I was with your grandmother when she bought this in India." Her eyes fluttered open, and she turned to Jess. "She always wore it."

Aruishi put her hands on her hips and said with a huff, "I would wear it every day if I could, but my Mummy won't let me." She retrieved the locket from Usha's hand, patted it gently, and tucked it back into her T-shirt.

Jess smiled at Aruishi's confidence and her spirit. She had the ability to lighten the weight of their sadness.

"Jessica, you can move over here beside me so we can chat." Usha tapped the benchtop near the stove.

Jess began chopping the bunch of fresh coriander, as instructed by Usha. "This brings back many memories, Auntie."

Usha gently bumped Jess's hip. "Ah, for me too. And it's been a long time since you called me *Auntie*."

"I'm sorry, it just slipped out," Jess apologised. "I've always thought of you as my aunt."

"Your mother and I were as close as sisters. When you and Ben were children, you always called me that. I don't understand why people act as though it's a derogatory term. We were taught it was a term of respect. So, don't apologise. We are family, are we not?"

Jess smiled and looked across to where Aruishi knelt on the kitchen chair, focused intently on her drawing. "Yes, Usha. It is wonderful spending time with you again."

"And now you have Aruishi. You are good with her."

Jess laughed. "Although I've worked with children, on a personal level, I've had very little experience with them." She glanced again at her niece. "She can be very…mischievous," she whispered.

"Remember, she is only four. You'll have to learn along the way," Usha said. "Just like everyone else. There are lots of books on the subject—I, for one, wouldn't bother."

Jess turned sharply to Usha. "Oh, really?"

"The experts can put things on paper, but real life is very different. Children can be incredibly astute. Fun. Full of surprises. Exhausting." Usha tore a small piece of leftover dough and dropped it into the oil. "It's ready." She added a puri and pressed it down into the oil with a slotted spoon. "Most importantly, they need honesty and unconditional love. I can see how you are with the child. You are very fond of her, and she of you."

Jess hesitated, unsure of how much to reveal. "Aruishi means a great deal to me. She's given me hope. I feel a strong desire to be there for my niece." She stirred the potato mixture in the wok, put the spoon down, and turned to Usha. "I'd like to continue to be part of her life, but London is far away. She may forget me."

Usha lifted the golden puri onto a paper towel and dropped the next one into the bubbling oil.

"I'm sure she won't. Have you spoken to Lili of how you feel about Ru? She must know—otherwise she wouldn't trust you with her daughter for an entire day."

Jess shook her head and sighed. "That's true, but she is so sure of herself, an *earth mother* with a life plan for herself and her child. I don't know if she'll want me to continue to be part of their lives from afar. And I think she believes what they print in the gossip columns and imagines me living a fast-paced, shallow lifestyle."

"You mean none of it is true?" Usha shook her head from side to side with a slight roll of her eyes.

"My sponsors expect me to be seen in public. And I am often photographed with people of note," she said. "You know what I mean."

"Ooh la la." She raised her eyebrows. "Yes, you mean actresses, models, and such. The occasional royal? That can't be so bad."

Jess groaned. "The problem is the papers add their own spin. They infer that I'm a home breaker and just a party girl."

"No. Lili may have thought that before she got to know you. Not now. She comes across as perceptive. She will see the real you." Usha turned off the stove and covered the food with a tea towel.

"Maybe," Jess said. "I still don't know where I stand with Lili. Things have been better lately, but we didn't get off to a good start. I haven't lived in such close quarters with a woman since boarding school."

"Ah, and you want to make a good impression because of Aruishi. Yes?" She shot Jess a sideways glance.

Jess swallowed. "Yes. Yes, of course." Lili's proximity the other night during the massage had ignited churning butterflies in her stomach—just like before a big race. But she wasn't going to admit that to Usha. At the café in Portarlington, Lili had managed to get Jess to open up a little about her past. Trusting another person to that extent was rare for Jess.

"Time to eat," Usha said. "Let us check on Aruishi. She can help you set the table, and I will serve up the food."

Usha's puffed fried puri bread with potato bhaji surpassed even the best available at the Borough Market in Southwark.

Aruishi was adventurous with her food and tried everything. Usha sent her home with a Tupperware container filled with vegetable puffs and a jar of coconut-mint chutney for her mother. It was a day Jess would treasure.

That afternoon, when Lili entered the restaurant kitchen, Alex and Tim had already checked off and put away the deliveries, prepared the vegetable stock—that would later be strained to form the base of the chilled spring pea soup—and explored Ailie's garden for the day's fresh pickings. Tim was in the prep kitchen, assembling tonight's addition to the tasting menu: a ballotine of free-range duck filled with sourdough crumbs, caramelised orange, anchovy, and leeks. The boned, rolled, stuffed, and trussed duck would be roasted to perfection; the skin crispy just caramelised, the meat tender, still pink. It would be served simply, with golden pan juices and ginger-carrot puree, and garnished with a sprig of fresh thyme. That was the plan.

With their sleeves rolled up, Alex and Lili worked together at the marble-topped bench. The pale-gold dough had rested for thirty minutes, and Alex used a bench knife to divide it into four equal portions. Lili lightly floured the surface of the counter and kneaded the dough with her bare hands.

"This happened when? At half past midnight?" Alex put the knife down and stared at Lili, her hazel eyes wide. "You were in your pyjamas, and she massaged your back?"

Lili turned her head from Alex back to the dough. "Don't look at me like that. Jess was very professional the whole time."

"Ah-ha. Sure. She had those very professional strong hands and long fingers on your body." Alex snickered. "Was that before or after you demonstrated the pleasure of single malt whiskey?"

"Why was I stupid enough to tell you about it?" She picked up the wooden rolling pin and evened out the dough to less than the thickness of a credit card.

"You were flirting with her," Alex said, passing over the next piece of dough. "You're not going to deny that, are you?"

Lili grinned, kept her hips still, and moved her upper body from side to side. She winked at Alex and laughed out loud. "She fixed my back."

"She did more than fix your back, my friend," Alex said. "It's been a long time since you've laughed like *that*." Alex punched her lightly on the arm. "Oh my *God*, you like her."

Lili shrugged.

"Ah, I had my suspicions. I mean—you *like* her. You find her attractive. Desirable."

Lili put the rolling pin down. "Come on, Alex. Get the filling from the under-bench fridge before the dough becomes sticky, and the ravioli cutter while you're at it. And could you scatter a little more flour on the bench."

"Yes, Chef." Alex poked out her tongue.

"Of course I'm attracted to her. Jess is gorgeous." A puff of flour erupted in a cloud around the bench as Lili blew out a breath. "I'm only human."

"Okay, I got a bit carried away. Sorry about that," Alex said. "So, what are you going to do about it?" Alex placed a teaspoon of goat's cheese mixture on the thin dough sheets two centimetres apart and then brushed the dough around the filling with egg wash.

Lili placed a sheet of pasta on top and pressed down around the filling, making sure there were no air pockets. "What do you mean?"

"With your attraction to Jess? What do you want to do?" Alex prodded her shoulder with her finger and picked up the crimp pastry wheel to cut the ravioli. She transferred the plump squares onto trays lined with baking sheets and sprinkled them with semolina flour.

Lili washed her hands at the sink, dried them on a tea towel, and placed them on her hips. "You've seen the media reports about Jessica Harris. She has her choice and takes it—often. Beautiful actress on her arm one week. Spotted having an intimate dinner with some *hot* athlete another week. Or a model or a scientist or an heiress." Lili raised her hands in the air. "You get the picture?"

"You can't believe what you read in those English tabloids," Alex said. "Anyway, why not?" She grabbed the cling film from the drawer, covered the trays lightly, and placed them in the refrigerator. She popped her head up. "She's certainly caught Haley's attention."

Lili's hands fell down limp to her sides. "Do you think they've slept together?"

"Well it's possible. Haley talks about her every chance she gets. I heard Jess has agreed to take part in that fundraiser Simon and Haley are helping organise through CycleMania. It's to raise money for the young Drysdale girl, the one who was knocked off her bike on her way to school."

"Oh, right. What a horrible accident. I read about Usha Joshi's charity event in the *Surf Coast Times*. I didn't know Jess was taking part."

"Now she is. I think it's fantastic she's involving herself with the local community, don't you?" Alex paused. "I bet Haley's planning to make the most of Jess's time here in Australia," she said with a hint of amusement in her voice.

"What's that supposed to mean?" Lili asked abruptly.

"I'm just saying. Jess is single. She's young. She's sexy. Some people might want to make the most of that." She shrugged in an exaggerated fashion. "Anyway, you've probably got the advantage."

"What does *that* mean?" The conversation had moved beyond embarrassing to seriously annoying.

"Hey, I've seen Jess around you. I think she'd be willing if you were. It would be a great way to break the drought. Why not have a little fun?"

She looked askance at Alex. "Alex, you're talking garbage. It's not going to happen," she said gravely. "It *shouldn't* happen."

Alex slapped at her forehead with her hand as if having a sudden epiphany, sending flour dust all over her hair and face. She coughed. "Oh *fuck*. Jess is Aruishi's aunt, and she's not staying here. That would be awkward later, wouldn't it? Sorry, Lili. I wasn't thinking."

"Hey, are you two ready for a break?" Tim called from the prep kitchen. "I could use a cuppa tea."

"We'll be with you in five minutes, Tim." Lili answered. "Put the jug on."

"Righto. Consider it done."

Lili swept the floor while Alex cleaned the bench. Her friend had finally shut up about Jess, and Lili busied herself getting into the nooks and crannies while she calmed herself down.

Alex was right about one thing: Lili supposed she did suffer from relationship anxiety since Dani had left her pregnant and alone. Maybe a fling would help her self-esteem—especially if she remained in control and set the boundaries. She'd have to let it go when Jess inevitably left, but still, she could enjoy herself for a while.

Alex was right about a lot of things, actually. Jess was single, young, and beautiful. She played the field, and would soon be jetting back to London. Not to mention, lots of people besides Lili found her alarmingly sexy. She'd certainly managed to turn heads yesterday at the bakery, wearing her silky abstract-print jersey and suspender-bib shorts.

But when Jess had removed her racy-looking, wraparound, mirror-coated sunglasses, she'd looked directly at Lili, and her brown eyes twinkled in a way Lili had never seen them do before.

Could Lili risk a fling, then return to her routine like nothing had happened?

No way, not with Jess. The thing to do was to remain level-headed and consider the consequences. She had to protect her daughter. It would be heart-wrenching enough for Aruishi when Jess returned to London. They'd already formed a strong bond. If she got involved with Jess, had a fling, it wouldn't be possible to brush aside and forget. Jess would always be in their lives. Lili would also have to answer to her parents, if they found out.

She shoved the broom back into the utility cupboard and looked around for Alex. She must have left quietly, sensing Lili needed her space.

Did someone say they'd put the jug on? Lili hoped so. She longed for a cup of tea and a little something to eat. She had a hankering for vegemite on toast.

Chapter 16

"Mama, look. Here comes Auntie Jess…with Simon and Haley. Look!" Aruishi yelled as she stood on the fence rail, with Lili close behind, and pointed to the last three riders crossing the line. As event organisers, Haley and Simon would have held back to ensure all the riders reached the finish safely. Jess must have decided to ride along beside them, because there was no doubt in Lili's mind that Jess could have completed the ride in a fraction of the time. Jess had mentioned that her role at the event was to encourage and support the less-skilled riders in the group. This was not a race, but a sponsored charity ride to raise money for the Russo family. Every dollar raised would go to paying for the medical bills and ongoing care for Cara, their nine-year-old daughter who'd suffered a serious spinal cord injury after a hit-and-run outside her school gate.

Lili and Aruishi, with Helen, Scott, and Usha Joshi, stood together under a banner that sported a brilliant image of Cara Russo and her Jack Russell puppy, Romeo. Local businesses, restaurants, wineries, and individuals had sponsored two hundred riders to complete the thirty-five-kilometre circuit. The idea for the fundraiser had come from Usha, who was Cara's doctor, and she'd rallied the Emmetts to help organise the event. There was no loser today. In fact, in Lili's eyes, everyone was a winner.

"Wonderful." Usha turned to the others. "What an amazing crowd. We couldn't have hoped for a better turnout." She smiled and clapped her hands. Her Indian-styled tunic swung in sync with her arms, and her long plait of dark hair tossed itself from side to side. Usha was a small woman with a slight frame. Nevertheless, she had a confident, powerful presence.

Lili lifted Aruishi from the fence rail and hiked her onto her hip. "Usha, I'm so glad we could help today."

"Oh, Lili. I am very grateful to you and your parents for your donation of produce." Usha turned to Scott. "Thank you for helping us set up the trestles and marquee this morning."

"No problem. I was happy to be of use." Scott's face coloured. "I didn't do much. It was Lili that sweet-talked her suppliers into donating the fruit, juice, and bottles of spring water."

"Well, thank you again, Lili," she said.

"It looks like the Community Association volunteers have the food ready." Helen nodded towards the row of gas barbecues sizzling with a variety of meat and vegetarian options for the riders and their supporters. The red-and-white-chequered tables were lined with bowls, baskets, and platters of salads, fruit, cakes, breads, and drinks.

Aruishi wriggled in Lili's arms. "Can I go and find Jess now? She must be hungry."

"In a minute, sweetheart. Jess is busy."

Aruishi struggled harder to escape from Lili's grasp, and Scott reached out and lifted her from Lili's arms. "Here, let me take her," he said.

"Thanks, Dad."

Lili glanced around and spotted Jess amongst the other riders. She'd removed her helmet and hair tie and loosened her braid. Her hair spread in glossy waves over her shoulders and moved subtly in the breeze. It shone rich and dark against her skin. Lili stared as Jess accepted a towel from Haley, used it to wipe her face, and patted down her shoulders, arms, and neck. Jess beamed at Haley as she passed her a bottle—probably some type of electrolyte replenishment. She guzzled the entire bright-yellow drink and put her hand to her mouth as Haley snatched the end of her towel and dabbed at Jess's chin.

Jess seemed to be enjoying the attention. *Maybe they have slept together. In that case, I'm definitely out of the picture.* Damn, could Haley get any closer?

Scowling, Lili jumped when Usha pinched her lightly on the arm.

"I'm sorry to interrupt your thoughts, but I have another reason to be grateful to you," Usha said.

Lili looked down as Usha stroked her forearm as though to soothe the small pain she'd inflicted. "The suppliers were more than happy to donate to Cara and her family."

Usha shook her head. "And yes, for that I am very grateful." She turned her gaze towards Jess. "But I want to thank you for letting Jess stay in your home, and for making her welcome."

Lili watched Aruishi slide out of Scott's arms, and as Jess crouched to greet her, she threw her arms around Jess's neck and nearly toppled them both to the ground.

Haley quickly stepped out of the way. Aruishi had created a diversion. *That's my girl.* "As you can see, Ru is already very fond of Jess," Lili said.

"Yes. And Jess is very fond of her niece." Usha tilted her head to Lili. "And you?"

There was no misunderstanding Usha's meaning. Lili crossed her arms in front of her chest and met Usha's gaze. There was no judgement, only genuine concern in her serious, dark eyes. "Jess will return to London soon," Lili said resolutely.

"She would be much better staying here where she has family. That child has been on her own far too long. Now that I have reconnected with Jessica, I will be very sad to see her go." Usha gave a resigned sigh.

"Ru will also be very sad when she leaves." Lili stared at Usha. Had Jess ever thought about returning to live in Australia? "Do you think—"

An earnest-looking, large-framed man in a polo shirt approached Usha, waving a notebook in his hand. "Sorry, Doctor Joshi. Martin Dean, *Bellarine Times.* Are you free for our interview now?"

Usha winked at Lili and said, "We'll talk later." She gave a friendly smile to the reporter and followed him.

Lili stood rooted to the spot, still contemplating Usha's wish for Jess to stay. When her daughter's hand nestled into hers, she turned towards her and saw Aruishi's other hand firmly attached to Jess's palm. Her heart skipped a beat. *Let's face it. I'm going to miss this woman too.*

"Mummy, I'm hungry. Can I have a sausage now? In bread with sauce, please?"

"Yes. Let's go." Lili blinked away her frustration and strode towards the food tables with Aruishi and Jess in tow.

Haley and Simon walked towards them, with Helen not far behind.

"Are you heading for the barbecue, Aruishi? I'm starving." Haley looked directly at Jess. "Why don't we all head for the food? Are you coming, Simon?"

Simon shook his head. "I promised the Russos I'd take Jess over to meet Cara." He turned to Jess. "She's in the marquee with her family, and they're really looking forward to meeting you. Is it okay if we do that now?" He pulled down his aviator sunglasses.

"Let's not disappoint them, then." Jess flashed an apologetic smile at Haley. "Aruishi, would you like to come and meet a very special girl?" Jess smiled at her, then glanced across to Lili for approval.

Aruishi leaned back against Lili's side and squinted up at her. "Should I, Mama? What about my sausage?"

"You can. But do you want to meet Cara?"

Aruishi nodded solemnly. "I think so. You must save me a sausage."

"Okay, I will. Be a good girl and stay with Jess, please."

"I promise to keep a hold of her." Jess lifted their still-joined hands. "Helen, Lili, would you two like to come with us?

"We'll go to the food marquee and see if we can help while we wait for you," Lili said. "I'll meet you back at the picnic area when you finish, and we'll get that sausage for Ru."

"Okay, she's safe with me."

"I know." Lili blew a kiss to her daughter.

"Hey, I don't have to be anywhere. I'll come with you, Jess," Haley called out, and trotted off to catch up with them.

"I thought she was starrr...ving." Helen laughed and linked her arm through Lili's. "That girl is seriously crushing on our celebrity cyclist."

Lili didn't bother to hide her scowl. First Alex, now her own mother. Did everyone have to rub her nose in it?

"What?" Helen asked. "Haven't you noticed? Not that it matters. I don't think Jess minds. She's probably used to getting plenty of attention from pretty women."

"Yes, Mother. I'm sure she is." Lili kicked the ground with the toe of her boot and almost tripped. "Come on. Let's go."

Jess dropped a broken beach chair on the pile of rubbish just outside the door and mopped the sweat from her forehead with the back of her hand. It was sweltering in Ben's garage, even though both doors were propped wide open. Lili looked as hot and sweaty as Jess felt.

Lili's playful side had emerged over the last few days. When she smiled, her entire face lit up. It had been hard to ignore the provocative and sexy way Lili had demonstrated her enjoyment of a single malt whiskey. The husky, slightly throaty timbre of her voice had made Jess a little giddy.

More and more, Jess enjoyed the time they spent together. At the bakery in Portarlington, Jess had talked more about herself that afternoon than she had with anyone. That was down to Lili's impressive skill at drawing Jess out of her shell. How had she done that?

She had been so thankful when Lili offered to help sort through the mountain of surfboards, fishing equipment, kayaks, and other paraphernalia in Ben's garage. After an hour of work, they had made some decent headway.

Jess let out a stifled breath. She tugged at the neckline of her jersey, pulled it over her head, and tossed it on a nearby workbench. "It's a hothouse in here," she said, turning around to face Lili, who was staring straight at her. *God*, she must look a sweaty mess.

Lili looked away quickly, but not before Jess realised what she saw in her eyes was interest. Lili snatched a bottle of water from her tote bag and passed it to her. "Here, this may help."

"Perfect. Just what I need." Jess opened the lid, drank most of the contents, and poured the remaining water into her open palm and splashed it over her face, neck, and arms.

"Jeez…" Lili hissed, bending down to pick up one end of a kayak. "Can you give me a hand with this? When you're ready."

Jess grabbed her jersey and wiped the droplets of water that trickled down the front of her tank top. "Sure, just a minute." She pushed back the loose strands of wet hair that clung to her face and caught hold of the kayak. When she looked up at Lili, her face seemed flushed. Was it just the heat in the garage?

With Lili's recent injury, Jess didn't think she should lift anything heavy and risk inflaming her lower back. But Lili assured her she regularly lifted sacks of potatoes weighing twice as much as the Superlite eleven-kilogram kayak. It wasn't heavy as much as awkward, but together they moved it out to the strip of lawn in front of the garage, alongside a sleek single-person canoe.

"Ben loved riding this thing," Lili said. "Loved taking it out in the big surf. He was constantly hunting the perfect wave for aerial moves."

"I wish I'd seen him do that." Jess sighed. She stretched her arms above her head, enjoying the warm breeze on her exposed midriff. "I'd like to give it go, but I should try a surfboard first. Haley did offer to teach me, if I was interested."

"She did, did she?" Lili marched into the garage, returning with two fibreglass paddles that she tossed onto the grass.

"She did. She's full of energy, a lot of fun," Jess said. Haley was keen to give her surf lessons, and *definitely* something else. The more Jess thought about it, though, the more she realised she wasn't interested in *something else* with Haley.

Lili kicked one of the paddles, and it hit the canoe with a smack. "Yeah, she's a regular live wire."

Was it Jess's imagination, or was Lili annoyed with her? "We can finish sorting the garage some other time if your back is still giving you trouble?"

Lili shook her head. "I'm good. Whatever you did the other night worked. Thank you." Lili's gaze travelled the length of Jess's body, but when their gazes met, Lili's eyes darkened and she looked away.

There was no denying it: there was a mutual interest. "Maybe you could teach me to use the surf kayak?" Jess tried. "When you have time."

"Maybe." Lili turned and walked back towards the garage. "That is, if you stick around long enough."

What was going on? Lili had seemed to enjoy flirting with Jess the other night, and Jess didn't want to quell her growing attraction to Lili, the attraction responsible right now for the spike in energy and the pleasant fluttering in her stomach. There was no sign of Lili's lighter, flirty side, however; she was not smiling now.

Jess instead focused on the scenery. This really was a postcard-worthy stretch of coastline—uncrowded, with clean, pale-golden sandy beaches. She loved the sound of seagulls squawking and the crashing waves. Jess took a deep breath of the salt-laden air, closed her eyes, and soaked in the sunshine. Following Helen's advice, she'd slapped on sunscreen; nevertheless, her skin had turned a healthy gold under the Australian sun.

She rolled her neck and shoulders and shook herself out of whatever trance she'd fallen under. Was Lili's change of mood to do with Haley? Surely not. She appeared jealous, but why? Jess didn't focus on the things she couldn't have or get too attached to something transitory, no matter how attractive she might be. She'd thought Lili was the same.

Jess walked the short distance along the path and stepped out of the sunshine, into the garage. She blinked as her eyes adjusted to the dimly lit space. "Lili," she called out.

Before she knew what was happening, Jess was in contact with the steel of the garage wall. Lili clenched Jess's tank top with her fist and pressed their bodies together. When she let go, she took hold of Jess's face in her hands. Jess trembled as Lili gently brushed her thumb over her forehead and along the line of her eyebrows.

She gripped Lili's hips and drew her close. Lili's lips parted, and Jess was overcome by the intensity of her stare.

"Kiss me," Lili said.

Jess dipped her head and pressed her lips lightly to Lili's.

Lili's blue eyes stared intently, then closed. She kissed Jess—fiercely, impulsively, like she couldn't help herself.

Jess was lost in the silkiness, the generosity, and the sweetness of Lili's mouth. When her tongue swept across Jess's lower lip, she opened her mouth with a low moan, hungry for more of the delicious sensations Lili's kiss elicited. Time stopped, everything else stilled. For a moment, there was only Lili and Jess.

Light-headed and breathless, Jess broke their kiss to trace the shape of Lili's ear with her tongue. She ran her fingers along Lili's cheek, trailed them down the length of her neck, and rested her hand near Lili's heart. She could feel the rhythmic *thump, thump, thump* under her hand, and hear her rapid breath. Jess closed her eyes momentarily. She'd imagined kissing Lili, and it was so much more than she'd expected. But what had driven Lili's sudden change of mood?

Lili quivered. "Jess." She moaned, resting her head in the crook of Jess's neck. "What are you doing to me?"

She lifted Lili's chin, in need of the heat of their connection again. She wanted her. She slid her hands under the hem of Lili's shirt and caressed the curve of her breasts.

The colour drained from Lili's face, and she pressed her hand firmly into the middle of Jess's chest. "Sorry, I can't." She pushed her away and took a step back. "I can't do this with you. I know I started it, but…"

Jess slumped back against the wall. "But..."

"I am sorry." Lili shook her head. "I won't risk..." She raised her hands as if to physically push temptation away. "No, I can't. Not with you, Jess." She looked up with a sad smile, turned around, and rushed out of the garage.

At the sound of the Subaru wheels spinning on the gravel driveway, Jess slid to the floor and put her head between her knees. *Breathe in, breathe out, breathe in.* The magic of Lili's lips claiming hers and the thrum of warm energy generated by their brief encounter spiralled through her entire body. She pushed her head back and banged it against the wall four times.

The moment they'd kissed, her destiny changed—she felt it with her whole being. But what did it mean that Lili had kissed her and then bolted? It was usually Jess who left after the fun. Didn't get involved. Didn't leave herself open for hurt. But Lili had run, leaving Jess bewildered, fighting the urge to run after her.

Chapter 17

FOR WHAT SEEMED LIKE THE hundredth time today, Lili's thoughts drifted to Jess, and their encounter in Ben's garage. She'd acted rashly, without thinking about the consequences, which was completely out of character. To make things worse, she'd run off like a thief in a jewellery store.

The memory of Jess's lips and her lush, warm mouth sent shivers through her. Shaking her head, she leaned over the garden bed. If she didn't concentrate, she'd be harvesting the half-grown cauliflowers instead of protecting their developing buds.

But how did Jess feel? Had she given their kiss even a second thought? Lili doubted she was used to women grabbing her unexpectedly, but Jess must be used to women making advances. Should she have pounced on her like that without warning? Probably not.

On the plus side, however, she hadn't kissed anyone so intensely for a long time—if ever—and the thought of kissing those lips again, of feeling that heat once more, was consuming her.

"Pass me another, please." Helen waved an empty seedling tray in front of her. "I've prepared the ground."

At the sound of her mother's voice, Lili snapped back to the job at hand. "Okay, Mum." She reached into the tiered garden trolley and picked up a tray of heirloom tomato seedlings. They would produce yellow-and-ruby-streaked fruit—perfect for the savoury tomato sorbet she planned for the summer menu.

Lili sat back and surveyed her mother. Dressed in jeans and a striped shirt, Helen wore her sleeves rolled up to her elbows. A weathered straw hat sat perched on her head, shading her pale skin. Her blonde hair had darkened slightly over the last few years, but only a few strands of grey were visible.

"I remember learning this trick from you. I must have been about five." Lili spread green leaves over an eight-centimetre head of cauliflower before edging along on her knees to the next one.

"And I learned how to keep a cauli head white from my dear old mum."

"I grew up with my hands in the dirt." Lili wriggled her soil-covered gloves. "You and Grandma inspired my love of the earth, for growing and nurturing. Soon, I'll show Ru." For now, her four-year-old was content to dig with her pint-sized gardening tools, pick and eat fresh berries straight from the vine, and chase butterflies.

Lili had once aspired to be the chef at one of Sydney's top restaurants. Now, she couldn't imagine bringing up her daughter in a crowded city, away from Faodail Farm.

Helen peered at Lili from under her wide-brimmed hat. "You know, don't you, that Jess's generosity has made things a lot easier for you?"

She swallowed down the lump in her throat and kept her eyes low. "Mum," she began, but words failed her. Silence was the only way to contain her guilt.

"I know Jess won't talk about it," Helen said. "She considers the whole matter done and dusted." She removed her gloves and squeezed Lili's forearm. "But as a family we have to acknowledge her magnanimity."

Lili extracted her water bottle from the trolley, removed the lid, and took a grateful swallow. Her mother had opened the door for her to explain why she found it difficult to accept that Jess had simply removed the debt.

"Having the loan completely wiped totally stunned me. She tried to explain, but I still don't fully understand why she did it. She doesn't owe us anything."

"No, she doesn't. It was for Aruishi's sake. You can tell from her patience and the warmth in her eyes how fond she is of her niece."

"The trouble is I'll be forever in her debt," Lili said with an exasperated sigh. "It would have taken years to pay her back, but it would have been the right thing to do."

Helen put her arm around Lili's shoulder. "It's really been taken out of your hands, darling. Is it that Jess seemed oblivious to the enormity of her gift—is that what you find so hard to accept?"

"You and Dad have been through tough times, especially when the large milk processor tried to force you to scale up. You found a way to become independent and stayed afloat. I can too. You raised me to be self-sufficient."

"Yes, and we are proud of what you've already achieved. Ailie is a thriving business." She hugged her close. "But don't let pride get in your way. Gratitude is just as important."

"I am really grateful, but it's hard to let go of old habits."

"Sometimes, we must accept things happen for a reason and just be thankful." Helen gave her a gentle shove. "You have a few things to think about."

Lili did have a lot of things to think about. Due to her lack of self-control, she'd been an idiot, pounced on Jess, kissed her—then run off like an adolescent. And she'd left Jess on her own to sort out the garage. Of course, her mother didn't need to know any of this. "I do."

"I'd better get a move on. I want to finish planting the seedlings before I pick up the little person from kindergarten," Helen said. "That will give you time to pull up some beetroot and sow the mustard greens."

"You're the best, Mum. I'll string new trellis lines for the peas; they've taken off with last week's rain. The green pea shot starters are getting positive feedback from our guests."

"There's nothing quite like the taste of fresh peas, straight from the vine," Helen said. "You'll have a busy afternoon, then."

The busier the better. Less time for thoughts of Jess. "We've already got a lot done, thanks to your help." Lili stacked the empty seedling trays and wiped her damp forehead with her shirt sleeve. "Phew, it's hot. After I finish off here, I'll tackle the mountain of paperwork on my desk." She lifted her peaked hat and ruffled her hair. "I have that information session with our apprentices at the college tonight. Is Ru's sleepover still okay?"

"Oh yes. We've got a plan," Helen replied. "She's requested bolognaise and zoodles for dinner. Then we have a date with Dory."

"Again?" Lili laughed. "Are you sure?"

"We'll be fine. Ru will be asleep within half an hour of the film starting."

Lili pulled off her gloves, brushed the crisp green leaves with her fingertips, and let her hands sift through the rich, dark soil around the beetroot bulb. She lifted it out of the ground and inhaled the woodsy, almost sweet, damp bouquet. She relished earthy flavours. Today, earthly delights, powerful and seductive, were intrinsically linked to Jessica Harris. The hollow at the base of her neck, where Lili's lips had lingered and she'd breathed in vanilla and orange blossom. She leaned back, closed her eyes, and lifted her face to the sun. Distraction was proving futile.

It was fortuitous that Jess was accompanying Usha on a two-night trip to Wylie, the country town in Western Victoria where she was born. Lili didn't want to face her right now. It was her fault that she couldn't hold back and had thrown herself at Jess, creating an awkward, embarrassing situation.

Jess was irresistible and challenging. Lili's gut instinct told her trying to suppress her attraction would be like drizzling a croquembouche with caramel on a humid day and crossing your fingers it would hold together. *Impossible.* When Jess left, life would have to return to normal. Forbidden fruit was always the sweetest, but once tasted, almost impossible to forget.

Sheltered under the sprawling branches of a giant fig tree, Jess sat on an old wooden bench close to the headstone marking her mother's grave. She'd not been there since the funeral, when they'd lowered her mother's casket into the ground. She recalled Usha's wiry arm around her shoulder. Ben had sobbed, but that day she couldn't cry. Tears rolled down her cheeks now, and she wiped them away with her sleeve. "Aruishi has your eyes, Mum," Jess said. "When Ben died, I felt so alone. Now, I have a niece. I gave her a bicycle. You should see her take off down the farm road." Jess laughed. "She's feisty and playful and so naughty; she reminds me of Ben in that way. She's beautiful and stubborn like her mother."

What would *her* mother think of Lili? She sighed. "I like being around them both, Mum. Lili is kind-hearted and generous. I enjoy her company very much."

Jess stood up and walked to the grave. "My body is healing, and I'm getting stronger every day. I feel good about being back in Australia, and I'm sorry it took me so long to get here." She bent forward, rearranged the small posy of roses displayed in a pottery jar, and pressed two fingers to her lips before placing them over her mother's name etched into the stone. "I'm going to pick up Usha at the hospital; she's the guest speaker at the reunion lunch. You know she hates to be kept waiting."

On her way to the car, Jess looked over her shoulder. Fine rays of sunlight dappled the neat rows of headstones, casting a warm glow over her mother's final resting place. "I miss you, Mum."

Next month would mark the nineteenth anniversary of her death, and waiting for Usha outside the Wylie Hospital made it seem like yesterday.

Usha climbed into the Jeep and fastened her seatbelt. "Thank you for collecting me, Jess. It was nice to see so many of my old friends again," she said. "Some of the guests knew your mother, and you may have met them when you were a child."

"I'm surprised there are still people in Wylie who remember Mum," she said, turning the Jeep left into the town's main street.

"We were a close-knit community, and Doctor Aruishi was well-respected and loved. You must remember Marion Neville. She was here when we first arrived in Wylie, and became our chief nurse and a close friend. She only just retired after thirty-two years of service."

Her mother and Usha had signed a five-year contract to work here in exchange for residency in Australia. Unmarried, with no family to support, they'd accepted the relatively poor pay conditions offered in a country practice.

"I do remember Nurse Neville," Jess said. "Everyone at Wylie Primary was petrified of Mad...Marion."

Usha chuckled. "Her bark was always worse than her bite. Did you children really call her that?"

"Yes. We were subjected to vision, hearing, and scoliosis screening and head lice checks on a regular basis. And Marion's tetanus jabs were the worst." Jess shuddered. "Thank goodness it was only Prep that received the full *undress* examination."

"She helped improve the health of our community. We had three doctors in the town. Even though most of the patients were nonsurgical or postsurgical, the doctors and RN's were responsible for everything. Marion was a town asset, and we relied on her to get a lot done."

"I understand." Jess smiled. "She was still scary to a child."

"You were always sensitive," Usha said. She rested her head back and sighed. "I should have come with you to the cemetery, Jess. Were you okay going alone?

"Yes. Someone's left roses near the headstone."

"Your mother loved roses." Usha sighed, again. "The Women's Historical Association look after the cemetery grounds even though it's been closed for years."

"They do a good job, then. Everything looks neat and well cared for."

"Did it help visiting your mother's grave?"

"It did. I found it comforting. It was a reconnection to Mum, and my childhood," she said. "Will you tell me what led up to Mum and Dad's divorce? I was too young to understand. I can hardly remember him then."

"Oh, child. Because of his commitments to his sport, he wasn't around much. I don't remember him being in Wylie for more than a few months here and there. Back and forward overseas." Usha tapped her hand on the dashboard. "Whenever he returned home, it was honeymoon time all over again. She was over the moon when she fell pregnant with Ben and they married, even though she knew your father would never be a stay-at-home dad."

"If he was away so much, why did they have me?"

"They loved each other, Jess," she said in a serious tone. "Your father returned from a successful Olympic Games. Two medals. He made a lot of promises to Aruishi about settling down. I tried to warn her, but what could I do when she was so in love?" She patted Jess's knee. "Your mother really wanted another child, and she was blessed with you, nine months later."

"Obviously he couldn't keep his promise."

"It was something your mother hoped." She shook her head. "He based himself in Wylie for nearly a year after your birth—only riding in Australian events. But he got restless and tried to convince Aruishi to give up her work and travel with him."

"Why didn't she?"

"She wouldn't do that with two small children. I think, also, by then his lack of commitment to the relationship and his family couldn't be ignored. Benjamin Harris could not be happy in one place," Usha said. "Your mother wanted to provide a stable home for you and Ben."

"Mum…did that." Jess stared straight ahead at the road.

"Yes. Her children were always her first priority. Work was important, but you and Ben were her world."

"Unfortunately, she didn't talk much about Dad, at least nothing personal."

"She didn't want to burden you with her troubles," Usha said. "The divorce was inevitable."

"After that, you were always there. Mum wouldn't have coped without your help."

They continued travelling towards their motel in silence until Usha said with a weary smile, "I don't know about you, but I could use an afternoon nap. I always feel like this when I have days off. Once I stop, I'm tired." She patted her stomach. "Mind you, eating a roast and all the trimmings in the middle of an unusually warm day doesn't help."

"I had forgotten how hot it can get here, even in spring." Jess parked the Jeep in the motel carpark. "I thought I'd do a few laps at the swimming pool, if there is still one in town. I need a workout."

"Good idea. The shire pool closed years ago, but there is a swim recreation centre near the botanical gardens," Usha said. "I'd join you, but I'd sink to the bottom like a stone after the lunch I've eaten." She laughed heartily.

Jess knew Usha and her mother had never learned to swim. "I'd be there to rescue you," she said.

"I'll stick to my nap, thank you. I'm tuckered out after standing up and talking in front of all those people. If you don't mind, I'll just nibble on the snacks I brought and have an early night."

"That's fine with me, Usha. That way you'll be well rested and we can head back early. I promised to look after Ru tomorrow night. Lili is working, and Helen and Scott want to go to the cinema." Jess jumped out of the driver's seat and ran around to the passenger side to help Usha, who accepted Jess's arm as she stepped onto the pavement.

Usha gave her hip a light squeeze with her hand, then looked up sharply at Jess. "Old age, Jess," she chuckled. "Not only have you grown into a beautiful woman, your manners are impeccable. You were an attentive companion last night at the town gala and turned many heads. I think a few of the women there would've liked to get to know you better."

Jess was sure she now wore a shocked expression. She looked away. Did Usha know she was a lesbian?

Usha squeezed Jess's arm. "I've kept track of your career and your London life, as you know. There are stories in the tabloids, my dear."

"Don't believe everything you read." Wasn't that what she'd said to Lili?

"I never read anything bad. Just stories of an athlete who's achieved a great deal," Usha said. "I guess it's open slather with your personal life. You are young, successful, and attractive. And you attract a lot of attention."

"You know that I'm…" Jess hesitated; she just couldn't say the word.

"Gay? Of course. Your mum and I talked about it when you were ten years old."

"But even I didn't know then." Jess couldn't believe she was having this conversation in a motel carpark.

"Your mother did." They'd reached Usha's room, and she put the key into the lock and opened her door. "Don't be surprised. We watched you win a handful of track and field medals at the school sports, and she commented that when you were old enough to have a boyfriend, it would be a girl."

Jess leaned against the doorjamb and rubbed her temples. She could only stare at Usha incredulously.

"Your mother was an astute woman." She ushered Jess into the room and wrapped her arms around her. "She loved you unconditionally."

"Thank you. I can't explain how much that means." She'd never doubted her mother's love, but learning she would have accepted her sexuality was immensely comforting.

Usha let go of Jess and yawned. "Your mum picked up on a lot of things. Anyway, I'll let you get to the pool." Usha covered her mouth with her hand as she yawned again, loudly.

"Have a restful evening, Usha. Call me on my mobile if you need anything." She turned, walked towards the door, and opened it.

"Jess," Usha called.

She turned back to face her.

"Your mother would have been so proud of you." Usha blew her a kiss. "Enjoy your swim."

Jess hummed all the way to her motel room, but when she reached the door, her eyes welled up. It made all the difference that her mother knew she was gay. At the cemetery, Jess would have told her about Lili's kiss and that she'd run off.

Why had Lili run off? Jess wasn't that bad a kisser. Maybe she was scared. That was understandable. Why would she get involved with Jess? She was Ben's sister. She was Aruishi's aunt, *and* she was in Australia fleetingly. Wasn't she?

Jess rested her forehead on the motel room door. Her head felt too small to contain all the conflicting thoughts and emotions spinning around inside.

She pushed the key into the lock. Had she really thought she was all cried out? Good thing Wylie still had a swimming pool. No one would notice her tears in the water; red eyes could always be explained by an over-chlorinated public pool.

Chapter 18

Lili wiped her hands on the towel that draped over her shoulder and moved to stand beside her apprentice at the plating station. "Keep the broth at eighty-eight degrees Celsius, ready for pouring," she said. "Fill the jug three-quarters full when the server is ready to collect."

"Yes, Lili." Sky took the food thermometer from her jacket pocket and wiped it on a cloth before inserting it into the bain-marie filled with tomato-and-mussel broth.

"It's sitting just above eighty-eight. I'll maintain the temperature until we serve."

The door swung open. Owen whooshed into the kitchen and approached the service bench. "Table twelve, diner four has requested to see you, Lili."

She tilted her head and frowned. "Oh? That's the table that arrived late. Is there a problem?"

"I hope not. It's those urban creatives from the big smoke. The woman's a looker and an affable guest, if anything. Maybe she wants you to share a recipe." Owen grinned.

"It's not the same woman who forgot to tell us she's lactose intolerant, is it?" Lili asked. "Can it wait until after we serve the snapper?"

"No, not her. This guest did say no rush."

"Okay, thanks, Owen. I'll take care of it."

"No problem." He turned and headed back to the dining room.

Urban creatives? Did that make them a table of *yuccies*? She shrugged. The children of yuppies? Whatever. Lili didn't know what category she'd fit into, if any.

Using an oven glove, Lili grabbed five shallow bowls from the under-bench plate warmer and lined them up in a neat row along the plating counter. The ceramic bowls had to be piping hot, as they would cool when carried out into the dining room. She swiftly spooned three poached mussels into each bowl before placing the julienne of gingered pear and purple onion alongside the plump, orange shellfish. Lili carefully sat a portion of golden, lightly salted snapper fillet onto the julienne and garnished the fish with crispy snap-fried rocket leaves. She wiped the edges of the bowls and placed them under the heat lamps. "Sky, fill the jugs now." Lili hit the service bell, and the apprentice poured the broth, releasing a light tang of lemon myrtle. Lili removed the order receipt and spiked it on the cheque spindle. "Four pork, and this table's done," she said, massaging the aching muscles in her lower back with both hands. It had been a long night, but so far, everything had run smoothly.

Sky had followed her instructions to perfection. "Good job," Lili said.

The apprentice looked up quickly, her face flushed crimson. "Thanks, Chef."

"I mean it. You've done well tonight."

"Shall I ask Alex if she needs help with the dessert and petit fours?"

"Good idea. I'm going to clean up before I see what our guest at table twelve has to say." Lili wiped her forehead with a towel from the laundry trolley and turned back to Sky. "I spoke to Alex, and she's rostered you to work desserts and pastry next week as you requested."

"Thanks so much." Sky's shy smile reappeared, and her dark eyes lit with excitement.

"You're welcome." Lili headed towards the change rooms. In some ways, her second-year apprentice reminded Lili of herself—passionate and driven. Earlier in the year, she'd won a silver medal for her Almond Praline Gateau in the Culinary Federation National Apprentice Competition. However, unlike seventeen-year-old Sky, Lili had never been timid. They'd have to work on building her self-confidence and encouraging her creativity.

Lili stared at the mirror and rubbed her eyes. She couldn't believe she was two weeks shy of turning thirty-seven. Nothing significant, just another birthday.

She was healthy and strong, with a beautiful child who filled her days with love. She had family, good friends, and a business that was rewarding— she truly enjoyed what she did. But she'd spent a long time last night lying in bed and staring into the darkness, finally reaching the conclusion that she wanted what Alex and Tash shared—a loving relationship. Spending time with them reminded her of what she was missing. She took a deep breath and then another before jiggling her shoulders and standing up straight. Just because one relationship had failed didn't mean she didn't want another.

When Aruishi had been a newborn, Lili was fully occupied—caught up in the wonders of motherhood, too exhausted and too busy for a relationship. What was her excuse now? The truth was that she did have time to date. How often had Alex and Tash tried to set her up? At least a dozen. How often had she accepted their offers? Twice, if that. Alex was spot on: she was scared.

Right now, there was an alluring woman sharing her house. A woman whose presence threatened her self-control, her equilibrium. Being around Jess made Lili wish for more than just friendly company, more than just a kiss. It was a damn shame that Jess would soon return to England; there was just no future for them.

She turned off the tap, dried her face, and glanced down at her jacket. It had remained surprisingly clean under the full-length apron. She quickly applied a touch of clear lip gloss, ran her fingers through her hair, and replaced the black skullcap on her head. "Here I go."

Lili walked through the swing doors and stood beside Owen at the bar. With the dessert plates cleared, the petits fours were about to be served with coffee and sweet wine. Mei entered from the kitchen, skilfully carrying three ceramic plates on one arm, with the fourth plate in her hand. She stopped briefly in front of Lili for her appraisal.

"Dark chocolate wattleseed brownie and lavender-honey macaron. Good to go," Lili said.

Mei headed for table three and placed the final offering in front of the diner. His eyes widened, and he smiled appreciatively. Without hesitation, he lifted the fudgy chocolate chunk to his mouth. Paired with the delicate lilac macaron, the bittersweet treat was created to make an enticing finale. By the look on his face, it worked. Lili couldn't suppress her grin. *I got it right.*

Owen subtly nodded in the direction of table twelve. "That's her with her back to us. The one in the sleeveless black dress," he said to Lili. The woman at seat four was talking to a bearded hipster in a navy-blue suit. Mr Hip looked up as Lili approached, a smile across his handsome face.

The woman straightened her tanned shoulders, and she reached up to tuck a curl of auburn hair behind her ear.

Lili smiled, as the other guests at the table looked up.

Mr Hip cleared his throat. "Your chef is here, Danielle."

Danielle turned around in her chair to face Lili. She smirked, pushed her chair back, stood up, and moved towards Lili in a sweeping movement. Her dress shimmered and clung to every curve of her body. Lili fought the urge to run and clenched her fists to her sides. Their gazes met, and as Dani took another step forward, Lili instinctively stepped back.

"Lili. *Gosh*, it's good to see you," she gushed.

Lili tried to speak, but nothing came out. She snapped her mouth closed—suddenly reduced to a speechless robot.

"You are as impressive as ever." Dani's wide grin showed off that tiny little gap in her two sparkly-white front teeth.

"Dani. What are you doing here?" Lili asked finally in a casual voice belying her anger and disbelief that her ex-girlfriend would turn up unannounced.

Dani gestured to her companions, who had resumed their conversations. "I'm here with friends. We're in Queenscliff for Jackson and Avril's wedding." She motioned to the couple wound in an affectionate embrace.

"No, I didn't mean that. What are *you* doing here? I thought you were still in London."

"I've been back for six months." Dani rubbed the palm of her hand down the side of her dress and caressed the silky fabric with her fingers. "I'm living in St Kilda, actually. The law firm is strengthening its Melbourne offices, and I have a better chance of making partner here." Dani leaned towards Lili and held out her hand as though she was about to touch her. Lili recoiled and stepped back again.

"Lili, could I please have a word?" Owen whispered in her ear. She'd been so preoccupied, she hadn't noticed him approach.

"Please, excuse me for a minute," she said to Dani before following Owen back behind the bar.

"Is everything okay?" he asked.

She tugged her ear and sighed heavily. "It will be."

"I'm so sorry. I honestly didn't think she was going to complain about anything. Their plates were clean, they were complimentary to the servers. I should have handled it, myself."

Lili placed her hand on Owen's forearm. "It's okay, there's no problem." Well, not in the way he thought. "I know her."

"My apologies." He looked sheepish. "I didn't realise she was a friend." He looked over Lili's shoulder in Dani's direction.

"She isn't," Lili said. "I haven't seen Danielle Taylor for four years."

Owen raised a questioning eyebrow.

"I'd better go back and find out what she wants. I'd like to get home as soon as possible. Jess is childminding."

"Understood," he said. "She must enjoy it."

Lili frowned.

"Jess. I mean Jess must enjoy looking after Ru. I saw them riding around in circles when I came past your parents' house this afternoon. Ru looks like she's mastered her new bicycle," he said. "Ahem, anyway, I'd better leave you to it."

"Thanks."

At table twelve, Mr Hip held the chocolate brownie to Dani's lips. Lili cringed as Dani giggled and nibbled it from his fingers.

Owen's interruption had given her a moment to calm down. She strode over to the table.

Dani looked up. "Wow, this is to die for—death by chocolate." She removed a crumb from her chin and put it in her mouth. "Would you like to meet up for a coffee on Sunday? I'll be around. We can talk about old times."

Lili stared at her. No. She shook her head. "I can't. I'm busy."

Dani narrowed her eyes and turned to her companion. "Have you got a pen and paper, sweetheart?"

Sweetheart?

"I'll find one," he said.

"I have an apartment in St Kilda near the beach, off Acland Street. It needs redecorating, but I have a great decorator. He's a treasure."

Was Dani always so superficial? Lili folded her arms and rocked back on her heels.

"Anyway, here's my number." Dani scribbled on a piece of paper. "Ring me when you have time. I'm sure this place keeps you busy. Loved the soufflé, by the way. You always did have a light touch."

The brazen look Dani gave her made Lili want to tear the piece of paper into confetti and throw it at her presumptuous face.

"Thank you," she said slowly and politely. "I'd better get back." She looked up to find Dani's friends focused on their exchange. "Congratulations to the happy couple, and enjoy the celebrations tomorrow."

"Thanks, I'm sure we will." Before Lili had a chance to retreat, Dani leaned forward and kissed first her left, then her right cheek. "Au revoir."

"Good night." Fuming, Lili turned on her heel and marched towards the sanctuary of her kitchen. "Bon débarras," she muttered through clenched teeth. *Good riddance.*

At the top of the stairs, Lili looked up at the dark, ominous sky and filled her lungs with crisp air. She exhaled slowly. The familiarity of her home surroundings had a calming effect, and the warm glow of the entry light was a welcome sight. She suddenly realised that Dani hadn't asked about Aruishi. Not at all. She hadn't bothered to ask about the child that could have been *theirs.*

On the landing, Lili removed her shoes and quietly unlocked the front door. She tiptoed straight to Aruishi's bedroom, unzipped her chef's jacket, placed it with her satchel on the floor, and entered the room. Soft rays of light fell across the bed from the giraffe lamp. Aruishi was on her side, fast asleep, with one arm flung above her head. Her breathing was deep and regular. A shuffling, whispering sigh came from the other side of the bed near the wall. Lili stooped down to peer under the bed, and there was Jess curled up on the carpet with Aruishi's Princess Teddy tucked under her head. Lili smiled. Jess had somehow managed to squeeze her tall frame between the bed and the wall, although it didn't look comfortable.

Aruishi sighed loudly and turned over onto her back. Jess reached up and patted the quilt. "I'm here, baby. Go back to sleep," she murmured, withdrew her arm, and wrapped it around the teddy bear.

Lili stood up and edged around the foot of the bed to kneel in front of Jess. She looked peaceful, without a trace of tension. Lili brushed a strand of silky hair from Jess's cheek and her fingers tingled as she caressed velvet skin.

Jess stirred and opened one eye. She squinted and opened both eyes. "Lili," she said drowsily.

"Shh…" Lili put her finger to her lips, then rested her hand gently on Jess's shoulder. "I'm sorry to wake you, but I can't leave you on the floor all night."

Jess eased herself into a sitting position, shuffled around to face Lili and touched her arm. "How is Aruishi?" she whispered.

"Sound asleep." Lili stood, offered her hand, and helped Jess to her feet. She squeezed Jess's fingers, reluctant to let go. Jess stretched and twisted her waist from side to side.

"It was the only way I could get her to sleep," Jess whispered. "She wouldn't settle, and insisted there were scuffling noises outside the window. She didn't want to be alone."

Lili stifled a giggle. "Cows, sheep, horses, rabbits, echidnas—we *are* in the country. She's having you on, Jess," she said. "It's one of her little tricks."

"Oh. I didn't mind. But I'll remember that, for next time."

They both hushed and glanced at Aruishi as she coughed and slid onto her side.

Lili placed her index finger over her lips again and motioned to the door. She leaned across Aruishi's bed, kissed her on her forehead, and turned off the lamp. The nightlight on the wall automatically lit. Lili yawned and followed Jess out into the hallway.

Jess was propped against the wall. She wore crumpled lightweight sleep pants and a crewneck T-shirt that barely reached her waist. Effortlessly seductive.

It had been a long night. The frustration from her encounter with Dani lifted and dissipated into the air, and all Lili could see was Jess. Tousled hair and dreamy eyes like a midnight sky—so imperfectly perfect.

Lili couldn't resist. She walked towards Jess and leaned in until their foreheads touched.

Jess's warm breath tickled her face, and her hands lowered along the curve of Lili's waist, down to her hips. When Jess tugged her closer, heat radiated from her body. Need coursed through Lili, tangled with her desire, as Jess stroked the base of her spine with her fingers in a slow, tantalising motion.

Lili lifted her head, and Jess's eyes fluttered half-closed, her dark lashes brushing her cheeks. She moved one hand to the base of Lili's neck and slowly pushed her fingers through her hair.

Lili leaned forward and parted her lips.

Jess took a step back and lowered her gaze to the floor. "Please, Lili. Don't run. Not this time."

"I can't, even though my head tells me I should." Lili swallowed.

Jess looked up to capture Lili's lips in an intensely demanding kiss. Waves of pleasure coursed through her as the caress of Jess's tongue became soft, slow, and teasing.

She wound her arm around Jess's neck and pulled her closer. She pressed into Jess's body—so lean and taut, so silky and soft. The worries of the day evaporated like ice on hot cement. Instinct took over. She deepened their kiss, matching Jess's hunger.

Jess's scent was sweet like honey, rich and heady as vanilla, warm and spicy like cinnamon. Lili nibbled gently on the corner of Jess's mouth and swiped her tongue along Jess's lower lip.

Jess moaned and slipped her hands from under the hem of Lili's singlet, but Lili grabbed the front of Jess's shirt to pull her back.

"Is that your phone buzzing?" Jess pointed to Lili's satchel.

"Oh. No one rings me this late."

"Someone does," Jess said. "They're persistent. It's been humming for a while." She tugged at Lili's singlet. "Don't answer it."

"Sorry, I'd better check." Lili retrieved the phone from her bag and looked at the screen. "It's Alex. It must be important." She reached out and took Jess's hand. What bad timing.

"Okay, then." Jess squeezed her hand briefly and let go. "Goodnight, Lili," she said.

"Don't go. Give me a minute?"

"It's okay. Answer your phone." Jess turned away and walked quietly down the hallway.

It was hard to ignore the disappointment in Jess's eyes. She'd asked Lili not to run, and yet here she was, not exactly running, but messing up again. She moved away from Aruishi's half-open door and put the phone to her ear.

"Hi, Alex, what's up?"

Chapter 19

A WARM NORTHERLY BREEZE MOVED through the tall, grassy meadow, with its scattering of daises and clumps of lavender. Jess dismounted her bicycle and wheeled it through the crop of apple trees dotted with pink-and-white blossoms. From the path along the water's edge, views across Port Phillip Bay and the hills rising above the flat Werribee Plains were framed by a clear blue sky and azure ocean with a hazy silhouette of Melbourne's skyscrapers just visible to the right. The McAllister farm, in this beautiful corner of the Peninsula, had provided a welcome shelter for Jess.

She'd miss all this when she returned to London, where she'd be walking back to…what, exactly? A lonely flat and the future of her pro career up in the air. Even if Jess regained full fitness, it seemed like a sensible progression to scale back the strict schedules, regimented diet, and constant travel, and start figuring out her future. She could do that here in Australia if she wanted. Moving from one continent to another may not be a bad idea.

A magpie lark swooped dangerously close to Jess's head. She ducked and waved an arm. "Oh no you don't. I've got your number." The black-and-white bird perched on a wooden fence rail, singing loudly—almost tauntingly—with its beak aloft and feathers bristled.

She didn't want to risk losing Scott and Helen's respect, or the close bond she'd developed with Aruishi, but Jess wished Lili had knocked on her door last night. She had gone to her room and debated about leaving the door slightly ajar as an open invitation. Remembering Lili's words, she'd opted to close it, giving her the choice to follow her *head*.

If they'd slept together, they'd be in a right pickle later if things didn't work out. The first kiss in Ben's garage could be attributed to wild impulse or a whim, but surely last night Lili had known what she was doing. It was getting harder for Jess to quash her attraction, and Lili's push-pull, pull-push behaviour was wreaking havoc with her sexual appetite.

In a difficult road race, having the advantage of preparedness, sharp focus, and well-rehearsed tactics was paramount. Jess probably conducted her dating life similarly to her cycling manoeuvres. Avoid sharp corners. Know your competition. Wait for the right time to make a move and get out in front. It was different this time; Lili was making the moves.

If Jess were in London, she'd have had a session with Doctor Waters today. Somehow, she'd managed with minimum damage to overcome a lot of obstacles without her psychologist's calm approach and guidance. She'd have to utilise the coping strategies she'd learned from her to negotiate this entanglement with Lili.

The opening fifteen minutes of a race were always fast and furious, but you had to use self-control, and not get excited too early. You had to have patience. But Jess also knew that to win the race, you must risk losing it.

Jess hesitated at the courtyard entrance before she unlatched the wrought iron gate, wheeled the bicycle near the staff entrance door, and propped it up against the wall. She knocked on the door and strode into the kitchen.

Alex stuck her head out from the cold-room. "Jess, come on in."

"Thanks, Alex," she said, then inhaled deeply. "Something smells really good in here."

"That would be me." Alex turned one corner of her lips up in what could only be called a smirk.

Jess leaned her elbows on the counter, rested her chin in her hands, and met Alex's gaze. "Hmm. In that case, you smell deliciously of rich, warm chocolate." Jess winked.

"Actually, it's the batch of brownies I just pulled from the oven," Alex said. "Are you here to grace us with your piano playing again?"

"If it won't disturb you?"

"No, it's great to hear someone play as well as you do."

"Thank you."

"By the way, how is Lili this morning?"

Jess tilted her head to one side. "I've been out riding; I haven't seen her. Is something the matter?"

"Just checking, after I spoke to her last night."

"Oh? How did she seem?" Jess frowned. Had Lili told Alex about what happened between them?

"Dani and her friends from Melbourne were at the restaurant last night and they—"

"Dani? As in Lili's partner, Danielle?" Jess took a step towards Alex.

"Ex-partner, yes. Dani had the cheek to summon Lili to the table. No one had a clue she was in the restaurant." Alex shook her head as though in disbelief.

"Okay," Jess said, lowering her voice. "Well, that explains…things."

"What things?" Alex touched Jess's forearm. "Look, I shouldn't have said anything. I thought she must have told you what happened. She didn't?"

Jess blinked. "No, she didn't." Long after she'd crawled into bed, she'd stayed awake, hoping for that knock on her door. Jess shrugged and turned quickly towards the piano. "I hope you like Wagner."

There was something comforting about arriving at Ailie. The bright, open kitchen that she and Ben had created was her second home. Every inch of space had its purpose. It worked well, whether she was alone throwing together an idea or, on a busy night, when the place was fully staffed and buzzing with action.

The warm, enveloping aroma of molten dark chocolate combined with coffee-like toasted wattleseed drifted through as Lili entered the kitchen. She sighed blissfully.

To a chef, a good olfactory sense was imperative in order to be able to combine aromas and flavours appealingly. She'd developed 'a good nose' and continually worked to refine her skills identifying foods and assessing their condition. Lili paused and closed her eyes.

"Hi, Lili." A voice called out from behind the mixing machine.

"Oh, hi there, Tim." She looked up sharply. "Where is Alex?" Piano music drifted faintly from the dining room. "I haven't heard this song before. Is she messing with my playlist again?"

"I think she's out the front."

Lili turned her head. "That's not her playing. As far as I know, she doesn't have a musical bone in her body."

"Hardly." Tim laughed. "It's your houseguest. The lovely Jessica."

"Oh. Are you sure?"

"Yep, it's her," Tim said, filling a piping bag with vanilla buttercream from the mixing bowl.

"Okay. I'll let you get back to what you're doing." She started towards her office but found herself detouring to the dining room, drawn to the soulful melody like a magnet. She stopped just inside the doorway. Alex leaned against the bar counter, half-hidden in the shadows.

Lili glided in beside her. "Hi," she whispered.

Without turning, Alex said, "She's been in to tinkle the keys a few times, but I've not heard her like this before. She was playing some really heavy stuff earlier, but I like this soulful stuff better. She's good."

"Yes, she's good." Lili sighed. Her mother had mentioned Jess played, but not that she was this talented. Here she was, in Ailie's tiny piano alcove, head held high, shoulders straight, and strong hands passing gracefully over the keys, like she was lost in another place and time.

Lili placed a hand over her heart as it started to race. She imagined those hands on her skin. Slow and skilled. Was there nothing the woman couldn't do?

A loud crash from the kitchen broke the magical spell. Jess turned around, clearly startled by the noise. Her gaze met Lili's briefly before she turned back to the piano.

"I'm sorry, but I may have put my foot in it earlier," Alex whispered to Lili.

Lili frowned. "What do you mean?"

"I asked Jess how you were after last night."

"Oh? What else did you say?"

"I mentioned about Dani being here. I don't know why, but she seemed agitated." Alex stared at Lili. "Anyway, what's going on between you two?"

"Nothing."

"Lili, this is me. If it's not about Jess, what is it about? You said last night on the phone you were okay after your encounter with Dani. But now you're acting funny. What is it?"

"I am okay. Believe me, it's not about Dani."

"So then it's about Jess."

"Let's leave it for now, please. I need to talk to Jess about Ru's new bike. I think it needs adjusting or something." Lili glanced down at her watch. "I'll be back here in half an hour."

"Okay, sure. But I have seen the way you two look at each other." Alex shrugged. "You are acting weird, and so is she. Don't think I haven't noticed." She turned and walked back into the kitchen.

Lili wanted to tell Alex she was wrong, but what was the point of denying it? She did have to talk to Jess, now. "This music is a bit pensive," she said, placing her hand on Jess's shoulder.

Jess's muscles tensed under Lili's fingertips. She closed the lid of the piano. "What? Don't you like Leonard Cohen?" She glanced over her shoulder to look at Lili, and her brow furrowed. "Did you kiss me last night because of what happened with Dani?" Jess asked in a low-pitched growl.

"No. I didn't." Lili folded her arms. Jess's obvious distress caused a heaviness in her chest. Is that what she thought? That Lili had kissed her because she was angry at Dani? She groaned inwardly. Time for damage control. "I was furious that Dani showed up unannounced after four years' absence and expected me to welcome her with open arms." Lili brushed Jess's arm gently with her fingers. "But that is not why I kissed you."

Jess tilted her head, and her expressive eyes filled with emotion. "Then why did you kiss me? Again?"

Lili focused on the fullness of Jess's mouth and let out a low whistle. "I couldn't help myself. I just couldn't help myself," she repeated.

The door flew open, and Josh barrelled in. "Hey, Lili," he said, and nodded in Jess's direction before disappearing into the kitchen.

"Hi, Josh. Don't run," Lili called out, watching the doors continue to swing backward and forward, forward and back. She turned to Jess. "Come outside and talk to me."

Jess's dark eyes were wary. "Okay."

Lili exhaled and realised she'd been holding her breath. "Let's find a spot in the garden where we won't be disturbed."

With Jess close behind, she led the way into a sheltered corner at the back of the courtyard. It was a peaceful nook filled with plants she'd struck from her grandmother's rose garden. Lili sat in one of a pair of old wooden chairs. She motioned for Jess to take the other.

She wasn't sure how to begin. Her feisty grandmother, if she were still around, would have advised Lili to trust her instincts. She picked at a loose thread at the end of her sleeve.

"I feel the same. I couldn't help but kiss you back," Jess said.

"You couldn't?" Lili looked up.

"I'm finding it increasingly difficult to be around you," she said, placing her hands under her thighs, as though to keep them steady. "I know there are a lot of reasons it's a bad idea for us. But I like you, Lili." Jess moved to the edge of the chair and took her hand. "What if? I've been asking myself, *what if?*" She caressed Lili's clenched fist with her thumb until Lili relaxed and allowed Jess to thread her fingers with hers. "Why didn't you come to my room last night?"

Lili's gaze scanned upwards and settled on Jess's face. "It was late." She reached forward and gently tugged Jess's braid, then traced a finger down the straight line of her nose, across her cheek, along the defined curve of her jaw, to the corner of her mouth. "Your door was closed. I was a coward. You have me so distracted... You have the most beautiful lips. I like you too."

Jess's mouth curved into a slight smile, and her warm breath tickled Lili's hand. Her eyes reflected Lili's desire, with a hint of shyness and an inkling of playfulness.

"I'm almost scared to touch you," Lili said.

"Shush," Jess murmured. "I'm not, and I want your touch." She leaned closer and lightly pressed her lips to Lili's, then pulled away. Her eyes twinkled with amusement. "See? Nothing bad happened." She held Lili's face in her hands. "In fact, I'm going to kiss your beautiful mouth again."

Lili tilted her head to meet Jess's lips, and the soft, sensual kiss awakened tenderness and longing. She closed her eyes and exhaled slowly.

"Where do we go from here?" Jess whispered.

Opening her eyes, Lili said, "You're doing it again."

"Doing what?"

"Putting my thoughts into words." Lili shifted back in her chair and motioned with her hand for Jess to do the same. "A little physical distance is good. We need some separation to talk."

"But..." Jess protested with a slight pout.

Lili held out her hand. "No. You stay right there. I can't think straight if you're close."

"Okay, but I don't see any advantage in thinking straight at all." Jess raised her entire body out of her chair, using her hands, and eased herself back down to sit ramrod-straight.

"Yeah, well." Lili laughed at the confidence Jess conveyed.

Jess leaned back and crossed her legs. "Okay, I'm ready to talk."

"At least we've agreed on one important fact." Lili glanced up as a noisy flock of cockatoos flew by.

"Yes." Jess grinned and stared directly at her. "You like me, and I like you."

"We need some rules."

"Yes, *Chef*."

Lili raised her eyebrows. "Seriously, Jess. We do need to agree on a few things."

Holding up both hands in a classic gesture of compliance, Jess said, "I'm sorry, Lili. Please, go ahead."

Lili rotated her shoulders. "You are really good with Ru."

"Aruishi is totally adorable, the little minx." Jess chuckled.

"Yes, and sensitive and intuitive. I'd rather she didn't know. She's fixated on you already. If she thought there was something going on with us"—Lili gestured between them—"she'd get her hopes up." She wouldn't want Jess to leave. "We need to keep things platonic in front of her."

"Platonic? Oh, you mean just friendly." Jess nodded. "I don't want to hurt Aruishi. I'll be careful."

It was a relief that Jess seemed to agree that Aruishi's sense of security was paramount. "We'll both be careful. I'd rather Mum and Dad didn't know either."

"Okay." Jess drummed her fingers on the armrest of her chair.

"Just okay?" Lili asked. "It is different for us, because it's not like we just met. You're already part of our lives. I am being overly cautious. And if I were you, I'd put us in the 'too hard' basket."

"It won't be a problem." Jess reached for Lili's hand. "You're protecting your family. I can understand that."

Lili relaxed her shoulders. She needed to lighten up a little and not scare Jess away. "Thank you," she said.

Jess kissed Lili's hand, carefully placed it back onto Lili's thigh, and patted it lightly with her fingers. "We can take it slow… There's a lot I'd like to learn about you."

Lili looked around. "I am kind of an open book, don't you think?" The movement of Jess's hand on Lili's thigh increased. She grabbed it and held it tightly. "Whereas I know very little about *your* life." She cleared her throat. "You were vague when I asked if anyone was waiting for you at home."

"No one waiting." Jess shook her head.

"Seriously, it's hard to believe you're not with anyone."

"Why?" she asked defensively. "If you read the British tabloids and believe what they say—just like dear old dad—I play the field and I've never been serious about *anyone*."

"Jess, I'm sorry. I didn't mean to—"

"They are partially correct," Jess interjected. "When I was first on the circuit, it was easy to fall into the casual hook-up culture, but I soon got tired of it. I do date, but there is nobody of consequence." She flashed Lili a challenging look. "How about you? Do you date much?"

Lili shifted uncomfortably in her seat. "Err…I've been busy with Ru and the restaurant."

"When was the last time you went out with someone?"

She narrowed her eyes. "Ten months. With one of Tash's friends."

Jess stared at her in amazement. "Ten months? That's a long time."

"Don't look at me like that. I told you, I've been busy." Lili shrugged. "Anyway, it was a disaster, so I wasn't in any hurry to try again."

This time Jess laughed, a soft throaty laugh, and her whole face lit up. "What was wrong with her? I mean you're so…" Jess raised her chin.

"Boring and tied down with responsibilities," Lili said.

"I wasn't going to say that."

Lili shook her head. "No. That's what the date thought."

"Well then, good riddance to her." Jess grinned, and Lili couldn't help but join her.

Jess waved her hand erratically as a bee zipped around her face and circled her head. She leapt to her feet, and jumped up and down, but the bee wouldn't budge. "Damn it, I'm allergic to bee stings."

Lili leaped up, took Jess's hands and held them to her sides. "Trust me," she said. "If you swat at a bee, they're honour-bound to sting. Hold still."

The little creature landed on the cap sleeve of Jess's T-shirt. "Now what?"

"Hold still," Lili repeated. She leaned in close and blew hard at the bee. It fell onto the ground, and then flew off into the rose garden. Lili brushed Jess's shoulders. "See? No damage."

"Only to my self-image," Jess said. She glanced around and inched closer to Lili.

Lili tapped her lightly on the nose, slipped her hands around Jess's waist, and pulled her into her arms. She rested her head upon Jess's shoulder. "I have to get back to work now." She sighed. "Otherwise someone will come looking for me."

"Can I kiss you first?" Jess asked, her voice low and playful against Lili's ear.

"Please."

This time, their kiss spoke of promise and left Lili's heart hammering in her chest. She watched Jess wind her way through the rose bushes with a spring in her step. At the courtyard gate, she turned to Lili and blew her a kiss.

Chapter 20

Usha dished another spoon of curry onto Jess's plate. "Eat up. Think how much you will miss my cooking when you return." She winked at Jess. "I know, I know. London is full of good Indian restaurants. Those British-Indian chefs think they can reproduce the best quality and authentic spiciness, but nothing beats home cooking."

Jess nodded and scooped up palak paneer with a piece of freshly made roti and popped it in her mouth. She took a sip of water to wash down the spicy spinach and cheese "It's hot. Definitely better than anything I've eaten in London."

"You flatter me, Jess." Usha's grin widened. "I'm glad you like it."

"I only speak the truth."

"You are also very sweet." Usha helped herself to a piece of roti and offered more to Jess.

"Enough, please. I've eaten much more than usual." Jess shook her head and pushed her empty plate away.

"Good. I am happy." Usha sipped her chardonnay. "Thank you for bringing this very palatable wine."

"It was Lili's recommendation."

"Ah, the lovely Lili. You can tell her I enjoyed it."

"I will," Jess said. "She hoped it would go with whatever you were cooking."

"Very nicely. I am a creature of habit and still prepare the dishes I enjoyed in my childhood. The clinic is busy, so unfortunately it is not often I make a proper meal for myself." Usha shrugged. "Now, tell me, how is it with Lili?"

Jess nearly choked on her wine and dabbed a napkin to her mouth.

Usha looked alarmed. "Are you okay, Jess?"

She coughed. "Yes, I am. The wine went down the wrong way. Things are very satisfactory. I have a spacious comfortable room, a beautiful bathroom with a huge bath, and panoramic views of the farm and ocean. I couldn't ask for more."

"That's good. What about Ben's friend, who is renting the beach house? If you decide to stay on for longer, can you move into the house?" Her forehead creased. "I imagine you cannot remain indefinitely at Lili's home."

"Nathan has a month before he and his girlfriend travel to South America. I don't want to upset their plans. I won't make any decision about the house until they leave."

"That seems fair. Is Lili comfortable with your living arrangements?" Usha eyed Jess with an inscrutable expression. "Two beautiful, single women under one roof. That must be difficult for you both?"

Jess rubbed at her forehead. "I enjoy Lili's company," she said. "And, of course, Aruishi. And Scott and Helen. They have all been very good to me."

"That is not what I meant, Jessica." Usha smiled and turned towards the window. "The weather here is getting warmer. Late spring, early summer is the best time on the Peninsula. But you must be missing the cold in England. I only spent two weeks at a conference in Oxford, but it was enough. Don't get me wrong: I loved being at the university, but it was dark *so* early, and grey every day. The wind ruined three umbrellas while I was there—turned them inside out."

Jess laughed, relieved Usha had veered away from the subject of Lili. "I love spring and summer in England. The parks and bike trails near my flat are lovely in the warmer seasons. Everything is so green and fresh. But I don't miss the English winters. My cycling team travels to milder climates in the cooler months to train, in the south of France, Spain, or Italy."

"You are lucky. I too have been fortunate to travel in southern Europe on more than one occasion. I can imagine you cycling past those castles and along those windy roads like in the Tour de France. How wonderful," Usha said. "It hasn't been very long since the crash. How is your recovery and rehabilitation progressing?"

Jess automatically pressed between her sternum and clavicle. "Good." She straightened in her chair. "The last set of tests showed no long-term effects from the concussion. I had a clean nondisplaced fracture of the clavicle. They don't usually operate, but without surgery, I would have been in a sling and immobilised for six weeks until it had healed."

"So you had surgery?"

Jess nodded. "My surgeon used titanium nails to put the clavicle together. Surgery was considered an aggressive choice, but it meant I could start rehabilitation on a stationary bicycle two weeks after my knee surgery."

"They really got you back on the bike quickly. You've made a remarkable recovery. In some areas, sports medicine has pushed general medicine to consider the way we treat musculoskeletal injury and pain management. Your physiotherapy degree must be an advantage in your own rehabilitation."

"Knowing the process was helpful, but I had to put my trust in others. The team's practitioners supervised an intense programme, and I'm now cycling more than three hundred kilometres a week".

"Oh my *gosh*. I don't know how you do it." Usha stacked the empty dishes into a neat pile. "But, it is in your blood." She stood and Jess helped her carry the dishes and leftovers into the compact kitchen. "Go and sit down and relax. I will clean up and join you."

"I'd like to help; after all, you did the cooking," Jess said, placing the dishes on the benchtop.

"I don't need help. I have a dishwasher. It will only take me five minutes to put away the food and stack the dishes in the machine." She gently pushed Jess out of the kitchen towards the living room.

Usha's house was cosy and modestly sized, with a postage-stamp garden, but inside, it was spacious and filled with light. An earthy hint of sandalwood and patchouli, mixed with the lingering zest of spices, tickled Jess's nose. She wandered around the living room that was decorated with richly dyed textiles and furniture. Brass floor lamps, a boldly coloured rug, patterned throws, and embroidered mirror cushions that reflected Usha's heritage blended surprisingly well in the Edwardian-era timber cottage.

The overflowing bookcase was dotted with framed photographs. Jess picked up a wooden surround holding the same picture of Usha and her mother in front of a huge ocean liner that she'd found at Ben's shack. She ran her finger over a photograph of herself, standing between her mother and Ben, taken at a Wylie Primary sports day. Jess held a gold ribbon and grinned like a Cheshire cat. Even at ten, she was already the same height as her mother. Ben, with his dark fringe across one eye, towered over them both.

Just as she replaced the frame onto the bookcase, her phone buzzed with an incoming text. She dashed across the room and plucked it out of her messenger bag.

Chopin by Candlelight, Melbourne Arts Centre. Sunday evening.
Early dinner? A glass of sparkling?

With a huge grin, Jess typed her reply, her fingers flying over the screen.

Yes, to all the above. Yes. x

She stared at the screen before tucking the phone back into her bag and taking a seat on the red sofa. Usha entered the room, balancing a tray of sliced fruit, a bowl of pale-orange cubes, a teapot, and two tea glasses.

"Help yourself to some mango and watermelon. And try this pumpkin and semolina halwa." Usha picked up a piece and popped it into her mouth. She poured the tea. "Cardamom. Very good for digestion."

"Thank you. I don't think I could eat another thing. But I will take some tea," Jess said, accepting the glass.

Usha settled into her armchair. "The halwa is made by one of my patients, Mrs Trivedi. Bless her." Usha pushed the plate along the wooden inlaid table towards her. "Go on, just one piece. At least we have a good Indian supermarket in Geelong now. We can get everything we need to make such delicacies without taking a trip to Melbourne."

Jess helped herself to the smallest piece and took a tentative bite. "Hmm...I do like the texture and the coconut."

"It's very tempting. Keep it away from me." Usha chuckled. "I am glad to see a smile on your face. I was worried all the talk about the accident would be distressing. You must miss everything, everybody?"

Jess finished chewing the halwa and sipped her hot tea. "No, I'm fine, Usha. I've had to accept that I won't be able to race for some time, but meanwhile I am enjoying cycling to build strength without the pressure of competition or the press." She gave Usha a warm smile. "Coming back here, has allowed me to reconnect with you. And I've made new friends."

"Ah...yes. This is good. Lili and her sweet daughter bring a smile to your face." Usha cleared her throat. "Call me a meddling aunt, but I saw the way Lili kept her eyes on you at the fundraiser."

"Lili is a very good-natured human being. Generous and kind." Jess looked down at her lap. "She's—"

"Yes, I know. Generous and kind," Usha repeated.

At the faintly teasing tone in her voice, Jess looked up quickly to see Usha grin mischievously.

"There are many reasons for you to stay on here, Jess," Usha said.

"I never intended to be here this long. Anyway, I have to get back now that Ben's estate is nearly settled." But even as the words left her mouth, Jess knew she didn't sound convincing.

Usha brought her hands to her face. "I'm so sorry. Here I am thinking of myself. I didn't even ask if you have anyone special at home. Is there someone you are wanting to get back to?"

"No. No one special." Jess smiled sadly. "But I do have friends in London, a flat and a car, my team and my manager, and my therapist." Jess stared at the ceiling. It was so easy to forget her responsibilities back home, especially when *home* had started to feel like somewhere completely different.

"Yes, I understand." Usha pointed to Jess's bag beside the sofa. "Your phone is making a noise. Maybe you should check it."

"I'm sure it can wait." Jess looked down at her bag. "Actually, if you don't mind, I will take a quick look." Jess retrieved her phone and stared at the screen. She turned slightly away from Usha's scrutiny, knowing she probably wore a silly grin again.

> *At farmers' market with Mum and Ru in the morning and must check in with the electrician at Ailie before we leave. We could head out around 3.*

"It's Lili," Jess murmured, looking up to see Usha's reaction.

"Ah, yes. Generous and kind." Usha watched her with smug delight.

Chapter 21

PUSHED ALONG BY THE SWARM of fellow concertgoers, Jess and Lili exited the Arts Centre in St Kilda Road. Their bodies jostled together every time an eager patron tried to squeeze ahead. Waiting for the lights to change at a pedestrian crossing, Jess pressed her lips to Lili's cheek. "Thank you," she said.

"You're welcome, but I should be thanking you. I probably wouldn't have gone to the concert without you, and I learned a lot about Chopin."

"How so?"

"I expected a full orchestra, but you explained that Chopin preferred playing to smaller groups in salons rather than concert halls. That's why tonight there was only a cellist, a violinist, and an..."

"Oboist," Jess said.

"Yes, oboist. Just the three instruments accompanying the pianist brought out something special. It was intimate. And the cellist was formidable in her black tux." Lili's eyes twinkled with obvious excitement in the glow from the street lamps and the spectacular palette of colours from the setting sun that bounced all around them.

"Kiss me," Jess whispered.

"Right here? With all these people watching, on one of the busiest streets in Melbourne?" Lili's tone was teasing, and she leaned in and pressed their lips together.

Jess gasped in surprise, then parted her lips to return the kiss.

After a few delicious seconds, Lili ended the kiss, smiled coyly as she grabbed Jess's hand and interlocked their fingers, giving her a gentle tug. "The lights have changed." She looked from left to right, then led Jess across the street and onto the riverside pavement. "Come on, we can walk along the Yarra River. But not for long. All that romantic music and candlelight made me ravenous. I'm taking you to one of my favourite inner-city haunts."

Jess stole a glance sideways and caught Lili's tantalising grin. "It was mouth-watering music."

"Exactly." Lili let go of Jess's hand, and they strolled side by side along the riverside park terraces until they reached Federation Square, where the crowd grew dense. She edged close to Jess. "This way."

Occasionally, she trailed her arm over Jess's shoulder as she guided her through the crowd. The casual intimacy, and hint of more, made Jess's body spark with energy. At the visitors' centre, Jess pulled her to a stop.

"Can we look at the map? I'd like to set my bearings. I'm usually the one leading the way, you know." She glanced at the list of restaurants, galleries, and theatres. "The Australian Centre for the Moving Image. That could be worth a look."

"You'll have to come back another day and explore," Lili said, so close that her breath tickled Jess's ear.

"I will, definitely." Jess laughed out loud, for no apparent reason. Lili's playfulness and her physical closeness made her light-headed, in the best possible way. She soaked up the atmosphere: the ultra-modern architecture, balanced with solid stone and metal; people chatting on their phones; shoppers weighed down by parcels; the laughter and clinking of glasses from clientele spilling out of wine bars.

Melbourne wasn't London, but it was an exciting and culturally diverse city. If Jess returned to Victoria, Melbourne would provide the big-city vibe when she needed it.

A siren blared in the distance, and Jess suddenly realised Lili was tugging at her arm.

"Move along, slow coach," Lili said, dragging her along fifty metres or so until they stood beneath a chaotically structured glass-and-steel atrium at the centre of Federation Square. They both looked up, and Jess snapped her head this way and that as crazy distorted patterns reflected in the mirror surfaces.

Lili was off again, and Jess jogged to keep up with her. Once again, Lili took her hand, and they zigzagged through stationary traffic and over the tram lines to the other side of Flinders Street. They entered a shadowy cobbled laneway.

The bluestone lane was set between a towering Gothic cathedral and a modern office building diagonally across from Flinders Street Station. Jess stared wide-eyed at the laneway's graffiti-covered walls before Lili gently ushered her through a doorway.

"I'll tell them we're here." Lili crossed to the other side of the restaurant in a few steps and tapped a robust bearded man on the shoulder. He turned and greeted her with a toothy grin and a one-armed squeeze before pulling out a notepad and pencil.

The red-bricked, dimly lit restaurant bar reminded Jess of the many tapas eateries she'd frequented during the cycling team's visits to Spain.

Lili wound her way back around the wooden tables. "Come on, you." She flashed her a relaxed smile. "I booked ahead, and Sam saved us a nice *quiet* table furthest from the bar. Follow me."

She gestured for Jess to be seated, peeled off her emerald military-styled jacket, and hung it on the back of her chair. "I hope you don't mind, since we had champagne with our Chopin, I took the liberty and ordered us a glass of Rioja—my current favourite juicy Spanish red. They have a particularly nice one to complement the tapas."

"Thank you. They seem to know you here."

"I guess. I have been coming to this bar for years. It's lively and friendly, whether you are alone or with a group." Lili edged her chair closer to Jess. "I love the bodega style. When I eat out, I usually, but not always, opt for simple and fresh, adventurous and flavoursome. This place ticks all the boxes."

The waiter delivered their wine, and Lili lifted her glass by the stem, swirled it in slow motion, held it to Jess, and waited for her to do the same. "Cheers," she said.

Jess lightly touched her glass to Lili's, took a cautious sip, and met Lili's gaze. She took a larger mouthful and let it swirl around before swallowing. "I approve. Can I leave the food selection to you too?"

"Do you trust me?"

Jess raised an eyebrow. She wasn't overly trusting with food—or leaving what she ate in someone's else's hands—but Lili made eating a fun adventure.

"No comeback? That's good, because I've already ordered," Lili said. "I have my favourites, but I've included something from the specials board."

"Thank you. I do trust you. And I'm trusting you to get me home as well." Jess took a sip and then another, and before she realised it, she'd drained the glass. "I'm feeling totally relaxed and prepared to put myself entirely in your hands." She lounged back in her seat with her hands interlocked behind her head.

Lili licked her lips. "I will get you home safely, I promise. It's just water for me from now on, but seeing how much you like the wine, I'll order you another." She nudged Jess's shoulder.

Jess enjoyed a pleasant buzz from the wine and the half bottle of Veuve Clicquot they'd shared at the concert. Surprisingly, she had an appetite. So far, the date with Lili was more than fun, but nervous energy simmered in the pit of her stomach. They'd be returning to an empty house; Aruishi was spending the night with Helen and Scott. She glanced up to see Lili regarding her curiously. "I am hungry," Jess said. Was Lili also imagining what might happen when they returned home?

They'd consumed three colourful savoury dishes when the waiter served up a wooden board with two golden balls wrapped in a white rubbery substance and dotted with something black. Jess stared at it. "Umm…what is this?"

Lili picked up one in her fingers and broke it in two. She dipped half into a glossy yellow sauce and leaned across the table. "Take a bite and tell me what you think."

Her eyes sparkled, and Jess couldn't resist the morsel held to her lips. Why not? She liked how in Lili's company, she was tempted to try new things. She bit through the crisp exterior, and as she reached the soft, gooey centre, a burst of flavour hit her palate.

As soon as she was able to speak, Jess said, "I don't know what this is, but it's yummy."

"*Croquetas de Choco en su Tinta.*" Lili winked.

Jess winked right back at her. "Your pronunciation is impeccable, but I haven't a clue what you just said."

Lili replied, "Squid ink croquette wrapped in a slice of cuttlefish."

"Cuttlefish?" Jess gulped. "Okay."

At around ten p.m., they left the tapas bar to head back to the car. "Let's hop on a tram," Lili suggested. "We'll get there faster."

She reached for Lili's hand. "I'm enjoying this, being with you. Let's walk."

It took some time before they reached the underground carpark, climbed into the Subaru, and headed for home. Jess shifted in the passenger seat so she had a better view of Lili. With her head against the headrest and the seat slightly tilted back, Lili's hands were placed solidly on the steering wheel at nine and three o'clock.

"What are you looking at?" Lili asked, her eyes still on the road.

"I'm glad you're driving. I'll probably doze off." She patted her stomach and sighed contentedly. "It was delicious, but I ate too much."

"It was a light selection. You didn't eat that much."

"Oh, I did. What was that crispy, smoky, salty thing? The one you insisted I try, and fed to me?"

"Ahh, you mean the thin toast with anchovy and smoked-tomato sorbet?"

"It sounds convoluted, but I did enjoy it," Jess said. "And believe me, I'm not one to be enthusiastic about food."

"No? Then who was that stranger at our table who licked the last sliver of crème caramel flan off the plate?"

Jess lightly pinched Lili on the leg and left her hand resting on her thigh. "I did no such thing, although it did cross my mind."

Lili changed into the left lane and steered the Subaru towards Geelong. She put her hand over Jess's. "We'll be home in about forty minutes. Are you really tired?"

"Not really." Jess's hand trembled, and she removed it from Lili's grasp, hoping she hadn't noticed. "You're the one who was up early. Do you ever get to sleep in?"

"I'm sure with the right incentive I would." She gave Jess a sidelong grin.

Jess laughed, then swallowed. They were getting closer to home, and she was edgy with anticipation. Escaping early the next morning was usually her main objective after a date. Not tonight. If she and Lili spent the night together, there'd be none of that.

Since their conversation a few days earlier, Jess had stuck to Lili's rules. Lili hadn't. When they'd met in the hallway, both ready for their trip to Melbourne, Lili had looked her up and down and stepped into her space.

She'd placed her hands upon Jess's shoulders, moved them down her arms, and then, with excruciating slowness, slid them beneath the silk-textured fabric of her pullover and curled her fingers just under her bare rib cage. Lili's steady gaze had held her captive.

"I was up early this morning to meet the electrician at Ailie, but he cancelled at the last moment."

"Is there a problem?"

"The lighting in the detached store out the back has been flickering since we had the temperature control system serviced. I need to have it checked."

"Sounds like a good idea."

Lili tapped her index finger on the steering wheel. "I can't remember the last time I lazed about in bed. Once I'm awake, my brain starts ticking, and I have to get going."

Jess smiled. She could take that as a dare. "Thank you for today. Everything was perfect—the concert, the food, the company." She angled the air vent to direct cool air to her flushed face. "Dining out with a chef was something new for me. I can't remember everything I ate, but I enjoyed your choices."

"Salty pork with brittle crackling, scallop ceviche, eggplant fritters, and the squid ink croquette." Lili flashed her a cheeky grin. "You nearly took my finger off coming back for a second bite."

Jess coughed. "There would be no advantage to that. Absolutely none."

"I'm glad you had a good time. I did too." Stopped at a red light on the outskirts of Geelong, Lili turned to Jess. She wrapped the palm of her hand around Jess's neck and leaned in for a brief kiss before returning her hand to the wheel and her eyes to the road. "You haven't let me cook for you yet."

Distracted by Lili's sensuous lips and yearning for more, Jess said, "Hmm. Yes, you did. A salad...from the garden."

"You haven't dined at my restaurant." Her voice held a challenge.

Jess cleared her throat, shaking off the mental images that played in her mind. "I'm ready and more than willing."

"So am I," Lili whispered. She pressed a button on the steering wheel, and Martha Wainwright's unequivocally gravelly voice filled the car.

"This makes a change from Chopin."

"I like to mix it up. Country, jazz, R&B, classical, and rap. No metal, though," Lili said. "I can't have you falling asleep." She drummed on the steering wheel, and just as the last raspy sounds echoed through, it automatically switched to the ringtone of an incoming call.

"It's Mum. I'll have to answer. It's on speaker."

Jess nodded. "Okay."

"Hi, Mum. How is everything?"

"Hi, Lili. Have you and Jess had a nice evening?"

Lili glanced over at Jess and smiled. "Yes, we have. Everything's been fantastic. We're about fifteen away. I think Jess would agree, we're tired and ready for bed."

Jess put her hand over her mouth to stifle the giggles that threatened to erupt.

"I'll bet you are. You sound happy. Anyway, I'm ringing because I had to bring Ru back to her own bed. She wouldn't settle, and her temperature is slightly raised," Helen said.

A flash of worry darkened her face. "We'll be home soon. What do you think it is? Is her breathing okay?"

"She is asleep now and breathing normally. You'll be able to check for yourself when you get home."

"We shouldn't be long. I'm sorry your night's been disrupted."

"Don't be silly. Drive safely, see you soon."

"Bye, Mum."

Jess knew Lili would be worried about Aruishi, considering her previous health scare and hospital admission. Jess too was concerned and glad they were nearly home. "Are you okay?"

Lili breathed out heavily. "I'm sorry. The evening hasn't turned out the way I'd planned." She brought the car to a slow stop outside the Faodail Farm gate.

"I'll get the gate. Please, don't apologise. I understand." She leaned back against the headrest and stared at Lili before opening the car door.

"Jess, wait." Lili reached for her, letting out an exasperated-sounding breath. "I want this." She kissed a path across Jess's cheekbones, over her eyelids, and down to her neck. A slow burn of want filled Jess before Lili's mouth covered hers. Silky, hot, and full of unspoken promises.

They ended the kiss and pressed their foreheads together. Jess looked down to where Lili's hand rested on her thigh. Her heart thumped in her chest. The passenger door was half-open, which was good, because she needed air. "I'll get the gate," Jess repeated, slipping out of the car.

Twenty minutes later, Lili saw her mother out of the house and secured the front door. Jess followed her down the darkened hallway to Aruishi's room but stayed just outside. Lili's socked feet barely made a sound as she tiptoed across the floorboards. She bent over Aruishi's bed, laid her hand on her daughter's forehead, and brushed back her curls. Turning to Jess, she nodded and smiled. The tension from earlier was gone. Her eyes shone with relief.

Lili carefully sat down on the bed and positioned herself alongside Aruishi. She stretched her arm over the sleeping child.

Jess moved silently into the room, gathered the quilt from the end of the bed, and gently pulled it over Lili's shoulders. At Lili's silently mouthed *thank you*, Jess kissed the tips of her fingers and placed them against Lili's lips. Lili closed her eyes, and Jess left to prepare for another night alone.

Lying in her bed, staring at the ceiling, Jess wondered if the way things had played out tonight was a sign. All her training told her to go after what she wanted, but this wasn't a road race or competition. Being so peculiarly conscious of another person, so tuned in to them, was a new phenomenon. She'd always thought that the power of a glance was overrated in romance fiction, often overused. Wrong. Lili's blue eyes were lethal—one glance was like a magnet, reeling her in.

In the car, Lili had told her she wanted *this*. Was that just a declaration of physical attraction? The chemistry between them was undeniable, and her attraction to Lili off the charts. Jess's realisation that it was more than physical was unnerving. What was she willing to risk? The stakes were high. It wasn't just about her fondness for Aruishi. It wasn't just about coming back to Australia. It was Lili.

What would be the cost if they had sex and then things went pear-shaped?

Chapter 22

"I HAVE A TEMPERATURE," ARUISHI said as Jess entered the kitchen. She wiped a hand across her forehead in a sweeping motion. A dollop of yoghurt slipped off the spoon she was holding and onto the front of her bright-red top. "Mama, look. I made a mess."

Lili reached across the table and swiftly scooped the yoghurt with her own spoon before it had a chance to soak through the cotton T-shirt. She removed the spoon from Aruishi's hand and placed it back in the bowl of cereal. "Be a good girl and show Jess that you're feeling better and you haven't got a temperature anymore: finish your breakfast."

She turned in her chair. "Good morning." She quickly scanned Jess's face to gauge her mood. Jess's hand skimmed across her shoulder on the way to the table, and Lili breathed a quiet sigh of relief.

"Good morning, sweet pea. It's nice to see you looking rested this morning." The warmth in Jess's eyes echoed in her voice. She pulled out a chair next to Aruishi's and sat down.

"I've had a good rest. Mummy spoke to Doctor Travis, but I don't have to see him, do I?"

"No, you'll be fine," Lili said.

"I'm glad you don't have to see the doctor. Are you feeling better? No fever?" Jess leaned forward and placed her hand upon Aruishi's forehead.

"No fever." Aruishi grabbed Jess's hand and held on to it. "Mama checked with a meter."

"A thermometer?" Jess gazed at Lili steadily, lifting an eyebrow.

Lili nodded in confirmation. "Ru's much better this morning."

Aruishi laid her hand upon her forehead. "Gran had to bring me back to my own bed because of the temperature."

"Yes, you came back to your own bed." Jess kissed the top of Aruishi's head and gave Lili a sidelong, wistful glance.

Lili smiled. "What can I get you for breakfast, Jess?"

"Don't you know by now? Coffee. Only." She grinned back at Lili.

"Coffee, coming up." Lili shook her head. "Ru knows having breakfast is an important start to the day, don't you?"

"Breakfast gives you energy for the whole day," Aruishi said sternly, and stared at Jess.

Jess jumped to her feet and was beside Lili in a second. She reached into the cupboard above the coffee machine and brought out a bowl. "On second thought, I wouldn't want to create a bad example. I will have cereal and fruit with my coffee."

As Jess's damp hair brushed against her, Lili caught her warm and inviting fragrance. She wanted to hook her thumbs into the top of Jess's loose-fitting yoga pants, pull Jess close, and bury her face in her neck. Instead, she enjoyed simply being close to her.

"I had yoghurt with my cereal," Aruishi advised loudly.

"Oh, and I may add some yoghurt too." Jess walked to the fridge, and took out the yoghurt container. She slid back in her chair and helped herself to cereal and sliced strawberries from the bowls on the table. "Would you like some more yoghurt, Aruishi?"

"No, Jess." Aruishi pushed her bowl away and grabbed the cord on Jess's charcoal hoodie. "I want a nice top like this."

Jess allowed herself to be pulled along. She leaned in and whispered into Aruishi's ear, something inaudible to Lili.

Aruishi squealed and yelled, "Orange!"

"I'll see what I can do," Jess said, and stuck a spoonful of cereal into her mouth.

The domesticity of the scene tugged at Lili's heartstrings. While Lili stacked the dishwasher with their breakfast dishes, she watched the pair giggle together like best friends.

Jess entertained Aruishi with her interpretation of *The Secret Garden* by Francis Hodgson Burnett. The multilayered story of a girl taken from her home in India to live in England after her parents died told of the healing power of nature, family, and friendship.

Lili couldn't imagine how traumatic it must have been for eleven-year-old Jess to lose her mother and be whisked away from her brother and home by a father she hardly knew, to a country across the other side of the world. She swallowed the lump of sadness in her throat. Jess must have been *so* alone.

Ben's death was heart-breaking, but maybe something could be salvaged from the tragedy. Jess was back in Australia and had discovered she had a niece.

Jess recited a line from the book. Aruishi's eyes grew wide and she clapped her hands. Jess had certainly charmed her daughter, but it was infinitely clear that Aruishi wasn't the only one who'd fallen under the spell of Jessica Harris. Lili was hooked, drawn to her like a honeybee to sweet nectar. Not just by her beauty—though she was gorgeous and sexy—but by how Jess balanced strength and eloquence, sensitivity, and grit with flashes of modesty and an ability to be fully engaged in the moment. Lili was falling. Hard.

"Mama, can we take Auntie Jess to our secret garden?" Aruishi jumped out of her chair and ran over to Lili.

"Whoa. I'm holding hot drinks." Lili hoisted two cups aloft as Aruishi clung to her thigh. She carefully passed Jess her coffee and shuffled to her chair with Aruishi still attached to her leg.

"Thank you." Jess smiled in appreciation as she accepted the coffee.

"You're welcome." Lili set her cup down, reached out with both arms, and lifted Aruishi onto her lap. "Now, what were you saying?" She pinched her lightly on the nose.

"Can we take Jess to the garden?" Aruishi asked in a pleading tone.

"Well, that depends," Lili said, glancing at Jess over Aruishi's head. "She may have other plans this morning."

Jess tilted her head and tapped at her chin, pretending to contemplate her options. Her eyes danced with mischief. "Nothing planned. I'm all yours," she said. "Should we go as soon as we finish our breakfast? Where is this garden?" She pushed Aruishi's glass of apple juice within her reach.

"It's a secret," Lili and Aruishi called out together. Aruishi giggled, jumped off Lili's lap, and twirled in a circle. "It's a secret, Jess," she repeated blissfully.

Jess raised an eyebrow playfully and was still smiling as she drained the last of her coffee.

They headed through the orchard, past an old wooden windmill near the creek before Aruishi stopped and insisted Jess's eyes be covered for the rest of the walk.

Lili took the silk scarf from around her neck, folded it, and tied it loosely around Jess's head, completely obscuring her vision. The captivating smell, unique to Lili, floated in the air around Jess, and for a delicious moment, her warm body pressed into Jess's back.

"Relax. It's only a short distance. Trust me." Carefully guiding her along, Lili kept a firm hold around Jess's waist. "Watch your step. Oops, I mean slow down." Lili tightened her grip when Jess stumbled.

She squeezed Lili's arm. "This is a first for me. I've never trusted anyone to lead me down a garden path, especially with my eyes covered."

"There's a first time for everything."

"Don't peek, Jess, till I tell you." Aruishi held Jess's other hand and tugged her along.

"I can't see a thing, Aruishi."

Soon after, the ground underfoot softened, and she heard a rustling like fallen leaves. There was the rattle of a metal latch, the creak of a gate's hinges, and the tinkle of a brass bell.

"We're here," Lili said.

"Mama, I want to take the cloth off."

"Okay. Hang on a minute. I've got you."

Lili must have lifted her daughter off the ground, because her small hands patted Jess's ears and pulled the blindfold over her head. Jess blinked in the bright sunlight. Two pairs of eyes stared at her, one dusky brown and the other brilliant blue. Lili's eyes sparkled, and her sensual mouth lifted in a half smile. She bounced Aruishi on her hip before lowering her onto the path.

"This is it," Aruishi cried out.

Jess turned around in a full circle. They stood in an enclosed garden with a higgledy-piggledy mix of informal plantings. Cheerful orange and yellow flowers covered the ground at her feet. White daffodils and purple daisies poked out from a half ivy-covered wheelbarrow, and rambling soft-pink roses covered the tall bamboo picket fences around them. "This is special," Jess said. "Where are we?"

Aruishi's hands went on her hips. "It's a secret."

The roofline of Helen and Scott's house was visible in the distance. "Yes, it is a complete mystery to me," she said and winked at Lili.

"How about we let Jess in on the secret? I don't think she'll tell anyone," Lili said.

Aruishi nodded solemnly. "Okay, I'll whisper in your ear."

Jess crouched and Aruishi cupped her hands around her ear. "This is where the secret garden is. It used to be Mama's when she was little. Now it is mine, and it can be yours too."

"I'll treasure it." Jess bit her lip, reached down, and selected a large white shell from an overflowing pile in a rusted blue bucket and held it to her ear. She smiled at the echo of waves and held it to her niece's ear.

Aruishi gave a delighted giggle and looked up at Jess. "It's magic. It's the sea."

The rest of the morning passed with a sprinkling of sunshine, a gentle breeze, a dozen secret glances, and clandestine touches. Even a brief stolen kiss when Aruishi climbed onto her treehouse platform a foot or so above Jess's head, and left Lili and Jess alone for a moment.

They lingered at the bottom of the ladder. Lili sat perched on the treehouse step, chin in hand, watching Aruishi. The light breeze ruffled Lili's fair hair, and her cheeks glowed with a flush of pink.

"Hey, Jess," Lili said. Their gazes met with a flare of heat, and a tingling swept up the back of Jess's neck. "What were you thinking?" she asked gently. "You don't have to tell me, but you look pensive."

"Spring's the best time of year."

Lili tilted her head and gave her a goofy grin.

Jess rocked back and forth on her heels before she strode the few steps to Lili's side, leaned down, and planted a kiss on her lips.

"Catch me, Jess." Aruishi appeared at the top of the treehouse steps and held out her arms.

"Aruishi, don't!" Lili called and jumped to her feet.

Jess turned quickly and reached up to grab Aruishi before she launched herself off the platform. She twirled her in the air and swung her onto her hip.

"Ru can fly!" Jess said with overdone amazement.

Aruishi laughed, wrapping her legs around Jess's waist and her arms around her neck. "Love you, Jess."

Jess was overcome by Aruishi's tenderness. "I love you too," she whispered.

Lili wrapped her arms around them both and squeezed.

Tears stung Jess's eyes as she pressed her face into the shelter of Lili's neck.

Chapter 23

JESS RAISED HER CHIN AS a whoosh of water sprayed over the deck. "This is awesome," she said, taking a gulp of salty air. She was thrilled to be out on the ocean having her first sea kayak lesson with Lili. Helen had taken Aruishi along on her shopping trip to Geelong, and she and Lili had seized the narrow window of opportunity to take advantage of the brilliant sunny morning.

Thank God Lili knew what she was doing, or Jess would have a lung full of water by now. Kayaking on open seawater was a new experience, but having Lili behind her with her feet braced in the footrests beside Jess's hips gave her a sense of security. She followed Lili's instructions absolutely, mindful they could be tossed into the foaming breakers at any time. For her first time in the tandem kayak, Jess was happy to let someone else be in control.

The waves were choppy enough to work her core, arms, and shoulders. Jess curled her fingers tightly around the paddle pole as a large swell came in behind the kayak.

"Hold the paddle out of the water," Lili called out over the lapping waves and squawking seagulls. "If we start too soon, we'll be paddling in front of the wave, and it will break on us. Don't you paddle. I'll guide us in."

Jess lifted her paddle in the air and quickly turned to catch a flash of Lili's confident grin. She'd seen that look before, when Lili greeted her guests at Ailie. She'd been attracted to her aura of self-confidence and prowess then—and, now, Jess liked it a lot.

The kayak skimmed over the water, as if weightless, while the wave surged underneath. Lili paddled and steered effortlessly towards the shore, and Jess sat back, enjoying the rush as they coasted in on the back of a large wave all the way to the beach.

"You get out first. Try and hold it steady," Lili said.

Jess scrambled off the kayak into the shallow water and steadied it for Lili to get out. "That was amazing. Almost as good as racing. Almost." Her adrenaline was pumping, and the words came out in a breathy gush.

"I agree, it was a blast," Lili said, reaching out to squeeze Jess's biceps.

They hauled the water-laden kayak out of the shallows and onto the dry sand. Jess winced as her leg muscles cramped. The discomfort in the quadriceps femoris was the result of her thigh muscles tensing during the more hair-raising moments of their morning on the water. All worth it, and nothing a few stretches wouldn't fix.

Lili pushed her sunglasses on top of her head. "You take instructions really well." Her eyes gleamed with amusement and shone a dazzling blue in the bright sunlight.

Jess held Lili's gaze. "Absolutely, because this is definitely something I'd like to do again." She followed Lili to the secluded sandy alcove, hedged with clumps of tall tussock and shrubs, where they'd stashed away their towels, shirts, and shorts. Jess pulled off her drenched flotation vest and sun visor and tugged off the half wetsuit, freeing her arms from the rubbery garment.

With the sun on her back, she adjusted her racer-back crop top and did a slow lateral neck stretch, rotated her shoulders and arms, and then bent her knee to take her left ankle in her right hand and pull back to stretch her thigh muscles. With a final straight-leg stretch, Jess touched her toes and reached up to the sky. She turned around to pick up her towel and found Lili watching her with dark, hungry eyes. Lili's hand was paused on the half-open zipper enclosure of her skin-tight two-piece wetsuit.

"Hey, you've thrown your gear all over the sand. Why don't you toss it in the wet bucket?" Lili's voice was just above a whisper and held a raspy edge. She pointed to where the large green bucket lay in the sand.

"Oh gosh, that would have been the sensible thing to do." It would be sensible to do it now, but sunlight glistened off the wet neoprene material and the exposed skin of Lili's chest, and Jess couldn't take her eyes off her.

Lili bit her lip. That little gesture made everything else fade into the background. Jess's focus narrowed to just the two of them. She couldn't hear anything past the thumping of her own heart.

They moved towards each other at the same time. Jess put her hand out and cursed as it trembled. Now was not the time to be nervous. She covered Lili's fingers with her own, and together they drew the zipper all the way down to expose more of Lili's skin.

With one hand, Jess traced a line along the damp flesh of Lili's abdomen and skimmed her fingers within the deep cleavage of Lili's bikini top.

Lili gasped. She grabbed Jess around her waist and hooked her thumbs into the tops of her shorts, tugging forward until their bodies collided and their lips connected.

There was nothing teasing or apprehensive about the way Lili's mouth matched Jess's—hot and demanding. The intimacy, the rawness, and the friendly duel for command made Jess nearly lose her balance in the soft sand. When they surfaced for air and pressed their foreheads together, they were both panting.

"Wow," Lili whispered.

"Not bad." Jess let out a slow breath. She tore her gaze from Lili to quickly scan their surroundings. The dip in the sand dunes and the foliage made it private, but you couldn't be too sure. She glanced up towards the path that led to Ben's cottage.

Lili followed Jess's gaze and shook her head. "Nathan or Julia could come home anytime."

Jess sighed. "Back to your place?"

"Thirty-five minutes away?" Lili moved her fingers across Jess's bare midriff.

Jess closed her eyes briefly as her stomach quivered.

The breeze ruffled Lili's hair, and Jess brushed the light-gold strands out of her eyes. Lili tipped her mouth into a provocative grin, and she ran her tongue slowly over her lips.

Jess groaned. They were alone, apart from a few seagulls circling above them.

She dropped to her knees onto the towel, pulling Lili down with her, then dragged the open half-wetsuit off Lili's shoulders and flung it into the bucket. She pulled up the bikini top as Lili helpfully raised her arms.

The nipples underneath were flushed pink, Lili's breasts full, and they rose and fell with her uneven breaths as Jess cupped her palms around their perfection. The need to taste her was so strong, Jess's body vibrated in anticipation. "Finally," she murmured, and buried her face in the valley, then closed her mouth over one firm peak and then the other.

A soft gasp escaped Lili's lips, like a murmur of encouragement, and she threaded her hands through Jess's hair, tugging firmly.

Jess lifted her head up and eased Lili sideways onto her back. She placed her knees on either side of Lili's hips. Grasping the waistband, she urged Lili to raise her hips and drew the shorts over Lili's knees before tossing them aside. She rested on her palms and gazed at Lili, who lay before her, completely naked, with an open expression and eyes full of desire. She was breathtakingly beautiful. An unfamiliar tenderness shot through Jess. She trailed her tongue along Lili's slender neck and across her collarbone. She bit gently into the muscle of her freckled shoulder. Jess inhaled Lili's fresh, natural scent. She tasted the salt on her skin. Crisp and clean, sultry and sweet.

Lili's hands slid from her lower back into the top of Jess's damp sport shorts. In their haste, there'd been no time to shed her shorts.

Jess lowered herself onto her elbows, settling her hips between Lili's thighs, and the warmth from Lili's centre was slick against Jess's stomach. Jess moved to create friction, eliciting a moan from Lili—a mixture of pleasure and frustration. Raw heat between them sizzled with each rolling movement of their hips.

Lili grazed her fingernails up Jess's spine to her shoulders and pushed, urging Jess to slide down her body, to where her need was greatest.

Jess inched lower to Lili's rib cage. A small tattoo in the shape of a delicate twig was underscored with the words, *Thyme on my side.* Jess smiled. It was corny, endearing—but at this moment, so not true. Lili wriggled under her, her breath short and fast.

"Impatient?" Jess flicked her tongue along the tattooed skin and down, teasing around her belly button to the apex of her thighs.

"*Crazy,*" she hissed, clenching her fist in Jess's hair. "You're driving me crazy."

Jess wanted slow and unhurried, but now was not the time for slow. She lifted her gaze, and their eyes locked in a moment of absolute awareness.

She lowered her head. The scent of Lili's arousal was intoxicating. She gripped her hips, holding her in place, and her mouth found her. Hot, silky smooth, and so sexy.

Lili cried out. Or did she? It could have been one of those nosy seagulls swooping and calling overhead. It hadn't taken long. Jess had her so fired, all it took was a few strokes of her skilful tongue before Lili came with a series of shudders. She drew one knee up to rest it against Jess's shoulder. The slight position change and the increased pressure of Jess's lips caused another more intense wave of pleasure to surge through her. Her muscles twitched as she tried not to move. With Jess's head against her thigh, the brush of her hair and the tickle of her breath threatened to set her off again.

She ran her fingers over Jess's head, down to where a tangle of hair spilled over her shoulders. "Are you okay?"

Jess moved her head and kissed her centre again. "Hmm...I am," she said. "How are you?"

The vibration of Jess's voice against her sensitive flesh made her tremble. She squeezed Jess's shoulder. "I think you should come up here—now."

"Is that you humming?" Jess asked. Lili could feel Jess smile against her skin.

"No, not me." Lili raised her head and squinted, temporarily blinded by the bright sunlight.

Jess made one last sweep with her tongue, and Lili shivered as Jess rolled off her and stared up, shielding her eyes with her hand. "Oh. That's the sound. What is that?" Jess asked. She dived across her, grabbed the other towel, and draped it over Lili's exposed body.

Lili wiped her hand over her face to get rid of the sand that fell from the towel. She sat up. "What? What is it?" She held the towel in place.

"Don't move." Jess got to her feet, pulled her shirt over her crop top and shorts, and stood with her hands on her hips, glaring up at the sky. "It's a bloody drone." Jess shook her head.

"A drone?" Lili brushed the sand out of her eyes and stared upwards. "A drone? You mean one of those things with a camera attached?" It circled above them, whirring and humming. It dipped closer and then steadily began to gain altitude and zoomed away. Dazed, she snatched her T-shirt that had somehow been part buried in the sand, drew it over her head, and dragged on her cargo shorts.

Jess combed her fingers through her hair and fanned it over her shoulders. "I hate it when sand gets into my hair," she muttered. "It probably does have a camera. Even the hobbyist drones have them."

"Shit." Lili took her watch out of her shorts pocket and fastened it around her wrist.

"Hey, don't worry." Jess calmly placed her hand on Lili's arm.

She glared at Jess. "That's okay for you. You weren't the one lying stark naked, exposed to the world."

Jess pulled Lili into her arms. "It was pretty high up. I don't think it would have got a very clear picture, if anything at all." She rubbed her hand up and down Lili's back in a soothing motion. "Anyway, I had most of you covered. Literally." She laughed.

Lili lifted her chin from Jess's shoulder and looked up at her. Jess's golden skin was flushed from the sun. She flashed her dark eyes and fluttered those thick lashes at Lili. Her luscious, slightly bruised lips tilted in a cheeky grin. Lili sighed, remembering just what those lips, that mouth, had been doing a few minutes ago. She nodded and smiled somewhat reluctantly.

"That's better," Jess whispered, tightening her arms around her.

Jess's phone pinged. "I wonder who that could be?" She reached for the safety vest, extracted the phone from the waterproof pocket, and checked her screen. Her eyes narrowed. "It's a message from your mother."

"Oh. What does she say?"

"She tried to ring you but couldn't get through."

Lili reached into her pocket and pulled out her phone. "Damn. I forgot I'd turned it off."

"I think it's okay. Helen is just reminding you she's volunteering this afternoon."

"She's at aged care today, helping with their bridge afternoon. I'll just text." She glanced at her watch. Crikey, where had the time gone? "If we hurry, we'll just make it back before she has to leave."

Lili typed that they were on their way and hit *send*.

The towels, water bottles, and sundry items were quickly gathered and placed in the bucket.

"Jess, where are my swim shorts? I can't see them."

"In the tub," Jess said. "With the rest of the gear."

Lili picked up the bucket. "Okay, let's go."

"Lili," Jess said.

"Yes?"

"The kayak is still on the beach," she said, holding out her hand. "Come on, let's carry it up to Ben's garage." She pushed a strand of flyaway hair from her face.

Lili dropped the bucket. "Damn, we really will be late." She took Jess's hand, and they ran towards the kayak as fast as they could on the soft sand.

She gave a small squeal as she realised her selfishness and ground to a halt.

Jess stopped and turned to her. "What's up?"

"I am so sorry, Jess. With that stupid drone, I didn't even get a chance... you know," she said sheepishly. She hadn't even had the chance to undress Jess.

Jess reached forward and placed her index finger on Lili's lips. "It's okay."

Lili grabbed her hand and drew it to her chest. "It's so not okay. I want to."

Jess snaked her hand free from Lili's grasp and ran her finger along her cheek and under her chin, tilting her head up. One eyebrow arched, and she leaned forward, giving Lili's earing a light tug as she whispered, "Have absolutely no doubt I want it too." Her breath tickled Lili's ear. "I can't wait to touch you again. I can't wait for you to touch me."

A little dizzy, a little light-headed, Lili closed her eyes and exhaled slowly. Words failed her.

"Let's go. We really should hurry." Jess laughed, dragging her towards the kayak. "Helen won't be pleased with us if she's late for her appointment."

Chapter 24

"I KNOW YOU SAID NOT to worry, but what if that drone took pictures of us on the beach?" Lili asked. "I just don't want to appear on someone's Facebook page, or YouTube."

Jess laughed, patted Lili's knee, and returned her hand to the steering wheel.

"Why are you laughing?" Lili wrapped her arms around herself. "Oh yeah, I forgot. Even if someone did get a picture, it would be the back of you, with your clothes on." She gave a short laugh and shook her head.

Jess was skittish and exhilarated from their morning together kayaking and from the great sex in the sand, but she had been thoughtless in her response to Lili's anxiety. "I am sorry. I wasn't laughing at you," she said. "I can't help feeling happy. I had a really good time, and I don't want the drone incident to spoil it."

"I had a great time too," Lili said. "I guess you're used to cameras flashing and microphones pointed at you?"

Jess nodded. "Not at first. With a father who often appeared in the newspapers and on television, I've learned to accept the paparazzi as part of life. When I was a naïve teenager, they tried and often succeeded to get to him through me. I discovered it was better to keep silent." Otherwise, she would have suffered from his angry outbursts.

"I'm sorry. I can't even imagine how hard that must have been. But what about you? You've had your share of coverage in the news and on social media."

Jess stopped the Jeep outside Helen and Scott's cottage. She engaged the handbrake and turned to Lili. "Yes, but being part of a team gives you a bit of protection," she said. "As for the other stuff—the gossip and innuendo—I've had to develop a thick skin." Jess reached for Lili's hand.

"I am sorry. It was inconsiderate of me to make light of the drone. I really hope it comes to nothing."

"It's okay." Lili placed her hand over Jess's. "I overreacted." She opened the passenger-side door, then suddenly turned back and kissed Jess on the cheek. "Let's let it go and remember the *awesome* things about the morning."

"It was awesome?"

She gazed at Jess for what seemed like forever. A wary gaze. "It was fun…and I'd like to do it again," Lili said eventually.

"I feel like there's a *but*," Jess said.

Lili sighed. "As I've said before, I like you a lot. You're incredible." She looked down at her hands in her lap. "It's been a while since…" She cleared her throat. "Since I've been intimate like that. You're amazing, and I'd like to enjoy this for what it has to be—fun."

Jess was about to protest—wasn't it more than just fun? But Lili held up her hand.

"You'll be going soon." Her shoulders drooped.

"Yes, but I—"

"Are you two coming in, or are you just going to sit in the car?" Helen yelled from the porch.

Lili jumped. She sprang out of the car and sprinted towards her mother. Jess closed her door and followed Lili at a more sedate pace.

Helen was obviously ready to leave. She'd dressed smartly and held a carryall in one hand and a covered tray in the other.

"Sorry, Mum. Have we made you late?" Lili asked.

Helen turned to Jess and smiled. "I'd like to get going. I promised to partner Mrs Lang this afternoon, and she gets a bit anxious if I'm not there right on the button." She held the tray aloft as Lili peeked under the gingham tea towel. "Savoury scones. I left a few on the kitchen bench in case you two came back hungry after all that exercise."

Lili coughed and looked sideways at Jess. "Thanks, Mum."

"Scones. I am ravenous," Jess said. "Thank you, Helen."

"You're welcome. I hope you both enjoy them." Helen turned to Lili. "Are you okay, love? You seem a bit flushed. Did you get too much sun? Just because it's only spring doesn't mean you can't get sunburnt."

"Yes, Mum. I'm good," Lili replied quickly. "Maybe we were in the sun too long. What do you think, Jess?" Her lips twitched.

Jess's gaze settled on Lili's smile. "We made sure you were well covered the whole time," she said with a straight face.

"Okay, ladies. I'm off," Helen said. "Oh, and you know the rules, Lili. Don't try and pry any information out of Ru about our shopping trip this morning. Enjoy the afternoon."

As Helen stepped past them and walked to her car, Aruishi raced through the front door and onto the porch to throw herself at her mother's knees. "Mama, I missed you." She peeked around Lili's legs. "You too, Jess. I missed you."

Lili scooped her into her arms and twirled her in a circle. "We missed you too," she said. "I'm hungry. How about you? Would you like to come into the kitchen and have one of Gran's scones?"

Aruishi shook her head. "No. It has that yucky cheese and olives in it. I already ate a special one with plain cheese. *Peppa Pig* is nearly finished. Can I watch the end?"

"Okay, off you go, then. But we'll head home after that. I need a shower."

Aruishi scampered back inside towards the sunroom. Strange noises—a xylophone and pig snorts—emanated from inside.

"Ru hasn't yet developed a taste for feta cheese or black olives. It'll take time for her to realise how delicious they are." Lili nudged Jess playfully. "I can't believe you told Mum you were ravenous. She'll think I never feed you."

Jess patted her growling stomach. "I am. Blame it on the sea air."

"Well, move along, then. Mum's savoury scones are the best for when you've worked up a healthy appetite." Lili smiled cheekily and started towards the kitchen, leaving Jess staring after her.

She was all upbeat and flirtatious now, but Jess didn't know what to make of Lili's see-sawing mood.

Lili persuaded Aruishi to take an afternoon nap so she'd be rested for Alex and Tash's visit. The shopping trip into Geelong must have exhausted her, because she didn't protest much. Jess seemed to have disappeared into her room while Lili settled Aruishi.

She was just about to knock on Jess's door when her phone rang. It was Owen with an update on their bookings for the next few days. The teachers from a school in Ocean Grove had chosen a four-course prix fixe menu for their principal's retirement luncheon, and the restaurant was fully booked the next day for both lunch and dinner service.

"Did you get my message? Are you okay with me placing Simon Emmett's last-minute booking for six at the chef's table?" Owen asked.

"Yes, that's the only option. We have nowhere else."

"Do we need extra staff?"

"Not back of house," she said. "Alex, Tim, and the apprentices will prep in the morning, and Nora and the kitchen hands will join us for the lunch service. If things go to plan, we'll all get a chance for a break during the afternoon before dinner service."

"I've called in a casual to replace Haley, front of house."

"Oh?"

"Yes, Haley's part of Simon's group, as is Jess."

Why didn't she know that? "That's right," she said firmly, hoping Owen didn't detect any surprise in her voice.

They went over the finalised lunch menu before she forwarded it via e-mail to Alex and to the restaurant.

In less than an hour and a half, Tash and Alex would arrive for dinner. Lili shut down her laptop and tiptoed down the hallway to the kitchen to gather the ingredients for the Balinese minced seafood satay and the simple accompaniments she'd chosen for tonight.

Alex had offered to bring dessert, so that was one thing she didn't have to worry about. She glanced at her watch. There was just enough time for that overdue shower.

Lili avoided the bathroom mirror as she stripped out of her clothes and stepped into the shower. It wasn't until she was under the gloriously steaming water that she noticed a small purplish bruise where Jess's teeth had grazed her hip. The painless bite had been amazingly arousing. She ran her fingers over her mouth. Her lips were slightly swollen, and her overly sensitive breasts still marginally uncomfortable under the shower spray.

She recalled Jess's body arched over hers. The brush of her soft skin, the way her hands held her still, the heat of her mouth. Lili closed her eyes, relishing the subtle muscle ache and the tingling that coursed through her body.

She flicked the temperature control and gasped under the icy water. She needed a wakeup call. It was only sex. Unbelievably good sex—and she wanted more. It was like her body had woken after a long sleep. What was that saying about riding a bike? Once learned never forgotten.

"Look, Tash, I don't need the training wheels anymore," Aruishi shouted. She did another circuit of the sun deck before jumping off her bicycle and propping it against the safety rail. She skipped over to where Tash and Jess sat at the wooden table.

"It didn't take you long," Tash said. "Maybe you can help Alex when she actually starts using her new bike?" she added, loud enough for Lili and Alex to hear her from where they stood at the grill.

Lili rocked back on her heels. "So, how long before you'll be off your training wheels, Alex?"

"I can help her. I have natural balance and *dextree*." Aruishi spread her arms out wide and tilted from side to side with one foot in the air.

"I think she means *dexterity*." Jess laughed and took a sip of wine.

"That's what I said, Jess." Aruishi reached out for Tash's bottle of pale ale, but Tash was faster and lifted it to safety.

"Oh no you don't. I'm not contributing to the delinquency of a minor." Tash placed the bottle out of Aruishi's reach. "I could get you an apple juice or water?"

Aruishi shook her head and leaned against Jess's leg.

"Ru, the food will be ready soon," Lili said. "Please go and wash your hands."

"Why? Do I have to go now?"

"Yes, please."

Aruishi played with Jess's hair. "Does Jess have to wash her hands?"

"Aruishi." Lili spoke in the low tone she'd learned was successful if she wanted her to comply.

Aruishi ran for the French doors. "Okay. I'm going," she said sombrely. Just before she hightailed to the kitchen, she called, "How come no one else has to wash their hands?"

Lili stared at her daughter, who quickly shut the door with a bang. She shook her head. "I don't know. I swear she's getting bolder by the day."

"She's got a point though, right?" Alex grinned. "I mean, what do we drill into new staff during health and safety training?"

Lili laughed. "Wash your hands."

With her arms outstretched and her hands splayed, Jess jumped to her feet and walked over to Lili. "Want to check them?" Her eyelids fluttered playfully.

Without thinking, she reached out and pinched Jess's cheek.

"Ouch." Jess rubbed her face, obviously play-acting. "I'm going to wash my hands and check on Aruishi while I'm there." She flashed Lili a taunting smile and headed inside.

For a few seconds, Lili stood in front of the charcoal barbeque, staring after Jess. She looked up at Alex, who was gazing at her with raised eyebrows.

"What?"

Alex put her hands on her hips. "What's going on?"

Lili rotated the skewers on the grill, slowly basting each fish satay with the spicy marinade. "You'll have to be a little more specific, Alex."

Alex leaned in close. "Blatant flirting." She smiled at Tash, who'd joined them at the barbeque. "Just because I've been in a relationship for nine years doesn't mean I don't recognise the signs."

Tash stood behind Alex, placed her arms around her waist, and kissed the top of her head. She glanced at Lili. "I did notice the looks between you two. The playful touching. The eye contact."

"You've slept with her."

"Alex, stop. No, I haven't *slept* with her." She wasn't lying. There had been no sleeping, although the thought of *lying* in bed with Jess was on her mind, despite everything she'd said to her.

Alex laughed loudly. "Oh, shut up. You're not denying it, then? We're about to eat dinner, but Jess looked like she's ready to devour *you*."

"Okay, you two." Lili glanced up towards the door. "Please, behave. And don't say anything around Ru."

"But you said—" Alex tilted her head in question.

"Shush..." Tash whispered. "Here they are."

Jess and Aruishi stepped out onto the deck, waving their hands in front of them.

Lili gave Alex a pleading look.

"I think we'd better follow their example, Tash," Alex said. "Come on, let's wash our hands, and we'll get the rest of the food on our way back."

"Thanks, Alex." Lili breathed a sigh of relief. "And please bring the cider from the fridge, and the champagne glasses."

"Cider in champagne glasses?" Jess asked.

"It's Cider Methode Champenoise. It's fresh and light and goes well with spicy food."

"I'm going to help carry out dinner," Aruishi announced loudly, and followed Alex and Tash into the kitchen.

"This smells incredible. What are they? And what are those green sticks? They're not wood." Jess hovered near Lili, watching her work.

Lili placed the skewers onto the platter and added the bowl of lime wedges and spiced peanuts at one end. "The sticks are lemongrass. The flavour permeates into the fish mixture during cooking, mingling with the kaffir-lime zest and sour-sweet of the tamarind."

As Lili lifted the platter, Jess placed her hands over hers. "Here, let me carry that for you. I can't wait to try it. You are making me a more adventurous eater."

Lili looked at her, raising an eyebrow. "But you've travelled all over the world. You must have tried lots of different foods."

"When I first arrived in England I was fussy. I'd hardly eat a thing." Jess sighed. "I missed my mum and Usha's cooking."

"That's hardly surprising."

"Plus, I have to be careful when we're competing. Things can be mislabelled, contaminated, or have banned ingredients that show up in tests," Jess said. "The team usually eats together, sticking with simple high-protein foods."

Lili released the platter in to Jess's hands. "Um," she said. "You didn't tell me you were having dinner at Ailie tomorrow with Simon and Haley."

"What? Haley?" Jess frowned. "Simon's invited me to dinner with a group of his cycling friends. He never mentioned Haley would be there, as a guest."

"Oh, I see," Lili said. "But you didn't even mention you were invited to *my* restaurant."

"I'm so sorry. Simon only rang me a couple of hours ago to let me know he'd managed a last-minute booking, and did I want to come? I've had no chance to tell you, Lili."

"Come on, you two. Everything else is on the table," Alex called.

"Are we okay?" Jess asked in a serious tone. "There is nothing going on between me and Haley."

She sighed with relief. They were okay. "Yes, we're okay."

"Mummy, I want some of the yellow rice, but do I have to eat this stuff?" Aruishi pointed at the large bowl of mixed-vegetable salad.

Lili sat down in the chair beside Aruishi, and Jess sat beside her. She heaped a small mound of rice onto Aruishi's plate and chopped a minced fish satay into bite-sized pieces. "I think you should try a few veggies. How about some green beans, sprouts, and carrot with a little grated coconut and some of the peanut sauce you like?"

Aruishi picked up a long bean in her fingers, dipped it in the peanut sauce, and munched. She picked up another bean and waved it in the air before taking a large bite. "Yummy," she said with her mouth full.

Lili jumped as Tash popped the cork on the sparkling cider and Jess squeezed her knee, the heat from her hand radiating through Lili's trousers.

"Lili, shall I pour you a glass?" Tash asked.

"Yes, please," Lili rasped as Jess's hand moved along her thigh. "I could use a drink."

"This is tasty." Aruishi shovelled a loaded spoon of fish and rice into her mouth.

Lili watched Jess take a sizable bite of the satay and lick the peanut sauce from the tips of her fingers.

Lili's hand shook slightly as she lifted her glass to her lips and she took a sip. "Eat up, everyone," she said, looking from Jess to Aruishi. "We have the approval of the fussiest eaters at the table."

Aruishi didn't even make it to dessert. She finished her main meal, then clambered onto Lili's lap and fell asleep. Lili carried her inside, put her pyjamas on, and tucked her into bed. Aruishi didn't stir when Lili placed Princess Teddy against her shoulder. With any luck, she would sleep through the night.

Lili stopped in the kitchen to collect Alex's tray. Miniature citrus tarts with dollops of tangy lemon curd, crisp coconut pastry, and a touch of candied orange peel. It would finish the meal perfectly.

With platter in hand, Lili rejoined the group on the deck. She sat quietly as Alex explained to Jess how she and Tash had first met.

"At a women's football game, of all things," Alex said. "We were barracking for different sides. When the ball sailed over the boundary line into the crowd, we both reached up to catch it and missed. Instead, we collided into each other."

It was a story often told, but Lili couldn't help but smile as Tash and Alex grinned at each other and playfully bumped their foreheads together. Jess put her head back and laughed along with them.

Lili felt her heart expand. Jess seemed to fit right in—like she'd known them all for years. She half turned in her chair to look out over the moonlit bay. She was skirting dangerously close to risking a deeper emotional connection with Jess.

Lili needed to know she could trust her. She could almost convince herself it was no big deal, but it was. Jess's explanation about the dinner engagement with Simon and Haley seemed genuine. Even where things stood between them now—with an uncertain future—honest communication was essential.

Tash and Alex went home just after midnight. Lili gently pulled Aruishi's bedroom door almost shut, relieved her daughter was still asleep. When she walked into the kitchen, there was Jess, stacking the dishwasher. It was mind-boggling somehow, having Jess in her kitchen doing tasks like she belonged there, in the house that she'd shared only with Aruishi for four years.

As if sensing Lili's presence, Jess looked over her shoulder. "She still asleep?"

"Like a log." Lili walked towards her. "You didn't have to clean up, but thank you."

Jess closed the dishwasher with her knee, wiped her hands on a tea towel, and turned around to face Lili. "Too late. It's all done now." She reached out and circled Lili's waist, and her eyes widened with a questioning smile.

Lili swallowed hard as a pleasant fluttering stirred in her stomach. "Would you like a hot drink? A whiskey? More wine?"

"No, I'm perfectly fine," Jess said. "The meal and the company were terrific."

"I hope Alex didn't ply you with too many questions? She's an inquisitive one."

Jess lifted the hem of Lili's top with her thumbs, stroking her bare midriff. "I enjoyed every minute of it." She pulled Lili close. "Everything."

Lili cupped Jess's face in her hands. Craving a closer connection, she leaned forward and kissed her. She linked her hands around Jess's neck and kissed her again with a deeper intensity that even she found surprising. Jess's tongue caressed hers with soft, sensual strokes. It was sweet and lush, and Lili tasted a hint of apple cider and lime.

Finally, out of breath, Lili lowered her head and buried her face between Jess's breasts. Kissing was wonderful, but it wasn't enough. She leaned into Jess, pushing her against the kitchen bench.

Their chests rose and fell together. Jess's heart pounded, and she seemed as breathless as Lili. She rested her chin on top of Lili's head. "Lili," she said, releasing a quivering sigh.

"Come to bed, Jess."

Jess's hands tightened around her waist. "Are you sure? To your room? What about Aruishi?"

Lili nodded, recapturing Jess's lips in a brief kiss. "If she wakes in the middle of the night, she'll call out. I wouldn't hear her at the other end of the house." She stroked Jess's cheek. "My room is best, and I have a way to secure the door."

"If you're sure?" Jess looked down to meet Lili's gaze, and Lili was stunned by the vulnerability and the desire reflected in her eyes.

"Yes, I'm very sure," she whispered. She slid her hand down Jess's arm, grasped her hand, and led her along the hallway.

Lili quietly closed the door behind them and switched on the light. She raised one finger. "Give me a second."

While Jess waited by the door, Lili opened her dresser drawer and rummaged around until she found what she was looking for. "Got it." She held up the small flexible bracket, walked back to the door, and fitted it into the ready-mounted block on the doorframe, which was well out of Aruishi's reach. "It's called a Houdini door," she explained. "Ru can open it a crack, but she won't be able to come in without us unlatching it."

Jess peered at the contraption, pressed Lili back against the closed door, and put her mouth to Lili's ear. "Brilliant. You did have me wondering." She flicked the light switch off. "Does that mean I've no escape?"

"Absolutely none." Lili pushed Jess backwards towards the bed. Moonlight seeped through the sheer blinds—just enough to illuminate their way. "No escape." She smiled against Jess's lips as they covered hers, and they kissed until Lili's breath came out in ragged gasps.

Jess wasted no time and started undoing Lili's shirt. She released the last button, slid the shirt off her shoulders, and let it fall to the floor.

Lili worked her hands under Jess's shirt and pushed it upwards just as Jess took hold of the hem, lifted the shirt over her head, and tossed it on top of Lili's discarded top.

"Hey, that's my job," Lili said in a commanding tone. She feasted her eyes on the swell of Jess's breasts, visible through her gauzy black bra, and marvelled at the way her shiny hair rippled sinuously about her shoulders in waves. She took pleasure in the curve of Jess's waist that tapered to slim hips and the defined muscles of her almost-flat stomach. She found her voice. "Jess." Her body pulsed with need. She wanted no more barriers between them.

As she urged Jess backwards onto the bed with a soft push and tugged off her already unbuttoned shorts, Jess let out a startled gasp.

"Want help with yours?" she asked with a grin at Lili.

Lili shook her head and quickly shed her trousers. She straddled Jess's knees and tumbled with her across the bed. "Are you suggesting that I'm slow?"

They wrestled playfully with their tangle of undergarments until they were both naked.

Jess inched her way up the bed. "You're not slow. I just want to speed things along." She laughed.

"I don't want to rush." Lili crawled over Jess, crouched above her, and rested her hands on the bed on either side of Jess's shoulders. She let her gaze linger on Jess for a few moments before trailing her hand across her shoulder, to her chest and down to her midriff. She paused purposefully, relishing Jess's skin glowing in the silvery light. Was she Nike, the goddess of strength and speed, reincarnated? Lili brushed the top of Jess's right thigh with her fingers—along five small, almost indiscernible lines. Jess flinched under her touch. "What are these from?" Lili asked.

"Cycling saved my life," she said slowly and deliberately after a deep breath.

Lili recalled Jess's nervous habit of rubbing the top of her leg when she was upset. She should have realised the scars were too regular to be the result of an accident. She used to cut herself. *Cycling saved her life.* She stroked Jess's cheek tenderly and saw no sign of anguish now.

Jess placed her hand over Lili's and gently moved it away from her face, down to where she obviously wanted her.

Lili refocused, responding to Jess's need and her own desire to connect. Jess arched up to meet her—their bodies intimately and inimitability aligned.

They moved in rhythm—adjusting, brushing, and pushing against each other. Lili slipped her hand between them, finding, caressing, stroking, and Jess lifted her head, her breath coming out in uneven gasps. She tensed and then called Lili's name, exhaling in a rush as her body trembled, then stilled. Their gazes locked. The unguarded trust she saw in Jess's eyes caused another wave of unexpected tenderness. Jess fell back against the bed, shielding her eyes with her arm.

She watched the rise and fall of Jess's chest and lazily drew circles through the faint sheen of sweat on her midriff. She kissed her there, teasing her belly button with her tongue, until Jess's fingers combed through her hair, stilling her movement.

Placing kisses along Jess's body, Lili moved up and rested her head on Jess's shoulder. Cinnamon, basil, and vanilla were known to be erotic stimulants, but the unique scent of Jess—spicy, rich, and smooth—was a heady mix, and, tonight, Lili's aphrodisiac. "Hey," she murmured.

Jess lowered her arm from her face and pushed herself up on one elbow. "Hey." She smiled. Her eyes were deep pools of emotion.

She prided herself on her pragmatism, but at this moment it was difficult for Lili to face the reality that whatever was between them could only be temporary. She lowered her head to Jess's breast, avoiding her gaze, unable to face her own emotions. "I tired you out," Lili whispered.

"You think so?"

She let out a puff of air as Jess nudged her shoulder and flipped her onto her back. She grinned, holding Lili's wrists on either side of her. "Don't you know athletes adapt to physical stress? We have superfast recovery. It's a skill."

"I'm out of practice," Lili murmured. "It's been a while since..." She hesitated, suddenly lost for words and a little dazed, not just from the tension building inside but the exquisite desire that surged through her.

Jess trailed her tongue along her neck and murmured in her ear, "Then let's not waste a moment. I am a firm believer in making up for lost time."

Chapter 25

JESS SLIPPED OUT FROM UNDER the sheet, collected her clothes off the floor, and pulled on her shorts and singlet as quietly as she could, careful not to wake Lili. She stole one more glance at her and laid a kiss on her shoulder as she recalled their steamy hours together, bodies entwined. The last thing she wanted to do was leave, but she couldn't risk Aruishi finding her in Lili's room. How would they explain that to her four-year-old niece?

Lili slept soundly, one arm tucked under her pillow, the other extended over the side of the bed. Jess adjusted the sheet over her and stealthily crept to the door. It opened a couple of inches, then jammed. Damn, she'd forgotten about the childproof device. She fumbled to get it unlatched, succeeded finally, and let herself out. She walked quietly past Aruishi's bedroom door, through the dimly lit house to her own room. She closed the door and leaned against it.

According to Lili, whatever was going on between them was just a bit of fun. But surely, after last night, it was more? She pushed her hands through her hair and inhaled deeply. Lili's scent was on her fingers, her skin, and on her clothes. They'd connected physically, but it wasn't just skin deep.

Jess sighed, collapsed into the chair close to the window, and stared out across the dewy meadow and the trees silhouetted against the morning sky. She knew with all certainty her attraction for Lili was beyond just fun and way beyond physical gratification.

Her phone sat on the dresser, and she reached across to check the time. It was only five o'clock. She wished she was still curled up in Lili's bed, wrapped around her incredible body. If she got into her own cold bed, she'd never get back to sleep, but it was still too dark and dangerous to take her bicycle out.

There were two missed calls, and an e-mail from Jonathan. If she couldn't sleep or ride, now was as good a time as any to return his call. She slipped on her hoodie, opened the balcony door, and stepped onto the deck. The air was crisp, and a sheen of dew covered the wooden handrail. Jess gripped the damp rail and stretched backwards, surprised her body was wonderfully fluid and free of tension. The thought of Lili naked in her bed made Jess want to sneak back to the room and start all over again. Lili was confident, sexually adventurous, and so responsive. She straightened her back, took her phone from her pocket, found Jonathan's number, and pressed call.

Descending the stairs, she placed the headphone in one ear, then strolled along the path that led to the beach. She pulled up her hood and tucked the phone back into her pocket.

"Hello, stranger," Jonathan said brightly.

"There you are. I wondered if you'd answer. Are you free to talk? I hope I'm not disturbing your Friday evening with the family."

"Not at all. I always have time for you, Jess." She could hear the smile in his voice. "I tried to ring you earlier."

"Yes, I know. Sorry I didn't get back to you." A gentle background cooing noise came through the phone. "Are you trying to sing?"

"No, never. Maxine's having a night out with the girls, and I've been left holding the baby. Literally."

"How are Maxine and little Rupert?"

"We're terrific, Jess. Rupert is growing in leaps and bounds. Sleeps pretty well, I'm happy to report."

"I'm glad for you all." Jess smiled.

"How are you?'

"I feel good, Jonathan. Getting stronger every day," she said. "The warm weather is a bonus. Lili even had me out on a sea kayak. It was brilliant."

"That's great. I hope you didn't see any sharks? Of course, we Brits think all Australian waters are shark infested."

"That's bollocks. Just like there are kangaroos on every street corner."

"Aren't there?" He laughed. "Any thought about coming home soon, or are you enjoying the Australian wildlife too much? We had a proper snow yesterday. The Heath is Christmassy white and bloody freezing."

Stopped at the edge of the grassy embankment, Jess waved to a couple jogging past, their bodies casting long shadows in the soft morning light. "Must admit, even though it is magical and I enjoy the odd toboggan ride at Kite Hill, I don't miss the cold at all."

"I don't blame you. Enjoy the warmth while you can," he said. "So, have you read my e-mail?"

"I've just glanced at it. Did Ashley contact you?"

"Yes. She hasn't heard from you in a while, and she's anxious to know what's going on—what your plans are. You should give your manager a call. Ashley would like an update."

"Okay, I will. You said something in your e-mail about pictures," Jess said. "What pictures?" She paced back and forth on the grass. "I haven't done any interviews. I doubt anyone knows, or cares, that I'm here."

"I wouldn't be so sure of that. There is a piece in the *UK Today* about you in Australia, and there are some"—he hesitated—"photographs."

His tone said it all. Jess stopped pacing. The drone. She'd forgotten about the bloody drone. What if it *had* picked up images of her and Lili on the beach?

"What photographs?"

"Hang on a minute, I'll send the screenshots," he said. "I just have to put Rupert in his bassinet. He's fast asleep in my arms."

Jess could hear gentle rustling and then silence. She jumped off the embankment and sat cross-legged on a large rock, waiting for the images to arrive.

"You there?" Jonathan asked.

"I'm still here, waiting." She adjusted her ear piece and stared at the screen.

"Okay, I've sent them," he said. "They should come through to you any minute."

A few seconds later, the Messenger app pinged. "I think they're here." Jess pressed on the first image and sighed with relief as it downloaded. It was taken at the fundraiser and revealed a clear picture of Simon, Haley, and herself on their bicycles under the finish line banner with their arms around each other's shoulders. The caption read, *Return Downunder: Aussie born elite Brit cyclist supports injured schoolgirl at local event.*

"There's nothing to be concerned about, Jonathan. It was just that. I took part in a local charity ride organised by an old family friend."

"Yeah, I agree. No problem with that one. Have a look at the others. I'm a little curious about them."

"Damn," she whispered. There was no doubt about the voyeuristic image appearing on her screen, now. A little grainy, probably snapped with someone's phone at the nightclub—the moment Haley Emmett lunged at her on the dance floor, plastering her lips over hers. Jess had disentangled herself soon after, but the image didn't show that. "It's not how it looks," she said flatly.

"Really? I'm glad you're having a bit of fun." He laughed softly, then cleared his throat. "It's the other photographs that might—"

"*What the fuck.*" She double tapped the screen to zoom in, using her finger to move the image around.

"Yes. I didn't think you'd be pleased."

Clenching her jaw, she scanned the title, "*Ready-made family?*" Nausea coiled like a twisted bike chain in her stomach. Her eyes focused on the photographs, complete with captions.

"How? Why? Damn it, Jonathan." She pounded her fist into the sand.

"I know. I am sorry," he said. "I would have expected better from that newspaper, but they haven't got anything on you lately and they're fishing."

"The picture in the nightclub was in Melbourne, and the woman should be okay with it, but the others are personal. Someone is paying for me to be followed," Jess said. "The next photo was snapped the day I gave Aruishi a bicycle and we went to Queenscliff with Lili's friends." They were standing on the wharf on either side of Aruishi, swinging her in the air. Alex and Tash were blurry figures in the background. "Lili's going to be furious they've published a photo of her daughter. How dare they?"

"I understand, Jess, but it's not your fault."

"Lili won't see it that way."

"Lili is an attractive woman," he said. "What about the next picture, of you and her—is that in Melbourne? I recognise the building in the background. Where is that?"

"Federation Square. How on earth did they even find us there? It was packed with people like Piccadilly Circus."

"You know how these outfits work. They comb social media and YouTube looking for anything. They pay scouts. You know the deal."

Jess dropped the phone in her lap and put her head in her hands.

"Are you still there?"

"Yes, I'm here."

"So I guess the way Lili's looking at you gives reason for the caption 'Aussie chef supplies star athlete with all the right ingredients'." He laughed.

"How can you make light of the situation?"

"It's not the first time you and your companions have been featured in social media."

"This is different."

"Well, I have to say you look happy. I mean, is there any truth in this? Lili looks like she's about to kiss you."

Jess closed her eyes. "She is special."

"Ah, and there you go," Jonathan said, a hint of resolve in his voice. "I'll wait until you're ready to tell me more, but I do urge you to warn Lili soon. There is a chance she will come upon the pictures."

"I will as soon as I can." Jess wouldn't make the same mistake twice. She had already upset Lili by not telling her about Simon's invitation to dinner at Ailie, tonight. "Lili has a really busy day ahead of her. She told me the restaurant is fully booked for lunch and dinner. She's got a lot on her plate."

"In that case, it's not likely she'll see anything today. Is this thing with Lili going to change your plans about coming home? What are you going to do?"

"I promise you when I know what I'm doing, I'll tell you."

"Okay. But just remember, I'm here for you."

"Yes. Thank you." Jess pushed herself up from the hard, cold rock and climbed back up the embankment. "I'll call you. Soon."

"You'd better. I don't want to read about it in the tabloids first," he said. "Good luck."

The call ended, and Jess stared at the picture of Lili and herself at Fed Square. They'd stopped under a sculpture of a huge metal bird, and Lili had pulled her under a wing. She *was* on the verge of kissing her. Jess shivered, recalling all that had happened since that kiss.

A gust of wind blew hair into her face, and she pushed it back over her shoulders. She closed her eyes and licked her lips. She could still taste her.

Chapter 26

"How do you feel about Jess dining with Haley tonight?" Alex asked Lili, as she peered through the small hatch that gave her a view across the bar into the dining room. "Did Owen seat them at table two so you can keep an eye on what they're up to?"

Lili untied her leather apron straps and retied the knot securely at her waist. "Jess is not dining *with* Haley. There is nothing going on between them," she said. "Simon invited Jess as his guest. I'm glad she is here, finally having a proper meal at Ailie. And we always seat VIPs at table two."

"Who are the other three women at the table?" Alex asked, still peeping through the hatch.

"Owen said they're pro cyclists, part of a group raising the profile of women's cycling in Australia," Lili answered. "Simon organised it."

"The cute woman with the short, dark hair sitting next to Jess looks familiar." Alex smirked. "I've seen her on TV."

Lili nudged Alex aside so she could check the other guests at Simon's table. "I don't recognise any of them."

"Well she definitely looks like she's on our team. I notice Haley managed to seat herself between the two most attractive women." Alex nudged Lili back. "How did things go last night after Tash and I left? How was the rest of your evening?"

"Good, thanks," Lili answered dismissively. Last night had been, well, incredible. But she wasn't going to discuss it at work, even with her best friend.

Alex turned around and scowled at Lili. "Good, thanks? That's it? You two looked ready to—"

Lili couldn't escape Alex's razor-sharp gaze. She starred back, unblinking, willing her to shut up about it.

"You did, didn't you? You really have slept with her." Alex reached out and squeezed her forearm. "I thought there was something different about you this morning. You came in all sparky."

Lili pressed her lips together, looking around to be sure they couldn't be overheard. Then she smiled. She couldn't help it. "Ah-ha."

Alex grinned. "I knew it. I'm happy for you, sweetheart," she said, in a low voice, giving Lili's arm a playful punch. "Just wow."

"Okay, okay." Lili gripped Alex's shoulder and steered her back to their workstations. "We can't talk now. Come on, they've nearly cleared first course. Get back on the line, woman."

Alex laughed, saluted, and play-marched to her station, right across from Lili. She stood with her back to the range, waiting for the next order. "Hey, it was inevitable. Attraction is an unstoppable force," she said over Lili's shoulder. "If you want to join Simon's party after we plate dessert, I can finish up."

"That's not going to happen."

The service door swung open with a whoosh as Drew, the casual server, strode into the kitchen, his tray stacked with dirty dishes.

"How's it going, Drew?"

"All good, Chef."

"I didn't have time earlier to thank you for coming in on such short notice."

"No problem, I'm glad to have the hours." He set the tray of empties on the returns bench. "Owen and Mei are looking after table two. Sort of strange having Haley out there as a guest, sitting with Jessica Harris, Simon and those pro cyclists. I'm glad I'm not serving them. I used to follow Simon when he was competing, and Jessica is just awesome. I hope she gets back to racing soon."

If another person pointed out that Jess was dining with Haley, Lili would scream. She fixed her eyes on the row of orders clipped in front of her and steadied her breathing. Naturally, Simon would include his sister, a wannabe cyclist herself. But what was the reason for the gathering tonight at Ailie?" She shrugged. Competitive cycling was Jess's world, one completely foreign to Lili.

Owen stuck his head through the bar hatch. "We'll be ready once Drew's finished clearing."

"On it, Owen." Drew straightened his jacket, picked up a clean tray, and headed through the doors.

"Ordering," Lili called. "Table two. Four scallops. Two ravioli."

"Heard that. Two ravioli, Chef," Nora confirmed from her station, next to Alex.

It would take Nora two minutes to poach the delicate goat's cheese dumplings and toss them with a smidgen of extra virgin olive oil. Lili was confident Nora had the experience to cook them to perfection. An extra thirty seconds would render the pasta stodgy and unacceptable.

"Heard. Four scallops," Alex called.

Lili watched Alex pull out the tray of plump sea scallops, pat them dry, season with pepper and sea salt, and place them into two pans sizzling with butter and a dash of olive oil.

On Lili's bench, four heated oblong dishes were lined up ready. She dropped three dollops of creamy fennel puree evenly spaced along each plate. When Alex transferred the seared scallops to Lili, the briny, buttery, sweet aroma tickled her nose. She pressed a scallop lightly with one finger. It was slightly translucent, crispy on the outside, but still tender to her touch. She set each golden morsel onto a puree circle with a sliver of grilled pancetta and trickled truffle butter over them. As Lili positioned the four dishes under heat lamps, Nora delivered the shallow bowls with ravioli and asparagus. Lili spooned red currant jelly cubes next to the slender asparagus stems, and as Owen stepped up to the kitchen pass, she criss-crossed lines of lemon vinaigrette cream over the small pasta envelopes.

"Table two. Good to go," Lili called, wiping a tiny dribble of sauce from the rim of a dish.

Owen expertly collected three plates in his right hand before picking up the fourth in his left. Mei stepped up beside him, lifted the ravioli bowls, and followed Owen into the dining room.

Wiping her hands on a tea towel, Lili read out the next order, "Ordering. Table four. Six scallops. Hold the truffle butter on one." The last bit of information was for herself, but she always read the whole order out aloud.

Lili remained focused and fully engaged during service, but after nearly three hours of plating, expediting, and helping with clean-up, she was flagging. There were moments when she'd allowed herself to remember last night. She hummed quietly and tapped rhythmically on the top of the bench with her fingers. It was tough having Jess so close and yet out of reach. There'd been no time tonight for her usual meet and greet, which was lucky because it would have been awkward. It had nothing to do with the hint of jealousy that shadowed her when she saw Jess and Haley together, despite what Jess had told her. At least that was what she told herself.

Lili's shoulders burned, her feet were sore, and her lower back cramped—not unusual after a hectic workday. Her thighs ached in an entirely different way, and that didn't surprise her, reminding her how long it had been since she'd spent the night with a woman. She yearned for another night with Jess. She ached to touch her and ached for her touch.

Perched on a stool at the end of the bench, Lili could just see Jess at table two, engaged in earnest conversation with the attractive woman beside her. She nearly jumped out of her skin when Alex tapped her knee.

"Sorry. I didn't mean to startle you," Alex said. "Whatcha doin'?"

"Just going through numbers with the new menu. The changes we made are producing minimal wastage." Lili reshuffled the already neat pile of order slips.

"Really? That's what you're doing? Looks to me like you are staring at Jess again." Alex placed a cup of black tea beside Lili, and, balancing a plate in her hand, hoisted herself up onto the kitchen bench. "You must be stuffed. I bet you didn't get much sleep last night." She waved a spoon of chocolate tart in front of Lili. "Want some of this?"

She opened wide, and Alex placed a spoonful of bitter tart into her mouth—a dense, creamy burst of energy.

"You need nourishment. It's been a long day," Alex said. "Your chocolate tart creation was popular at lunch. It went down a treat with the mandarin sorbet and honeycomb popcorn. I like it on its own—bitter and squidgy and so decadent." Alex lifted the remains of the tart with two fingers and popped it into her mouth. "Yum." She ducked her head and peered through the hatch. "*Are* you keeping tabs on her?"

Lili clipped the order slips together. She saved the open spreadsheet document with tonight's entries and closed her laptop. "They're the last table. Looks like Owen's in for a late finish. He's just served more coffee and port." Lili glanced around the empty kitchen. "Everyone else done?"

Alex nodded. "Apart from Owen and Mei out front, just Eddie out the back sorting the garbage."

Owen walked through the swing doors. "Here's a treat," he said, loosening his tie. He placed a half-empty bottle of red, three glasses, and his iPad on the bench near Alex. "Mei is giving you a lift home, isn't she, Alex? So you're okay to drink? How about you Lili?" He picked up the bottle and waved it in front of her. "It's a good one, shame to waste it."

Alex took the bottle out of his hand. "Yeah, not driving. Tash needed the car tonight." She peered at the label. "It's a 2015 Terindah Estate Shiraz. Should I pour one for you, Lili?"

Stifling a yawn, Lili shook her head. "Not tonight. Just one sip would put me to sleep." She stood and picked up her laptop. "I'll take this to the office. You still okay to lock up, Owen?"

"Yes, no problem," he said, and picked up the iPad he'd carried in from the bar. "Lili, you may want to look at this." His voice was calm, but insistent. "I was doing my usual check on social media to see if we featured on any of the sites. These pictures are on Twitter. Take a look." He pushed the device across the bench and turned it around to face her.

Lili narrowed her eyes. "That's Jess and Haley here tonight. And that woman next to Jess, what is her name?" She glanced up at Owen.

"Tara Green."

"And she is?"

"Founder of SwitchedOn Women's Racing, an Australian-based racing team," he said. "Simon mentioned it when he made the booking. The other two women are also part of the team."

Lili's eyes widened as she read out loud the hashtags under the picture, "#jessicaharris, #switchedonWR, #girlsonbikes."

Alex leaned over Lili's shoulder and read, "Is Aussie women's racing poaching Brit champion?" She tapped Lili's arm. "Did Jess tell you what the dinner was about?"

"Nope. She didn't really know," Lili answered. "Who is posting this stuff?"

"Let's check the Twitter handle on that," Alex said.

"Handle?"

"The username, in front of the line," Owen explained.

"You mean this? *Dot at cycleongirl.*" She pointed to the symbol and name preceding the line. "Why is there a full stop in front of the *at* symbol?"

"It's a Twitter thing. A full stop in front allows all followers to see the post." Owen shrugged his shoulders. "Could be posted by a fan of Jess's. Scroll down a bit, Lili, but be prepared, because you're not going to like what you see. Whoever cycleongirl is, she's reposted Instagram photos and retweeted from other sources to her post."

Lili pressed on the first link. The image that appeared was of Aruishi, Jess, and herself in Queenscliff. "How the hell did someone get this photo? No one was around that evening at the wharf."

"Tash and I didn't take any photos," Alex said. "Someone must be following Jess."

The caption made Lili wince. *Ready-made family.* "How do they know Ru is her niece? It's just bad. People shouldn't post pictures of children without permission." She opened the second link and zeroed in on the picture of herself and Jess in Federation Square. "There were scores of people in the square. Anyone could have snapped this. But why?" She put the iPad down on the bench in disgust.

Owen handed Lili a glass of wine. She accepted it gladly and took a large mouthful.

"Maybe this is to be expected. There is heaps of stuff about Jess out there in the media," Alex said. "Remember, you told me about it before she even got here."

"On her, yes." Lili downed the rest of her wine in one gulp. "But not me, and definitely not Ru. Jess should have warned me."

"Lili, this is not Jess's fault," Owen said. "She probably hasn't seen these yet. Anyone could have posted those photos. Cycleongirl is probably taking advantage of Jess's notability to attract more followers."

"But the photo taken here, at Ailie, had to be posted by one of the guests." Lili picked up the device again and peered at the screen.

Alex lifted the iPad out of Lili's hand. "Yes, and counting Simon's table, there were forty-four guests tonight. Everyone uses their phones to take pictures of the food, themselves, each other, and the restaurant to post stuff on Facebook, Instagram, Twitter, and YouTube."

"Alex is right, Lili," Owen said. "And people like, share, and repost constantly. Must be hell for anyone trying to keep a low profile."

Owen and Alex were spot-on about the lack of respect of people's privacy. Jess had travelled across the world to settle her brother's estate.

Wasn't she allowed to have a private life of any sort? But the meeting with the Australian team indicated there was more going on with Jess. Things she hadn't yet shared with Lili. What was she planning?

Owen looked at his watch and adjusted his tie and jacket. "I'd best go and see if table two are ready to settle up."

Lili nodded. "Thanks, Owen."

"Oh shit," Alex said, making a hissing sound through her teeth.

"What now?"

Alex clutched the iPad to her chest with both hands.

"Just show me."

"It's probably not what it looks like. You know what people are like at a nightclub. Moody music, dim lights, and all that."

"Alex. What is it?" Lili slapped her palm, down on the bench. "Show me."

She passed the device to Lili. "Okay, if you insist."

Lili looked at the screen and bit her lower lip. Haley and Jess on the dance floor. Kissing. It looked intense. Their bodies were pressed together. Haley held Jess around her waist, and Jess had her hand on her shoulder. It wasn't a chaste kiss.

She sat down heavily on the kitchen stool. "That was a while ago. She was a free agent." Lili gave a resigned moan. "Like you said, things happen in clubs." She *had* seen them kissing in the car. But that was then.

"Yeah, things do happen in clubs," Alex said. She put her arm around Lili's shoulder. "Don't worry about it."

They both turned as the swing doors opened.

"Hi, Alex, hi, Lili," Jess said in a happy sing-song voice, her face lit up with a wide grin.

"Hello, Jess." Alex propped herself against the bench.

Jess approached them with a spring in her step. Her eyes danced, bright, almost eager. "Thank you both. I had a great evening. The food was delicious. I'll definitely be back again." She sidled over to stand closer to Lili. The ivory rib-knit top she wore was draped about her neck. It flowed down over her shoulders, sat snug around her breasts, and hung loose over her hips. Her hands were tucked into the side pockets of her black pleated trousers. Jess looked dazzling even under the kitchen's LED downlights, and Lili was at a loss for words.

This morning, Jess had taken off for a bike ride even before Lili was out of bed and probably cycled for sixty or seventy kilometres. Yet, here, she stood bright-eyed and bushy-tailed. Where did she get her energy?

"Have the others left?" Alex asked.

"Most of them. Haley and Simon are still here."

Lili flinched. For a moment, she'd been so hypnotised by Jess, she'd forgotten about the photos.

"Is it okay to catch a ride back to your place? Haley did offer, but if you don't mind, I'd rather go home with you."

An ache formed in the back of Lili's throat. She drew her bottom lip between her teeth as Jess's warm fingers closed around her forearm.

"We're all done, aren't we, Lili?" Alex asked, raising an eyebrow. "I have to wait for Mei, anyway. Why don't you two take off?" She grabbed the empty wine bottle and glasses from the bench. While heading for the dining room, she turned back to face them. "Lili, I'll talk to you tomorrow." Her gaze darted to Jess. "Um, have a good night, you two." The doors swung closed.

Jess seemed so happy, oblivious to the social media circus she'd created. It would be a shame to spoil her mood. Lili knew she could be short-tempered when overtired, and she was running on empty. The last thing she wanted was a confrontation.

"Hey, Lili?" Jess's voice interrupted her thoughts. Her hand brushed along the bare skin of Lili's forearm.

"Yes?" Lili shivered and met Jess's dark, penetrating gaze.

"How are you holding up? You've worked all day, after very little sleep."

Lili blinked; she couldn't ignore the genuine concern in Jess's eyes. "Yes, very little sleep," she repeated, smiling wearily.

"Is Aruishi staying over with your parents tonight?" Jess asked. "Will you be able to sleep in tomorrow morning?"

"Yes, she's at Mum and Dad's all night. I knew it would be a late finish." Even though she was exhausted, she'd hoped to make the most of a night alone with Jess. Not a total repeat of last night—even though, up to half an hour ago, she could have been persuaded. She'd wanted to fall asleep with her arms around Jess, or Jess's body spooned against hers. Now, she wasn't sure. It seemed like their bubble of uncomplicated joy had already burst.

She stood and collected her laptop from the bench. "I have to get my keys. Why don't you say goodnight to the others, and I'll meet you at the car?"

"Okay. I'll see you out the back."

Lili walked towards her office but stopped when Jess called her name. She turned, surprised to find Jess at her side. "Yes?"

"Are you sure everything's okay?" Jess asked.

She glanced down where Jess's hand rested on her hip. Lili stared up at her. "Yes. It's been a really long day."

Jess raised her hand and lightly stroked her thumb across Lili's cheek. She leaned in and kissed her. It was a soft caress. Just a brushing of Jess's lips against hers.

"I'll be ready in five minutes," Lili said, and stepped back out of reach. She turned and walked into her office.

After closing the door behind her, she placed the laptop into her bag and sank into the office chair. The photo in the nightclub was disturbing, but Jess wasn't sleeping with Haley, so she'd have to get over it. The glimpses she'd had of Simon's party gave Lili the impression of an animated group hatching a plan. She had noticed Jess and Tara Green engaged in an intense conversation. Was there any truth in the caption? Was something brewing between Jess and the Australian team? It was frustrating not having a clue what Jess's plans were. Lili had no idea when she intended to return to London.

They were growing closer, but Lili was prepared for the fact that Jess would leave eventually. If Jess was thinking of changing her plans, why didn't she share them with Lili?

It was less than a ten-minute drive back to Lili's house, but as each minute passed with no communication, Jess became more anxious. When they reached the house, the awkward silence still hung between them, broken only by the faint roar of the sea in the distance. At the top of the landing the sensor lights illuminated the deck, and Lili fumbled with the key before Jess heard it slide into the lock. Lili swung the door open, not bothering to switch on the entrance hall light, and strode down the hallway. Jess pushed the door closed and peered after Lili's silhouette, lit by moonlight filtering through the large window at the end of the hall. Lili stopped, and Jess clicked on the light just as she turned around to face her. She looked like she wanted to run, or cry—or both.

"Lili, why haven't you spoken to me? You didn't say a word in the car."

Lili held up her hand. "I'm just overtired. I need to have a shower and go to bed."

"*Rubbish*. There is something wrong. Do you regret sleeping with me? Are you having second thoughts?" She knew her voice was unnecessarily raised, but she couldn't help it.

"No. No, I don't." Lili's voice cracked, and she looked down at her feet. "Jess, there are pictures all over social media. Of you and Haley. Of us. And Aruishi." She looked at Jess with a frown, as though accusing her of something.

Jess pressed her eyes shut for a moment. Damn. Lili had seen the bloody pictures. She should have told her.

Lili pulled her phone out of her pocket, tapped on the screen, strode over to Jess, and held it under her nose. "Look at this. You haven't bothered to share with me, but what you're up to is all over Twitter and Instagram. According to this site, you are romantically linked with two women, having a whale of a time down under." Lili lifted the phone out of Jess's reach and jabbed her finger at the screen. "This is what it says, and I quote, 'Not only does the alluring athlete like to flex her muscles with an attractive young Aussie cyclist, she has found time to throw herself onto a hot grill with Bellarine Peninsula chef.' And it goes on."

Lili narrowed her eyes and tilted her head to one side. "I should have known. You're twenty-nine years old, for crying out loud. You'll go back to England, go back to your friends and social whirl, and think, well, that was a bit of fun, what's next?"

Jess's heart pounded in her chest. "What are you talking about? You know me, Lili. Does that really sound like me? You know there's nothing going on with Haley. I don't think you're being very fair. I can't control what's posted on those sites." Jess shoved her hands in her pockets. "People make up all kinds of things."

"You were definitely kissing Haley." Lili waved the phone in front of Jess. "That wasn't made up, was it? And in the car when you got home."

Well, Lili had seen them kiss in the car. Damn. There was no point denying it. "That was before anything happened between you and me," she said. "We were in a nightclub and—"

"Yes, I know. Things happen in nightclubs."

Jess took a step closer, and Lili cut her off with a wave of her hand. "Anyway, what's going on with the Australian cycling team? Aren't you still rehabilitating? As far as I know, you're based in London. You haven't bothered to share your new plans with me."

"I don't *have* any new plans yet. But even if I did, why would a plan to stay here closer to you and Aruishi be a bad thing? Don't you think *you're* being unreasonable under the circumstances? I wasn't aware of Simon's agenda. It was a friendly get-together with fellow racers. I didn't know they would approach me. As you pointed out, I'm not in top form. I'm still recovering, and I've got to look at all my options."

Lili expelled a long breath, turned away, and walked over to the window at the end of the hall. She slumped against the frame and pressed her forehead to the glass.

"What do you want from me?" Jess asked quietly, wishing Lili would look at her. "We slept together. That's what we both wanted. You think it's okay to sleep with me and keep it secret from your family." She lifted her chin. "I respected your wishes and did what you asked. I haven't told anyone about us."

Lili turned around to face her but still wouldn't make eye contact.

"So, let's leave it at that, if that's what you want," Jess said, shrugging. "We slept together."

Lili crossed her arms in front of her chest. "I didn't want to tell anyone we're sleeping together because you don't even know how long you'll be here." Her voice dropped to a whisper, "Dani kept things from me, and I didn't pick up the signs until it was too late.

"I am not Dani. I'm sorry she did that to you." Jess rubbed her hands over her thighs. "I honestly didn't know Tara and the cycling team were going to approach me tonight. I didn't know what to expect when I came back here to settle Ben's estate. I thought I'd be out of here within two weeks." She looked towards Aruishi's bedroom. "I didn't know I had a niece. I didn't know I'd meet *you.*"

"That's just the problem. You don't know anything," Lili said with a deep sigh. "This is too hard for me."

"Too hard for you? So, what does this thing between us mean?" Jess swallowed the lump in her throat as Lili finally met her gaze. "Does it mean enough to you to tell your parents about us? Does it mean enough to tell Aruishi?"

Lili rested her head in her hand. Finally, she looked up again. "I think it's best for all of us if we stop this now." Lili looked totally crestfallen, but her words were clear. Her eyes softened. "You have decisions to make. They are *your* decisions to make. You've had a tough time, but you're on the mend. The way things are going, you'll soon be back in top form. Racing again," she said. "Cycling is your life. I've been selfish wanting to keep you here. It's been wonderful for Ru, and for me. But you have a life I can't compete with."

Jess blinked back her tears. She wanted to pull Lili close and comfort her. She'd looked forward to having the house to themselves and making love to Lili—slowly, unhurriedly, and holding her while she slept.

"I'm going to bed before I fall over." Lili pushed herself away from the window. "I'll see you tomorrow." She walked towards her bedroom, then stopped and turned back to Jess—her expression unreadable. She hesitated at the door for a moment, pushed it open, lowered her head, and was gone.

Jess stared out into the night. A sliver of moon was shrouded in thick cloud. Lili was right; she had urgent decisions to make. She placed her forehead against the window glass where, minutes ago, Lili's face had rested. The window was icy cold. A shiver ran down her spine.

Cycling competitively had taught Jess some important lessons that could be applied to life in general, ones that had helped her get past the harsh clutches of uncertainty she'd experienced throughout her youth, paralysed by self-doubt and the fear of her father's disapproval. Cycling had taught her that sometimes in the peloton you relaxed and coasted along in the slipstream, while at other times you gave it all you had and jockeyed for front position.

If she wanted Lili and Aruishi in her future, she had to give it her all to convince Lili she was worth the risk.

Chapter 27

LILI LAY ON THE COUCH with her head propped in her hand. The two pain killers she'd swallowed earlier had barely taken the edge off the persistent drumming in her skull. She lifted her head as she heard the front door open, and Aruishi's high-pitched squeal was accompanied by the fast thudding of her footsteps as she ran along the wooden floorboards into the living room. Lili grabbed the end of her T-shirt and wiped her eyes, then quickly folded Jess's note and tucked it into the side pocket of her grey sweatpants. The note explained simply that Jess would stay overnight at Usha's, as she had an early ultrasound appointment tomorrow with her sports physician in Drysdale. The friendly tone of the note made her feel worse about the way she'd treated Jess last night. She pushed herself up and swung her bare feet over the side of the couch onto the floor.

Aruishi threw herself on top of Lili.

"Oomph." Lili fell back against the cushions.

"Mama, I'm here," Aruishi announced, wrapping her arms around Lili's neck. "I love you."

Lili closed her eyes and gave her daughter a fierce hug. "I love you more."

"No, I love you more." Aruishi giggled and patted Lili's cheeks. "Why are your eyes red? You look sad, but I'm home now, so you can be happy."

Taking a deep breath, she lifted Aruishi onto her lap and kissed the top of her head. "I'm okay, munchkin. I missed you."

"Morning, Lili," Scott called from the hallway, his voice echoing through the house. "Where did that little rascal get to?"

"We're in here, Dad," Lili called back. She stood up carefully with Aruishi still clinging to her. "Thanks for bringing—oh, hi, Mum."

Helen walked towards Lili, rustling the contents of a brown paper bag. "Ru helped me make muffins this morning," she said, holding the bag up in front of Lili.

"They smell delicious. Apple and honey?"

"Yes." Helen nodded. "Apple, honey, and oat. How about I put the kettle on?" She walked towards the kitchen. "Cup of tea, anyone?"

Aruishi jumped up from the couch. "Maybe Auntie Jess would like a muffin? I'll go ask her."

Lili grabbed her hand. "Wait a minute, Ru."

"You won't find Jess here," Scott said. "She was away early this morning. I spotted the Jeep when I opened the top gate for the cows. It had that fancy bike of hers on the rack." He patted Aruishi's shoulder. "You can save one for Jess and give it to her when she comes home from her ride, darling."

Aruishi looked at Scott and frowned. "Just one? She'll be hungry. Jess goes very fast."

"Jess has gone for a big ride and is staying overnight at Usha's," Lili said. "We'll save her a muffin for tomorrow."

"Are you sure, Mama? She didn't tell me she wasn't coming home tonight."

Lili combed her fingers through Aruishi's soft hair. "Maybe you can ring her later today," she said, giving Aruishi a gentle nudge towards the kitchen. "Let's help Gran make a pot of tea."

Lili carried the tea tray and followed her mother out onto the deck. Helen sat down on the bench seat and Lili placed the tray in front of her. She pulled her sunglasses from the top of her head, slid them onto her face, and adjusted the umbrella to give Helen some shade at the table.

"Look at those two, they're having their own tea party," Helen said.

Aruishi and Scott sat cross-legged on the deck. Aruishi lifted her tiny melamine tea pot and pretended to pour tea into his matching polka-dot cup.

He lifted the cup with his little finger extended and made loud slurping noises.

"That's not how you hold it, Papa. Do it like this." She instructed, using her thumb and index finger to pinch in between the handle, and sipped delicately from her own cup.

"Well, excuse me," he said in a posh English accent.

"Unlike my husband, I prefer the real thing," Helen said, taking the cup Lili handed her.

They sat at the table for a few minutes watching Aruishi entertain Scott.

A cloud blocked the sun, and Lili pushed her sunglasses on top of her head. "When Jess and I took Ru to the Hi-vis shop in Geelong to pick up that funky little vest Jess ordered in for her, they thought she was Jess's daughter," she said. The incident had taken her by surprise.

"People see what they want to see and make assumptions," Helen said. "With your fair colouring and blue eyes, it wouldn't register immediately that you are Aruishi's mother."

"Yeah. People do make assumptions." Talking about Jess brought tears to her eyes. Lili should have known to steer well away from the subject. She replaced her sunglasses before her mother noticed her watery eyes.

"You're not hiding much behind those sunglasses, you know," Helen said carefully. "I could tell you'd been crying when we got here. Want to talk about it?"

Lili shook her head. She wasn't ready to tell her mother what had been going on between her and Jess.

"You always get a little melancholy just before your birthday. Is that what this is?"

"No, it's just another day." The truth was, she'd barely given her birthday a moment's thought.

Aruishi was now dancing around Scott doing pirouettes, making Lili dizzy just to watch her.

"Ru's excited about your birthday. She's got things planned."

That brought a smile to Lili's face. "Is that why she asked you to take her to Geelong?"

"Correct. But I've been sworn to secrecy, so don't ask any questions. When will Jess be back from Usha's?"

"Tomorrow, I think. She has an appointment at the Sports Clinic in Drysdale for an ultrasound in the morning."

"An ultrasound? Is something wrong?"

"It's just to check her progress, and Jess uses the gym at the clinic. She's been working out with one of the sports physicians who has a background in cycling."

"Has Jess told you when she's going back? Is that what you're upset about?" Helen fixed her with a penetrating gaze.

Had her mother guessed there was something going on between them? She didn't know what to say. After having pushed Jess into a corner last night, she wouldn't be surprised if Jess left very soon. She bit her bottom lip and averted her gaze. Sunlight sparkled like tiny jewels on the bay.

She was falling in love with Jess. There—she'd finally admitted it to herself.

"Fine, I'll stop beating around the bush, shall I?" Helen asked. "Last night, Ru confided that she saw you kissing Jess in the secret garden. She was up in the treehouse."

Lili turned back to Helen, wide-eyed. "She did? What did she say exactly? Was she upset?"

"No. She didn't seem upset," Helen said. "She said it was funny, and that you and Jess laughed a lot. I've wondered for some time if you have feelings for her. But she'll go back to London, eventually, won't she? What does that mean for you? Do you know how Jess feels?"

"I don't know, and I don't know when she plans to go back." She sighed. "Actually, we had a fight about it."

"A fight?"

"Look, Mum, there are pictures on social media, of Jess with me and Ru. And other photos. I didn't know about them till last night—"

"What kind of pictures?" Helen interrupted. Her eyes narrowed.

Lili glanced at her father, who'd turned towards them at the sound of Helen's raised voice. She reached for her mother's hand across the table. "Mum, hold on," she said. "They weren't that bad. The picture of Ru was taken in Queenscliff on the pier. It's of us swinging her in the air."

"But how did this happen? Is Jess being followed?" Helen asked, keeping her voice low. "I want to see them."

"I'm sure you won't be able to escape them soon. The articles and pictures insinuate that Jess is playing the field with women here."

"What do you mean, 'playing the field'? Who with? I assume you are one of the women."

"Yes, but there is a picture of Jess kissing Haley. Or Haley kissing Jess. Whatever."

"You mean our Haley?" Helen scowled. "No wonder you are upset. Is Jess sleeping with Haley?"

"*Shush*. No, Mum. She isn't. The kiss thing happened at the nightclub when they went to Melbourne. Jess said it wasn't anything. There is also a Twitter post of me and her in Fed Square."

"Of you two kissing?" Helen asked, raising her eyebrows.

"It may as well have been."

"Okay, then." Helen nodded sagely. "So, if the picture with Haley was nothing, why were you and Jess arguing?"

"Because last night, Jess had dinner with Simon and his guests from the women's racing circuit. According to Twitter, the rumours are that an Australian team is trying to recruit her. She hadn't even told me that she's considering staying, or joining a team here."

"Well, are you sure the rumour is true? Is that what Jess told you? You should ask her what her plans are. That would be the simplest solution."

"That's the problem, Mum, I tried to," Lili said, "and she couldn't tell me. She is unsure of so many things."

"I know that must be disconcerting, but Jess has a lot on her plate. She's dealing with Ben's death and settling his estate. She's still recovering from her injuries. It can't be easy having to cope with so much. On top of that, she found out about Ru."

Lili clutched her teacup, then quickly placed it down on the table. "And that's another thing. I know she adores Ru, but when she goes, Ru will be devastated."

Helen turned towards her granddaughter. "God knows, she thinks Jess is a cross between Wonder Woman and the princess from *Brave*, on a superfast bike." She turned back to Lili. "Does Jess know?"

"What?"

"That you're in love with her?"

Lili tightened her arms against her chest. "Oh, Mum." She loosened her grip and sighed. "I was stupid to react to the photos the way I did. It wasn't Jess's fault someone posted a picture of Ru. But what about her dinner with the Australian racing team? What's that about? I don't know what's going on with her. She doesn't share things," Lili whispered.

She'd convinced herself letting Jess go was the right thing to do—ending what they had before she got in deeper and left herself wide open for hurt. All the same, she ached with regret whenever she thought about it.

"Every day I've been expecting her to say she's leaving," Lili said, gazing across the rolling valley to the sweeping expanse of ocean.

"You need to tell her how you feel, Lili. She could have gone home by now. Ben's estate is all but settled, and Jess has agreed to Nathan and his girlfriend's request for a one-year lease on the shack when they return from South America. I didn't think she'd stay this long. You must have asked yourself why she has. Maybe it has something to do with Ru. And you."

Lili looked up into her mother's searching eyes. "She does care a lot about Ru." But just because she'd bonded with her niece didn't mean Lili had allowed herself to imagine Jess would want to stay *for her*.

"It's not just about Ru, though, is it?" Helen asked. "You and Ru, me and Scott—we're Jess's family now. And Usha. That must mean something?"

"I don't know, Mum."

Jess could probably do just about anything she put her mind to, even the Tour de France, so why was she so indecisive about her future?

While they'd been chatting, Scott and Aruishi had moved to the table and helped themselves to the remaining muffin. Aruishi stood on the bench across from Lili, nibbling her piece slowly.

Scott perched himself on the seat next to Helen and placed one hand over hers. "Everything all right here, girls?" he asked.

Lili wanted to kick herself. She should have told Jess how she felt, but what if her feelings weren't reciprocated? Their physical attraction was definitely mutual—an already intoxicating sexual connection. But for her, it went beyond that. Lili hadn't met anyone since Dani who was worth the effort, or the risk, of something more.

If she wanted this, she had to be brave, didn't she? To take a chance and risk Jess's rejection. That was, if she wasn't already too late.

The cadence sensor on the bicycle's GPS confirmed Jess's pedal revolutions per minute were continuing to improve. Her rhythm had returned, and her legs were a lot stronger. She felt great. Assuming the diagnostic ultrasound scheduled for tomorrow gave her encouraging results, she'd contact Tara Green and arrange a meeting to find out what exactly they had to offer.

Jess was at the tail end of her forty-nine-kilometre ride. Her bicycle tyres hissed on the wet asphalt as she rode into a headwind along 13th Beach Road near Barwon Heads. The brief spring rain shower had passed, and sunlight peeped through the clouds, streaming across the river estuary and the broad ocean beach with its huge crashing waves. She steered around a surfer strapping his board to the top of his utility, and headed in the direction of the Point Lonsdale Lighthouse where she'd parked the Jeep.

During her ride, she'd thought long and hard about Lili's accusations. It was obvious why Lili was frustrated and didn't trust her. In road racing, Jess learned to handle the ups and downs and unexpected obstacles. But Lili's outburst last night about her indecisiveness had momentarily stopped her in her tracks. She had procrastinated long enough.

It was just after five o'clock when she knocked on Usha's door.

"Jess, come in," Usha said with a welcoming smile as she beckoned her into the house. "Have you been listening to the radio? There's a storm blowing in across Port Phillip Bay." She drew Jess in for a quick a hug. "I worried you'd be out on one of your hundred-kilometre rides and get caught in the downpour."

"It was forty-nine-point-five kilometres," Jess said, and smiled at Usha's exaggeration. She followed her into the living room. "There were light showers earlier, but it's bright and sunny now. No sign of rain."

"Well, it is coming very soon," Usha said. "The rain app on my phone predicts a heavy downfall, accompanied by gale force winds, thunder, and lightning."

At that news, Jess exhaled with relief. She should have taken more notice of the forecast, instead of rushing out of Lili's house early this morning, unprepared for a change of weather. "Even more reason to be here, in your warm welcoming home," she said.

"It is nice to have you stay." Usha picked up Jess's overnight bag and then put it down again. She tapped her forehead. "I almost forgot. You hoped it would arrive in time for Lili's birthday, and it is here." She walked to the dresser near the front door and returned holding a yellow-and-white package. "It's arrived. Oh, and do you want to change out of your riding gear? We can put your things in the guest room too."

Jess took the parcel from Usha and tucked it under her arm. "Thank you. That's fantastic. And yes, I wouldn't mind a quick shower, if that's okay?" She tugged at her bib shorts and jersey before picking up her bag. "Sweaty post-ride lycra."

"Yes, of course, make yourself at home. There is an en suite for you through here." She indicated the door inside the bedroom, between an antique carved wardrobe and a small writing desk. "You are very colourful in your cycling gear, but I don't know how you wear that skin-tight elasticised clothing." Her eyes twinkled with amusement. "I will leave you to have your shower. When you are ready, there is a nice red wine waiting for me to pour. Then we can talk about dinner and what you'd like me to cook for you."

"Usha, you didn't want me to take you out, but you did agree to a takeaway meal," Jess said. "And considering the storm, it's a good idea to have it delivered. That way we're safe and will have plenty of time to talk. I need your advice."

"Okay, okay, child." Usha held up her hands and tilted her head from side to side. "We will talk and have takeaway, if you insist. I have some menus in the kitchen drawer. Will pizza suit? Or do you need more protein after your long ride?"

"I fuelled up with a protein smoothie this afternoon, so we can have whatever you wish."

"Good, all settled, then. Pizza it is." As she pulled the door closed behind her, she said, "Take your time."

Jess unzipped the overnight bag, took out her change of clothes, and laid them on the bed, alongside the small package. She collected her toiletries, stepped into the en suite, and flicked on the light. Usha was right about the coming storm. Out of the small bathroom window, Jess saw how the sun had retreated behind a thick bank of clouds. The wind had picked up, and she heard the creaking sound trees made when branches scraped against each other. She quickly shed her clothing, wrapped her arms around herself as she shivered, and stepped under the welcoming hot water. Another thunderstorm. She was relieved Usha's home was cosy, a shelter from the storm.

About a half hour later, Jess was flicking her damp braid over her shoulder and sitting down on the sofa across from Usha, who handed her a glass of wine and glanced at her watch. "Our pizza should have been here by now. I expect the storm has caused the delay."

"At least we're safe," she said, raising her glass to Usha. "I still can't bear these spring storms, but if I'm considering staying here, I'll have to get used to them."

Usha stared, wide-eyed. "Oh Jess, are you really contemplating moving back to Australia?"

Jess nodded slowly. "Hmm. I can't imagine being truly happy anywhere else." She really couldn't. "But do you think I'm doing the right thing?"

Usha tapped her fingers on the rim of her glass. "It would be wonderful, but what if it doesn't work out? I mean, with Lili?" She regarded her with a shrewd gaze. "You've had a difficult time this year, adjusted to many changes. It's a risk, Jess."

"It's one I'm willing to take. I've never been so sure of anything before. I know Lili and I can make things work." Jess sat up straighter in her chair. "Since my father died, I have no direct family in England, only my cousin in France, but we've never been close. Even though Lili is the catalyst, she's not the only reason I want to come...home."

"You won't be able to cut off your life over there," Usha said, concern in her voice. "What about your team, your manager, your friends? Won't you miss them?"

"I will, but cycling teams, no matter what country of origin, are truly international, fielding riders from everywhere. Whichever team I race for in future, I will have to travel and spend time away. That's one of the great things about competitive cycling, Usha, you meet up with friends all over the world. Anyway, I'm exploring all my options here."

"I'm going to refill our glasses. This happy news calls for another toast," Usha said with a huge grin, just as a loud hammering sounded at the door. "Our pizza has arrived."

Jess exhaled, and as her hand trembled, she placed her wine glass down on the coffee table beside her. Saying the words out loud was the first step. Now, she had to make it happen.

Chapter 28

WHAT THE HELL WAS THAT? Lili sat bolt upright, awakened suddenly by a loud boom. Brilliant flashes of light shot through the open blinds, momentarily illuminating the living room. She stretched out her numb, tingly arm, rubbing it vigorously. Falling asleep on the couch was not very smart. A few seconds later, another even louder rumble rolled across the valley. Wind roared through the eaves and heavy rain pelted the tin roof, sounding like hundreds of marbles rolling over the corrugated surface.

The second bolt of lightning came with a resounding crack, and streaks of silver danced across the sky, followed by a few seconds of complete silence as the room was plunged into darkness. Power out.

"Mama, Mama." Aruishi's cry could only just be heard above the storm.

Lili jumped to her feet, reached for her phone, swiped the torch icon, and used the light to guide her way to her daughter's room. Aruishi enjoyed the drama of a thunder storm during the day, but they really spooked her at night.

Although the power failure nightlight had come on automatically and Aruishi's room was bathed in a soft light, Lili couldn't see her daughter. "Ru, Mummy's here. Are you hiding? Where are you?" She moved quickly towards the bed.

"Mummy." Aruishi's soft whisper had escaped from a small mound under the bedclothes.

Lili perched on the side of Aruishi's bed, lifted one corner of the blanket and peered under. "I see Princess Teddy's with you," she said as two pairs of eyes stared back—one pair glassy and unblinking.

Aruishi had her arms securely around the pink soft toy. "She doesn't like the noise. I'm protecting her."

A bright flash of lightning lit the room, followed by rumbling thunder.

Aruishi huddled further under the covers. "Ooh, that's loud," she whimpered.

Lili lifted the bedclothes, squeezed in beside Aruishi and pulled the covers over them. She illuminated the small space using the phone torch. "This is cosy," she said, putting her arm around Aruishi. "Clackety-boom. Clackety-boom. Just like in your book *Rumble Boom.*"

"It is loud. Thunder and lightning just like in that story. Teddy is afraid of the thunder." Aruishi rolled on top of Lili and tucked her head under Lili's chin.

Lili tightened her arms around Aruishi and Princess Teddy. "In the story, the little boy and his puppy were safe in Mummy's bed, just like we're safe in here." She kissed the top of Aruishi's head. "Listen to the sound of rain on the roof. Do you remember what I told you about thunder?"

"It's just the sound that lightning makes."

"That's right, and the rain is good for the trees and our vegetables. The storm is feeding the plants." If it didn't create a flood, the rain would set off a massive growth spurt in the vegetable gardens.

"Mama." Aruishi's voice was a little panicky. She lifted her head, and gripped Lili's arm tightly. "Is Auntie Jess home safe?"

Lili covered Aruishi's small hand with her own. "Jess is safe. Remember, she's at Usha's house tonight."

"She should be here with us."

Lili was sure Jess had chosen to spend the night with Usha to give herself space. Why would she want to be around Lili, who'd accused her of being indecisive and ambivalent?

Aruishi's eyes fluttered closed and her head nestled into her pillow. Lili shifted her cramped arm and turned on her side, towards her daughter. Aruishi had phoned Jess at lunchtime to remind her about the birthday dinner tomorrow night. She hoped Jess would still come.

Jess hated storms, and she would be okay with Usha, but Lili wished she was home with her and Aruishi. She stared at her phone screen for a moment, unsure, then hit the messenger app and typed out a text before she changed her mind.

Hope you are safe. Ru, Princess Teddy, and I are in bed, huddled together. Your niece is worried about you and wants to know why

*you are not here. I'm sorry you're not here with us. We hope to see
you at dinner tomorrow night. You will come, won't you?*

Lili lowered the blankets under her chin, tucked them carefully around
Aruishi, and clutched her phone, waiting for a reply. Rain beat a steady
pattern on the rooftop. The wind had died down, but there was still the
intermittent flicker of lightning and rolling claps of thunder.

She kissed Aruishi lightly on her forehead and snuggled closer to her
sleeping daughter. Still no reply from Jess.

Lili had fallen asleep on the couch at eight-thirty, and it was now two
hours shy of her birthday. Running her fingers gently over Aruishi's back,
Lili let out a slow, deep breath. She already had so much—was it selfish to
want more? To want compassion, intimacy, and a future with Jess? But what
would a future—a relationship—with Jess mean? Even if Jess was willing to
give it a try, was Lili prepared for life with an elite athlete? How would she
handle the times Jess would spend away chasing her dreams? How would
she cope with her fame and public status?

The softness of the mattress, the warmth of the sheets, Aruishi's steady
breathing, and the soothing sound of rain distracted Lili from her worries
and lulled her into a restful state. She let her mind drift, imagining Jess's
gaze upon her. How her dark eyes grew ebony just before she kissed her,
and how her long, thick eyelashes tickled her skin. Lili closed her eyes. She
knew what she wanted for her birthday, what she wished for.

Chapter 29

JESS PRACTICALLY SKIPPED OUT OF the Sports Clinic. The diagnostic ultrasound showed definitive improvement of ligaments, tendons, and muscles around the knee surgery, and her clavicle was fully healed. She'd survived the prodding and poking from the stress and strength tests carried out by the sports physician. These were small steps, but she was moving forward in her recovery and beginning to feel like an athlete again.

Doctor Johnson had recommended Jess begin low-intensity pulsed ultrasound therapy on her anterior cruciate ligament reconstruction. The therapy would fully heal the tendon graft in the bone tunnel, allowing Jess to continue her aggressive rehabilitation to pre-injury activity.

Jess climbed into the Jeep, tossed her satchel on the passenger seat, and remembered she'd turned her phone off at the clinic. The phone powered up and pinged with two incoming messages. They were from last night. There must have been a problem with transmission during the storm. One was from Helen, the other from Lili, sent at 10.30.

What did she mean, *you will come, won't you?* Of course she'd be there. She quickly replied.

> *Sorry. Just got your message. Last night was a bit hair raising, but I survived. Thank you. I will be at your birthday party tonight!*

She attached a dozen silly birthday emoji's and a row of smiley faces. Next, she phoned Helen. "What should I bring with me?" she asked.

"Just yourself," Helen replied.

"Where is Lili today? I expect she's working?"

"Yes. The birthday girl is in the storeroom at Ailie, working on inventory with Alex."

She smiled. "Why am I not surprised. Thanks, Helen. I'll see you this evening." Jess finished the call, set her phone aside, and turned the key in the ignition.

Half an hour later, she turned left off the main road at Faodail Farm and left again up the long gravel drive that led straight to the restaurant. She'd passed Alex in her red car travelling the other way, a kilometre up the road, meaning Lili would be there by herself, if she hadn't already left.

Jess leaned back against the headrest and took in a deep breath. The back seat of the car held a large bouquet of snapdragons, sea holly, and coral rosebuds, with flowering wild mint, purple basil, and raspberry greens. The florist had gone overboard when Jess suggested an earthy combination to suit Lili's wholesome cheffy sensibilities. The fragrance was delicious, and the arrangement was colourful and fun.

Warm sunshine streamed through the Jeep windows, intensifying the perfume and making it a bit overpowering in the confined space. Jess rolled down the window fully, rested her elbow on the window ledge, and enjoyed the breeze dancing over her bare arm.

A nervous laugh escaped her, and she moistened her lips with the tip of her tongue. Her throat was suddenly dry. So many things depended on Lili's response, her willingness to take a risk on Jess and to trust her. She couldn't imagine making such monumental changes in her life, if there wasn't trust on both sides.

In the rear-vision mirror, she caught sight of a shadowy figure in the bushy trees to her left, fast approaching the Jeep. She eased her foot off the accelerator and slowed to a crawl. She stuck her head out the window to greet the black-and-white dog that approached the car and barked loudly. Pulling over onto the grassy verge she greeted Rhona, Scott's dog. "What's the matter, girl?" she called as Rhona yipped, barked, and whined, then turned on her tail and took off towards the restaurant. Rhona was never without Scott. She was clearly distressed about something, and Scott was nowhere to be seen.

Rhona stopped suddenly a hundred metres up the road, turned back to Jess, barked again, then raced ahead, obviously urging Jess to follow. She put the car in gear and gripped the steering wheel tightly, her gaze glued to the dog sprinting ahead.

As Jess reached the top of the rise, she glimpsed plumes of smoke billowing up behind the restaurant complex. It was dark grey and yellowish, emitting a sharp, chemical odour. She pulled the Jeep into the front carpark alongside Lili's orange Subaru. A shiver of dread crept over her. Where was Lili? Where was Scott? Was he in the storeroom with her?

She jumped out of the Jeep, grabbed the barking dog by the collar, and picked up her phone. *Not nine-nine-nine, Jess, you are not in England— think.* She hit *emergency* on the locked screen, while keeping a firm hold on Rhona's collar.

"You have dialled emergency Triple Zero. Your call is being connected," the operator's voice was clear and calm through the phone speaker. "What is your location? What is your emergency?"

"Victoria. Ailie Restaurant. Bellarine Peninsula. It's a *fire*." Her voice broke. She must have sounded panicked.

"Street name? Your name, Ms?"

"I don't know the street name. It's Faodail Farm. A-i-l-i-e Restaurant. Hurry!"

"Your name?"

"Jessica Harris."

"Stay on the line please, Jessica."

"Come on," Jess yelled at the phone as the seconds ticked by.

"Jessica. The fire department dispatched two vehicles to Ailie Restaurant five minutes ago."

"They're on their way?" Jess asked, with relief.

"Yes, Jessica," the operator said calmly. "Stay on the line, please. They should be there soon. Stay on the line."

"I have to go," Jess cried. "Lili could be in there...I have to go."

"Jessica. No. Under no circumstances—"

Jess shoved the phone into her jeans pocket, lifted Rhona onto the car seat, and slammed the car door shut. "Sorry, girl. You'll be safer in here." Her head was spinning. This was no time to panic. She pushed herself off the car, wobbled slightly, then steadied as she heard the harsh, but welcome, peal of sirens.

She dashed around to the restaurant's main entrance and thrust the door open. "Lili, where are you?" she shouted. "Lili? Scott? Where are you?" She ran through the dining room, circumnavigating the tables and chairs that seemed to be placed directly in her way, as she scanned every corner. She pushed through the kitchen service doors with such force they swung back at her and nearly threw her off her feet. "Are you in here?" She raced towards Lili's office. Surely she would have heard her by now. Not surprisingly, the office was empty. There was no point ringing Lili—her phone lay on the desk. *Oh God!* A wave of nausea shot through her as she imagined Lili and Scott lying unconscious on the storeroom floor.

She charged down the passageway and out the back door into the service carpark. Her gaze darted to the black smoke that poured from the storeroom's broken window. "Lili," Jess called again.

Sweat dripped down the side of her face. Her chest tightened. She coughed as the acrid smoke reached her throat and stung her eyes. Using her sweater sleeve to cover her nose and mouth, she edged closer to the storeroom. She had to find them before it was too late, but the fumes were overpowering, and she sheltered behind the large industrial bins to catch her breath. The sound of approaching sirens grew louder. *Why aren't they already here?*

"Jess. Jessica." It sounded like Scott, yelling from somewhere close by.

Thank God, he's safe. "I don't know where Lili is. I have to find her. She must be in the store," she screamed back to him.

"Jess, stop."

She pulled her sweater up over her face and stepped out from behind the bins. Just as her left foot hit the ground, her world shook with a deafening boom. A flare of heat was followed by a loud thud, and she threw herself backwards onto the ground. A sob escaped, and she forced her eyes open to stare up through the dust. She struggled to breathe and tried to lift her head, but a hand on her forehead held her in place. A flash of yellow passed over her, then red lights flickered and voices shouted around her.

"Get her out of here. Now," a voice echoed in her buzzing ears. "All of you. Get out of here. There may be more cylinders. Hoses coming through. *Move.*"

Two hands curled around her armpits; two hands grabbed her calves. She was lifted bodily and carried aloft.

"Steady, lass." She recognised Scott's voice. "We're moving," he said.

"Where's Lili, Scott? Please tell me Lili is safe." Jess's throat hurt, and her voice was rough and shaky.

"I'm right here."

It was Lili's voice. She closed her eyes with relief.

Jess was jostled up and down before being placed on some kind of solid board, and again lifted and carried. The movement caused her to tense, but there was nothing to grip onto.

"Hurry," someone said. "Into the front carpark." She didn't recognise the man's voice. "Should be safe enough there."

Where was Lili? She tried to push herself up but could only raise a few inches before falling back against the hard board.

"Keep still," the unfamiliar voice commanded.

A hand rested in the centre of Jess's chest. "Lie still, Jess. Please lie still." Lili's voice cracked in a husky whisper.

"Down here should be okay, mate. Let's put her down…easy does it. That's it."

"You need to lie still, you may be hurt," Lili said. "You were thrown onto your back."

"Lili." Jess inhaled sharply and placed her hand over Lili's. She was dizzy and her eyes flickered shut. She forced them open again, desperate to see her. One side of her face was streaked with dirt, and her hair and clothes were covered in grey powder. She was beautiful. "Are you okay? What happened? I called for you. Rhona was on the road. I thought you were in the storeroom, I couldn't find you, or Scott, anywhere." She gripped Lili's hand. "Thank *God*. I thought…you were…in there." She gasped for breath, wheezing between words.

"Try not to talk. I'm okay. I was in the garden, getting the hose. I didn't hear you call." Lili crouched and hovered over her, her brow wrinkled. "Sweetheart, please lie back and let the fireman check you out."

"I'm okay, really. I need water, though," she said, reluctantly dragging her gaze from Lili to the large grey-haired man who kneeled beside her. "Don't go," she whispered to Lili, when she lost hold of her hand.

"I'm right here," Lili said. "I need to give the fireman space."

The fireman brushed her face with a cool damp cloth. "Hi, Jess. I'm Andrew," he said. "Let me check you first, and then we'll get you some water. You're lucky you were close to the dumpster when the door blew out." He smiled kindly.

"I'm all right. I threw myself out of the way." Jess lifted her head. "The explosion—"

"Yeah. Something blew the door out," he said. "The empty cardboard boxes you landed on broke your fall." He shook his head. "Very lucky."

Jess winced as Andrew prodded her shoulder. "Cycling injury," she said, gritting her teeth.

Lili was back by her side, lightly squeezing her hand.

"Sorry, love. Just checking," Andrew said. He skimmed over her torso and down her arms and legs with his large hands.

"What happened?" Jess asked.

"Not sure yet. The fire is contained. We'll find out more soon," he replied.

"It didn't spread to the main building," Scott said. "It was confined to the prefab store, bit of a mess."

Jess turned her head towards Scott, who was standing behind Lili, resting his hand on her shoulder. "But the explosion? What was that?" she asked.

Scott hunched over her. "We don't know yet for sure. Most likely the gas cylinders. We're lucky it's not worse."

"Are you experiencing pain anywhere?" Andrew asked.

Jess shook her head. "Nothing new, just a slight headache."

"Okay, let's sit you up," Andrew said, placing his arm carefully around Jess's back and easing her into a sitting position. He lifted a small penlight from his breast pocket. "I'm just going to examine your pupils. Look straight ahead."

After a few seconds staring at the light, Jess blinked, her eyes sore and gritty. "Can I please have some water now?"

"I'll grab some," Scott said. "Hang on, Jess."

"You're wheezing. Do you suffer from asthma?" Andrew asked.

"No, none."

Andrew stood up and turned to Lili. "It may be a good idea to take Jess to the local clinic for a check-up, just in case. And *you* need to have that cut on your arm attended to."

"I'll give the locum a call," Lili said.

Jess noticed the bloodied bandage around Lili's forearm and gasped. "You're hurt."

"It's just a superficial wound," Lili said. "I'll clean and dress it when we get home."

"All the same, get it checked," Andrew said. "You cut it on some rusty metal, didn't you?"

Lili lowered her head. "Yeah, I tripped and fell on the old hose reel. I was in a hurry to get the hose unwound. Stupid mistake. It's just a graze."

"More than a graze. It's bleeding and the cloth you've wrapped around it is dirty," he said. "I'd better go and see what's left to be done, if you two are okay." He looked from Lili to Jess, and back again to Lili.

Scott appeared, water bottle in hand, with Rhona trotting beside him. He removed the lid and passed the bottle to Jess. "Thanks for putting her in the Jeep," he said. "She took off like a rocket when she smelled the smoke. I couldn't stop her."

"She was corralling the Jeep. Insisted I follow her." Jess sipped the cool liquid. "Oh, that's good." She took a large gulp and spluttered.

"Just sip it. Take it easy," Scott said.

She stood the bottle on the grass beside her and attempted to stand. As she wobbled unsteadily, Scott grasped her elbow.

"Thank you."

He wiped his hand across his forehead. "I'm just so grateful you're both safe," Scott said, slipping his phone into his pocket. "Your mother is frantic. I told her I'm sending you and Jess straight home."

Andrew returned, picked up the stretcher board, and tucked it under his arm. "Lili, you may need a tetanus shot," he said, then looked directly at Jess. "I don't know what you were thinking, running towards a burning building. I know you were worried about your friends, but it could have ended a lot worse had you been any closer when that cylinder went off. Luck's been on your side today, ladies." He tipped his yellow helmet, smiled, and strode off towards the fire truck with Rhona at his heel.

"Rhona, get in behind," Scott called, pointing to the ground next to his boot.

Rhona scurried back obediently and sat down beside Scott.

"Must be the uniform," Scott said with a shrug.

"Thanks, Andrew," Lili shouted to the fireman's retreating figure. She turned to her father. "Dad, I need to stay," she said. "If you take Jess back to the house and tell Mum I'm all right, I'll talk to the fire crew and make sure everything's secure."

"I'm not leaving you," Jess said. Their gazes locked for a second, and her heart skipped a beat. "I'm so sorry, Lili. The storeroom is gone."

Lili leaned forward and brushed Jess's lips with the tips of her fingers. "Shush," she said, circling Jess's waist with her arm. "We're safe. That's all that counts."

Scott placed his hand on the top of Rhona's head. "I've told Helen, you are both on your way. She insisted you go straight to the cottage for showers and she'll sort out a change of clothes. I will stay here with Rhona and make sure everything is secure," he said with finality. "The fire chief says the storeroom—what's left of it—is a forbidden zone. The fumes are toxic. Their photographer will be here sometime tomorrow."

Lili looked like she was about to protest, but Scott held up his hand. "Darling, take Jess home. You can't do any more here today. I'll see you both later. And I'll lock up." He shook his head. "Not much of a birthday, Lillian, but..." Scott shrugged.

"It could have been so much worse, Dad," she said, pulling Jess closer to her side with her uninjured arm. "Thanks. Be careful, and we'll see you at home."

Jess sent a reassuring smile Scott's way. "Thank you, Scott. We'll be fine now."

With Scott out of sight, Jess leaned into Lili's side and gently took hold of her bandaged arm. "How is it? Will you need a tetanus shot?"

Lili rested her head against Jess's shoulder. "No, it doesn't hurt much, and I had my booster just over a year ago."

"Usha will examine and redress it. She should be at the cottage by now."

Lili tilted her head back and met Jess's gaze. "Right, but only after she checks you out," she said. "Come on, let's get going, or Mum will bring everyone here, and I don't want Ru to see the mess." She took Jess's hand and gently tugged her towards their cars. "Although she would love to see the fire trucks and the crew in their gear."

They stopped between the Subaru and the Jeep. "Can we please take the Jeep?" Jess asked.

She saw the questioning look on Lili's face. "There are things inside it I need." Jess turned away, hoping Lili hadn't seen her blush.

Lili peered into the back seat of the Jeep, smiled coyly, and opened the passenger door for Jess. "No problem. Get in."

"Are you sure? What about your arm?" Jess climbed into the passenger seat knowing full well she was in no state to drive.

Lili leaned across Jess, grabbed the seatbelt, and clicked it into place. "It smells a lot better in here. Let's get going." Lili smiled and placed her hand on Jess's thigh.

Jess looked down where Lili's hand rested. "It's your birthday. I haven't even had a chance to wish you—" Before she could finish her sentence, Lili's lips captured hers, and Jess's parted instinctively. They kissed gently for a few seconds, simply enjoying the heat that simmered between them, before Lili pulled away.

"Well, that takes care of that." Lili patted Jess's thigh, backed out of the car, and pressed Jess's door closed. She raced around to the driver's side, opened the door, and jumped in. "It is my birthday," she said, turning the key in the ignition. "I get to do whatever I want."

Jess stared at her, a little breathless. "I guess you do. Happy birthday, Lili," she whispered.

Chapter 30

LILI CRUNCHED INTO FIRST GEAR and slowly released her foot from the clutch. "Sorry, about that," she said as the Jeep bunny-hopped a few metres, then sped forward. At the end of the drive, she pulled over to allow one of departing fire trucks to get ahead. The driver waved and tooted the horn. Lili called out, "Thanks, guys." They watched the fire truck amble down the dirt road.

"I'm so glad I didn't leave with Alex," Lili said, resting her head on the steering wheel. She sat up and turned to Jess. "I was in the car, ready to go, when I suddenly remembered the wine I had to take to Mum's. If I hadn't gone back, I wouldn't have smelt the smoke. Just think what may have happened if I hadn't called the fire brigade." Her stomach knotted at the thought.

She drove out onto the farm road, and soon after took the lane that branched to her parents' cottage. Lili slowed the four-wheel drive and peered into the rear-vision mirror, where the back seat held the massive flower arrangement she'd seen earlier. "Beautiful flowers," she said, inhaling the blend of fragrances. "Jess, why did you come to Ailie this afternoon? How did you know I was there? I didn't expect to see you until tonight."

Lili parked the Jeep beside Usha's small white Honda hybrid and turned fully to face Jess, who still hadn't responded to her questions. Jess's hands were tucked under her knees, and even with a dust streaked face and her hair dishevelled—the usually neat braid was now tangled over her shoulders—to Lili, she was the most heavenly sight.

She rested her hand on Jess's shoulder, just wanting to connect. "You could have been badly hurt." Lili slid her hand to the back of Jess's neck and massaged gently. "You rushed towards the burning storeroom like a superhero."

Jess gazed at Lili through puffy eyes. She looked down at her knees. "I had to find you," she said with a gravelly voice, and coughed. "I thought you were in the storeroom." When she looked up again, her eyes were wet with tears. "I didn't have time to think. I had to find you."

"But you could have been burnt." She stroked Jess's tear-streaked cheek with her fingers.

"I love you, Lili," she said, removing Lili's hand from her face to turn it over and kiss her palm. "I know this complicates things. This may not be what you want. But I am here. My indecision wasn't because of how I feel about you. I've been alone for so long, and I'm not used to sharing what I'm thinking, or how I'm feeling. I came to Ailie this afternoon to tell you I love you." She searched Lili's eyes. "If you are willing, we can make this work. I'd like to give it a try."

Lili was stunned. She gazed down at their joined hands. Her heart pounded in her chest. Jess was giving her the reassurance she needed, and yet she was paralysed. It was so unexpected. She leaned back against the headrest and closed her eyes, giving herself a moment to think. Jess had just declared her love, and there was no doubt in Lili's mind it was true after the way she had acted today.

"Am I too late?" Jess squeezed Lili's hand.

She opened her eyes wide and saw a flicker of fear on Jess's face.

"Wait," Jess said, and reached into the back of the Jeep.

Lili's first thought was that Jess would give her the flowers, but instead she held a colourfully wrapped parcel in her hand.

"I was going to give you this later tonight, but...I think you should have it now," she said.

Lili accepted the package, turned it over, and removed the sticky tape carefully. "What can it be?" It was the size and shape of a small hardcover book.

"A pair of socks?" Jess gave her a half-smile.

"Wonderful." She tore at the package and revealed a book, as expected. But not just any book. On the cover was a photograph of Aruishi on her shiny lavender bike, with Jess crouched behind her, and Lili in the background looking at them with a silly grin on her face. "I remember that day, but how on earth did you get that photo?" she asked. "I love it."

"Magical hands," Jess said with a smirk.

Lili knew her cheeks were rosy red. She prodded Jess's shoulder with her finger. "Oh, you."

"Come on, there's more."

Opening the book, she slowly began to leaf through the pages. Aruishi on the deck, in her pyjamas and her favourite slippers, pointing to a flock of birds in mid-flight. Lili holding Aruishi aloft as she reached for a mandarin from a tree in the orchard. Helen and Scott dozing in matching wicker chairs on the front porch of their cottage. And there was the view from Ailie's terrace, with Jess's bicycle propped against the newly installed metal weathervane she'd purchased at the farmers' market.

"Jess, I don't how you took all these without us knowing." The photos were visible proof that Jess was truly invested in her, Ru, and the family. She'd taken the time to organise them into this wonderful book. Lili sucked in a calming breath and put her hand out to turn Jess's face towards her. "You're not too late. I love you too."

A loud tapping on the Jeep window startled them both, and they drew apart. There was Helen. Lili looked back at Jess and mouthed *Sorry* as Helen prised the driver's door open.

"Thank goodness," Helen said, almost throwing herself into the car. She pulled Lili into a fierce hug that threatened to squeeze the air out of her lungs.

Lili winced. "Mum," she said. "I'm okay, you can let me go now."

"I'm so sorry." Helen released her and stepped back out of the car. "Oh, darling, you're bleeding. What have you done to your arm?"

"It's not serious. Really, Mum."

"Well, it's a good thing Usha is here. She's anxious to look you both over."

Tash rushed down the path, opened Jess's door, and helped her from the Jeep. "Your eyes look really bloodshot, Jess."

"Just a bit of soot," Jess replied. "I expect I need a shower."

Lili turned to her mother. "Where's Ru?"

"In the kitchen with Alex. She heard the sirens. Tash and Alex arrived in the nick of time. She's demanding to see you and Jess, but Alex is keeping her distracted, decorating the cake."

"I hope they're not attempting to put all thirty-seven candles on it." She raised her eyebrows. "We've seen enough smoke and fire to last us a long, long time."

"I couldn't agree more," Jess said as she and Tash joined Lili and Helen on the front porch.

"Okay. Let's get you two inside," Helen said. "We'll sneak in. It would be better if Ru didn't see you until after you've both cleaned up."

"You're absolutely right, Mum."

"Come on, girls," Tash said. "Scott's left me in charge of his wood-fired slow-cooked lamb. But I couldn't concentrate until you got here. Not much of a birthday surprise, eh, Lili?"

They quietly followed the others into the house. Lili ran her hand through her hair. Jess must think they were crazy, wanting to get on with the evening and celebrate her birthday. Sure, she'd lost the storeroom, equipment, and stock. But they were all safe. And Jess loved her.

"Hey, now that your mum is out of earshot," Tash said. "Tell me: is everything okay?"

Lili smiled and leaned against her friend. "Count me hopeful. Things look promising."

A light breeze filtered into the room through the open French doors, moving the colourful balloons that hung in twos and threes around the sunroom. The enormous bouquet of flowers from Jess, placed artfully on Helen's antique dresser, made an amazing backdrop for the already cheerfully decorated room, and the air was perfumed with the fragrant flowers and aromatic herbs. The anxiety of this afternoon was already fading from Lili's memory.

Aruishi had no doubt orchestrated the birthday preparations while Helen did the work. Lili caressed the superfine merino scarf she wore draped around her shoulders. It was handmade and illustrated with a delicate design of roses and vines. Although the gift and the accompanying crayon drawn card were from Aruishi, she knew for certain that Pinkie Piggy bank would not have yielded enough coins for this luxurious present.

With Tash's help, Scott had managed to produce a melt-in-the-mouth roast lamb shoulder with crispy garlic potatoes and honeyed carrots. The near disaster seemed to only increase their appetites, and every morsel was soon gone. A sweet smell of ginger-caramel custard lingered along with the buttery scent of Helen's freshly baked rhubarb crumble—two of Lili's favourite dishes.

"Well, it's been a rather eventful day, and a birthday you won't forget." Helen held up her glass of bubbly to Lili in salute and plonked down in the overstuffed floral armchair beside her, nearly spilling the contents of her glass over them both. "It's nice to get off my feet," Helen said, placing the glass on a side table.

"Thanks for everything, Mum. Dinner was delicious."

"You're welcome. After this afternoon, I'm so glad we could still celebrate your birthday."

Lili had barely taken her eyes off Jess all evening. Her long hair curled at the tips and was pinned to one side with a silver comb. She wore the lightweight pale-indigo pullover and loose-fitting grey trousers Helen had selected for her.

Jess looked up, as if sensing Lili's gaze upon her. Her eyes lit up and her lips curved gently in a hesitant smile.

She smiled back at Jess, her heart skipping a beat.

Her mother nudged her in the ribs. "Would you like us to keep Ru overnight?"

"Err...no. I don't think that's a good idea," she replied, surprised by Helen's question. "She's unsettled and it's better if she sleeps in her own bed." She turned to her mother and raised an eyebrow. "Why do you ask?"

Helen frowned and gave a slight shake of her head. "You've hardly taken your eyes off Jess all evening, and I see her giving you clandestine looks." She smiled. "You two can't hide a thing. I'm so happy for you, Lili."

"You're very observant," Lili said, nudging Helen in the ribs. "Thank you, but I'd rather have Ru with us."

"Of course." She patted Lili's uninjured arm.

They continued their observation of Usha and Jess seated on the sofa, diagonally across from them, with Aruishi perched on Jess's knee.

"I wonder what Jess and Ben's mother, Aruishi, was like," Helen mused. "I've seen photos of their parents. No wonder Benjamin Harris Senior was bowled over by her beauty. She had that quintessential classic Indian elegance, just like a film star."

"Who's like a film star?" Alex asked. She crouched on the floor beside Lili and leaned her arm on the chair. "I presume you mean Jess?"

"She could easily be a film star." Scott perched on the armrest next to Helen and draped his arm over her shoulder. "Do you remember how we used to tease Ben, that if he got tired of working as a chef, he should try out for a role as the first surfing, dancing Bollywood star?"

"Surfing, definitely." Lili smiled sadly. She felt a sharp pang of sorrow as she watched Jess wipe Aruishi's fingers with a paper towel, then lift her onto Usha's lap. "Not so much the dancing part. Ben had two left feet on the dance floor."

Alex squeezed Lili's arm. "Gosh, wouldn't he have loved to be here with us. To see Jess and Ru together."

Lili could only nod her head in agreement. Perhaps Ben had had a hand in the way things turned out.

"I'm ready for a cuppa, but first I'll have some more cake." Scott stood up and strolled towards the dining table.

"Go easy on the sugar, darling," Helen called, peering at him over her reading glasses. She resumed leafing through Lili's gift. "I can't believe Jess snapped these photographs with her phone," she said to Lili and Alex. "There are some fabulous shots in here." She turned a page and giggled, half covering her eyes with her hand. "Oh, that one's not entirely flattering."

Lili leaned across to look at the picture her mother pointed at and laughed. "When was that taken? You've been caught on *Candid Camera*, Mum."

"We were helping Scott move the cows to a dryer paddock, and I slipped." Helen gestured with her arm. "*Swish*. I was off my feet and onto my bottom."

"Looks like the mud was winning. You and Ru are both covered from head to gumboot in the sludge."

"And cow poo," Helen shrieked. She covered her face with her hand again.

"I think Mum's a bit tipsy," Lili whispered in Alex's ear.

"The photo book is pretty cute," Alex said.

"It is. I love it." She looked across the room and smiled. Aruishi was feeding Jess a spoonful of raspberry-mousse sponge.

Alex bent forward, resting her chin in her hand. "Do you have any idea what caused the fire?"

"We won't know until the fire inspector's been. The lights were flickering again yesterday," Lili said. "It must have been something to do with the storm, maybe a power surge."

Alex gasped. "Oh *shit*. You're right. Thank goodness those big barbeque cylinders weren't in there."

Jess walked across the room and placed her half-eaten plate of cake on the dining table. Scott was hoeing into a slice of rhubarb crumble and looked up guiltily as Jess leaned towards him and made a comment that Lili couldn't hear.

"What are those two plotting? Your father looks pleased about something," Helen said. "I wonder what Jess said to him."

Alex grinned at Lili. "Maybe she's asking your father for your hand in marriage." Even though she sat next to her, Alex spoke loud enough to make everyone in the room turn their heads.

The colour rose in Jess's cheeks. Lili had never seen her blush so deeply. Jess shoved her hands in her pockets and said, in a clear voice, "And now I could."

A hush came over the room, and at that moment everyone's attention focused on Jess.

Lili sat up straight in her chair, reached for her glass of champagne with a trembling hand, and took a large gulp to settle her nerves.

Aruishi jumped off Usha's lap, ran to Jess's side, and clutched her leg.

Tash entered the room quietly, a damp tea towel over her shoulder, and sat next to Usha on the couch.

Lili returned Tash's quizzical gaze with a shrug of her shoulders and a silly grin.

They both turned to focus on Jess, who placed one hand lovingly on Aruishi's shoulder, then looked up and blinked, seemingly aware now that everyone was staring at her.

Scott cleared his throat loudly. "Jess has something she'd like to tell us," he said.

Alex grabbed Lili's hand and squeezed.

"Thank you, Scott. I do." Jess glanced around at the small gathering. "It's been an extraordinary day, and you are an exceptional bunch." She stared down at her feet briefly and looked up again. "I came here under a cloud after Ben's death. A stranger to you, really. You've all made me feel at home. I don't want to leave."

Lili didn't want Jess to leave either. She prised her friend's hand from hers. Alex's grip threatened to cut off her circulation.

"I don't want you to leave," Aruishi said, taking the words out of Lili's mouth.

Jess looked down at Aruishi. "I have to go away for a little while, but I will be back, soon. I promise."

Aruishi yelled, "Hooray!" She jumped up and down on the spot. Lili was tempted to join her.

"As some of you already know"—Jess gazed at Lili—"I was recently approached by an Australian team to join their outfit for the next season."

"Well, there have been those rumours on social media." Alex exchanged a quick glance with Lili.

"Yes, there are rumours, Alex." Jess's head was held high, and her voice was steady. "When I return to elite cycling next year, I will be racing with SwitchedOn, the Australian team." She spoke with sureness and self-confidence.

As the room erupted in applause, Lili didn't know whether to cry or burst into song. She noticed the glance that passed between Jess and Usha before the doctor grinned at Lili with a knowing nod.

Aruishi tugged on Jess's trousers and stared at her with a rapt expression.

Jess crouched beside Aruishi, and her face softened as she looked from Aruishi, back to Lili. "I could never have dreamed that coming across the world to settle Ben's estate…" Jess's voice broke. "When I came back to Australia, I had no idea my world would change so dramatically. I never dreamed that I would find family or that I would make new friends. Or that I would find love."

Aruishi launched herself at Jess, toppling them both onto the floor. "I love you too, Auntie Jess," she said.

Jess looped her arms around her niece and rolled them both into a seated position.

Lili's gaze darted to her mother and father, who stood at opposite sides of the room, then back to Jess and Aruishi. She wanted to savour the moment—to be thankful for her friends and family and the happiness and love that surrounded her.

She jumped out of her chair, flew across the room, and fell onto her knees beside Jess who was laughing now also as she held Aruishi close. She leaned in and kissed her daughter's forehead before she reached for Jess and cradled her face in her hands. Jess's lips parted in surprise.

"I love you so much, Jess. Thank you." Tears welled up in Lili's eyes, and despite her determination not to cry, they spilled down her cheeks.

"Why are you two *crying*?" Aruishi asked.

"Because we're happy," Jess whispered, against Lili's lips.

"Well," Alex said, "if this isn't the best Bollywood ending *ever*."

Epilogue

Two months later.

"Last night, the Australian television networks replayed footage of your horrific crash in the Netherlands," the British reporter from *The Guardian* said. "Did it concern you, Jessica?"

"I don't watch television the night before a race." Jess sat forward in her chair and rested her chin in her hand. "It's all part of cycling: the crashes and the media's recounting of the event. I am in great form and look forward to the rest of the season."

"But didn't it rattle you today when at the final descent a touch of wheels brought down Hübl? On a psychological level, it must affect your confidence."

"I am sorry Claudia's day ended with an ambulance ride to the local hospital. But I've heard she's okay," Jess leaned back in her chair. "It's not unusual to have some jitters and doubts before a first major ride after an injury. However, with proper preparation and training, they can be contained. As I said, crashes are a part of my sport."

"Considering your success today, is it safe to say you've made a full recovery?"

"I feel amazingly strong. I look forward to continuing to wear the SwitchedOn jersey this season. The team's tactics and planning set me up perfectly for the sprint finish. It is exciting to be part of this squad," Jess replied.

"This season?" he repeated, raising an eyebrow. "Would you like to shed some light on the rumours that this may be your last year on the World Tour?"

"Ahh…rumours are just that, Mark. Rumours," Jess said. She'd come to respect Mark Samson's coverage of the pro cycling circuit, but there was no way she would feed speculation about her future.

Jess was clear with herself about the direction in which she was heading, with Lili and Aruishi taking precedence in her life, but that information was not for public knowledge.

Mark nodded and turned over a page in his notebook. She was relieved he didn't pursue that subject. He scratched his beard and continued with his interview. "Due to your injuries, you missed almost a full season. How will it influence your ranking?"

"It won't. As you know, the ranking system is calculated on a fifty-two-week calendar year. It's January, the start of a new year." Jess stretched her limbs, feeling like a lazy cat basking in the warmth of the dappled evening sunshine. "I'm focusing on my fitness, not titles or ranking," she said, looking across the outdoor table to meet Lili's gaze.

"You achieved such a good result today. What secrets can you reveal about your pre-race preparation?" Mark asked.

"Hmm…" Jess twirled a strand of hair and tore her gaze away from Lili to reply, "The details will remain a secret, Mark. But you know that a week of easy spins—with occasional intense workouts, great sleep, and good food—is the best preparation for race day."

Lili arched an eyebrow, reminding Jess how and where they'd spent most of their free time since she'd returned from the UK. Jess sighed, recalling the ways Lili had managed to keep her both on the edge and blissfully relaxed over the last week.

It was hard for Jess to take her eyes off Lili. She'd changed from her chef's uniform and now looked refreshed in tailored grey shorts, a sleeveless mint-green shirt, and sandals. Her eyes twinkled when she laughed, and her slightly tousled hair seemed lighter and shone like gold. She was captivating in every way, and more than anything, Jess wanted to feel her close again. Now she was ready for them to be alone. After a gruelling, exhilarating race, Jess felt both light and pleasantly sore, and she was one hundred and one per cent willing to test Lili's post-race recovery strategies.

The heated looks between them generated a spark and sizzle that had Samson flicking his gaze between Jess and Lili. "Jess." He cleared his throat to get her attention. "A change of countries? A change of teams? Big changes. Have you made the right decision?"

"Yes, most definitely. I believe I proved that today."

"All eyes were on you when you broke away and charged towards the finish line. Well done." With that, Mark gave a quick nod and put away his notebook. Clearly, the interview was over.

"May I get you another drink, Mark?" asked Lili.

"Thank you, but no thanks. I have a deadline to meet, and tomorrow I must be up bright and early to cover the men's race." He adjusted his straw fedora hat, stood up, and held out his hand to Jess. She reached out to shake it firmly. "I covered your father's racing career, and it is a pleasure to cover yours. I was at the scene of your crash at the Ronde van Drenthe last year, so it's tremendous to witness your return. The very best of luck for the future."

"Thank you, Mark." Jess walked around the table to stand behind Lili. "I'll see you at my next event?"

"You will. And La Route de France Féminine, in July?" Mark asked.

Lili looked up, and Jess squeezed her shoulders. "That's what I am working towards, if it doesn't get cancelled like last year. Maybe, you'll see me at RideLondon instead."

"Hmm, that was an almighty disaster for women's cycling," Mark said with a frown. "Not to be repeated. Yes, RideLondon is a fantastic choice for a sprinter. It would be a thrill to see you win in a city that for many years claimed you as its own." He tipped his hat to Jess and reached for his leather briefcase. "Cheerio. Best of luck to the both of you. Thank you, again."

They watched him make a beeline towards Bianca, the Italian sprinter, and her partner, a member from SwitchedOn, who sat together at one of the terrace tables.

"Alone at last." Jess leaned down and kissed the top of Lili's head, ruffling her hair with her hands.

"Is that the end of the interviews today?" Lili pouted. "Do I really have you to myself finally?"

Jess lifted Lili's chin. "For about ten seconds at the most." She brushed Lili's lips lightly with her own. "Oh, and maybe not even that, because, look, here come Alex and Tash and Owen. And your parents with Aruishi, back from… Where was Ru again?"

"Camping," Lili said. "At the Children's Music Festival in Port Fairy."

The timing of Aruishi's vacation, when Jess had arrived back from the UK, had been opportune, giving her and Lili space alone to reconnect.

"Jess," Aruishi called out, breaking away from Helen's grasp. Jess squatted and held out her arms as Aruishi barrelled towards her.

Lili placed her hand on Jess's shoulder. "You do realise Ru is coming home with us tonight?"

Aruishi covered Jess's face with kisses. Jess looked up at Lili and tightened her hold around Aruishi. "I wouldn't have it any other way."

What a way to start the day. Lili and Jess lay exhausted, their limbs tangled and damp with perspiration—but Lili couldn't resist touching her again. She tenderly ran her hands along the contours of Jess's body, from her neck to the swell of her hip. She inched slowly down the bed and kissed the row of small horizontal scars along Jess's silky thigh. This time, Jess didn't flinch and slid her fingers through Lili's hair, coaxing her closer. She was trusting and open; Lili needed no further encouragement. Within minutes, Jess's supple back arched in surrender. She called Lili's name, her voice trailing off to a low moan as she convulsed around Lili's fingers.

Lili crawled up the bed to lie beside her. She nuzzled into Jess's shoulder before sweeping her tongue over her breast. "Stop," Jess pleaded, moving her hand to the back of Lili's head and holding her still, while her breathing slowed. "Your stamina amazes me."

"Darling." Lili placed a gentle kiss in the curve of her neck, then looked up and was caught in Jess's soft gaze. "*I* didn't ride over a hundred kilometres yesterday or stand on the podium afterwards."

Jess propped herself on one elbow, reached for Lili's arm, and squeezed her biceps. "You have plenty of staying power. Chef's work is physically hard, hauling heavy pots and bags of potatoes," she said. "Ooh, feel those muscles." She tossed her head in the cheeky way Lili had come to adore, and her hair flew out of her eyes. "Aruishi is not exactly a lightweight, now, either."

Lili tugged Jess's hair playfully. "Have you noticed how much she's grown in the last two months?" She closed her eyes, relishing their closeness and the sensual flow of energy between them. She'd missed all this: the intimacy, sensational sex, the easy, high-spirited banter that they'd shared for those two heady weeks last year before Jess had returned to England.

Resting her head upon Jess's breast, Lili marvelled at how easily she'd succumbed to Alex's insistence she take the week off. With Jess just back, she would have been unable to focus and a total klutz in the kitchen anyway.

They were hardly apart. They'd kissed—she'd spent hours appreciating Jess's sensuous lips and their limitless talents—made love, talked, and made plans. Every morning, Jess went out for a ride. Otherwise, they were inseparable.

"Where did you go?" Jess asked. The tips of her fingers traced over the nape of Lili's neck and down her spine.

Lili shivered, at Jess's touch. "Nowhere. I'm right here. Exactly where I want to be."

Jess pushed herself up onto her knees and hovered over Lili, her expression bright with mischief.

"Oh, found your second wind, have you?" Lili asked. "You're adorable, but get that look off your face." She pushed Jess onto her back, reversing their positions. "I need food and a cup of tea." She held Jess's wrists and kicked at the dishevelled bedclothes to untangle them from her legs. "I bet you've worked up an appetite. There's a lot of growling and rumbling going on in here." She leaned down to kiss Jess's midriff. "You must be hungry."

"I am hungry…for you."

Jess freed her arms from Lili's grip, ran her fingers along Lili's rib cage and up to clasp her shoulders. Her kiss was sensual and fiery—demanding, yet slow and lingering.

Lili lifted her head slowly. "I love you, Jess, and I'd love nothing more than to stay here in bed with you all day and explore every inch of you." Lili glanced at the clock on the bedside table. "But Ru will be awake any minute."

Jess moaned and cradled Lili's cheek in her hand. "I love you too, and I look forward to the next time, and all the times after that."

Lili rolled over and propped herself on her elbow. "Don't go away, I'll be back." She swung her legs off the bed, reached for her robe, and slipped it on. She picked up the nightshirt off the floor where Jess had discarded it last night and tossed it onto the end of the bed. "I won't be long," she said, opening the childproof latch. She left the door slightly ajar before heading towards the kitchen.

On her way back, Aruishi's animated voice made Lili stop outside the bedroom door. Tea tray in hand, she leaned against the hallway wall, curious to know what stories Aruishi was telling Jess.

"But you were away for such a long time," she heard Aruishi say. "I really missed you, and so did my mummy. We were lonely for you."

So true.

"And I missed you both very much." Jess's voice was soothing. "But we talked on FaceTime, and we shared videos. Remember the one I made when I rode past Buckingham Palace?"

"Where the queen lives."

Jess chuckled. "Yes, exactly. Oh, and hey, I saw you riding your bicycle along the farm track, past the brand-new storeroom."

"I'm almost as fast as you. Grampa took that video. I like the iPad you gave us, but I like it best when you are here. Don't go away again, Jess. Please."

Aruishi sounded so sad, Lili sighed heavily and nearly dropped the tea tray.

"Well," Jess said, slowly, "you do know I have to travel sometimes to race. But don't forget there will be times when you and your mama can come and watch me."

Lili decided now was a good time to rescue Jess and pushed the bedroom door open with her foot. "Well, what have we here?" She set the tray down on the dresser. "Good morning, munchkin." She leaned over and kissed her daughter, who sat next to Jess on top of the blanket. Jess had her nightshirt on and had straightened up the bedclothes.

"There's room for you here," Aruishi said, patting the empty space on the bed beside her.

Lili moved the tray to the bedside table and handed Jess a cup of tea. She sat down beside Aruishi and held out the plate of toasted honeyed-almond brioche. Jess lifted a golden slice and took a bite.

"Hmm...."

Lili's gaze was focused on Jess's mouth, and the way her tongue darted out, collecting the sliver of butter at the corner of her lips.

"This is so delicious. Crispy, chewy. Yum." Jess took another bite.

Lili rapidly closed and opened her eyes. She wanted to kiss her, and it didn't help that Jess sent her inviting, sexy grins.

"Mummy, can I please have some of that?" Aruishi tugged her arm.

Lili bit her lip, dragging her gaze away from Jess. "Sure," she said, holding a piece of brioche to Aruishi's mouth.

She took a tentative bite. "Hmm…" she said, imitating Jess. "It is yummy. Can I have a whole slice?"

Lili grabbed a tissue from the box on the bedside table. "Only if you hold this under it." She handed her a slice of the brioche. "I don't want crumbs in my bed."

Aruishi nodded, nibbling carefully whilst holding the tissue under her chin.

Lili sat back and rested against the headboard.

Jess helped herself to another slice, chewed happily, and finally washed it down with the last of her tea.

"No crumbs," Aruishi told Jess seriously.

Jess just rolled her eyes at Aruishi's comment but quickly checked the sheets.

"Mama?" Aruishi stared at Lili intently, her head slightly tilted.

"Yes, Ru?"

"This is *your* bed. Is this Jess's bed too? I mean, does Jess have two beds? Can I have two beds?"

Lili almost choked and glanced up to meet Jess's look of surprise. Jess edged closer to Lili and rubbed her back soothingly.

"Well," Lili said. She put down her cup and lifted Aruishi onto her lap. "Do you mind Jess sleeping in here with me?"

Aruishi shook her head. "No. Jess loves you." She patted Jess's hand and pulled it onto her leg. "You do still love my Mama, don't you?"

"Yes. I love you both very much, sweet pea."

"Good. Gran already told me that Jess is going to live with us from now on. Properly. She doesn't have to sleep in the guest room."

"And what do you think of that?" asked Lili.

"I think it's a good idea," Aruishi said matter-of-factly. "If Jess is living with us, she can sleep in here with you. She'd be too lonely on the other side of the house all by herself."

Lili breathed a sigh of relief. "Yes, yes, she would."

"The guest room can be for guests again, can't it?" Aruishi turned to Jess. "It will be ready for your friends from England when they visit us."

"Yes." Jess's eyes widened. "I am looking forward to Jonathan, Maxine, and Rupert's visit in May, and they can't wait to meet you."

"You can play with Rupert. Maybe share some of your toys?" Lili ran her fingers through Aruishi's curls. "That will be fun, won't it?"

"Oh, Mama. He is *just* a baby," Aruishi said, then crawled from Lili's lap and snuggled in with Jess. "Jess, I will start school this year."

Jess clearly wasn't used to a near five-year-old's split-second ability to change the topic of conversation. She looked startled. "So I heard," she said finally. "Are you looking forward to it?"

She nodded. "I met my kinder teacher for this year already. Ms Sprout. Like brussel *sprout*." Aruishi jiggled up and down on Jess's lap.

Lili grabbed Aruishi's hand. "Jess's legs are tired. Why don't you collect your clothes and meet me in the bathroom? After breakfast, we're going to pack the car and head for the beach."

"Really?" Aruishi's eyes lit up. "Are you coming too, Jess?"

"Yes, definitely. Just try and stop me."

"Yeah," Aruishi yelled, jumping off the bed and racing out of the room.

"Oh, me." Jess fell back against the headboard. "She's a whirlwind."

Lili put her arm around Jess. "Yep. She can be exhausting." With her other hand, she turned Jess's chin towards her. "It's not all too much, is it?" Lili asked, unable to keep the hint of insecurity out of her voice.

Jess leaned into her. "No. I'm a little sore after the ride, but a swim in the ocean will be perfect for my tired muscles."

Lili rolled over, straddled Jess's thighs, and gripped her shoulders lightly. "Yes, I'm looking forward to a swim too," she said. "But that's not what I mean." She searched Jess's face.

What she saw completely dispelled her fears. Jess's eyes were truly the window to her soul. Warmth and desire shimmered there, giving Lili all the strength and assurance she needed.

"I love you, Lili McAllister," Jess said, holding her gaze. "And I'm ready for everything that it means. Everything."

Lili kissed her purposefully. Longingly. A sense of calm flowed through her. She pressed her hand against Jess's chest, just inside the top of her nightshirt, over her heart. Jess's pulse was steady, strong, and pure.

About C. Fonseca

As a small child, C. Fonseca had imaginary friends. She told these friends stories and her family set them places at the dinner table. When she grew up, she lost the imaginary friends but she continued writing stories and poetry.

She was an executive chef for many years until a car accident stopped her in her tracks and forced her to change direction.

She lives by the sea, with her Kiwi partner and their beloved Burmese cats. She is an expressionist landscape painter and can often be found at a cliff-top platform overlooking the Southern Ocean, daydreaming, plotting and planning her creative adventures.

CONNECT WITH C. FONSECA
Facebook: www.facebook.com/cfonseca1au
E-Mail: cfonseca1au@gmail.com

Other Books from Ylva Publishing

www.ylva-publishing.com

Where the Light Plays
C. Fonseca

ISBN: 978-3-95533-421-5
Length: 285 pages (97,000 words)

Dr. Caitlin Quinn is a sophisticated, self-assured Irish art historian visiting Australia on sabbatical. That doesn't mean she can't enjoy the local scenery—especially sun-kissed Surf Coast artist Andi Rey. Their attraction is unstoppable, but their lives are moving in opposite directions. Andi doesn't need distractions, and a woman that eschews commitment spells trouble, with a capital "T".

Code of Conduct
Cheyenne Blue

ISBN: 978-3-96324-030-0
Length: 264 pages (91,000 words)

Top ten tennis player Viva Jones had the world at her feet. Then a lineswoman's bad call knocked her out of the US Open, and injury crushed her career. While battling to return to the game, a chance meeting with the same sexy lineswoman forces Viva to rethink the past...and the present. There's just one problem: players and officials can't date.

A lesbian romance about breaking all the rules.

Contract for Love
Alison Grey

ISBN: 978-3-96324-086-7
Length: 301 pages (97,000 words)

Sherry lives in a trailer park with her son, trying to make ends meet.

Madison's life couldn't be more different. Her only goals are partying and bedding women.

When her grandmother threatens to disinherit her, Madison has to find a way to prove that she's cleaned up her act.

After a chance encounter with Sherry, Madison comes up with a crazy idea: she wants Sherry to play her fake girlfriend.

Up on the Roof
A.L. Brooks

ISBN: 978-3-95533-988-3
Length: 254 pages (88,000 words)

When a storm wreaks havoc on bookish Lena's well-ordered world, her laid-back new neighbor, Megan, offers her a room. The trouble is they've been clashing since the day they met. How can they now live under the same roof? Making it worse is the inexplicable pull between them that seems hard to resist.

A fun, awkward, and sweet British romance about the power of opposites attracting.

Food for Love
© 2018 by C. Fonseca

ISBN: 978-3-96324-082-9

Also available as e-book.

Published by Ylva Publishing, legal entity of Ylva Verlag, e.Kfr.

Ylva Verlag, e.Kfr.
Owner: Astrid Ohletz
Am Kirschgarten 2
65830 Kriftel
Germany

www.ylva-publishing.com

First edition: 2018

Credits
Edited by Michelle Aguilar and Amanda Jean
Cover Design and Print Layout by Streetlight Graphics